Tor Books by David Drake

*Forthcoming

THE LEGIONS
OF FIRE

DAVID DRAKE

TOR®
fantasy

A TOM DOHERTY ASSOCIATES BOOK
NEW YORK

This is a work of fiction. All of the characters, organizations, and events portrayed in this novel are either products of the author's imagination or are used fictitiously.

THE LEGIONS OF FIRE

Copyright © 2010 by David Drake

All rights reserved.

A Tor Book
Published by Tom Doherty Associates, LLC
175 Fifth Avenue
New York, NY 10010

www.tor-forge.com

Tor® is a registered trademark of Tom Doherty Associates, LLC.

ISBN 978-0-7653-6045-8

First Edition: May 2010
First Mass Market Edition: May 2011

Printed in the United States of America

0 9 8 7 6 5 4 3 2 1

To Sarah Van Name, a fellow Latinist

ACKNOWLEDGMENTS

Dan Breen is my first reader. He catches things that I miss and, even more important, forces me to look at things that I passed as "Well, that's about right." When I tell myself that something's about right, it means it really isn't right.

Dorothy Day and my webmaster, Karen Zimmerman, archived my texts as usual, protecting me against electronic disasters, my own screwups, and the possibility of a moderate-sized asteroid targeting my part of the country. (Don't laugh: there are a lot of asteroids up there!)

Karen (again) and Joe Benardello each provided extremely specialized information that I couldn't have gotten in any other way. I hope I have used their help in fashions that won't embarrass them.

Computers died in the creation of this book. I'm sorry, but they did. One I simply worked to death. As for the backup machine, I was working away (outside on the porch, as usual) when a squall hit, blowing the rain in horizontally. My son, Jonathan, replaced the first with its nearest modern equivalent; he then got the backup working again, to my great delight.

My wife, Jo, continues to feed me extremely well and to keep the house running, while also reminding me of the normal incidents of human society (a birthday party tomorrow night, the dental appointment next week, and so on).

I could work without my circle of friends and family. The books would not be as good, though, and I would certainly not be as good.

My thanks to all those above; and thank *heavens* that I'm not alone.

AUTHOR'S NOTE

First and foremost, *The Legions of Fire* is a novel about a fictional city named Carce (pronounced CAR-see) and the empire which Carce rules. It is not a novel about Rome and the Roman Empire in A.D. 30, under the emperor Tiberius.

Having said that, a reader who knows a little about Roman history and culture will find similarities with my Carce. A reader who knows a great deal about Rome will find even more similarities. I'm not writing a historical novel, however, or even a historical novel with fantasy elements.

The fantasy elements which I've used here, like the historical and cultural elements, are real. The Cumean Sibyl did exist; so did and do the *Sibylline Books*, which a committee of senators examined when Rome was in particularly grave danger (for example, after the disaster at Cannae).

I prefer to use real things instead of inventing pastiches which I hope will sound right. The magical verses of this novel come from the *Sibylline Books* and (for reasons which will become clear to the reader) from the *Völuspá*, a Norse prophetic poem. (Occasionally you will find lines from other poems of *The Elder Edda* as well.)

There are various literary borrowings throughout *The Legions of Fire*. This wasn't research on my part, exactly: I read classical literature for fun, and I found it easier to snatch something from (for example) the elder Seneca, or the Homeric Hymns, or Silius Italicus, than to invent it myself. (This is the first time in forty-odd years that I've found familiarity with Silius Italicus to be useful knowledge.)

One final note: the word "servant" occurs frequently in this novel. In Carce as in ancient Rome, the word generally means "slave."

I've heard intelligent people state that classical slavery wasn't as bad as slavery in America's antebellum South. You can make a case for that, but I consider it along the lines of arguing that the Spanish Inquisition wasn't as bad as the Gestapo.

A Roman householder had the power of life and death—and sexual control—over the slaves in his or her "family," and this power could be extended to freed slaves as well. I'm not writing a political tract, but the reader should be aware of this background in order to understand the social dynamics of *The Legions of Fire*. A servant in Victorian England might lose her position if the mistress became angry. A servant in Rome—or Carce—could lose considerably more.

I've had a lot of fun in trying to make a foreign culture accessible to modern readers. The fact that the culture is (pretty much) real and is one of the major underpinnings of Western civilization made my task even more fun.

But I'm not an educator. I'll have succeeded if you readers also have fun with my story.

DAVE DRAKE
www.david-drake.com

THE LEGIONS
OF FIRE

CHAPTER I

Corylus had ordered Pulto to wear a toga because he thought that he'd need his servant to swell the audience for the poetry reading by his friend and classmate Varus. Pulto hadn't complained—he'd been a soldier for twenty-five years and the batman of Corylus's father, Publius Cispius, for the last eighteen of them.

On the other hand, the young master hadn't specified footgear. Pulto had chosen to wear hobnailed army boots with the toga.

Corylus grinned as they turned from the Argiletum Boulevard onto the street where the town house of Senator Gaius Alphenus Saxa, Varus's father, stood. Pulto clashed along beside him, muttering curses. Hobnails were dangerous footwear on the streets of Carce. The stone pavers had been worn smooth as glass and were slimy besides: the last rain had been almost a month past, so more recent garbage hadn't been swept into the central gutters and thence to the river.

Corylus wasn't an army officer yet, but he'd learned a few things growing up on the Rhine and Danube frontiers, where his father had been first centurion of the Alaudae Legion and then tribune in command of the Third Batavian Cavalry. Sometimes letting your subordinates do just what they pleased was the most effective punishment you could visit on them.

Pulto caught the young master's smile and—after an

instant of bleakness—guffawed in good humor. "By Hercules, boy," he said, "you *are* the Old Man's son. I keep thinking you're the sprat I paddled for having a smart tongue. It'll serve me right if I fall on my ass, won't it? And have to get this *bloody* toga cleaned!"

Corylus laughed. "Maybe you're setting a new fashion trend," he said. "Carce is too stuffy about style, I think."

He'd never have ordered Pulto to wear his boots, but the ring of hobnails on stone turned out to have an unexpected benefit. Wagons weren't allowed inside the city until after dark, but peddlers, beggars, loungers, and other pedestrians clogged the streets, especially old ones like these in the very expensive Carinae District. To people who came from regions recently annexed to the Republic of Carce—and many of the city's poor did—the soldiers who'd done the annexing were still figures of terror.

As a citizen of the world educated by Pandareus of Athens, Corylus was disturbed by the implications of why people scuttled to the side or even hunched trembling with their heads covered. As a citizen of Carce and a soldier's son . . . well, he'd have been a liar if he'd claimed he didn't feel a touch of pride. And it did make it easier to walk without getting his toga smudged.

"How long do you guess this is going to go on, Master Corylus?" Pulto said, sounding resigned now instead of huffy. "Lord Varus's reading, I mean?"

When Corylus went to Carce to get the first-class education which Publius Cispius wanted for his son and heir, Pulto had come with him. Corylus knew that his father didn't expect him to live like a Stoic philosopher—Cispius had been a career soldier, after all, before he retired to the Bay of Puteoli and bought a very successful perfume business.

He didn't want his son to get in over his head if it could be avoided, however. The young master wouldn't be able to bully Pulto into letting him do something stupid.

And if trouble couldn't be avoided, well, Pulto was a good choice there, too. He'd stood over the Old Man when a Sarmatian lance had knocked him off his mount. By the time the rest of the troop rallied to relieve them, the servant had seventeen separate wounds—but when the tribune woke up, he had only a headache from hitting the frozen ground. Pulto limped and his fringe of remaining hair was gray, but neither Corylus nor his father knew anybody who was more to be trusted in an alley in the dark.

Pulto would rather face Sarmatian cavalry than listen to an epic poem, even if Homer himself were singing it. Unfortunately . . .

Varus was an erudite scholar and the only one of Pandareus's students with whom Corylus could deal as a friend. He put enormous effort into his verse; nobody could've worked harder.

But Varus wasn't Homer. Dull didn't begin to describe his poetry.

"I expect he'll finish by the eleventh hour," Corylus said, feeling a pang of guilt. "I, ah, think so. I may stay longer to chat, but you can change out of your toga as soon as the reading itself is over."

"We stood a dress inspection for the Emperor the onct," Pulto said stolidly. He settled the fold of his toga where it lay over his left shoulder; it wasn't pinned, which was all right if you were standing on a speaker's platform but less so if you were striding along at a military pace. "That was at Strasbourg. I guess I can take this."

"We're just about there," said Corylus soothingly. "Ten paces, soldier."

He didn't blame Pulto for disliking the toga, but it was the uniform of the day for this business—and in Carce generally, though the city was the only place in the empire where the old-fashioned garment was still in general use. In the provinces a citizen wore a tunic in warm weather and a cloak over it in the cold and wet. In Gaul a gentleman might even wear trousers in public without anybody objecting. The toga was for lawsuits and other formal occasions, like weddings and a son's coming-of-age ceremony.

Everything was formal in Carce. Even the slaves wore togas, at least the ones with any pretensions.

And speaking of pretentious slaves, Saxa seemed to have a new doorman, whose lip was curling upward as he watched Corylus and Pulto approach. In the year Corylus had lived in Carce, he'd learned what to expect from that expression.

Saxa let ground-floor rooms to shops on either side of the house entrance. There was a dealer in upscale leather goods for women on the far side; on the near side, a Greek jeweler named Archias bowed low to Corylus as he passed. Corylus had never done business with Archias, but the jeweler was unfailingly courteous to a friend of his landlord's son.

If the doorman had been more observant he would've noticed that. He'd been picked for his impressive appearance rather than his brains, though: he was broad-shouldered and well over six feet tall, with blond, lustrous shoulder-length hair.

Sneering at the two narrow purple bands on the hem of Corylus's toga, he said with a strong South German accent, "Around to the back entrance if you're looking for a handout. The Senator's hours for receiving riffraff are long past."

"Do you suppose he's one of the scum my father dragged to Carce in chains?" Corylus said, speaking German in a louder-than-conversational voice.

"Might be a bastard of mine, young master," Pulto rumbled back. "Venus knows the brothels at Vetera were mostly staffed with Suebian whores. About all the use I ever found for a Suebian, come to think."

From deeper inside the house, a female servant called cheerfully, "Agrippinus, you'd better get out here fast or you're going to have to replace the new doorman!"

The German had reached for the cudgel behind him, but the maid's voice penetrated his thick blond hair as the jeweler's deference had not. Red-faced, he straightened. "Whom shall I announce, gentlemen?" he croaked.

"Publius Corylus, a knight of Carce"—as indicated by the twin stripes on the toga; a member of the middle class and very much below a senator in rank—"and his companion, Marcus Pulto, by appointment to attend the public reading by their friend Gaius Alphenus Varus," Corylus said, speaking this time in formal Latin.

He was shaking with reaction. For a moment everything had blurred to gray in his sight except the necessary parts of the German's body. *Grab the left wrist and twist hard so that the blond head crashes into the transom. Pulto would kick the German's knee sideways, breaking it, so Corylus could topple him into the street where they would both work him over with their boots. . . .*

"Master Corylus, how delightful to see you again!" said Agrippinus, Saxa's majordomo: plump, oiled, and *very* smooth. He spoke Latin like an aristocrat of Carce and Greek like an Athenian philosopher, but he was a former slave who'd been born in Spain. "And how pleased Lord Varus will be that you're present for his literary triumph! Please, let me lead you into the Black-and-Gold Hall, where Lord Varus will be reading."

Corylus had visited the house scores of times. Agrippinus knew he didn't need a guide, but it was important that the doorman learn that the youth was a friend of the family rather than being one of the parasites who haunted great men's doors in hopes of an invitation to fill out the dinner party. To underscore the fact, the majordomo said over his shoulder, "I'll want to have a discussion with you, Flavus, when Gigax relieves you at nightfall."

Agrippinus minced quickly through the entrance hall. Half a dozen servants stood there around the pool which caught rainwater from the in-sloping roof. They bowed, but Corylus suspected the gesture was paid not to the visitors but to the majordomo. Agrippinus's present aura of pompous formality was even more impressive than his toga of bleached wool with gold embroidery.

Instead of continuing on into the office which was in line with the entrance, Agrippinus turned right to enter the portico surrounding the large garden in the center of the house. Saxa's house had no exterior windows on the ground floor, but the garden acted as a light well and also provided flowers and fruit in a bustling city. The roofs over this main section of the house fed the pool in the middle of the garden, but they did so through downspouts and sunken pipes.

The Black-and-Gold Hall interrupted the portico in the middle of the east side, opening directly onto the garden for the maximum of light. Ornate frames of gold paint separated the black panels of the walls, each of which had a golden miniature of a fanciful creature in the center. The dais on which Varus would read was against the back wall, but there was a triple lamp stand to either side.

Just now Varus stood stiffly beside the dais. He was talking with Pandareus, who taught public speaking to a class of twelve youths including Varus and Corylus.

Varus and Corylus also learned to love literature and Truth. Their classmates saw no value to literature except to add colors to an oration—and as for Truth, if they ever thought about it, was a danger which successful attorneys shunned.

"By Hercules, the bloody room's full!" muttered Pulto.

He sounded amazed. So was Corylus, because the statement was undeniably true.

"Please come to the front, Master Corylus," Agrippinus said, starting down the center aisle. The room, thirty feet wide and nearly that deep, now held two files of benches which must have been rented for today's event. The seats weren't packed as tight as the bleachers of the Circus during a program of chariot races, but people were going to have to move if the newcomers were to sit down.

"A moment, if you please," Corylus said with a curt gesture to the majordomo. "Pulto, you can suit yourself. While you're welcome to listen to the reading with me—"

"Venus and Mars, young master," Pulto said, grinning broadly. "If you don't mind, I'll be in the gym chewing the fat with my buddy Lenatus till you're ready to go home."

"Dismissed," said Corylus, falling into military terminology naturally. Between Cispius and Pulto, "Army" had been the household tongue when Corylus was growing up. His mother had died in childbirth; his nurse, Anna, had taught him the Oscan language and a great deal of superstition, but she hadn't cared any more for roundabout politeness than the men had.

Anna was now Pulto's wife. She was just as superstitious as she had been when Corylus was a child; but as he grew older, he'd come to realize that quite a lot of Anna's superstitious nonsense was in fact quite true.

Corylus nodded to Agrippinus; they resumed their way to the front. Gaius Saxa had obviously done what he considered a father's duty to his son: he'd sent invitations to all his senatorial friends. They hadn't come, of course, and Saxa wasn't present either. They'd sent clients and retainers, though, men who were beholden to them and who made a brilliant show in the hall. Some of the senators' freedmen here were not only wealthier than Cispius, they had a great deal more power in the Republic than a retired tribune did.

Varus would appreciate his father's gesture, but the expensively decorated togas drove home the fact that Corylus and Pandareus were the only people in the audience who'd come to hear the poetry. And even they—well, Corylus was here out of friendship and Pandareus might well regard his presence as a teacher's duty.

Corylus grinned, then quickly suppressed the expression. The thought behind it was unkind to a friend. It was traditional that poets suffered. In Varus's case, the problem wasn't poverty or a fickle girlfriend: it was lack of talent. Which, for somebody who cared as deeply about his art as Varus did, was a far worse punishment.

Agrippinus gestured toward the place which had just opened in the front row, on the right side of the center aisle. "Or would you care . . . ?" he said, tilting his head delicately toward Varus, whose back was to the room while he talked with his teacher.

"No, I'll speak to him after the reading," Corylus said. *Varus is nervous enough already. . . .* He settled himself carefully onto the bench.

Togas weren't really intended to be worn while sitting down. Ancient Carce had transacted all public business while standing. A less stiff-necked people would've changed to a more comfortable formal garment before now, but a less stiff-necked people wouldn't have conquered what was already the largest empire in history. A soldier's son could get used to wearing a toga.

Corylus had met Varus when they both became students of Pandareus a year before. Pulto had already known a member of Alphenus's staff, however: Marcus Lenatus, the household's personal trainer, was an old soldier and an old friend of Pulto's from the Rhine. Corylus would have been able to exercise in the private gymnasium in a back corner of the house even if the Senator's son hadn't invited him to do so.

The man on the bench beside Corylus was, from his conversation with the fellow to his other side, the steward of another senator whose master was planning a banquet in a few days' time. It was the sort of thing that would've bored Corylus to tears even if the servants had tried to make him a part of the discussion. Agrippinus might feel it was politic to show deference to a friend of the family, but these men had no reason to pretend a mere knight was as interesting as a hare stuffed with thrushes which had been stuffed in turn with truffles.

Corylus smiled faintly. He supposed he wouldn't turn down a portion of the lovingly prepared hare—so long as it came with bread and onions. *That* was a soldier's meal. It wasn't an accident that the frontiers of the empire stopped at the edge of where farmers plowed fields instead of grazing goats or cattle.

Lenatus and the gym wouldn't get much use if it weren't for Corylus. Saxa saw the trainer only during the Saturnalia festivities, when he visited each post of duty to give the servants their year-end tip. Varus sometimes tried to exercise, but he'd begun coming regularly only to keep Corylus company. Even then, he often sat on the masonry bench built out from the dressing rooms and jotted poetic inspirations in a notebook.

Saxa didn't care about the waste of money, of course. A private gymnasium was a proper facility for a man of his stature, so he had one.

He also had day and night shifts of servants servicing the water clock in the central garden: a man to empty the quarter-hour tumblers; a man with a rod to ring each quarter on a silver triangle; and a third man with a bugle to sound the hour. Each servant had an understudy, ready to take over the duties in case the principal died of apoplexy while pouring, ringing, or striking.

Alphena, Saxa's daughter by his first wife, used the gymnasium too. Corylus felt his face stiffen out of the smile that was its usual expression.

The girl was sixteen, a year younger than Corylus and Varus. Alphena and her brother were both stocky and of middling height like their father, proper descendants of the sturdy farmers of Carce who had spread from their hilltop village to conquer a great empire.

Alphena would never be a great beauty, but she was cute and full of an energy that would have made people notice her even if she had behaved with decorum. Which she most certainly did not.

Corylus had realized even before he came to Carce that the only people who really set store by proper behavior were the solid folk in the middle ranks of society: peasant farmers and small businessmen. The poor were too busy scraping out a living to worry about such things; even a youthful moralist could understand their attitude.

But the very rich were if anything worse.

Alphena wasn't promiscuous, but that at least would have been an ordinary feminine failing. Alphena *wasn't* feminine. She acted as though she were Saxa's son, not his daughter, and the more masculine son besides. With Varus as her brother, that wasn't much of a stretch.

The stewards beside Corylus were discussing ways to make counterfeit mullets out of minced pork. At first that sounded reasonable to the part of Corylus's mind that was listening; mullet was a very expensive fish. As the conversation continued, he realized that the fake fish were even pricier than the real thing, and that the greater cost was the reason they'd been chosen for the banquet. It wasn't about food at all, just status.

Corylus would much rather be in the gym with the

two old soldiers, hacking at a post with a practice sword. He'd even rather—

He eyed Varus's stiff pose critically.

Corylus would *almost* rather be preparing to read bad poetry to an audience of strangers and his teacher.

VARUS FELT A rush of gratitude when he saw Publius Corylus and his man at the entrance to the hall. Corylus had said he was coming and he'd never given anyone reason to doubt his word, but even so the relief of having a friend present was greater than Varus would have guessed.

Pandareus wasn't an enemy, of course, but just now as the teacher glanced over the poem Varus felt a sort of blind hatred. He imagined that a worm might feel the same way about the robin whose beak had just plucked him from a leaf.

Varus smiled broadly. Pandareus shuffled the scroll expertly with his left hand, taking up the pages he'd skimmed while his right in perfect unison opened the unread portion. He glanced up from the verse and said, "A happy thought, Lord Varus?"

"Master Pandareus . . . ," Varus said, chilled as if he'd been asked to expound on a passage he'd read only moments before. "I know that I take myself far too seriously; I can't help it. But at least I can laugh at myself for taking myself too seriously."

Pandareus said nothing for a moment, then smiled as broadly as Varus had ever seen. "The first rule of a philosopher is 'Know thyself,' Lord Varus," he said. "I would say you've come further in that study than many of my long-bearded colleagues who expound their wisdom in the Forum and at the dinners of the wealthy."

He went back to reading *About the Heroic Life and Martyrdom of Publius Atilius Regulus*. Varus intended it as his first trial at his life's work: the epic of Carce's struggle with Carthage. Indeed, perhaps it would still be unfinished at his death, as Vergil had left his immortal *Aeneid*.

Literature was a proper arena for a gentleman; especially for a gentleman who had no talent for war. Varus wasn't a coward—he wouldn't be declaiming his own verse to an audience if he were a coward—but the sight of blood made him squeamish.

While Varus was writing, he could *feel* the thing beyond the words. Somewhere out there was the true ideal that he was striving for. But he couldn't see it, *nobody* could see it, and no poet would ever reach it.

Sometimes Varus told himself he was blessed above other men because he knew there was an ideal. At other times—and this was certainly one of those other times—it seemed to him that lucky people didn't torture themselves by chasing the unobtainable. That was obvious when he looked at Pandareus's other students.

Corylus had an interest in literature, but he didn't hold it in the sort of religious awe that Varus did. The other ten students were wellborn—six, like Varus, were the sons of senators—but they were at most interested in learning how to argue a case in court. That was a matter of extravagant language, flashy figures of speech, and skeins of logic which had been twisted until they screamed.

But half the class didn't care even about learning tools to use in court. They attended classes—or their fathers sent them to classes—because there was a cachet in saying you'd been taught by Pandareus of Athens—Pandareus the Sage, some of the parents called him, though Varus had never heard Pandareus himself use that boastful title. For them *everything* was appearance, not a pursuit of the ideal.

Pursuit of the unattainable ideal.

Varus's mind was lost in a very present philosophy of

life, but his eyes must have been focused on Pandareus. The teacher looked up and said mildly, "A very well-prepared manuscript, Lord Varus." He gave the volume a twitch to emphasize it.

"Yes, master!" Varus said. He was relieved that he hadn't squeaked; he felt seven, not seventeen. "I, ah, thought it would give a better impression to the audience if it was, ah, neat."

One of the clerks in Saxa's business office had a fine hand, but in the end Varus had decided to go to Marcus Balbius, who produced manuscripts for sale. In the main Balbius specialized in cheap reading copies by popular poets, but he had a sideline in presentation volumes; he'd been more than happy to produce a manuscript of the very highest quality for Varus.

Pandareus went back to reading. Varus realized that his teacher was deliberately preventing him from compulsively going over the document during the last quarter hour before the declamation. He'd have worked himself into a state if he'd done that, and he wouldn't have been able to prevent himself from doing it even though he knew better.

Pandareus was being kind to him. Varus would still rather have been standing on a dune in the Libyan desert than watching his teacher roll the volume forward and stop, roll and stop; his lean face all the while as expressionless as that of a vulture.

The volume shimmered. The roller sticks had been gilded, and red silk ribbons fluttered from their ends. The papyrus had been pumiced smooth before being whitened, and the calligrapher's hand was flawless as well as being unusually legible for a work of art.

Varus honestly didn't know what the manuscript had cost. Whenever Balbius presented the account, Agrippinus would settle it just as he did those from vintners, poulterers, fullers, and all the rest of the tradesmen who supplied the household of a wealthy senator. Saxa wouldn't notice the amount any more than he noted what Hedia, his new young wife, spent on dressmakers.

"Ah . . . ?" Varus said, struck by a sudden fear. "Master, though the manuscript was professionally prepared, I really did write the verse myself. On wax notebooks. Every bit of it."

Pandareus paused and stared at him. "You may set your mind at rest, Lord Varus," he said. His dry voice was all the more cutting for not having any emotional loading whatever. "I did not imagine that this—"

He waggled the volume again. The gesture gave the impression of the mistress of the house holding a dead rat by the tail as she gingerly removed it from the kitchen.

"—had been plagiarized."

Varus felt his face glow. "Sorry, master," he muttered. He shuffled, glancing toward the audience just to avoid looking at his teacher. His eyes caught Corylus in the front row. He looked up toward the ceiling immediately. It was bad enough being here as Pandareus judged him; it would be even worse to be judged in front of his only friend. Being reminded that Corylus was present helped settle him again, though.

Corylus's father, Publius Cispius, was wealthy by the standards of most people—but not by the standards of the senators' sons who were the majority of Pandareus's students. Besides facing ordinary snobbery, Corylus was an army brat—raised in camps along the frontier instead of the relatively civilized surroundings of a provincial city. He might have had a very difficult time of it in school, especially since Piso, the acknowledged leader of the class, had a cruel streak.

It wouldn't have helped Corylus that he was a real scholar instead of a numskull more familiar with swagger sticks than with the rollers of a book; his scholarship might even have made it worse. And it certainly didn't help that he and Varus had become friends. Gaius Alphenus Saxa was powerful enough that his son wouldn't be bullied, even by a Calpurnius Piso, but to extend his protection further would require that Varus have an active personality instead of being a loner, and a rather puny loner besides.

Corylus was tall and had fair hair from his Celtic mother. Presumably he'd gotten his slender build from her also, but Piso had learned the first afternoon following class that "slender" didn't mean "weak." He'd shoved Varus and found himself with his right arm twisted up behind his back and his thumb in a grip that could obviously dislocate it any time Corylus wanted to.

Another boy—Beccaristo, son of a wealthy shipper from Ostia and Piso's chief toady—tried to jump Corylus. He fell screaming when Corylus brought his heavy sandal down on his instep.

Piso had shouted for his entourage of servants to help. None of them moved. Corylus's man hadn't said a word, just watched with his right hand under his toga. The thing he was gripping would be about the right length for an infantry sword.

Corylus had released Piso then. He'd straightened his toga and grinned, not saying a word. And Varus had said, "Master Corylus, would you care to come home with me for some refreshment? I'd like to discuss the *Epilion* of Callimachus, which the master cited in his lecture."

Varus warmed at the memory. It was probably the smartest thing he'd ever done in his life. It had cemented his friendship with Corylus at the very beginning of their relationship.

Pandareus rolled the volume closed with the same smooth grace as he'd been reading it with. "Thank you for the early look, Master Varus," he said formally as he handed it back. "I await your reading with interest."

The water clock reached the tenth hour, the time set

for the declamation. The bugler called over the ringing of the quarter-hour gong.

Apollo and the Muses, be with your servant, Varus whispered under his breath as he mounted the podium.

As if to make him even more uncomfortable than he already was, his sister, Alphena, came marching down the aisle without so much as a maid to accompany her. She gave a peremptory gesture to the freedmen beside Corylus and sat down in the front row, glaring up at Varus.

She looked furious.

THE REAL PROBLEM was Nemastes the Hyperborean, but Alphena wasn't allowing herself to think about that. She was as angry as she ever remembered being. *How dare my stepmother tell me that I need to get married! Why doesn't Father stand up to her?*

This was one of those times that Alphena wished she weren't quite as smart as she knew she was. Much as she fumed over Hedia—who was only six years older, even though she was on her second husband already!— Alphena knew that underneath she was afraid, not angry.

She was afraid for her father. Ever since he met the Hyperborean wizard, Saxa had been acting strangely. He'd always been, well, a bit of a fool about the supernatural. Her father was a senator of Carce and one of the most powerful men on earth, so it was unkind of Alphena to suspect that he was unusually willing to believe in higher powers because he knew how incapable *he* was of intelligently exercising the authority he'd been given.

Alphena stamped into the Black-and-Gold Hall without any clearer notion than knowing that she would shock everyone by being the only woman in the audience—and that Hedia wouldn't follow her here. As soon as she was inside, she remembered seeing Publius Corylus coming up the street a moment before her stepmother drew her aside for an unwanted discussion.

Corylus was in the front row, so Alphena strode down the aisle toward him. When one of the wealthy freedmen seated there glanced up, she showed him her left fist with the thumb raised. That was the way the audience voted death in the amphitheater.

The freedman shot from the bench like a lion prodded into greater liveliness with a torch; he'd obviously understood Alphena's mood. Very possibly he had heard stories about the would-be poet's sister when he asked about the event he'd been ordered to attend.

The freedman to whom he'd been talking looked up in surprise; he saw Alphena bearing down like an angry weasel. He scampered also, though his fat friend's absence had cleared enough space already.

Corylus looked startled, then faced front and pretended not to notice that Alphena had sat down beside him. For a moment, she'd started to let fear break through her mind's surface of anger; Corylus's action brought the anger back to full blazing life.

Alphena wasn't interested in Corylus; not *that* kind of interested. He was only a knight after all, and even that by sufferance: his father had managed to stay alive for twenty-five years in the army and had his status raised from ordinary lummox to knight. She knew that soldiers were necessary on the frontiers to keep out the even cruder barbarians beyond, but it seemed to Alphena that they should stay in the border districts instead of coming here to Carce.

Of course Corylus wasn't a soldier himself; and though Alphena knew he intended to become one, she found it hard to imagine the youth as what she imagined a soldier was. Maybe . . .

Alphena didn't blush, but she pressed her lips together more closely. She *was* smart, not bookish smart like her brother but in the way that let her look at people and things and understand how they fit together. When parts didn't fit, one had the wrong shape. In this case, she knew that the mistake could be in what she thought a soldier was, instead of in the shape of Corylus who planned to become one.

She still wasn't interested in him. Of course!

Alphena had been the only person to use the gymnasium for over a year. Lenatus had informed Saxa that Alphena wanted the sort of lessons he'd expected to give Varus. He'd hoped his employer would order him to do no such thing. The Senator instead acted as though he hadn't heard the statement.

Lenatus had been angry and embarrassed to train a woman, but Saxa paid well. The first thing a new servant in his household learned was that the master wanted to have a quiet life—and that if the daughter of the house was angry, she would make her father's life a living hell until he did what she wanted.

Lenatus had thereupon gotten on with his job, which, in the household of Gaius Alphenus Saxa, turned out to be training a young girl as though she were to become a soldier—or a gladiator. After a while he'd more or less gotten used to it. Alphena had heard him tell the cook that it was like learning to drink ale instead of wine when he'd been stationed in Upper Germany: it wasn't the way it ought to be, but that didn't matter.

Then Varus had offered his new friend use of the facilities.

Alphena had watched Corylus the first time he exercised. Corylus had protested, but Varus wouldn't stand up to his sister. In part she was being contrary—she did quite a number of things because she knew that other people would rather she didn't—but she was also proving that nobody in the household could prevent her from doing what she wanted.

As for Lenatus, he'd taken his master's lesson to heart: he pretended he didn't hear either party to the argument.

Corylus had at last gone ahead with his basic drills, despite the audience. He couldn't order around the family of the man from whom he was accepting a favor. Alphena had colored when he said, "When in Carce, one follows the customs of Carce," and bowed low to her, however. He'd made the light comment sound more insulting than a tirade from a bearded Stoic philosopher.

"Gentlemen of Carce!" squeaked Varus. *Oh, Venus and Mars, he sounds so young!* "I welcome you on my own behalf and on behalf of Senator Gaius Saxa, my noble father and patron!"

The audience shuffled its feet dutifully, indicating its appreciation of the greeting. Alphena turned and glanced back, wondering if Saxa had come in after she did. She couldn't see the whole room—she was shorter than most of the richly dressed freedmen—but she knew that the Senator's presence would have caused a stir.

Saxa was probably off with Nemastes again; he seemed to spend all his time with the Hyperborean. He had never pretended to care about literature, of course, so he probably wouldn't have been present at his son's reading regardless.

Saxa was a good father in most fashions. He never ranted at his children about their behavior, and he supplied the money for their whims without objection or concern. He even seemed to care about their well-being, though he viewed them from a foggy distance.

Alphena didn't love Saxa; that would be like saying she loved the ornamental pond in the garden. But she liked him a good deal, and she certainly didn't want her existence to change so that he was no longer part of her life. One way or another, Nemastes the Hyperborean meant change.

"The filthy River Baroda slowly plows the sandy wastes

of Libya," Varus said, beginning to chant his poem. His voice had settled out of its initial squeak, but it had no more life than the plash of rain into the cistern in the entranceway.

Alphena had heard established poets and professional singers whom her father had invited to dinner parties. Some of them were better than others, but she couldn't compare even the worst of them to what she was hearing now. Her brother's delivery was as dull as watching concrete set.

Nemastes had appeared two weeks earlier as a petitioner at Saxa's morning levee. The Hyperborean was only a short step up from the outright beggars who crowded every rich man's doorstep until the servants ran them away, but because he claimed to be a wizard he'd been admitted to the office after Saxa and his more important clients had exchanged greetings.

Nobody seemed to know what had happened then, but Saxa and the Hyperborean had spent most of their waking hours together ever since. Indeed, Saxa had announced that Nemastes would be moving into the town house—

But that plan had collided with Hedia. Nemastes might well be a wizard, but Saxa's third wife had proved a match for whatever magic he was using on the Senator. There'd been a blazing argument—Hedia was petite, but her lungs and projection could match a professional actor's—at the end of which the two men had left the house. Saxa had returned alone later that evening.

"A dragon a hundred cubits long lived near that fateful bank, in a grove like the Avernian entrance to the Underworld," chanted Varus. His expression mingled terror with resignation. Alphena wondered in a clinical fashion whether that was how men looked when they were waiting to be executed.

She hadn't respected her brother until she realized that

Publius Corylus *did* respect him. Of course a rich man's son would always have men—and women, of a sort—crawling about him. Varus had stayed free of parasites, however, in much the same fashion in which he had the mud wiped from his shoes when he'd been caught outdoors in the rain.

Corylus wasn't a toady trying to cadge wine and dinners at the tables of the wealthy. He treated Varus with the respect owed a senator's son—and treated Saxa, when they occasionally met, with the greater respect owed a senator; but it was always the respect which a free man owed his social superiors, not cringing servility. He'd befriended Varus as a still-more-learned scholar.

Corylus didn't behave in an improper fashion toward Alphena. She'd have cut him off at the ankles if he had, but with a sense of smirking satisfaction; he was, after all, a handsome youth though a member of the lower orders. Instead, ever since their first loud argument about her presence in the gym, he pretended not to be aware of her existence. *Which is just what he's doing now.*

Alphena's lips set in a hard line. With the two freedmen gone, there was room on the bench for three Alphenas. She squidgled closer to Corylus, bringing her left thigh in contact with his right.

He didn't twitch, not even to move away. She would have gotten as much reaction from a statue. He seemed completely lost in her brother's poem, though how anybody could really listen to that twaddle was beyond her.

"The monster split the earth and raised its glittering head to the stars," Varus chanted. His hawk-featured teacher was jotting in a notebook of waxed boards, though his eyes never left the boy's face. Judging from Pandareus's expression, he wouldn't have anything pleasant to say to Varus at the end of the session . . . but maybe that was unfair. He might be serious rather than fierce.

Alphena hadn't taken well to Hedia when Saxa brought his new wife home. His first wife, Marcia, had given him both his children but died of fever a week after Alphena was born.

Sometimes Alphena wondered what it would be like to have known her mother, but now that she was a teenager, she knew that she had seen as much of Marcia as most of her acquaintances did of their mothers. Even when the parents remained married, the wife's social life was more important than the child-rearing duties, which could, of course, be delegated to a slave or an inexpensive peasant woman.

Saxa had then married Secunda, her mother's younger sister. Alphena remembered seeing her several times in the three years or so the marriage had lasted. Secunda had flitted occasionally through her life with a train of maids and pages, perfectly dressed. Each time, she dipped her fan toward the children, gave them a gracious smile, and continued on her way.

Alphena imagined that Secunda had a lovely, melodious voice, but she'd never heard it. She wondered if Varus had.

After the divorce—Alphena couldn't even guess when that had been; she'd been young, and neither the marriage nor its dissolution seemed to have been matters of great moment, even to the couple itself—the affairs of the Senator's household had gone on in a very placid fashion. Alphena's nurses and other female servants had made sure that she learned What Men Are Like—but frankly, her father had never struck her as that sort of man. Indeed, often he didn't seem to be any sort of man.

Thus when Saxa suddenly married the widow of his cousin, Calpurnius Latus, the mere fact had been a terrible shock to Alphena. Hedia herself had been a much worse surprise. Unlike Secunda—and probably Marcia—she had immediately become involved in every aspect of the household, including her husband's sixteen-year-old daughter.

Even a girl brought up to prize the feminine virtues of good breeding and decorum would have found the situation a wrench. Alphena had early on set out to be the son which her brother certainly was not. The new marriage had made her blaze like a funeral pyre even before she heard the stories about her stepmother which the servants were only too happy to retail. If so many as half of them were true, Hedia was a fast woman and no better than she should be.

In addition, rumor said that not fever but poison offered by his wife had carried off Calpurnius Latus. Was her father out of his mind?

"The monster filled its vast gullet and its poison-pregnant belly with full-grown lions which it snatched as they came down to the Bagrada to drink!" chanted Varus. The snake that lived in the Temple of Feminine Fortune—the spirit of the temple, the priest said—ate morsels of bread sopped in milk, but you were expected to provide a silver piece to the priest also if you wished to be certain that your prayer would be honored.

It would take a great deal of bread and milk to feed a snake the size of the one Varus had invented. Alphena wouldn't have thought lions were so common in Libya that they made a reasonable alternative, though.

She felt the solid presence of Corylus's thigh, but his mind seemed to be in another world. He wasn't so much avoiding Alphena as unaware of her existence.

Alphena had intended to ignore her stepmother, but Hedia hadn't permitted that to happen. The day after Saxa brought his new wife home, she had made an inventory of the town house. Agrippinus had guided her, but even then Alphena had realized that Hedia was in charge.

The servants treated Alphena like a small dog with a

tendency to bite; they respected and feared their new mistress, which was quite different. That had been another case in which Alphena would have been less angry if she hadn't seen the reality of things so clearly.

Hedia was all the things Saxa's daughter was not: beautiful, sophisticated, and sleek. Alphena had thought it would be easy to hate her; and perhaps she did, but she found she respected Hedia as well. The older woman was as much at war with society's view of Proper Womanhood as Alphena was, though their techniques could scarcely have been more different.

And Hedia was a lot more successful in her revolt.

"The monster roared!" sang Varus. "It was louder than the booming East Wind, more violent than the tempest which shakes the sea bare to its depths!"

Why does she insist that I get married? Alphena thought. And then with a silent wail she added, *And why does Corylus ignore me? I've seen him look at* her!

She shivered. The room was crowded and should have been uncomfortably warm at this time in the afternoon, but she'd felt a chill touch her spine. Corylus was as cold and distant as the image of Jupiter Best and Greatest in his temple on the Capitoline Hill.

Alphena tried to be angry with her stepmother, but she knew in her heart that Hedia meant well by her. *So why does she insist I get married?*

She was afraid she knew the answer.

"We fled," sang Varus, "breathless with terror—but in vain!"

HEDIA STOOD IN the doorway to the portico around the central garden. Her expression was as calm and aristocratic as those of the death masks of her husband's noble ancestors hanging from the walls of the reception room behind her. Both had been whitened, her face with rice flour, and white lead for the wax which decades and even centuries had turned black.

Hedia doubted that the ancestral masks were angry. She made it a point of pride that people around her couldn't read her emotional state, but obviously she wasn't as successful as she would have hoped: her personal maid, Syra, was in a state of terror.

Hedia patted the girl's wrist with her left hand. "It's quite all right, dear," she said. "It's nothing to do with you."

Syra's lip quivered. Her eyes were fixed on the great purple flowers of the cardoons in the garden, but tears dribbled from their outer corners.

Does the fool think I'm going to have her tortured to death because my stepdaughter won't listen to me? Hedia thought in a fury. *How dare she!* She raised the folded fan in her right hand—

And caught herself with a sudden giggle. Syra had been with Hedia for five years, through her first marriage. She was a perceptive girl. Sometimes rather too perceptive for her own good.

There were over two hundred servants in Saxa's town house. Syra was the only one Hedia could see at the moment, and the maid would have fled too if she had dared. They all knew that the mistress was angry, and they weren't sure that there was any limit on the kind of punishments that anger could lead to.

Normally servants swarmed in every room unless you ordered them out, and even then they'd be listening at doors and from outside under the windows. A rich man and his spouse had no more privacy than did the members of a poor family crammed six or ten to a tenement apartment.

Which was why Hedia was furious about her husband's *stupid* behavior. She didn't know what this Nemastes was doing, but she was quite certain that when the Emperor heard about it—when, not if—he and his inquisitors would take a dim view.

If Saxa had been carrying on at one of his rural estates—he had a score of them, scattered from Spain to Syria—he might have gotten away with it at least for a while. This was the middle of Carce. Every time Hedia heard horses in the street outside, her heart leaped with the thought that it was a troop of the German Bodyguards come to arrest everybody in the house and carry them to the palace for questioning.

They'd start with the slaves, of course, but neither Saxa's lineage nor Hedia's own would spare them from torture when the Emperor's safety was at risk. So *stupid*.

Hedia gave Syra a look of calm appraisal. The maid didn't look away, but she squeezed her eyelids shut. Tears continued to dribble from beneath them, and it was obviously taking all her strength to stifle the sobs.

Hedia didn't have anybody to talk to. If she said, "Syra, what do you think this Nemastes is really after?" the girl would simply stare like a rabbit facing a weasel. And Syra didn't have an answer; none of the servants had an answer, no more than Hedia herself had an answer.

As if she were reading Hedia's mind, Syra whispered, "Your ladyship, do you think the Senator's new foreign friend is a real magician?"

Hedia smiled wryly. Syra's eyes were still closed. She'd spoken because she was more afraid of silence than of speaking; and she'd asked the same empty question her mistress would have asked if she'd permitted herself the weakness.

"Oh, I don't imagine so, Syra," Hedia said lightly. "No doubt there are real magicians in the world, but I'm afraid my dear Gaius Saxa is more the sort to attract charlatans and confidence men. I suppose that's all right so long as it amuses him. He can afford his whims, after all."

By Astarte's tits! she thought behind her bland smile. *How I wish I thought Nemastes was a charlatan.*

Hedia had met—and had done various other things with—quite a number of charismatic, powerful men at one time or another. Nemastes wasn't simply a foreigner who had fasted himself thin and shaved his scalp clean.

For one thing, he wasn't shaven and it wasn't his scalp alone: his whole body was as hairless as an egg. The linen singlet the Hyperborean—wherever and whatever Hyperborea was—wore had few secrets from eyes as practiced as Hedia's at assessing men.

If she'd seen him only once, she could think he'd had his body waxed to impress the gullible. There was no sign of regrowing hair on any of the later visits, however. That didn't prove Nemastes was a magician. Hedia was quite sure he was something, though; and Hedia hadn't needed to feel the hatred boiling from the fellow's eyes to know that he was something dangerous to know.

Varus began to recite; Hedia looked toward the entrance of the hall. From where she stood, the words were a drone with an irritating timbre. She suspected—she grinned at Syra, but the maid didn't grin back—that the audience heard a louder version of the same irritating drone.

When Alphena had turned and scurried into the hall, Hedia had seriously considered striding in herself and retrieving the girl. Saxa's daughter was used to being the only person present who didn't mind a scene. That had changed when her father remarried, and the sooner the girl learned it, the better off they all would be.

"I thought of dragging Lady Alphena out by the ear," Hedia said in a low but conversational tone.

Syra's eyes were open again; the words made her blink. "The young lady is very athletic," the maid said carefully. She obviously wasn't sure whether her mistress was joking. "She practices in the gymnasium almost daily."

Hedia let her smile spread slightly. "I wasn't proposing to put on armor and duel her," she said. "If you haven't had it happen to you, Syra, you can't imagine how painful it is to have someone twisting your ear. You'll walk along with them rather than do anything that pulls harder on it."

She mused on the Black-and-Gold Hall. It wasn't anything to do with Alphena which had stopped Hedia from acting on her first impulse; rather, it was the embarrassment the scene would have caused Varus.

He wasn't the kind of man—boy—that Hedia would ordinarily have paid any attention to. He was a quiet little fellow, bookish and above all *earnest*. Sometimes that was a pose: Hedia had let one of her first husband's philosophical friends grope her beneath a bust of Zeno in his library because the split between appearance and reality amused her.

In Varus's case, it was poetry rather than philosophy— they were much of a sameness, of course, just words either one—but Varus couldn't have been more serious about His Art. Hedia took her duties as mother seriously. She wouldn't think of turning the boy's first public recital into a farce.

She listened critically a little while longer. Varus seemed to be doing quite well at creating a farce on his own. Perhaps tomorrow she could take him aside and discuss with him more suitable ways for a young man of his station to become part of public life. Misery might have made him malleable.

Her lips tightened. Syra noticed the minute change in expression and winced, so Hedia forced herself to smile again. *If I move quickly enough, I can marry Alphena off and save her from her father's ruin.*

There was nothing she could do for Saxa's son, though. Varus was doomed even if Hedia encouraged him to go to the right sort of drinking parties and perhaps introduced him to women who would like to polish the education of a boy who seemed younger than his years.

Hedia didn't care about Varus, but she cared quite a lot about Saxa. If there'd been a way to snatch her husband's male issue from the disaster, she would have done so.

Saxa was a bit of a mystic and a bit of a fool. The best Hedia could say for his physical approaches to her was that they were well intentioned and perhaps not the clumsiest of her considerable experience. But he was *kind*, a genuinely decent man, and one who could see the real heart of things more clearly than anyone else she knew.

Saxa's offer of marriage close on the heels of the death of his cousin, Calpurnius Latus, had been as surprising as it was welcome. Hedia hadn't murdered Latus—indeed, it was likely enough that fever, not poison by his hand or that of another, had carried her husband off. It wouldn't have been hard to suggest otherwise, however, and Latus's well-connected family had a considerable legacy to gain if the widow was executed for his murder.

All the whispers had stopped when Saxa married the widow. A cynic might suspect that he had simply scooped the legacy from the other relatives. Nobody who knew Saxa would believe that, however: he was not only staggeringly rich, he was as little interested in money for its own sake as any man in the Senate.

Perhaps Saxa had seen an excitement in Hedia which his life had lacked to that time. As for Hedia herself—

She paused, thinking. Saxa had given her safety, a debt which she would repay to the best of her ability. But he unexpectedly had brought her a kind of sweetness which she hadn't to that point imagined.

Saxa was a silly old buffer, but she loved him. Which was something else she hadn't imagined would ever happen.

There were voices at the front door; the German accent of the handsome new doorman was unmistakable. Immediately servants appeared from nooks and crannies. This sometimes made Hedia think of the way roaches scrambled if you walked into the pantry at night with a lamp.

She stepped into the reception hall. A pair of the attendants who'd left with Saxa in the morning were jabbering directions to Agrippinus. The majordomo must have been in the office . . . though how he'd gotten there without Hedia seeing him pass completely escaped her.

"Mistress," he said with a bow. "Our lord the Senator has requested that a lighted brazier be placed in the back garden for him and a companion. They will be arriving shortly."

"Then you had better do it," said Hedia, dismissing him with a crisp nod.

The two messengers started off with Agrippinus. "*Not* you, Bellatus," Hedia snapped to the one whose name she remembered.

Bellatus froze as though he had taken an arrow through the spine. "Mistress?" he quavered.

"Will my lord's companion be Nemastes the Foreigner?" she asked.

"I, ah, believe he might be, noble mistress," the servant said. He knelt, more to hide his face than to honor her, she thought.

"You may go," Hedia said, her tone mild and ironic.

Bellatus scampered away. *That's just as well,* thought Hedia with a faint smile. *If he'd stayed a moment or two longer, I'd have slashed him across the face with my fan.*

Clicking the ivory slats open and closed, Hedia took her position in front of the tiled pond in the entranceway. The edges of the fan had been painted while it was slightly ajar, then closed and gilded. If you ruffled the slats *just* right, you saw a nude girl on one side and a simply charming youth on the other.

Hedia continued to smile as she watched through the open outside door at the end of the hall. The messengers couldn't have been very far ahead of Saxa and the Hyperborean.

The servants had vanished again, all but Syra, who was looking determinedly toward the garden instead of out into the street. The maid couldn't flee, but she could pretend she was somewhere else.

There was a bustle outside. The doorman stepped into the street and bellowed, "All hail our noble master Gaius Alphenus Saxa, twice consul and senator!"

That was what Flavus meant to say, at any rate. Between his poor grasp of Latin and a German accent that made everything sound as though he had a mouthful of pork, you had to know what the words should be to understand him.

The crowd of clients bowed and saluted in the street. There were forty and more of them on a normal day, men who either owed Saxa service or hoped for a favor. Favors could range from occasional dinners and a small basket of coins during the Saturnalia, to support in an election or during a court proceeding. The Senator would never have to face the dangers of the streets alone.

Indeed, for poor men out at night a rich man's entourage was one of the greater risks. A band of enthusiastic clients would beat a tipsy countryman with the same enthusiasm that they would lavish on a real footpad. More, in fact, because the robber would probably be armed and dangerous to tackle.

Saxa entered, his head cocked over his shoulder to talk with the man behind him. He didn't notice his wife for a moment. When he did, he stopped, looking startled and embarrassed.

"Good evening, dear," he said. "I, ah . . . I'm afraid I don't have time to chat just now."

Saxa was fifty-two years old; plumpish, balding, and with the open face of a boy. At the moment he looked rather like a boy caught masturbating when his mother walked in. Hedia smiled with more humor than she'd felt before that image came to her.

Nemastes the Hyperborean stepped to Saxa's side; the outer doorway was too narrow for them to have entered together. He dipped to one knee to acknowledge the mistress of the house. He must have been at least six and a half feet tall—he towered above the German doorman—but he was skeletally thin.

Nemastes' eyes were large and pale. There was nothing very remarkable about them at a quick glance, but Hedia had never seen the fellow blink.

"We have family business, my lord, regarding the future of your daughter," Hedia said. Her words were those of a subservient wife, but her tone would leave a stranger with no doubt regarding the real distribution of power in the household. "Perhaps you can meet with your acquaintance some other day."

Nemastes rose and waited impassively. He didn't bother to scowl at Hedia or sneer; rather, he waited for her to get out of the way as he might have done if a herd of swine had blocked his path.

Normally Saxa's clients would have entered the hall with him and taken their leaves individually in ascending order of rank. It was Nemastes' presence that had held them outside. In the street they could keep their distance from the Hyperborean while still accompanying the Senator, but the hallway might have squeezed them into closer contact, which they all preferred to avoid.

"Ah, my pet, not now, I'm afraid," Saxa muttered, staring at his hands as he wrung them.

"My lord, *now*," Hedia said. Paving stones would have

more give to them than her voice did. "I intend to hold a marriage divination for Alphena at the full moon, which is tomorrow night. She is your daughter and we must discuss the arrangements."

"Whatever you decide, dearest," Saxa said, fluttering his hands miserably. "We have to, that is, I have to—"

"Husband," said Hedia. She didn't raise her voice, but each of the syllables she clipped out could have broken glass. "We—"

"Hedia, I really must go!" Saxa said. "Master Nemastes and I have business to transact now, men's business! Good day!"

Head high, back straight, and face set in misery, Saxa stamped through the door to the courtyard and continued around the pool to the rear suite of rooms. The back garden was the end of the lot on which the town house stood, closed on three sides by high walls.

Nemastes stalked along after him, looking more than usually like a praying mantis. He didn't bother to glance at Hedia, any more than a traveler would be concerned with the pigs which had briefly delayed him.

Hedia sighed. There was very little that she couldn't get a man to do without help, but this business was exceptional.

She walked into the courtyard, staying on the far side from the Black-and-Gold Hall so as not to disturb the reading.

Hedia was going to the gymnasium. She needed a magician, and that meant she needed the aid of Corylus's servant.

CHAPTER II

Corylus let his left fingertips slide along the wooden bench. He couldn't touch the wood with his right hand, because Alphena was there. *She's pressing so hard that if I stand up suddenly, she'll go shooting into the aisle.*

"Fiery as always with love of war and battles and struggles with foes," Varus recited, "our heroic general snatched up his arms!"

As best Corylus could tell, a giant African dragon had just attacked Regulus's army. He'd been expecting to hear more about the Carthaginians, though he supposed it didn't matter much. Varus would have made real history ludicrous, so starting with an absurd notion was perhaps a more efficient plan.

"Shouting encouragement to his cavalry, tried by the war god on every field, he ordered them to charge the foe," said Varus. His eyes were staring; Corylus didn't think he was reading the manuscript at all. He'd committed the work to memory and was letting it spew out like water from a tap.

Corylus was trying to stay awake. The room was warm, and the rhythm of his friend's voice affected him the way a tree shivers in a breeze. Corylus would nod off if he concentrated on the poem, and he didn't dare let that happen.

It would be awful if he fell asleep during Varus's reading. It would be far worse if he collapsed in giggles, and that was the likely result if he viewed the verse against the reality of war that he'd grown up with on Carce's distant frontiers.

The bench, the touch of wood . . . that was salvation. The boards were merely pine, but they'd been well seasoned and they were joined with mortises and tenons as clean as those of a ship. Corylus felt sunlight on the north slope of the valley where the pine had been felled. It was fitting that a straight-grained tree like this one should have been shaped by an expert.

The Emperor in his wisdom had nominated Saxa to be governor of Lusitania, the province on the Atlantic coast of the Iberian Peninsula. The Senate had agreed by acclamation to the Emperor's slate of recommendations—which *was* wise, since the Emperor had never been of an easy disposition and was becoming steadily more irascible as he aged.

Saxa would need a considerable staff to govern a province. Corylus was pretty sure that he could wangle a junior judicial position through Varus. Saxa probably didn't know his son's friend from his cook's brother, but there was no reason he *wouldn't* grant the appointment.

That might be a quicker route to success than the path Corylus had intended: becoming a staff tribune in one of the legions and following the legionary commander at increasingly higher rank on his future postings. A civil career might even be safer, though Corylus guessed that a judicial gofer in a province as wild as Lusitania would have plenty of opportunity to get his head knocked in.

He liked the idea of working with words and ideas, and of convincing people to work together rather than forcing them to do as he said . . . but his father had been army, and Corylus's own upbringing was army. Also, he'd met enough barbarians—that wasn't just a term of insult on the frontiers—to know that force was the *only* convincing argument to many Germans and Iazyges and Sarmatians and Jupiter-knew-who-all-else.

Maybe it was different in the East. There the cultures had been ancient when Carce was inhabited by shepherds who lived on separate hills and stole one another's sheep, but Corylus knew the Rhine and the Danube.

"Hunching high and then low again," Varus said, apparently visualizing his monster as a giant inchworm, "the creature rushed toward the attacking men."

Corylus tried to imagine how you would fight a snake that big. A smile twitched the corners of his lips, so he quickly let his thoughts return to the grain of the wood.

Unexpectedly he entered a world of trees, cool and silent and perfectly graceful. They marched across plains and climbed hills in ragged columns. They sprouted from cliffs, their roots clinging to cracks where no animal could grip; they spread their branches to embrace birds and the breezes.

He forgot about Varus's poem; it became as meaningless as the whirl of dust motes in yesterday's sun. Human activities flashed and vanished before Corylus's new sensibility registered them.

The world was an enormous green unity, all times and places in a single spreading carpet of trees. In the distance ice glittered north to all eternity. Fringing that sterile mass were cold marshes sodden with meltwater; spruce and cedars and larches grew there in packed profusion. Dead trunks slanted into the branches of their living kin and rotted in the air.

Snow had fallen deeply around the trees. Frost drew traceries from the coarse grasses, but the runoff from the glaciers was too vast to freeze over as yet. Corylus understood that. He was part of the forest's sluggish omniscience.

Elephants with thick black hair and curved tusks moved through the trees in a loose herd. They were bigger than the species from the North African coast that Corylus had seen often in the amphitheater, bigger even than the occasional Indian elephant which had been trekked overland to tower above its African kin.

The creatures' feet were the size of storage jars, but for all their bulk they made less sound than men walking. Corylus could hear the deep rumble of their bellies, like sheep only many times louder; their trunks moved constantly to sweep in crackling branches. The elephants' jaws worked side to side, pulverizing sprays of conifer needles and occasionally dribbling the green mush out the sides of their lips.

The herd moved on, squealing brief notes to one another. Their dung was green and steamed where it splattered onto the snow; it had a resinous odor.

A lynx watched from a high branch, showing the same careful interest in the elephants as in the ice cap distantly visible from its perch. It didn't move. If the cat was aware of Corylus, it gave no sign of the fact.

Corylus drifted across the dank landscape, fully aware but having no more volition than a tree. The forest exists, but it neither plans nor cares.

Something cared. It was drawing Corylus along.

Before him was a grove of twelve great balsams. Water dripped from their dangling fronds, but the ground in their center was higher than the surrounding marshes. There stood two foggy human figures, bending toward a tripod where herbs smoldered on a bed of charcoal.

On the inward-facing sides, the bark of the balsams had been carved with elongated human features. Corylus drifted into the circle; the trees' slitted eyes turned to follow his invisible presence.

The scene sharpened as though someone had opened the shutter of a dark lantern, throwing light on what had until then been shadowed. First Corylus registered the ornate bronze tripod: three Chimeras gripped the edges of the brazier; their snake-headed tails were looped up into carrying handles. The piece was striking and unique, easily identifiable as part of the furnishings of Gaius Alphenus Saxa's town house.

Saxa, wearing a toga with the broad stripe of a senator, stood on one side of the brazier. Sweat glistened on his pinkish bald spot. He stared at Corylus in amazement.

The other man was inhumanly tall and so thin that his arms and legs made Corylus think of a spider. He wore a garment pieced together from small skins sewn fur-side in. He was barefoot, though the ground he stood on was frozen; his long black toenails resembled a dog's claws.

He glared at Corylus. His irises were a gray so pale that they were almost indistinguishable from the whites of his eyes.

The cadaverous stranger pointed. Corylus didn't have a hand to raise to defend himself nor a body to move away.

The forest fell out of reality. Saxa and the stranger were in Saxa's back garden. Cold had shattered the pear tree beside them; frost sprang from the pebbles of the walkway. The old coping around the natural spring in the far corner glowed with a faint saffron light.

Corylus gripped his bench. He was in the Black-and-Gold Hall with the aisle to his left and Alphena beside him. His head buzzed with pulsing whiteness, and everybody seemed to be shouting.

He was shouting too. "Where am I? *Where* am I?"

OFF-DUTY SERVANTS—MOST OF the household staff was off duty most of the time—leaped to their feet and bowed as Hedia entered the suite of small rooms leading to the exercise yard. There'd been a game of bandits in progress. An under-steward now sat awkwardly on the game board, but one of the knucklebones they'd been throwing had escaped into the middle of the terrazzo floor when the mistress unexpectedly appeared.

"Go away," Hedia said in apparent disgust. She didn't care that the servants were gambling illegally. She knew, though, that if her tone suggested that she was thinking of crucifying them, she would get a degree of privacy that was otherwise beyond imagining.

The twenty-odd people in the four small rooms scattered like blackbirds startled from a barley field; at least one was still tying his sash. The under-steward ducked out but paused in the doorway. One hand stretched toward the loose knucklebone but his eyes were on Hedia; he suddenly vanished after the rest.

Hedia glanced at Syra. The maid looked studiously innocent. Very likely she was more than a casual friend of one of the people routed by their mistress's appearance.

"What's the name of that under-steward, Syra?" Hedia asked in a conversational tone.

"Ursus, I believe, mistress," Syra said without meeting her mistress's eyes. She kept her voice calm, but she blushed down to the top of her tunic.

Hedia smiled, not from what she'd learned—she didn't care about that—but because she'd learned it using observation and her mind. She nodded, silently directing Syra to open the door into the exercise yard.

Knowing that Pulto and Lenatus were comrades from the army, Hedia had expected to find them sharing a carafe of something from Saxa's storeroom and chatting about old times. Instead she'd heard slams and grunts as she entered the rear apartments.

When the door opened, the men sprang apart and faced her. For a moment they were nothing human: they'd been sparring in full armor and now glared at her with eyes slitted between shield tops and the beetling brass brows of their helmets.

"Hercules!" the man on the right said. He threw down

his fat wooden sword and straightened, sweeping off his helmet. He was Lenatus, which meant—

"Mistress, very sorry!" the trainer said. He hadn't done anything more than marginally improper, but he obviously considered it a sign of trouble when the lady of the house visited his domain for the first time. "I, ah, needed to keep my skills up, so I asked a friend of mine to exercise with me!"

—that the other man was Pulto, whom Hedia had come to see. He set his wooden sword in the rack and took off his helmet. He stood with it in his right hand and his shield, a section of cylinder made from laminated wood, still in his left.

Pulto was politely expressionless, but his stance was wary. He was a freeman and not a member of Saxa's household, but he obviously felt that Hedia's lack of direct authority over him wouldn't be much protection if she wanted his hide. She supposed soldiers got used to being in that sort of situation.

"It's quite all right, Lenatus," Hedia said breezily. "I was hoping to have a few words with your guest here. Master Pulto, isn't it? That is, while your master is attending my son at the reading." She waved a gracious hand. "If you'd like to go on, please do so," she said. "I only need a minute or two after you've finished."

Syra looked at her in shock; that made Hedia want to slap her. *Of course I don't mean it, girl, but these men aren't stupid enough to think that I do!*

"Time I quit anyhow, ma'am," Pulto said in evident relief. "I'm so out of shape I embarrass myself. It's a bloody good thing the Old Man wasn't watching me waddle around just now!"

He placed his helmet on top of a post in a wall niche, then unfastened the stout leather thong stretching from the top of his shield to a hook in the armor over his right shoulder blade. That spread the shield's considerable weight to the other side as well as taking some of it off his arm.

"Oh, you weren't doing too bad, buddy," said Lenatus as he disarmed also. "If you take a couple weeks to shape up, you'll be ready for carving up Germans and all the other fun and games."

Hedia watched the men without expression. They were pretending that things were normal and that the lady of the house wasn't about to make some unfathomable upper-class demand that they would have to obey. She had spoken only of Pulto, but they were friends; neither was going to leave the other alone in the soup.

With abrupt decision, she looked at her maid. "Syra," she said, "go back to my suite and set out clothing for dinner. I'll wear the violet synthesis, I believe, and the gold jewelry from Ephesus."

The men had been unlacing each other's armor; they paused. Syra blinked in surprise and didn't move either.

"Now, girl!" Hedia said. The maid squeaked and vanished back toward the front of the house.

"You gentlemen can relax," Hedia said, letting her voice take on a slight throatiness. She closed the door. "I need a favor and I hope you can help me, but you won't either of you be harmed by this business whatever your answer is."

The men looked at each other. "Ma'am?" Pulto said, carefully.

Hedia picked up the sword which Lenatus had dropped. It was startlingly heavy.

Her surprise must've shown. Lenatus took it from her with a grin and set it in the rack below the one Pulto had been using. "They're wood right enough, mistress," he said, "but there's lead in the hilt and they're double the weight of an issue sword."

"You practice with these," said Pulto, "and it's like going on leave when it's the real thing. Well, that's the idea."

"Yeah, except for the spear points coming the other way," grunted Lenatus.

Both men chuckled. Their grins made them look both reassuring and ugly beyond words. Well, they were reassuring if they were on your side.

Hedia nodded toward the rack of swords. "Does my daughter, Alphena, practice with those swords also?" she said.

Pulto stiffened into professional blankness. Lenatus clacked the heels of his cleated sandals together and straightened to attention. "Yes, your ladyship," he said, his gaze directed at something past her left shoulder. "She does."

Hedia nodded. The trainer hadn't lied or made excuses, just stated the flat truth and waited for what would happen next.

Nothing, or at least nothing bad, would happen to him, because he had proved he was a man. Therefore his friend Pulto was probably equally trustworthy.

"As her mother, I hope she'll grow out of it," Hedia said in a mild, conversational voice. "But I'm very much afraid that if I tried to forbid her, she'd go off to Puteoli and enroll in one of the gladiatorial schools. Not so, Master Lenatus?"

The men were smiling again. Pulto's cheeks swelled as he suppressed a guffaw.

"Your ladyship," said Lenatus, "I think you're wise. She can't get into any real trouble hacking at a post here at home."

He nodded to the armored dummy, which could be put in the middle of the yard for solo practice.

"But if she goes outside, she'll be sparring or worse. And that I won't let her do here, not if the master come down and ordered me to."

"I do not believe my lord and master will give you such an order, Lenatus," Hedia said, speaking carefully.

Nothing in her tone could be read as mockery of her husband, but neither did the words allow any doubt that she meant them.

She made a moue. She was here to deal with her domestic problems, but not by discussing them with a pair of commoners. Switching the topic slightly to lower the emotional temperature before she got to the real question at issue, Hedia said, "Does anyone else practice here, Lenatus?"

"Well, the young master does sometimes," the trainer said, just as careful in choosing his words as Hedia had been a moment before. "And—"

His eyes flicked left to his friend, but the men didn't exactly exchange glances.

"—sometimes he brings his friends here. Master Corylus, for one."

Pulto nodded with stolid enthusiasm. Corylus was the only friend Varus brought here, of course: the only one interested in military-style exercise, and probably the only friend Varus had.

"The boy's bloody good," said Lenatus, lifting both fists to display his thumbs.

"Which the Old Man's son bloody ought to be," said Pulto. "And you know, the other kid—sorry, ma'am, Lord Varus . . ."

He shook his head, angry with himself to have referred to the son of the house in a patronizing manner. "Sorry!" he repeated, twisting the toe of his right sandal against the sand floor.

"Lord Varus gets a lot more exercise because of his friend," said Lenatus with forced calm. "He says he knows he ought to, and having Corylus here helps him do the basics."

"Do they spar?" said Hedia, suddenly curious.

"No, mistress," said Lenatus, "that wouldn't be fair. But Corylus spars with me. There's tricks I can teach him, but I'll never be as young as he is again. And every time we mix it, there's less he doesn't know."

"Your son gets a good workout, ma'am," Pulto said earnestly. "At the start, you don't want to push them too hard. Then he watches some more and works on, you know, writing on tablets."

"He asks Master Corylus words sometimes while he's sitting there," Lenatus said, grinning. He nodded at the stone bench built against the wall between the two dressing rooms. "Remember the time he said he needed a word for spear that he could use in a line ending in a spondee?"

Both men chuckled. They were at ease again, treating Hedia as one of them. They didn't understand what she was about, but soldiers didn't expect to understand things. She had known a number of them—officers, all the ones she could think of, but that was the same thing with an upper-class accent.

Soldiers learned to adapt to situations, though; and if something seemed to be good, well, they were thankful. It would change soon enough, depend on that!

"I said, 'A bloody spear has always worked all right for me,'" said Pulto. "And Mercury bite me if the kid don't say, 'Yes, *my bloody spear*. Two spondees! Perfect.'"

"And Corylus doubled up laughing so I caught him a ripe one on the helmet," said Lenatus. "Which hadn't been the way the match was going before then, let me tell you."

Hedia joined the laughter. Still smiling, she said, "The problem I have is a specialized one, Master Pulto. And of course it requires discretion—"

"I'll get right out of here," Lenatus said. He was still holding his corselet of steel hoops. He turned to swing it into the alcove beneath his helmet.

"No!" said Hedia. "Master Lenatus, I said discretion. If Pulto wouldn't discuss the situation with the friend on whom his life has depended, he'd be a fool. I don't need fools."

She looked between the two men and said, "That's correct, isn't it?"

Pulto shrugged. He didn't meet her eyes. "I guess neither of us would be standing here now if it wasn't for the other, a time or two," he muttered.

"Yes," said Hedia crisply. Then, "Master Pulto, I need magical help. I understand that your wife is a witch."

Lenatus grunted as though he'd been punched low. Pulto grimaced and said to the sand, "Your ladyship, Anna is a Marsian and they always say that about Marsians. You know that."

"I'm in need, Master Pulto," Hedia said. "We all in this family are in danger, as I suspect you know. I would like to speak with your wife, Anna."

Lenatus played with the sash of his sweat-stained tunic, then looked at his friend. Pulto raised his eyes to Hedia and said, "Lady, Anna has rheumatism and can't manage stairs very well. Even if she, you know, did know something. We're up on the third floor, you see; not a, not a private house like this."

"In fact I intend to visit Anna rather than bring her here," Hedia said, which hadn't been her plan until the words came out. It really was a better idea, though. There'd be whispers that Saxa's wife was looking for a love charm or an abortion—but nothing nearly so dangerous as the truth. "Tomorrow, shall we say? At about midday?"

She phrased the statements as questions, but of course they weren't.

"Ah . . . ," said Pulto. His friend was watching but keeping silent. "Ah, I guess all right if, you know, if the Senator is all right with it?"

"My husband does not insult me by trying to control my comings and goings, sirrah!" Hedia said. She hadn't raised her voice but there was a whip on the end of her tongue.

The men straightened to attention. "Yes *sir*!" Pulto said.

There was shouting—screaming, some of it—from the front of the house. "Whatever is that?" Hedia said.

Lenatus tossed one of the practice swords to Pulto and kept the other. They went out the door together.

Hedia ran after them. Lengths of hardwood wielded by these old veterans were good things to have in front of you in trouble.

"IF THE MONSTER'S breath has unmanned you, I will ride on boldly and fight it alone!" Varus said. As he declaimed, he heard a distant rhythm. He supposed it was his fearful heart beating.

Pandareus took notes with an odd expression. He didn't suffer fools gladly, and surely Varus was proving himself a fool like few others.

Varus's soul had shriveled in misery. He was a clumsy wordsmith. He'd managed to conceal that from himself until now, but when he performed his work in public, his mind compared it with all the other literature he'd read or heard.

Varus had known he wasn't Vergil, but he wasn't even Ennius, who had the excuse of antique coarseness. His words had no soul, and because *he* did have a soul, he couldn't deny his failure.

I can see you, Varus whispered to the Muse. *I see you, but my tongue doesn't have the words to describe you.*

His voice sang on, empty and pointless. He wished the earth would open beneath him, but the poem continued to roll on like the Tiber in muddy spate.

Varus's mind slipped, step by shuddering step, out of the present. The insistent rhythm was outside of him, outside of the world. Its beat filled the empty vessel which failure had left of Gaius Alphenus Varus, would-be poet. Voices were chanting.

A cone of raw, rust-colored rock lifted from the ocean. It was hard to see. A dank northern mist bathed it, but there was something wrong with the air also. It was as though Varus were watching through layers of mica.

Things moved on the narrow beach below the cone. Portentous things, but they were invisible except—

The cosmos toppled like a lap marker at the race-track, bringing up a different face. Varus still felt the disjunction, but he was on the other side of it.

The cone was a great volcano. The sides were too steep to have a real beach where they rose from the sea, but waves had battered a notch in the coarse rock. On it, licked by spray, twelve tall men danced about the ivory image. They were nude and hairless.

Hyperboreans, Varus thought, for they were all so similar to his father's friend Nemastes that they could have been copies of the same statue. Their expressions were cold and angry, and they looked more cruel than stoats.

As the tall men danced, they chanted. At first the sound was as raucous as crows calling in a field of stubble and seemed empty, but Varus began to understand its patterns. Similarly, the rhythms of the dance wove together into a great whole and merged with the dancers' wild cries.

In the center of the ring was an ivory carving of a man's head. It wore a fur cap over its ears and was no bigger than a thumb. The figurine drew Varus inward.

The dancers watched Varus as they shuffled on their round; their eyes were hungry. Flickers like the blue flames of sulfur began to lift from the broken rocks. The wisps waved in time with the dance, rising and keeping pace with the jerking feet of the dance.

The flames brightened and became demons of blue fire. Ribs showed beneath their tiny scales, and their very bodies were translucent. Their skulls were like those of lizards, and their lipless mouths twisted in grimaces of fury. They danced like marionettes, under the compulsion of the Hyperboreans.

The chant roared in Varus's ears. The dancers, human and demon alike, stared at him as they paced their circle.

Varus reached out to the ivory miniature. He wasn't sure he had a body, but he could feel the vague, slick warmth of the yellowed ivory.

Almost Varus could grasp the pattern of the dance. That pattern was that of the whole cosmos. He raised the figurine, staring into the carven eyes of someone more ancient than Varus could grasp even with his new understanding.

The Hyperboreans grinned, and the demons licked slaver from their pointed jaws. The chant was too loud for the cosmos to hold. Varus almost—

There was a crash and blinding light; the pattern burst. Varus pitched forward. He was shouting.

"FEARLESSLY WITH A winged arm our Regulus hurled his spear through the air like a thunderbolt," Varus droned.

Does that sort of thing make sense to men? Alphena wondered. Certainly the freedmen farther down the row from her looked comatose. As for Corylus, he might as easily have been carved from a tree trunk.

When Varus spoke normally he sounded, well, normal. His voice had been spiky and nervous when he started his reading, but it was lots worse now. He seemed dead, or at least like he wished he were dead.

Though at this moment, Varus's voice sounded like blocks of stone being dragged across one another at a building site. Alphena remembered that she'd come here by her own choice when nobody would've forced her to come. Listening to her stepmother go on about Alphena having to get married didn't seem like such a bad thing now.

She couldn't walk out once she'd sat down, though. She and Varus hadn't been close, exactly, but they'd bumped around together in a household where their father didn't pay much attention and there wasn't anybody who even pretended to be their mother. Varus had never tried to tell his sister how to behave. There were plenty of brothers who tried to be stricter than their fathers were, she knew.

Alphena didn't feel that she owed Varus support in this silly poetry business, but it would be stabbing him in the back if she came to his reading and then walked out in the middle of it. He cared about his poetry, though Juno knew why. Insulting it publicly would be the worst thing she could do, and he didn't deserve that.

What was wrong with Corylus? Alphena pressed her thigh against his again, but it was like hitting a padded wall. He didn't even feel warm anymore. His eyes had narrowed to slits, and his breathing was so light that she had to watch carefully to see the tiny flutters of his chest.

"The earthborn monster blazed with rage," Varus said. "He was a stranger to fear and had never before known pain."

He recited like he was running through the list of vegetables which he'd been asked to return with from the family villa just east of Carce. His eyes were open and staring, but he'd stopped turning the scroll forward. His body was as rigid as that of Corylus here on the bench.

Why *doesn't Corylus notice me?* Alphena had seen the way he looked at Hedia out of the corners of his eyes when they happened to meet. When Corylus realized Alphena was watching him watch her stepmother, he blushed. He trotted toward the gymnasium so quickly that he trod on the heel of his own sandal and almost fell.

I don't care about Publius Corylus!

She went white with rage—at herself, though she was imagining Corylus strapped to a wooden colt so that she could flog him bloody with a switch. With her own hands!

Pandareus was seated at the left end of the front bench. Alphena leaned forward so that she could see him. He was jotting notes, using a brush and a notebook of thin boards. His outer garment was a light cape instead of a toga, because he wasn't a citizen of Carce. He'd hung a miniature inkwell fashioned from the tip of a cow's horn to the broach pinning the neck closed.

Varus stumbled. His recitation had been so dull that his stuttered "horny-hoo . . . horny . . . horny-*hoofed*—" almost passed unnoticed. The audience was asleep or lost in a world where this wasn't happening.

Varus released the book's take-up wand. The tension of the coiled papyrus made the glistening roll spring closed. He stopped speaking.

Alphena glanced around the hall. Pandareus looked quizzical, his brush poised; no other member of the audience appeared to have noticed the change. Corylus remained in his silent reverie.

"*Comes Surtr from below,*" said Varus, his voice suddenly thunderous. "*With him comes Fire, which sings in the forest!*"

Members of the audience came alert, mumbling in surprise. The hall had been uncomfortably warm with the press of bodies, but a clammy breeze made Alphena shiver.

A short freedman wearing a simpler toga than most of those present stood and pushed toward the door. Sweat gleamed on his high forehead.

Varus gripped the top and bottom of his scroll and twisted. The winding sticks crackled like the bones of a strangled chicken. One of the gold knobs popped loose and rattled to the floor.

"*Surtr's sword is drawn*," said Varus. Or at least the words came from his mouth. His eyes were wide and staring, and veins stood out on his throat. "*Like the sun it shines!*"

The room shuddered. It was dark as night save for a sort of yellow-green fox fire which came up from the earth itself. The doorway was a blur and the light sconces had become dull sparks as though their wicks were starved of oil.

The air was cold. At the edges of her consciousness, Alphena was aware of watching figures.

Alphena heard an angry squeak. The central image of the wall panel to her right was a sphinx no larger than a clenched fist, painted in the same delicate gold as the dividers which mimicked lathe-turned rods. It fluttered its wings. With another peevish cry, the little creature flew off the plaster and circled upward.

Instead of a molded ceiling, there was open sky. Storm clouds flashed lightning across it.

Alphena stood and took a step forward. The look on her brother's face stopped her. His eyes were bright with a wild malevolence which she'd never seen before. The figure shredding the lovingly prepared scroll *wasn't* Varus; it wasn't anything human.

"*Surtr's legions will feed on the flesh of fallen men!*" shouted her brother's mouth. "*Their blood will dim the summer sky forevermore!*"

Alphena stumbled forward, crying with the effort. Lightning as red as banked coals flashed. That and the glow where the floor should have been were the only light in the room.

Men shouted; benches toppled over. Alphena supposed the audience was trying to escape. Did the door to the courtyard still exist? All she could see over her shoulder was blackness.

"Varus!" she said. Something tangled her feet. The fetid light from below was getting brighter; she could see things moving in the depths. "Brother, you have to stop this!"

"*From the Iron Woods comes the Wolf's brood!*" thundered the speaker.

Pandareus gripped Varus by the forearm. "Lord Varus, attend to me!" he said in a voice of command.

Alphena reached them. The dais seemed a steep wall, but she forced herself up it. The shapes in the greenish light were crawling upward.

Circling the terrified audience, skeletally thin figures danced in the shadows. Almost visible, they leered in the darkness.

"*In Hel's dark hall the horror spreads!*" shrieked the white-faced youth. Alphena slapped him with all the strength of her right arm.

There was a thunderclap. Varus staggered; he would have fallen if Pandareus hadn't held him upright. There was no storm; the triple lamp stands seemed brighter for the hell-lit dimness which Alphena had imagined a moment before.

Her palm stung. Her brother's cheek was crimson and already swelling around the imprint of her hand; that much at least was real.

Varus blinked in dull wonder. He held something, but she couldn't see it properly.

Corylus joined them on the dais. He clasped his friend warmly, but Varus could only mumble in reply.

Alphena looked over her shoulder. The audience milled in confusion, bleating. The freedmen were afraid to go or stay, despite the sudden return to normalcy.

Saxa and the wizard Nemastes stood in the doorway.

The Senator looked puzzled, but naked fury blazed on the Hyperborean's face. He stared at Corylus.

Nemastes turned and rushed from the scene, drawing Saxa with him. They would have trampled Hedia in their haste if Lenatus and Corylus's servant Pulto hadn't put themselves in the way.

Alphena met her stepmother's eyes. Hedia looked calm and very cold; as cold as the blade of a dagger.

CHAPTER III

Alphena hugged herself. When the light returned to normal, the hall had again become warm and muggy; she shuddered from reaction to what had just happened. Whatever that was.

The members of the audience had rushed out as soon as they saw the sunlit courtyard again. Alphena smiled despite herself: if her brother had wanted his reading to be talked about, then he'd succeeded beyond his wildest dreams.

The smile slipped. She didn't want to think about dreams. She was afraid she'd see—she'd feel—this afternoon's events every time she closed her eyes for the rest of her life.

Varus and Corylus were still clinging to each other; they looked stunned, as though they'd been pulled from the water when they were on the verge of drowning. Their teacher, Pandareus of Athens, seemed unaffected by the visions. He frowned and said, "We should get out of this room, even though it seems to be all right now. Lord Varus, perhaps we can go into the courtyard?"

Though the guests for the reading had vanished, Saxa's own servants peered furtively through the doorway or hunched low on the second-floor balcony opposite to see into the Black-and-Gold Hall. If Varus and his companions adjourned to the courtyard, the spectators would have an even better view.

Alphena didn't want what had just happened to be discussed any more than it had to be. That would surely be enough as it was. Acquaintances would ask her what had happened, and she wouldn't know how to answer.

"I suppose—," said Varus.

"No," said Alphena. "We'll go into the gymnasium. It's bright, and Lenatus and your man Pulto can keep everyone away from the door. Come, I want to get into the sun."

Pandareus and the three younger people stood in a tight group on the dais. The veterans, each holding a wooden sword lightly, stood between them and the hall proper. They were turned slightly to keep the others in the corners of their eyes, but their real concern was anyone who tried to bull his way through to the courtyard.

When Lenatus and Pulto heard their names spoken, they nodded slightly. Neither spoke, but the trainer grinned. Alphena had practiced daily with him for over a year. That grin showed her a man she hadn't imagined.

"All right, where is it?" said Pandareus. "And quickly, if you would, though I don't think the room itself was the problem."

Pulto led; Lenatus brought up the rear. Alphena wondered why Lenatus wasn't in front; then a bulky understeward crowded too close. Pulto kicked him in the stomach. Corylus's servant was freeborn and outside the household hierarchy. That permitted him to act—with the authority of the owner's children, of course—without fear of retribution, either formal or informal. The old soldiers were coarse men and uneducated, but they weren't unsophisticated about the way things worked on the hard edges of society.

Varus rubbed his eyes as they crossed the courtyard. "Did I see Father come in?" he asked. "I'm not sure what happened."

"Father was here but left again," Alphena said. "It

was—there was shouting. I guess, well, I guess that a lot of people heard it."

Servants stared. They didn't appear to be so much frightened as excited and curious. They hadn't been in the hall when Varus was reading, and apparently all they knew was that there'd been a noisy to-do of some sort.

Alphena smiled again; her expression was wan but not forced. Hercules knew that she really couldn't say much more about it than that either; but from where she'd been, it certainly *had* been frightening.

Pulto strode into the gymnasium and looked about it. Alphena hadn't meant for the soldiers to be part of the discussion. Before she could speak, he came back out and said, "All clear, missy. You go ahead and talk all you like. Nobody will bother you."

Lenatus smiled again without speaking. *They're on our side,* Alphena reminded herself. She entered the yard, feeling the sun's touch relax her.

Pandareus shut the door with a thump and barred it. The gymnasium was open to the sky, but its walls were ten feet high. The yard wasn't overlooked by anyone outside the property, and the rooms facing it on the upper floor of the house were windowless.

"What happened?" Pandareus said. His voice was even, and he glanced between the two young men.

Corylus grimaced, then faced his teacher; the sun caught blond highlights in his hair. His features had been cut with a sharper chisel than those of Varus or Alphena.

"Master," he said formally, "I didn't see anything, I'm afraid. I must have—I'm sorry, Varus, I must have fallen asleep. I dreamed that I was flying."

"Flying?" said Pandareus. "Flying where, boy?"

He faced the two youths as though he were questioning them after a declamation. Alphena had watched the class once when it met in the Forum. It irritated her that her gender had excluded her from the further education her brother got, but she didn't miss the education itself. She would rather weave like a woman of ancient Carce than spend her time spouting high-toned twaddle about pirate chiefs and heiresses.

"Master, there were trees," Corylus said. He stood stiffly upright, his hands clenched. Alphena thought he would have liked to knuckle his eyes to squeeze the vision back to life. "Huge trees, firs and spruces mostly, and there was heavy snow."

He gestured, not with the sweeping arm of an orator but rather a circular scoop of one hand as though he were digging out the right word. His hair was a golden crown from where Alphena stood.

"Not snow like some winters here," Corylus said. "Snow like it falls in Upper Germany, but there weren't the hardwoods like German forests. It was all conifers." He pursed his lips and added, "And birches. Little ones."

"What did you see in the forest?" Alphena said. The men had been ignoring her, but she'd seen the look on Corylus's face as her brother boomed lines that he certainly hadn't written. "It wasn't just trees, I know it wasn't."

Pandareus looked at her without expression; Varus was still shrunk within himself. Corylus smiled faintly and said, "You're right. I saw elephants, but they had long hair. I was dreaming, as I told you."

He lost his smile, but he continued to face her. It was the first time he had really engaged Alphena as a person.

"And just before I woke up," he said, "I saw your father with a man I didn't know. He was the same man who came to the door of the hall with the Senator after I woke up. But when I saw them first, I was dreaming."

Corylus shook his head and looked at his teacher again. "Master," he said, "it was just a dream. But I've never had a dream like it before."

Pandareus nodded to close that portion of the discussion. He turned to Alphena's brother. "Lord Varus?" he said. "What's that in your hand?"

Varus blinked. Ever since Alphena had slapped him, he'd been acting as though he'd just woken up. His cheek still glowed.

"I don't know," he said, unclasping his hands. "I had the scroll. . . ."

They all stared at a two-inch-high head carved from—no, not stone as Alphena had thought. It was ivory, with the honey brown patina that old ivory got. The image was narrow-faced and wore a bulbous hat or turban. There was a loop in the back so that the figurine could be hung from a neck cord.

"Where did that come from, boy?" Pandareus asked sharply. He stretched out two fingers of his left hand but stopped well short of touching the object.

"I . . . ," said Varus, frowning with concentration. "I've had it, sir."

"Not that I've ever seen," said Corylus. There was harsh certainty in his voice.

"Nor I," said Alphena. "Brother, you know you didn't have that when you were reading. You were holding your poem!"

"I don't know, then," Varus said. He closed his left fist over the figurine again. In sudden anger he snarled, "It's mine now, anyway."

"Varus?" said Corylus in surprise.

Varus winced. "I'm sorry," he muttered, rubbing his temples with his right fingertips and the knuckles of his left hand. "I have, I guess it's a headache. My head throbs."

"Brother?" said Alphena. Varus wouldn't meet her eyes. "What did you see? You weren't the person reading at the end, were you?"

"I don't know," Varus whispered. "I don't know! I saw

a dance; I think I remember dancers. But I don't remember anything about it."

He looked up. "What did I do with my manuscript?" he said. He opened his left hand slightly to peer at the figurine again, apparently making sure that it hadn't changed back into a roll of papyrus. "Did I leave it in the hall?"

"You destroyed it on the dais, Lord Varus," Pandareus said. "In a very thorough and determined fashion. Why did you do that, do you suppose?"

"I did?" said Varus in amazement. "Why on earth did I do that?" He looked up with a wan smile and added, "I don't suppose much was lost by that. I don't think I'm going to gain fame as a poet."

Corylus put his hand on his friend's shoulder. Pandareus smiled coldly and said, "Regarding the heroic exploits of Regulus, I agree with your estimate. The lines you sang after you departed from your prepared manuscript, however—those had elements of real power. Did you compose them on the dais?"

"Master, I don't know," Varus said simply. "I don't have any memory of what happened after I started to read. Except that I think someone was dancing. Maybe I was dancing myself?"

"Not that we in the audience noticed," said Pandareus.

He pursed his lips, tapping his notebook against the palm of his left hand. "There is a great deal going on," he said, "and I can see only the surface. From what you boys tell me, you saw even less."

Varus grimaced; Corylus nodded firm agreement. Both were alert now.

"Therefore, I want both of you to join me tomorrow night at the Temple of Capitoline Jupiter," Pandareus said. "My friend Priscus—"

"Atilius Priscus?" Varus said in surprise.

"Yes, Senator Priscus," Pandareus said. "Are you surprised that a mere teacher of rhetoric would claim a respected senator as a friend?"

"No sir, not at all," Varus mumbled, lowering his eyes again.

"You might well wonder," the teacher said in a milder tone. "The Senator has a remarkable library. I applied to read his copy of *On the Stars* by Thrice-Learned Hermes. Our acquaintance ripened through a mutual love of scholarship."

He coughed, then continued. "He's on duty tomorrow. I'll send a messenger to him to expect us at the temple at the beginning of the second watch. You're both agreeable?"

Varus nodded. Corylus grinned and said, "I'm glad somebody has a plan. I don't, and . . . Master, I'm not a fearful man, I hope. But the dream I had disturbed me."

"Master Pandareus?" Alphena said. She spoke without the humility the youths, his pupils, put in the title. "Why do you think Priscus will understand the business better than you do? You were there, after all, and he wasn't."

"I don't think my learned friend *will* understand it," Pandareus said, allowing his lips to spread in a slight smile. "We won't be visiting him for that. He's one of the commissioners for the sacred rites, however."

"Oh . . . ," whispered Corylus, who must have seen what Alphena so far did not.

"Yes, that's right," said Pandareus, his smile still broader. "Tomorrow night Priscus will have the *Sibylline Books* in his charge."

A PAIR OF servants at the top of the back stairs gaped as Hedia stepped quickly toward them. She was forcing herself to keep a ladylike demeanor and not to skip steps.

"Where's your master?" she snapped. The servants didn't speak, but one nodded toward the suite behind him. His Adam's apple bobbed.

There hadn't been much doubt in her mind. When Saxa was badly pressed, he fled to his private apartment at the rear of the second floor. That had been an inviolate sanctum in the years before he had remarried.

Hedia found herself smiling as she swept past the servants. She wasn't sure whether she was more angry than frightened or the other way around, but she was quite sure that she and her husband were going to discuss what had happened today. Propriety and wifely subservience be *damned*.

The door to the suite was closed—but not barred, which was good. Hedia flung it open and strode inside. If necessary she would have brought the porters to batter the panel down with the poles from the sedan chair.

Half a dozen body servants fluttered at her entry. They were pretending to be busy and also pretending not to be staring at their furious mistress.

Hedia made a quick shooing motion as though she were flicking something unpleasant from her fingers. "Get out," she said to the servants collectively. She didn't raise her voice. "Close the door behind you."

Saxa stood at the window, his hands gripping the ledge. His pretense was that he was absorbed in the view up slope of the Palatine. Hedia waited till the servants had scuttled out, the last of them banging the door shut, before she said mildly, "Husband, what's going on?"

"Dearest, there are things you can't understand," Saxa mumbled without turning around. "I'm sorry, but you simply have to trust me."

The bedroom was decorated as a seascape. The small stones of the mosaic flooring were set in a stylized wave pattern, and water nymphs cavorted with fish-tailed Tritons on the walls. Plaster starfish and crabs were molded into the ceiling coffers.

Hedia rather liked the room, but the decoration puzzled her. Saxa didn't care for the sea; she'd had to press to get him to go with her to Baiae in the Gulf of Puteoli this past spring. Perhaps a previous wife had chosen it for him. . . .

"I do trust you, dear heart," she said, putting a hand on her husband's shoulder. He was trembling. "There's no one in the world with a better heart or with greater loyalty to the Emperor."

That last was for any ears listening at doorways or through the floor with a tumbler to amplify sounds. In truth Saxa probably didn't think about the Emperor twice in a week; he was about as apolitical a man as you would find in the Senate. But the deeper truth beneath that lie was the fact that Saxa *certainly* wasn't involved in a plot.

Not that the truth would matter if somebody laid a complaint. And Juno knew that it wouldn't be hard at all to show the Senator's behavior in a bad light.

"I don't trust your Nemastes at all, though," Hedia said, letting her anger show in her tone. Saxa had started to relax; now he tensed again. "He's a viper, and he'll bite many people besides you unless you scotch him immediately. But he'll certainly bite you."

She paused before adding, "And your son. As he did today."

"Hedia, that's not true!" Saxa said, whirling to face her for the first time. "You don't understand, I tell you. Without Nemastes' efforts, we're all lost. The world is lost!"

He's not lying, Hedia thought. She wasn't sure her husband could lie; certainly he couldn't lie successfully to her. But he thought he was telling the truth now.

"I understand that Nemastes plays at being a magician," she said aloud. "How do you think the Emperor will feel if he hears about that, Husband? *And* I understand that the viper you brought into the house with you today caused your son to speak words that terrified everyone who heard him. You *know* that."

Hedia hadn't waited to question the audience pouring out of the hall, so she didn't have any idea what had happened during Varus's recital. The wealthy freedmen were running as though Parthians galloped behind them with their bows drawn, but she could have stopped one if she'd seen the need to. Oh, yes, she most certainly could.

But their abject fear was all Hedia needed to know. Whatever happened, it hadn't been Varus's unaided doing: the boy didn't have it in him to frighten a mouse from the pantry!

Knowing that Nemastes was in the house, she hadn't had to search far for a villain. She was confident that the blame was deserved in this case, but she didn't particularly care. A threat to Varus was the best tool she'd been offered for prying her husband away from this dangerous magician, so she would have used it even if she'd thought she was being unfair.

"Nemastes had nothing to do with whatever you're talking about," Saxa said uncertainly. "He and I were together while the reading was going on."

"Together doing what?" Hedia snapped. "Tell me, Husband, what was your so-called magician doing? Besides tricking you out of money, I mean, because I know he's robbing you!"

That was a lie. She'd originally believed Nemastes was a charlatan—anybody would have believed that. She became really worried—really frightened—only when she realized that the Hyperborean's magic wasn't just tricks and suggestion.

"No, you're quite wrong, dear one," Saxa said, sounding relieved. "Master Nemastes hasn't taken a single coin from me. He's a king in his own land, you see."

Hedia wanted to slap him. *How do you know he's a king, you puling child? Because he told you so?*

And yet Saxa wasn't a fool or even unsophisticated in most respects. This was just something that he desperately wanted to believe.

"He pays for his needs with gold that he brought with him," Saxa continued earnestly. "All I did, dear heart, was introduce him to my own bankers, the brothers Oppius. Because Hyperborean gold isn't coined; it grows in blocks of quartz. But it's pure, the brothers assure me it is. They wouldn't lie to their own cost."

No, unless they are part of the swindle themselves, Hedia thought. But she didn't believe that, much as she wished it were true. The Oppii and their ancestors had served the Alphenus family for three generations.

"The money I withdrew isn't for Nemastes," Saxa said, the first time Hedia had heard about a withdrawal. "I'm renovating the Temple of Tellus at the entrance to the Carinae District. As a public service, you see."

He tried a smile. "That's why I suggested you and Alphena hold the marriage divination there, you see," he said. "The chief priest is a freedman named Barritus who owns the laundry on the same block. I knew he'd jump at a chance to do anything for me, since I haven't decided the scale of the renovation yet."

"Why are you . . . ?" Hedia said, as startled as if Saxa had just announced he was going to retire to his villa in the Campania and spend the rest of his life as a gentleman farmer. "That is, it's commendable that you're fixing up an ancient temple, Husband. But I hadn't previously noticed signs of your religious inclination."

"Well, it was Nemastes who made the suggestion," Saxa said diffidently, watching his wife to see how she took mention of the Hyperborean's name. Hedia didn't react. Even in the silence of her mind, she filed the fact and waited till she had more information.

Saxa cleared his throat and continued. "He believes it's important to the coming struggle that Carce's most ancient temple of Tellus, Mother Earth, be renovated. Because he's a foreigner, he would have to ask permission of the Senate to carry out the repairs in his own name."

"Ah," said Hedia. "I see."

Applying to the Senate—which meant to the Emperor—would call attention to the Hyperborean and to his patron, Gaius Alphenus Saxa. Hedia certainly didn't want that to happen, but the fact that Nemastes was trying to avoid it also was very disquieting.

"We're going to store the objects that have been given to the goddess over the years here," Saxa said. "In the back garden. There'll be some wagons coming by shortly. Bringing things for safekeeping, you see; there are some quite valuable dedications, though mostly from a number of years ago."

Hedia felt an aching fear. *If I could name what I was afraid of, it wouldn't be so bad. But now—*

Saxa swallowed. His face had briefly been animated as he talked about the antiquities which he so loved. It went waxen again and he turned away.

Seeming to gather strength from an image of Neptune blowing on a conch with a pair of Nereids, fish-tailed and bare-breasted, supporting him, he said, "My dear, you don't know what I have seen. *Seen.* Yes, in a vision, but it was *real.* It was—"

His hands lifted as though he were trying to squeeze an image into life.

"I saw fire," he whispered. The words sounded like dry leaves rustling. "I saw fire rushing across the whole world. Everything burning, everything dying in fire, and the fire god was laughing as he watched."

Hedia licked her lips, then embraced him. She hugged herself close, but Saxa didn't respond except to wriggle like a hooked fish.

"Husband," she pleaded.

"Please, dear," Saxa muttered to the wall. "Things will come out right. You have to trust me."

She stepped away and wrapped her arms around herself instead. She was cold with fear—not for the mythical fire, but from the certainty that Nemastes had caught her husband in a net she could not break him free of.

"You will do as you please, Husband," Hedia said. "I only hope that you come to your senses in time to, to . . ."

To escape the Emperor's torturers, but even in this awful moment she couldn't bring herself to say that.

"For my part," she went on instead, "I'll hold the marriage divination tomorrow as planned. I only hope that I can save Alphena from the wreck of her father's life."

Despair was crushing her down. She turned and strode from the room, leaving the door open behind her.

A waist-high plinth supported a small marble faun in the corridor. It stuck out slightly from its alcove. Hedia deliberately stubbed her toe on the base, then bent over shouting curses.

It was an acceptable excuse for the tears that were about to burst out regardless.

PANDAREUS HAD PAUSED to write a message on a sealed tablet for one of Saxa's servants to carry to Priscus, and the children of the house were staying home; Pulto and Corylus left the town house alone. On the doorstep Pulto paused. "Kid," he said, "I need a mug of wine before we go home. Or maybe a whole jar of wine. You up for that?"

"Sure," said Corylus. He grinned. "I don't know that

I'll be downing much of the jar, but I don't mind trying to carry you home."

Pulto chuckled, a pleasant change from the bleak glare he'd worn since they'd left the gymnasium. He turned right toward the bar two doors down, the Blue Venus, instead of left to go home.

"The Old Man's done it more than once for me," he said, "and me for him. Never both of us falling-down drunk at the same time, until he got enough rank that we stayed home instead of crawling the strip."

A masonry counter faced the street and ran down the right side of the central aisle. Three men stood at it. On its corner was the little statue of painted terra-cotta which gave the bar its name; Pulto patted her for luck. Thousands of other clients must have done so over the years, because the paint was worn from her bosom. Most of the times Corylus heard the bar spoken of, it'd had been as the Blue Tit.

To the left of the aisle were three small masonry booths, empty at this hour. "Bring us a jar of the house wine, Maura," Pulto said. "The better stuff, mind. We'll settle up when we leave."

He led the way to the farthest booth. "Now, boy, sit down," he said. "Because I'm going to talk to you."

"Yes, sir," Corylus said obediently. He felt as though he'd been punched in the stomach.

Pulto was his servant, the social and intellectual inferior of a well-educated knight of Carce. However, Pulto was also the fellow who had taught the Old Man's son the things a young man needed to know in and around a military camp. Sometimes the teaching had involved a switch or even a fist, because failing to learn the lessons could mean the next time they were rehearsed with steel in the hands of people who definitely wouldn't have the boy's best interests at heart.

Pulto hadn't touched the boy in years, of course. From

the tone of his voice, though, Corylus was afraid that the discussion was going to be more unpleasant than a beating.

The barmaid brought over cups, a mixing bowl, a bronze carafe of water, and a jar that must have held at least a gallon of wine. It had a tapered base to be set in sand or a hole in the counter sized for it; here she leaned it into a corner of the booth. She was a slight, older woman with crinkly hair—probably a Moor, as her name suggested—but she handled the awkward load with less trouble than Corylus would have taken with it.

He grinned; there were tricks to every trade. Some of Pandareus's other pupils, who'd been schooled only in words and literature, hadn't learned that. The education Corylus had gotten on the frontiers was broader; and in some fashions, he thought, much better.

Pulto hefted the jar onto the crook of his right elbow, his index finger through one of the loop handles, and poured a generous slug into the bowl. Corylus added water from the carafe, mixing it two parts to one without asking Pulto if he wanted it stronger. *If we're going to have a difficult discussion, we're going to have it sober.*

Pulto didn't comment, but he drank down his first cup and refilled it before he looked at Corylus across the table. "So, boy, I'm going to tell you about your mother, Coryla."

"The Celt who Father married when he commanded the fort on the Upper Rhine," Corylus said. Until the wine touched his lips, he hadn't realized how very dry he was. He forced himself to sip instead of slurping it down as instinct urged him to.

Strictly speaking, soldiers on active duty weren't permitted to marry. It was common for men in the frontier garrisons to enter into permanent arrangements with local girls, however. These would be recognized when they got their diploma of discharge.

That required both parties to survive, of course. Coryla had died giving birth, but her son had become a citizen of Carce as soon as Cispius had lifted him outside the door of the hut and named the child as his legitimate offspring.

"Right," said Pulto, "only she wasn't a Celt. And she wasn't a Helvetian either, which is what most of the folk in the district were—stragglers, those that come down from the mountains after Caesar chopped the main lot of them back in his day, and maybe some that hightailed it ahead of his cavalry."

"Not Celtic?" Corylus said. He finished his wine. There were any number of tribes in the empire, of course, not to mention those—like the Hyperboreans—who lived beyond the borders but mixed with civilized peoples. The fact that he'd been told a lie about his mother's race was much more disturbing.

"No, and don't ask me what she was," Pulto growled. "She and her mother had a language they spoke to each other sometimes, and it wasn't anything I've heard elsewhere."

He emptied the mixing bowl to fill both their cups; there was plenty more in the jar, and if they ran out of water, the barmaid would bring another carafe. "They tended a hazel coppice—government property, you know. Growing straight saplings for spear and arrow shafts. It was a big plantation and just the two of them to work it, but they didn't seem to have any trouble. Only the locals, you see . . . the locals, they didn't like them."

"Go on," Corylus said. His mouth was suddenly drier than before he'd had the first cupful.

"There was a sacred grove, two big hazels, along with

the saplings," Pulto said. "The Helvetians had brought their religion from the mountains with them, and the grove wasn't part of it. Coryla and her mother didn't need help, so it didn't seem to matter a lot. The Old Man—"

Pulto gestured with his cup. He would have sloshed wine onto the table if he hadn't drunk it down so far already.

"—his dad, and *his* dad before him had been nursery-men down on the bay"—Puteoli—"so he started spending time with the women. I guess something might've happened anyway, but one night there was Pluto's own storm, lightning and hail and more wind than I'd ever seen. We lost the roofs of half the barracks and thought we were lucky."

"And the grove?" Corylus said, not raising his voice.

Pulto poured more wine deliberately into the bowl, then added the water himself. He kept the mixture the same, two waters to the slug of wine.

When he had finished, he looked up and said, "A lot of the saplings lost their leaves, but the wind wasn't a problem even when it bent them double. The biggest hazel came down, though, struck by lightning, and then the whole thing blew over. And the old woman, she died too. Had a seizure."

Pulto grimaced and guzzled the cup of wine he'd re-filled while speaking. "Hecate knows how old she was," he muttered. "Mostly barbs are a lot younger than they look right off when you meet them, but I'm not sure the old lady was. Anyway, the Old Man took up with the daughter, that's Coryla, and things went along pretty much the way they had. And it wasn't too long before you—"

He gestured, then refilled the cup.

"—were on the way."

Pulto had splashed wine when he last filled the cups. He used his little finger to draw a line with it before the last of the puddle settled into the terra-cotta surface. Corylus waited silently, sipping from his own cup. The story was coming at the speed Pulto was comfortable telling it.

"It was just Coryla to work the coppice and her pregnant besides, but that didn't seem to be a problem," Pulto went on, continuing to play with the tile. "Just about every sapling kept straight and they didn't have a bug problem. Coryla—her and her mother—had a right good sum put by from bonuses when the assessors from the Quartermaster's Department accepted each crop. And then come the night you were born."

Corylus nodded to show he was listening. He tried to take a sip of wine and found his cup was empty. He set it down and reached for the mixing bowl. He gave up on that because his hands were shaking.

"Well, there was other women in the cantonment," Pulto said to the table. "Women who'd come with the cohort from previous stations. The local women, even the ones who'd shacked up with troopers, they wouldn't have anything to do with Coryla, but there wasn't trouble finding help with the lying-in. It all went pretty well, not that the Old Man nor me was looking at anything but the bottom of wine cups—and we *weren't* mixing it, boy, you can count on that. But everything was fine. Only the barbs"—he waved his left hand before him—"the locals, I mean, but they was barbs, they got into the plantation while Coryla was out of action and they cut down the other big hazel. And your mother, she died."

"In childbirth?" Corylus whispered.

"Sure, in childbirth!" Pulto said. "Hecate knows, boy. She'd born you and she died. Women die all the time, right?"

The bowl was empty. Instead of refilling it, Pulto lifted the jar and drank directly from the spout. Still balancing the heavy jar on his arm, he said in a raw growl, "Well, that was destroying army property, right? The hazel tree. So the army held their investigation, that was the Old Man. And there might've been some complaints to higher authority about just *how* he did the investigating, but as it turned out the locals were all killed while resisting the duly constituted authorities."

"All of them?" Corylus said. He could scarcely hear his own voice.

Pulto nodded emphatically. "Every bloody one," he said. "And the girls in the cantonment who must've known what was up but didn't warn anybody, they resisted too."

He poured unmixed wine into Corylus's cup, then swigged more from the jar. "Your father was a popular officer, boy," he said. "Not lax. Troopers don't respect a lax officer even when he's easy on them in peace. It won't always be peace, you see, and the veterans know it. But the Old Man always looked out for his men, so when this happened—"

Pulto shrugged. His grin was much like the one he'd had at the door of the gymnasium when he said nobody was going to disturb Corylus and his friends.

"—nobody questioned his orders. And afterward, nobody talked to outsiders about what had happened. Till I did just now, because after that business today, I thought you maybe ought to know."

There was a hint of challenge in Pulto's voice as he met his master's eyes.

"Yes," said Corylus with a crisp nod. "I see that. Thank you for—"

For what, exactly?

"—for your loyalty to my father and myself, Pulto."

He cleared his throat and went on. "Now, do you think we're ready to go back to the apartment? Because I'm to meet Pandareus and Varus at Jupiter on the Capitol tonight, and I'd like to get some food in me before that."

He patted his cup, empty again. "To settle the wine," he said with a grin which after a moment became natural.

Pulto set down the jar and stood, grinning even more widely. "Ready and willing, young master," he said. "And I'll pay the score here, if you don't mind."

The old soldier shook his head with a look of wonder. "For seventeen years I've wanted to tell you the story," he said. "Doing it now, well, it's a weight off me that I'm bloody pleased to be shut of."

Hooking his left index finger through one loop of the wine jar, he sauntered toward the counter, where Maura would measure the damage with a rod. He was whistling "The Girl I Left behind Me."

Corylus followed. His mind was full of more questions than he'd had before this sudden dose of truth from his servant.

And he wondered even more about what they would learn tomorrow from the guardian of the *Sibylline Books*.

VARUS SAT ON the curb around the spring in the back garden. The stonework beneath him was ancient; the garden wall kinked to enclose it. Instead of marble or even patterned tiles, the blocks were volcanic tuff: porous and sometimes light enough to float, but able to support more than an equal weight of concrete. The stone looked black, but it was light gray beneath the stains of algae and centuries.

Varus's hands were in his lap, closed over the ivory head. He wasn't looking at the figurine, nor was he really conscious of anything else in the present world.

A wagon drawn by mules pulled up in the alley behind the house. As it did so, a flock of house servants led by Agrippinus entered the garden from the house proper.

Waddling self-importantly with them was a middle-aged man with Greek features.

The majordomo saw Varus. "Quiet down!" he rasped to his companions.

Instead of obeying, the stranger bowed low to Varus and said, "My noble lord, I am Decimus Livius Gallo, chief attendant of the Temple of Tellus. I—"

"Shut up, you fool!" snapped Agrippinus. Unasked, a pair of husky under-stewards grabbed Gallo by the shoulders and jerked him back so that he was no longer addressing Varus. "You don't speak to your betters in *this* household unless they give you permission first!"

Varus turned slightly, his eyes tracking the freedman—he would have been the slave Gallo who took the name of Livius, his former master, when he was freed—without interest or full comprehension. He was in a reverie of sorts.

Servants unbolted the back gate, then stepped away. Agrippinus held a low-voiced discussion with Gallo and the wagoneers. The streets were supposedly barred to wheeled traffic during daylight hours, but the wagon in the alley had edged the law by an hour or so. Perhaps Gallo figured that because they were temple servants, or because they were carrying the goods to the home of a prominent senator, they didn't risk confiscation by the magistrates as lesser mortals did.

Varus dreamed, though his eyes were open. *He was riding past a great hound; it strained at its tether as it bayed with bloody jaws. The thunder of its fury shook the universe, and its open maw could swallow the world.*

"Don't look at me!" said a wagoneer to Gallo. He spat on the pavement in emphasis. "Our job is to drive the mules, not muscle around the crap in the wagon."

"All right, get with it," Agrippinus said in a low snarl to the waiting house servants. "And if any of you in the

Senator's household think that you're too good to carry temple treasures, then you can spend the rest of your lives on one of his estates following a team of oxen and learning to break clods with a hoe!"

The servants shambled into the alley without muttering. The conscious part of Varus's mind noticed that a few directed troubled glances toward him, but he didn't react.

Varus rubbed the ivory with his thumbs. *A powerful man clad in sealskin stood on a rocky shore, looking out to sea. Behind him at the tide line hunched a female whose body was covered by her own coarse hair. Her breasts hung to her waist; they were hairy also. Four children, halflings with her flat features but less hair and that of the blondish shade of the man's, stood to either side of her, looking puzzled.*

The man raised his face. He howled to the choppy sea in an agony of soul.

Six servants eased through the back gate, carrying a tusk. It was enormous, easily eight feet in length if measured along its sweeping curves. The part of Varus which remained in the present wondered if it really came from an elephant. Did the world hold some vastly greater creature whose tusks resembled those of the beasts he had seen in the amphitheater?

"Get that bench out of the way, Callistus," the majordomo snapped to the servant standing nearest the summer bedroom on the right corner of the garden. These, one on either side, were masonry-framed structures. They had tiled roofs but walls of wooden louvers. "We'll put the tusks under the portico and the bronze and silver in the summer houses."

"But where do I stand if it rains, hey?" asked one of the men carrying the tusk. He was half bald and paunchy, though his shoulders were impressively wide. Varus didn't remember the fellow's name, but he was one of the low-ranking watchmen; he wasn't handsome enough to be put at the front door, at least during daylight.

"Then you'll bloody get rained on, Castor!" Agrippinus said. "And by Hercules! I'll have somebody checking you every hour, so you'd better stay alert. This is the god's treasure you're watching, do you understand?"

The servants shuffled under the portico attached to the wall of the main house. Through the louvers came Castor's muttered, "I'm no Latin, so she's no god of mine!"

The ivory figurine had a sizzling warmth, like amber rubbed with a cloth. It made Varus's fingers prickle.

A man hung by one leg from a branch. His other leg crossed the tethered one, knee to ankle. His gray beard fell over his face, but through its cloud his one eye blazed like blue lightning. A babble of voices surrounded him, speaking all the knowledge of all time, and the Tree extended forever.

Beside the well curb was a pear tree. Its blackened leaves lay on the grass, where the killing frost had dropped them. Some twigs had split, and bark was already beginning to slough.

The pear had been healthy as recently as this morning. Two weeks ago it had been covered in white flowers, but their petals had fallen and they were beginning to set fruit.

"Watch that!" Gallo said, stepping forward; he pumped his forearms upright beside his face. "You're going to scrape it on the pillar!"

"Shut up, twinkie, unless you want this up your bum!" said the assistant gardener at the front of the group bringing in the second tusk; it was slightly shorter than the first, and the tip had been worn to a wedge by grubbing in the ground. "And if you don't get out of the way, you'll be lucky if that's *all* that happens to you!"

The men doing the work were members of Saxa's household. Whether slave or free, they had a clear awareness that no temple flunky was going to give orders to a senator's servant.

Varus stroked the ivory figurine. He knew what was happening in the garden; beyond the present he saw ice and fire, and monsters moving through them.

But close about Varus in the shadows of time were the twelve hairless men whom he had seen during the reading. They danced with jerky motions of their legs and arms.

Demons with furious faces danced among them, and together they whispered: *Nemastes is a traitor. Nemastes must die.*

CHAPTER IV

Alphena took a deep breath. Porters were fitting the polished maple poles into the sockets of the family sedan chair in front of the house, and a gaggle of attendants milled in the street.

Hedia, wearing an ankle-length linen tunic and a short wool cape dyed bright yellow, waited on the steps. Alphena had thought her stepmother might wear a thin silk synthesis as she did when she went out in the evenings, but apparently at midmorning that was too blatantly racy even for her.

The slut. Looking down her nose at everything and everybody, like a perfect ivory statue!

At this hour there was little traffic on the cul-de-sac where Alphenus Saxa and seven other wealthy families lived, though people traveling between the center of Carce and the northeastern suburbs thronged the boulevard at its head. The Senate was in session; Saxa had gone off to the session, accompanied by the throng of clients who'd arrived at dawn to pay their respects to him.

Venus be thanked, Father really *was* at the Senate House instead of with his Hyperborean friend. The Emperor was addressing the Senate today. Any senator present in Carce who didn't attend would be marking himself for quick attention of a bad kind.

Alphena marched past the doorman, startling him.

"Good morning, Hedia," she said. She was trying to sound coldly sophisticated, but she heard her voice wobble like a wren trilling. Her face went hot and she hoped she wasn't blushing.

Hedia turned; her maid hopped to the side with a twitter to avoid standing between them. Hedia wasn't tall, and Alphena stood on the step above her besides. Even so, the older woman gave the impression that she was staring down from a great height.

"Good morning, Daughter," Hedia said. "Usually at this time of day, you're at your exercises, aren't you?"

Her voice was pleasant and cultured and cool. The only insult in it was "your exercises," but even that was a gibe only if you felt that it was unwomanly and improper for a girl in armor to swing a sword at a post.

I have every right to exercise whatever way I want to! My brother could and I can too!

"I'm coming with you to Master Corylus's apartments," Alphena said, hearing her own shrillness. "That's where you're going, isn't it?"

I've practiced this! I'm going to be calm. But she wasn't calm, of course.

"I'm going to see Anna, Master Corylus's cook and housekeeper," Hedia said. She sounded amused, but Alphena had seen her eyes narrow. "I presume her master will be in class in the Forum with your brother Varus, dear. I'm sure you have better things to do."

"Well, *dear*," Alphena said. "You seem to think that you're spending your time properly when you interfere in *my* life, don't you? So I'm returning the favor. I guess you could say that I'm learning from you, do you see?"

Hedia lifted her chin slightly. "I'm your mother, girl," she snapped. "Keep a civil tongue in your head!"

The attendants in the street had stopped chattering among themselves. They shifted so that they all stood with their backs toward their master's wife and daughter.

The rooms facing the street would be filling with servants also, crowding close to the window louvers and trying not to breathe loudly.

Alphena was sure that if they were asked, everyone in the street would claim he—they were all men—hadn't heard a word of the discussion between the women. The rest of the servants would claim to have been in the back of the house while it was going on. She was also sure that the row—and it was certainly becoming one—would be the only topic of conversation among the servants tonight and with neighboring households. Well, she didn't care!

"You're my mother?" Alphena said. Her voice rose shrilly, and that made her even more angry than she'd been already. "You're five years older than I am, that's all! That's pretty young for motherhood, isn't it, *dear*?"

Hedia was actually six years older that Alphena, but she knew that she wouldn't be called on the petty falsehood. Hedia wasn't petty.

"Or do you mean that you've got so much more *experience* than I do?" Alphena went on. Words were bubbling out of her; she couldn't control them any more than a cloud could control the rain sluicing down. "I've heard that you do. Is that where you're going now, to get more experience? Is that why you don't want your husband's daughter along?"

"Dear," Hedia said calmly as she walked to the bottom of the steps directly below Alphena. "I don't think this is a good time or place for the discussion. I understand your being upset by the business yesterday. I'm upset too, and when I return we can talk about it quietly."

The German doorkeeper had vanished into his alcove; Alphena didn't think he was smart enough to understand how dangerous this was for a slave, but at least he'd figured out that he shouldn't stand obviously gaping at his betters.

"I've heard that Master Corylus's cook is a wise woman too!" Alphena said. She was listening to herself as though she'd just stumbled onto the conversation of two complete strangers. "Does she make potions, do you suppose? Does she make the sort of potion that your first husband swallowed the night he died?"

For a moment, Hedia's face had no expression at all. Alphena's breath sucked in; she'd shocked herself with her words, an accusation of poisoning screamed in public. If anybody took it to the authorities, not only Hedia but Corylus would be in serious trouble. *Hecate, make my tongue not have spoken!*

Hedia laughed, a silver trill that broke the brittle silence. Smiling, she patted Alphena on the arm and said, "You're quite right, dear. You're an adult, and you're a part of this business—the whole household is. I shouldn't have been treating you as a child."

"I'm sorry," Alphena whispered. "I shouldn't have . . . I didn't know what I was saying."

She'd been looking into her stepmother's eyes. For a moment Hedia had considered all aspects of the situation and all possible responses. She had chosen to laugh, but that was a *choice*.

"Nonsense, dear," Hedia said with another affectionate pat. She wasn't hiding anger under pretense of cheerfulness: the scene really did amuse her. "Someone seems to be attacking your father by magic, attacking all of us I shouldn't wonder, and of course you're upset. I couldn't be more pleased that you're willing to help me get to the bottom of the business."

She turned to the sedan chair. The bearers were facing up the street. They must've been watching the women in the polished bronze fittings, though, because they stiffened immediately.

"Scylax?" Hedia said. "Is the chair ready?"

Pairs of men carried the chair, but another pair would

trot alongside to take over every fifteen minutes—or less, if they were climbing hills. The chief bearer rose and turned, standing at attention.

"Yes, milady!" he said. "We just finished putting the poles in, milady. It made a lot of noise, it did, and I almost didn't hear you calling me!"

"Well, run up to the boulevard and find another chair as well," Hedia said, accepting the lie with an icy smile. "My daughter will be gracing me with her companionship. She'll go with you and I'll ride in the hired chair. Promptly, now!"

The bearer trotted toward the Argiletum at the head of the cul-de-sac. He didn't run, and his arms dangled instead of pumping back and forth as most people would have done. The chairmen were used to moving at a particular speed in a particular way, for as long as they needed to. Scylax wasn't going to change his technique simply because he'd been told to do something other than carry the front half of a sedan chair.

As they watched Scylax, Hedia slid her fingers down Alphena's arm and let them rest on the back of her hand. "We're going to be friends, dear," she said. "It's important that you and I be friends."

Alphena forced a smile. "Yes, Mother," she said, curling her hand around Hedia's.

The previous afternoon she'd realized that Lenatus and his friend Pulto had been killers, for all their politeness and the way they now bowed and scraped to the young mistress. They had been ready to kill again if they thought they should.

What Alphena had seen a moment ago in her stepmother's eyes was a colder version of the same thing. Hedia could be a *very* bad enemy.

VARUS WORE THE ivory head around his neck on a thin leather thong. Though he didn't reach under his toga while he listened to Piso's class exercise, his fingers curled with memory of how the talisman had felt.

"You were a prostitute!" Piso said. His left arm was crossed over his chest, while he swept his right out to the side as though he were pointing at a meteor plunging toward the Forum. "You say that you remained chaste and begged for alms instead of surrendering your body to your clients, but the only evidence we have is your word. The word of an admitted prostitute!"

Piso was declaiming from the rostrum in front of the Temple of Julius Caesar, facing his teacher and the remainder of the class in the Forum below. Pandareus and some of the students—Piso's friends and sycophants, at least—had notebooks out, either waxed boards or thin sheets of wood to write on with a brush.

Varus didn't need notes to remember clever twists that his fellow classmates came up with. Besides, in Varus's estimation, the chances of Piso doing so were slim to none.

The subject set for Piso's speech was whether a woman who remained chaste after being captured by pirates and sold into prostitution could legally become a vestal virgin. The situation was improbable, but it taught logic and technique as clearly as an ordinary case of legacy fishing.

"Your children would be barred from becoming priests," cried Piso. He clapped his right arm to his chest now and flung the left one outward. Like his voice, his gestures attempted by enthusiasm to make up for their lack of grace. "Because their mother had carried on a sordid occupation. Are we therefore to say that you are worthy of becoming a priestess yourself?"

The varied business of the Forum went on untroubled by the declamation. At least three other classes were going on nearby, though the babble of business was enough to drown the speeches in the general noise.

Occasionally passersby would glance toward them, but the exuberant gestures had probably drawn their eyes. Piso looked enough as though he were hurling things from his raised vantage point that a prudent man would take heed.

"Should the consul give way to you if he meets you as priestess in the street?" Piso bellowed, changing the angles of his arms yet again. "To you, a woman whom a crippled Levantine properly approached if he still had two copper sesterces in his begging bowl!"

There were cheers and stampings of applause from behind Pandareus and the semicircle of his students. Though the Senate was in session, the Emperor hadn't made his appearance yet. Piso's father and his political cronies had chosen to attend the boy's declamation, doubtless planning to rush into the session if the glittering progress of a guard detachment warned them that the Emperor was on his way. The session was being held in the huge Julian Basilica today; the entrance was within fifty yards.

What did the senators really think of the declamation? Perhaps they were impressed by it. This wasn't an age which valued subtlety, and Piso certainly displayed the present virtues of noise and color to an impressive degree.

"Do you say, 'The pirate who captured me can attest my virginity'?" Piso demanded. He'd initially shown some variation in his gestures, but now he seemed to have settled on mirrored pairings of one arm crossed, the other extended. "Perhaps, but your witness won't be able to visit you in your temple should you become a priestess!"

Saxa had never come to one of Varus's declamations. He'd attended early classes occasionally, though he wasn't an orator himself and didn't pretend to care about technique or about literature more generally.

Varus had never cared for argumentative declamations like the present one anyway. They were the stuff of courts and public assemblies, where a bold lie which couldn't be uncovered was more effective than any amount of calm reason.

Philosophical declamations were far more attractive to him. Varus had been quite pleased with the way he'd brought his audience to consider whether Alexander should sail from the mouth of the Indus River and turn east, attempting to cross the globe-girdling ocean. He'd summed up on the one hand that water was the first element and should not be conquered by any man, even Alexander; and on the other that this would be the longed-for moment when human civilization and the world should have the same boundaries. Pandareus had spoken highly of some of his figures of speech, and even Piso's claque had jotted notes.

But Saxa hadn't been present. Varus smiled with rueful affection. For as far back as he could remember, his father had been an antiquarian: a man who enjoyed unearthing odd scraps of knowledge. He had a great deal of information, but he hadn't been able to organize it in any fashion more complicated than a vertical stack.

More recently, though, his researches had descended into what could only be described as blatant superstitions, sillinesses that were unworthy of the attention— let alone the belief—of an educated man. And Saxa did believe in them. He not only practiced magical rituals himself, he let a self-proclaimed Hyperborean wizard lead him in the gods knew *what* directions.

Though Varus no longer saw the twelve dancers, they chanted in his mind as their demon companions hissed in unison. It was a dream, but it haunted his waking hours. It was a dream!

"You wheedled would-be customers to give you as alms what they had intended to pay as the price of your body!" said Piso. "Well and good—you remain a virgin. But is this the art which a priestess uses when speaking to the goddess of the hearth? Surely not! Yours was a whore's trick and a whore's manner. Your very demeanor is an affront to chaste Vesta!"

Corylus stood to Varus's left. His notebook was out for courtesy's sake, but he wasn't jotting anything down. Varus knew that his friend disliked Piso even more than he himself did, but he was unfailingly polite when they interacted.

On the frontier where Corylus had been raised, life was harsh and weapons were never far to seek even in the most civilized surroundings. As the chant seethed in his blood, Varus realized for the first time that his friend was always courteous because he was constantly aware of violence, not despite the fact. Varus didn't doubt what Corylus was capable of if the necessity arose, but Corylus understood better than the other students the difference between what was necessary and what was simply possible.

Corylus's declamations were forceful and closely reasoned, but he didn't gesture nor did he use the flourishes and allusions that would have made his speeches more striking. His wide reading—he wasn't as widely read as Varus, of course, but given the limited opportunities he would have had on the frontier, his knowledge was remarkable—would have allowed him to sprinkle colorful passages from the great poets and historians whether Latin or Greek.

It didn't seem to bother Corylus that Piso and his cronies sneered—behind the backs of their hands—at what they called his lack of erudition. As a knight of Carce Corylus wasn't eligible to enter the Senate, and he'd been bluntly dismissive when Varus had asked if he hoped to make his name as a lawyer.

Corylus spoke as a military officer would when suggesting a course of action to a superior or explaining it to his juniors. Varus decided that if the sneers didn't bother his friend, he could learn to ignore them also.

"This court, this goddess—"

Piso thrust out both arms to point at the round temple of Vesta beside where his audience stood. He looked like a bad statue of Phaethon dragging on the reins as the horses of the Sun ran away.

"—this sacred sky of Carce—"

He pointed straight up, though his face still glowered at his audience.

"—allow only one answer: you must be barred from the priesthood!"

Piso's father and his fellow senators called "Huzzah!" and stamped their feet loudly. The other students applauded also, ranging from the enthusiasm of the speaker's cronies to the polite tap of Corylus's right foot. Even Pandareus gave a nod which could be taken as approving.

Piso stepped down from the rostrum and bowed at the waist, sweeping his arms back to the sides as though he were about to dive into a swimming pool. He was smiling with triumph; the neck of his broad-striped toga was as wet as a used towel.

There's never only one answer, Varus mused, lost in his own thoughts. *There are often thousands of answers, and all of them may be wrong.*

In his mind the dancers whispered *Nemastes must die.* They had no other answer, and their voices were compelling.

HEDIA'S CHAIR ROCKED to a threatening halt. The hired bearers looked scrawny compared to Saxa's team, but they were fit and they got much more experience than the household slaves did. They hadn't slipped once on the way to Corylus's apartment on the Viminal Hill.

Judging by Alphena's cries from the following vehicle, the girl hadn't been so lucky.

Though Hedia had no complaint about the bearers, the chair itself was another matter. Syra had thrown a cushion over the stains on the wicker seat, but one of the clamps attaching the poles to the chair frame was loose or possibly broken. Hedia swayed unpleasantly at every turn on the way, and as they stopped she was afraid that she was going to pitch over on her face with the chair on top of her.

"Right here, your ladyship!" cried the courier who'd run ahead to point out their destination. He was new to the household; a young fellow from somewhere in Spain, with curly hair and a good build. "On the third floor, right here!"

He seemed to fancy himself. He had some reason, but not as much as he thought.

Hedia smiled coldly. That was generally true of men, she'd found. Women too, she shouldn't wonder, but they didn't interest her in the same way.

Instead of squatting with his partner to take the weight of the chair off their arms, the leading bearer looked over his shoulder at Hedia. She supposed he'd found that raising the weight was more work than simply holding it balanced till he was sure about what his fare intended.

"Mistress?" he said. "Are you sure about this? The block looks all right, but it's not the kinda district we usually take quality folks like you."

"By Nergal, Blaesus," grunted the bearer behind her. He spoke in trade Greek, but his accent came from much farther east than that. "We never took anybody like her *anywhere* before, did we?"

"My man seems sure," Hedia said, "so put me down and—"

"Yoo-hoo, your ladyship!" called a woman on the tiny

third-story balcony jutting from the building to the right. "I'm here, bless you for coming!"

She waved frantically with her right arm and gripped the railing with her left. If Hedia judged correctly, the way she hunched involved more than just that she was looking at someone below her. The rheumatism Pulto had mentioned wasn't an excuse to try to avoid a visit that embarrassed him.

Hedia got out; Alphena was climbing from the household chair. Local people stared at the visitors, but they seemed to be cheerfully interested instead of hostile. The score of attendants accompanying the women could have kept them away regardless, but even the children seemed satisfied to gawp at a respectful distance.

"Wait for my return," Hedia said to the lead bearer. "And if you've managed to attach the chair more firmly before I go back, there'll be a silver piece for you."

"Ahura's balls!" said the rear man. "We'll take care of it, lady-sir. We bloody well will!"

"I'll lead, your ladyship!" cried the Spaniard. He strode to the door, swaggering and making shooing motions with both arms. "Make way for the noble Hedia, wife of our noble senator Gaius Alphenus Saxa! Make way!"

Hedia frowned; that might've been a good way to catch a handful of rotten cabbage. Instead the three old women sitting on the doorsill got out of the way with an appearance of good humor.

They bowed low to Hedia. She smiled graciously as she swept past and said, "Thank you, good ladies. I hope you're well on this fine morning."

The staircase was lighted by street-facing windows at each floor and a mica-covered skylight above the fifth landing. It was clean, though the large jar for night soil on the ground level must not have been emptied that morning. Hedia climbed briskly, but even so Alphena's slippers *shuff*ed on the treads too closely behind her.

The door on the third floor swept open and the woman from the balcony stepped out. "Your ladyship!" she said. "I'm Anna, Master Corylus's nurse from the very day he was born. I'm honored, we're all so honored, that you're coming. I told the girls in the building, but I don't think they believed me till you stopped just now."

The materials used to build an apartment block became increasingly light—which meant flimsier—at each story upward; rents went down in the same proportion. This third-floor suite was large and well lighted, and though it was above the masonry level, the walls were wood rather than wicker.

Anna must have understood Hedia's glance of appraisal. She said, "Yes, if Master Corylus wished, he could've had something on the second floor and closer in to the Forum. Master Cispius is a careful man but not tight, and he's doing right well in the perfume trade, I don't mind to tell you. But the young master liked this one. You can look right over to the Gardens of Maurianus."

She surveyed the apartment possessively. The wooden floor had been brought to a high polish instead of being covered with a mosaic design as would have been more common, and the furniture, including the storage chests, was tasteful and of simple, excellent design.

"It looks very nice," said Alphena to call attention to herself. She'd sent the Spaniard and the other servants down to wait in the street, which showed better judgment than Hedia would have expected.

"My daughter, Lady Alphena," Hedia said coolly. "I've asked her to accompany me. I trust that is all right?"

"Bless me, your ladyship!" said Anna. "If you want to bring the whole Senate with you, I'm just honored. Though there'd be trouble finding them seats."

Anna's outfit—a blue tunic, a cape which must've been cut down from an officer's red traveling cloak, and a yellow silk scarf to cover her hair—was neither tasteful nor simple. She wore rings on all her fingers, a mixture of silver and iron washed with gold. She had two necklaces, one of rock crystal and the other of painted terracotta manikins each no bigger than a thumbnail. The tiny dolls were individually ugly, but they had an unexpected force as their stubby hands clicked into contact and separated.

Alphena laughed. Anna smiled in a bemused way, but Hedia wasn't sure that she had intended a joke.

Anna touched the yellow scarf, patting it against her bun of hair. The strands that had escaped to the back and sides were frizzy and yellowish gray. "Though your ladyship?" she said to Hedia. "There are subjects that I wouldn't talk about in front of a senator, you know?"

Hedia sniffed. "Not in front of a senator or any other man," she said. "But we're all girls together here, aren't we?"

Alphena was looking between the older women, her eyes flicking from one to the other. She looked younger when she was confused—as she was now.

Anna chuckled. "Here," she said, pushing aside the curtain covering the pantry alcove beside the door. She lifted out a bowl of wine which she'd mixed before her guests arrived and set it on the small table in a corner of the room. The circular top was a section of pine trunk, carved and stained to look like expensive desert cedar. "We'll have something to drink while we talk."

"Are there no servants?" said Hedia, raising an eyebrow toward the folding screen across the doorway to the adjoining room of the suite.

"Bless you, no there's not," Anna said, bringing out the cups. They and the bowl were of layered glass, colored to look like the expensive murrhine ware turned from a British mineral which the locals called Blue John. "The boy was raised in camp, you see. He's offered to get me some help, but truth is I'd rather handle it myself."

"But how do you do the shopping?" said Alphena as their hostess filled the cups. It was a tactless question, but it showed the girl had sharp eyes and could think.

Anna chuckled. "Crippled up like I am, you mean?" she said. "Well, that's true enough, but a couple of the girls on the fourth floor take care of that for less than it'd cost to feed a gofer of our own. I've done them a favor or two, you see."

Love potions, Hedia thought as she took the offered cup and sat down. *Love potions and herbs to cause abortions; the two went together, after all.*

The two storage chests in the corner had been covered with cushions for use as seats, with the table in the angle between them. There was a proper couch against the outer wall, but even at formal dinner parties women were more likely to sit than to recline on their left side as the men did.

Alphena hesitated; Hedia patted the cushion beside her and gestured Anna to the other chest. Anna settled onto it with a grunt of relief.

Turning her head as though she were looking out the window—there were three pots of herbs on the balcony— Anna said, "That's part of the reason I didn't want another pair of hands in the household, you see. They'd come with a tongue attached, you see, and there's stories enough already. Me being Marsian"—she met the noblewoman's eyes—"and all. Like every Marsian woman's a witch! Ah, begging your pardon if I've misspoke, your ladyship."

Hedia laughed. "You haven't, not at all," she said. "And I think you'd best call me Hedia while it's just the three of us. As I said, we're all girls together here. As for witchcraft—we women can't do things the way men do, so we have to find our own ways."

She sipped her wine. It was a good enough vintage to have appeared at her husband's table. She looked at Anna over the rim of her cup and raised an eyebrow in question.

The old servant sighed in relief. She drained her cup with less ceremony than wine so good deserved. "Aye, that's so, your ladyship," she said, wiping her mouth with the back of her hand. "We don't have the strength that men do—"

She grinned at Alphena; Hedia thought for a moment that she might reach out and pinch the girl's cheek. The standards of an army camp were different from those of a noble household.

"—not even you, little one. I've heard about you, sure, but that's not the way. You listen to"—she nodded forcefully toward Hedia—"your mother here. She knows a thing or two, I'll be bound."

"What I know at the moment . . . ," said Hedia. Even without the cheek pinch, she thought her stepdaughter might burst like a dead dog. This wasn't the time to laugh at her, though. "Is that Nemastes the Hyperborean is a danger to my husband and our whole family. I presume you've heard about Nemastes?"

Anna snorted. "Not from my man or the boy either," she said, pouring more wine for herself when her guests waved it off. "But that something was going on, sure. I could smell the magic on them each time they'd been to your house, milady. Though I hate to say it."

"Smell?" Alphena blurted in amazement. Her cup was raised, but Hedia didn't think the girl had begun to drink. "I don't understand?"

Anna shrugged. "Smell, feeling, call it what you like," she said. "I don't know how to name it if you haven't noticed it yourself. And you haven't?"

"No, I don't think so," Hedia said. She placed her empty cup on the table, a little closer to Anna to answer the question the hostess would surely ask. "We've come to you because you know things that we don't, mistress. But we're not in doubt that there's something wrong with Nemastes and whatever he's doing."

Alphena took a gulp of wine. "He's awful," she said, glaring at her companions as though they were going to argue with her. "I can tell when he's around because my skin prickles. And when he's looking at me, I feel *slimy*."

Hedia smiled, though she found the girl's comments—and Anna's knowing glance at her—disquieting. "Well, I've been called insensitive before," she said. "Nonetheless, I knew something had to be done even before the business yesterday at my son's reading."

She looked at Alphena. "I wasn't in the hall when it happened," she said, "but you were, dear. What did you see?"

"I didn't see—," Alphena began angrily, but she stopped herself. She swallowed, forced a weak smile of apology, and continued in a quiet tone. "I'm not sure what I saw. I thought a painted sphinx flew off the wall. And I thought things were coming up from a pit underneath me."

She's young, but she's no more flighty than I am. Nevertheless something has frightened her.

Alphena licked her lips. She seemed more composed now that she'd forced herself to think about what had happened. She said, "There wasn't really a pit. The floor was the same to my feet, I just couldn't see it."

"If you'd been my daughter, girl . . . ," Anna said, giving Alphena a look of sharp appraisal.

Hedia bit back a harsh—well, harsher—response and said only, "Which of course she isn't, mistress, she's the daughter of the noble Alphenus Saxa. Whose Hyperborean companion concerns at least me and Alphena."

"I spoke out of turn, your ladyship," Anna said, nodding into as close to a bow as she could manage while seated at the table. "Sorry, I'm an old fool who never had a child of her own, you see."

"Quite all right, my good woman," Hedia said. The thought of Alphena being brought up as a witch had taken her aback in a very unpleasant fashion. It was bad enough that the girl dressed as a gladiator! "This business is enough to put anyone on edge."

Anna looked at Alphena again, this time pursing her lips in thought. "You say the floor was still there, child," she said, "and in this world that must have been so. But there are other worlds than ours, you know. It sounds like this Nemastes was bringing another one close—or maybe closer than that. It's good that it didn't go on beyond what it did."

"I don't think it was Nemastes," Alphena said toward the mixing bowl on the table. "I think it was my brother, or something using my brother. He was saying funny things about fire. And I could see the fire, but—" She lifted her hands, then laid them flat to either side of the cup before her. She still didn't look up. "I don't know how I saw it. Not with my eyes."

"When Pulto and me got married after his discharge," Anna said carefully, "I promised him that I wouldn't do anything, you know, serious. A little charm or a potion to help friends, well that's just neighborly."

She gave her companions a lopsided smile and shrugged. "But after he and the boy come home yesterday—and they didn't tell me a thing except that you might be coming by, your ladyship. But it was all over them, especially the boy, like they'd been rolling in pig shit. Begging your pardon."

"That's how it felt to me too," Alphena said. Her smile was real, though faint. "Not that I've ever rolled in pig shit really, but what it seemed like."

Acting on instinct instead of by plan—and she usually planned things, particularly the things that other people thought were done without thinking—Hedia put her arm around the girl's shoulder and gave her a hug. Then she opened her short cape and removed the little fabric-wrapped object she'd pinned there. She handed it across the table to Anna.

"I would have brought you some of Nemastes' hairs," she said, "but he's as bald as an egg. His whole body's bare so far as I could see—and I assure you I've seen as much of it as I care to, no matter what you may have heard about me."

Alphena lifted a shocked hand to her lips. Anna guffawed as she undid the bundle, a twig from the frost-killed pear tree.

"Nemastes—Nemastes and my husband, that is," explained Hedia, "were in the back garden when this tree was killed. It was the same time when Varus was reading. I think—well, there must be some connection, mustn't there?"

Hedia was uneasily aware that the gymnasium where she'd been talking to the veterans was adjacent to the garden. The masonry wall was high enough to block words unless Saxa and the Hyperborean had been shouting, but she felt that she should have had some inkling if, well, a tree-killing storm had been going on a few feet away.

She hadn't been aware of anything unusual going on during the reading either, not until she listened to the frightened babble of the audience pouring out of the room. She looked from Anna to Alphena and smiled wryly.

Anna held the twig between the tips of her index fingers. She felt Hedia's eyes and looked up.

"I'm apparently not sensitive at all," Hedia said. "But I suppose I don't need to be, since both of you are."

Alphena turned to her. "You were sensitive enough to try to stop Nemastes before anybody else did," the girl said. "That's why we're here. I don't see any use in the way I feel." She shrugged with her whole body, her face scrunched up. "Slimy. Awful."

"We've a long way to go before we know what's useful and what isn't," Hedia said briskly. She turned to Anna and continued. "Will the stick be helpful, mistress?"

This was the first time Alphena had spoken to her in a tone that wasn't either angry or sullen. Hedia didn't dare remark on the fact or she would spoil the moment—the start of an improved relationship, she hoped.

"It may," Anna said judiciously. She eyed her companions. "It should. It's the full moon tonight. I'll be off to the old graveyard on the Aventine to gather some things I'll need."

"Herbs, you mean, Anna?" Alphena asked.

The older woman looked at Hedia—who kept her face expressionless—and then to the girl. "Things, dear," she said deliberately. "Some herbs, yes."

"Oh," said Alphena. "Oh, I'm s-s . . ." She turned her head away as her voice trailed off.

"I'll need your help, your ladyship," Anna said. "Not with my end—I wouldn't ask you for that, of course. But I hope you'll talk to my Pulto. When we were married, like I said, I gave up serious business. He didn't tell me to, but it's what he wanted and I did it. Now, though . . . ?"

"Yes," said Hedia. "I'll make it clear to your husband that I've asked you to do certain things for me."

Pulto would accept anything a noble demanded, Hedia knew. If she asked *him* to dig up ancient graves, he would obey. He wouldn't like it, but—her smile was cold—he'd been a soldier. As he'd said, he was used to doing things he didn't like.

"That will be helpful, your ladyship," Anna said,

nodding in relieved approval. "And now, if my ears haven't tricked me—"

The door opened. Corylus strode in, followed by Pulto.

"—I'd say my men were home!"

CORYLUS STEPPED TO the side as he entered the apartment; if he'd stopped in his tracks he'd have blocked the doorway for Pulto. That was training, however. His first instinct had been to freeze when he walked in the door talking over his shoulder to his servant and saw Alphena out of the corner of his eye.

"Hercules!" Pulto blurted as he saw the visitors. They'd known that the women would be visiting Anna, but they—or at least Corylus—had put out of their minds the possibility that Hedia and Alphena might still be present when they returned from the Forum.

Corylus hadn't fully realized how much he counted on the apartment being a safe haven in a city of strangers. He felt a flash of violent resentment, which embarrassed him just as violently. Nobody looking at him could've guessed he was more than normally startled to find company in his front room, though.

"Oh!" said Alphena; she jumped up. She looked as startled as Corylus was. To his surprise, that made him feel worse than he had before.

"Master Corylus," said Hedia. She rose as supplely as a cat stretching. He wouldn't have thought there was room for her to get out without shoving back the seat or the table, but she did it easily. "Lady Alphena and I were just taking our leave. Thank you for your gracious hospitality, and please convey our appreciation to your servants."

"Ah," said Corylus. He hadn't expected the formality, but of course it was the right course under these unusual circumstances. *Hedia likely picks the right course every time, at least by her own lights.* "Your presence honors my dwelling, your ladyship."

"I've asked a favor of your Anna here," Hedia said. She nodded vaguely in the old woman's direction, but her eyes continued to hold Corylus's own. "I trust you won't regard this as too much of an imposition?"

"No, your ladyship!" Corylus said. "Anything you need, just ask!"

The words tumbled out so quickly that he almost got his tongue tangled in his teeth. Alphena colored again.

"And I hope you'll direct your servant to provide what help Anna may require?" Hedia continued, raising an eyebrow.

"Umph," said Pulto as though a blow had gotten home on his belly. Hedia hadn't looked at the old veteran, and he didn't respond to the indirect order he'd just gotten, but Corylus knew how he felt about it.

Pulto would do what he was told, though. Duty was duty.

"I'm sure that whatever you ask will be important to my well-being, your ladyship," Corylus said carefully. "Some recent events seem to threaten not only Carce but the world. I—"

He stopped. He didn't know how to phrase what was a feeling and a memory rather than a considered opinion.

"That is," he said, "I trust your ladyship's judgment, and I'm sure that you have the best interests of the Emperor and the Republic at heart."

"Thank you, Master Corylus," Hedia said. Her smile was cool, but it quirked like a fishhook at one corner of her mouth. "Now I wonder, sir; would you mind walking partway back to the house with me? I know it's out of your way, but you seem a healthy young man. I have some questions about perfume, you see."

"Why, of course," said Corylus. He felt the way he had on the morning when the ice had broken and dumped him into the Rhine. *Venus and Mars, what is she really asking?* "Ah, though I don't really, I mean I'm not an expert . . . though my father, I mean . . ."

"I'm sure you'll be able to enlighten me sufficiently," said Hedia. There was laughter in her eyes, but it didn't quite reach her tongue. "And it will be quite decorous, as you'll be walking beside my chair through the public streets. You know the way, of course."

Alphena stared at her as though she'd walked in on her stepmother looting a temple. Anna had been bustling in the pantry, but now she stuck her head out and said, "Pulto, I have things to talk to you about. The boy can make his way to Senator Saxa's house and back without you to hold his hand this time."

"Yes, I know the way," Corylus said. "I, ah . . ."

"Then we'll be going," Hedia said, nodding at the door to the stairs. "My daughter and I have business to attend to tonight, so we need to get back."

"I wonder, *Mother*," said Alphena, her voice pitched higher than it had been when she spoke a moment before. "Why don't you take our chair and I'll ride back in the one you hired?"

"Not at all, dear," Hedia said, looking toward the girl with soft amusement. "I'm sure Master Corylus doesn't mind that he's walking beside a rented chair. It's not as though he's going to be talking to the bearers, after all, is it?"

As he listened to the interplay, Corylus realized that the bearers would be total strangers, not members of the household staff who might gossip to their fellows. Had Hedia planned this all along?

Alphena stood stiffly with her fists clenched at her sides. Then without a further word or a look backward, she marched out the door. Hedia, still with a faint smile that could have meant anything, drifted after her.

Corylus glanced over his shoulder as he followed the women. Pulto met his eyes and shrugged. "Keep your shield up and your head down, boy," the veteran muttered. "You're on the east bank now, believe me."

The German side of the river. Corylus grinned as he trotted down the stairs. He intended to be a soldier, after all, and soldiers had to take risks.

Outside somebody was shouting, "Bring the vehicles for the noble ladies Hedia and Alphena!" When Corylus got outside, he saw it was the oily-looking pretty boy who'd been standing in the stairway when he and Pulto came home.

One of Saxa's servants, he supposed, though not one he remembered seeing before. There were two sedan chairs, one of them Saxa's own with the burl maple inlays. They'd been parked down the side street in the shade rather than at the front of the apartment block. Even so Corylus felt a fool not to have noticed them, especially with their coveys of servants.

Pulto hadn't noticed the chairs either, though. The business yesterday had made them both jumpy—and apparently in the worst possible way: they so focused on cloudy fears that they weren't seeing things around them that might be important.

Alphena pushed a servant out of the way and threw herself onto the household vehicle. She couldn't make the bearers drop it—which seemed to have been what she intended—but she did make it sway to the side. The bearers were braced to take her weight, so she had shoved the chair from an angle.

The smarmy servant placed himself beside the hired chair and offered Hedia his arm; the bearers watched the byplay with bored disinterest. Hedia flicked a finger and said, "Iberus, run back to the house and announce that Lady Alphena and I are on the way."

She turned to Corylus and said, "Will you please hand me into the chair, Master Corylus?"

The servant gaped transfixed for a moment, but

judgment smothered his bruised ego in time. He spun and jogged down Long Street before Hedia took further notice of him.

"Your ladyship," Corylus muttered. He thrust his arm out for Hedia to grip. In fact her fingertips barely brushed his skin; Hedia didn't work out the way her stepdaughter did, but she was obviously fit.

The vehicles and attendants started toward the center of the city with Alphena's chair leading. There were servants both in front and behind, but none of the household were close to Hedia and Corylus.

Alphena seemed to be urging her bearers to speed up. That was a bad idea: trained pairs had a fixed pace. If they changed it they were likely to get out of step with one another, making for a rough ride; in the worst case they might even fall.

"Ah, you wanted to know about perfume, your ladyship?" Corylus said.

"Of course not, dear," Hedia said with a throaty chuckle. "And I don't want to know about Vergil's poetry either, which I suspect would interest you a great deal more."

She turned to look at him. The hired bearers were keeping a good pace, but to the left Corylus matched it easily by lengthening his own stride by a thumb's width from route march standard.

"And I'd like you to call me Hedia," she said. "In fact, I insist on it. You wouldn't refuse a lady's request, would you, Corylus?"

"Ah . . . ," said Corylus. "I would comply as best I could within the bounds of propriety. Hedia."

Her laugh trilled. "You're a diplomat," she said. "And much more intelligently cautious than I would expect from someone your age."

She looked him up and down, leaning toward him slightly to watch his legs scissoring on the pavement.

Just as glad for the silence, Corylus looked ahead and to his side of the street.

Old two- and three-story buildings lined the boulevard. Though Carce was growing with the expansion of the empire, the need for taller structures hadn't generally moved this far out from the Forum yet. Corylus's own apartment block was an exception, a replacement for three smaller buildings destroyed by fire only a year and a half ago.

"You don't move like a lawyer," she said, raising her eyes to his face again. "You move more like a wolf."

"I don't plan to be a lawyer," Corylus said. He was aware of her to his right through the corners of his eyes, but he continued to look forward. "I'm going to enter the army as a tribune next year"—he started to say, "your ladyship," but caught himself—"Hedia. Master Pandareus teaches us to speak, but he also teaches us to think, those of us who want to. Varus and I are learning a lot besides rhetoric."

"Umm . . . ," said the lady noncommittally. "At your age, I'd been married for a year. The first time, that is. I suppose you've heard various stories about me, Corylus?"

Corylus remembered how Pulto had grunted when Hedia had told him to help his wife with her magic. He felt the same now. The breath went out of him; he didn't miss a step, but his right foot slipped a trifle because he didn't place it with the care that the slick-worn paving stones required.

It's probably best to tell the truth. It's always best to tell the truth. Usually.

"Your ladyship," Corylus said. He looked at her as they paced along; their eyes were on a level. "*Hedia*, I'm sorry. Hedia, I'm not from Carce and I don't run in the same circles you do. Early on there was some talk in class from the other fellows, but I think they were just

trying to ride Varus because he and I were friends. And"—
how much to say?—"because that did kind of involve
me, I got involved in it and it stopped. Anyway, I wouldn't
trust Piso if he walked into the room wet and said it
was raining."

He didn't know how Hedia was going to react to
what he'd just blurted. After an expressionless moment,
she gave him a slow smile and said, "Piso, yes. Well, he
wouldn't like me, dear. I was married to Calpurnius
Latus, his uncle, you see. And I'm afraid the marriage
wasn't a success."

"Well, if Latus was anything like Piso . . . ," Corylus
said. His voice had dropped to a growl. He looked
ahead again because he didn't want Hedia to mistake
the hard anger in his expression as something directed
at her. "Then it wasn't your fault. Hedia."

"That's very sweet of you, Corylus," she said, "and my
first husband was certainly a nasty little thing. But there
were faults on both sides. There generally are, dear."

"Well, it's none of my business," Corylus muttered to
the air. He wanted to break into a run. He wanted to be
back in the apartment. He *wanted* to be back in the clean
forest glades in Germany; either side of the Rhine would
have been all right.

He remembered the forest he'd dreamed of while
Varus read his epic; the place with the shaggy elephants,
where Saxa and the Hyperborean had been sacrificing.
But the men had been in the garden of Saxa's house here
in Carce then. What had Corylus really seen?

"I'm sure some of the stories you heard were true,"
Hedia continued calmly. "Even if you heard them from
my nephew by marriage. In some cases, I doubt dear
Piso could have made anything up that would have been
more, well, colorful. Did he accuse me of poisoning
Latus, though?"

"I didn't believe it," Corylus said.

The snarl was on his face as well as in his voice. A fruit seller who'd dodged toward the chair through the screen of attendants now jumped back, breaking off his spiel at "These're the finest—"

"I'm glad to hear that," said Hedia, "because it's not true. *I* didn't poison him, at any rate. Latus had other interests, you see, and it's been my experience that men of a certain sort are more likely to be jealous bitches than real women are. But there was fever about in Baiae that summer, and I honestly believe that a fever carried away my husband."

Corylus coughed, then swallowed, to have something to do other than speak. He didn't know how to react when a woman he knew only slightly—a noblewoman!—started talking about, well, these sorts of things.

Which he *had* heard about, of course. And if he was really honest, he'd have to admit that he'd believed at least a little part of what he'd heard.

"I care very deeply for my husband Saxa," Hedia said. "He's a wonderful, kind, old man. By marrying me he saved me from being beggared if not worse after Latus died, and he truly loves me for what I am."

Corylus risked a glance at her. She smiled impishly and said, "Or despite what I am, if you want to put it that way. I'm sure a lot of people would."

"M-ma'am, I don't know about that," he said. "I don't know anything about, well, that."

"I doubt that's true," Hedia said with another chuckle, "but let it stand. Saxa is a very sweet *older* man. And he wouldn't have been an athlete even when he was younger, I'm afraid."

Corylus didn't speak. He thought about the subject of Piso's oration and began to grin despite himself. He wondered how Pandareus would react to a declamation on the subject "A freeborn lady offers her body to all comers. She then asks to become a priestess, claiming that because she refused payment for her services she did not carry on a sordid occupation."

"You're laughing, Corylus?" Hedia said with the least bit of edge in her voice.

"Piso was declaiming this morning," he said truthfully. "He struck me as mechanical and bombastic. But very loud."

"I'm not surprised that it remains a pattern in the family," Hedia said. Her lips pouted slightly, then relaxed into a grin. "Corylus, dear, I really do care about my husband and my family. My first concern is to remove the danger which threatens them. You're my ally in this, a valuable ally. I assure you that I won't do anything that makes it difficult for us to work together."

Corylus sighed with a combination of relief and an embarrassment greater than he'd felt earlier. "Thank you, ma'am," he said. "Ah, Hedia. I don't know what's going on, but it scares me. I'm glad I have friends like you and Varus to, well, help figure it out."

"The noble ladies Hedia and Alphena are home!" cried the runner, Iberus, from the steps of Saxa's town house.

Corylus looked around in surprise. They'd arrived, all right. A good thing there hadn't been a German war band lurking in ambush.

He grinned broadly. He wasn't sure that a dozen Germans would be more dangerous than getting involved with Hedia might be.

Agrippinus came out to pay the hired bearers, but Alphena took him aside before he got off the porch. The majordomo handed the purse he was carrying to an underling, who in turn came toward the chair.

Hedia got out and looked at Corylus over the vehicle. "Would you care to use the gymnasium now?" she asked. "I find that sometimes exercise is the best way to deal with a day of mental frustration. Or just a drink?"

"No thank you, your ladyship," Corylus said. It had

been a faster trip than he'd expected. "I'll be meeting Varus and, ah, friends tonight, so I have things to get ready."

Hedia glanced at Alphena, who was still talking forcefully to the majordomo. "I understand," she said. "I'll be going out with my daughter tonight also. But perhaps another time."

Corylus turned and started back. He heard Hedia call, "And may all our endeavors prosper, Master Corylus!"

CHAPTER V

Hedia swept out of her suite. Syra was just behind her, and in the maid's train followed a gaggle of lesser servants. They included two male lantern bearers, though the lamps in the hall had already been lit.

"Is my daughter ready?" Hedia snapped to the group of maids chatting beside the half-sized bronze copy of Myron's *Discus Thrower*. She thought one of them was assigned to Alphena's suite; and regardless, all of the upstairs servants probably knew where the family members were. They rarely had anything to do except gossip, after all.

The servants had flattened stiffly against the wall when Hedia strode into view. "Your ladyship!" said a henna-haired maid who must be nearly fifty. "Lady Alphena is already gone to the street to inspect the new litter!"

"Indeed?" Hedia said without raising an eyebrow.

"It's just been delivered," volunteered a new under-steward. The older men to either side grabbed him by the elbows and hustled him backward through a doorway and out of sight.

Hedia stepped briskly down the stairs, her face expressionless. She knew nothing about a new vehicle, and she doubted very much whether her husband did either.

"Travel safely, your ladyship!" the night doorman boomed. He wasn't so much greeting the lady of the house as warning the large number of servants in the street that she was about to appear in their midst. They straightened and formed into neat blocks, sorted by their duties.

In the center where Alphena stood was the object of everybody's interest, a huge two-passenger litter. It had a canopy and isinglass curtains which would allow those inside to get a cloudy view of their surroundings while staying dry in a storm.

The vehicle must be heavy, but not too great a burden for the two teams of four bearers. They were Cappadocians, judging by their features and stocky bodies. Their matching tunics seemed to be green, but that might be a trick of the yellow lamplight on blue fabric.

"Are we ready to go, Mother Hedia?" the girl said with brittle cheeriness. "And how do you like the new litter? I told Agrippinus to get one immediately so that you and I can ride together in the future!"

"A commendable show of initiative, dear," said Hedia as she walked over to examine the vehicle and its crew. "I should have thought of it myself."

Alphena had no authority to purchase a vehicle like this. With the bearers, it must have cost as much as a farm in the south of the peninsula. Even Hedia herself should have gotten the approval of her lord and master before she did anything of the sort.

Realistically, though, the servants knew that Saxa wouldn't have objected. If his daughter went into hysterics, as she'd given ample proof that she could, the life of nobody within earshot would be quiet. Alphena wasn't above demanding that a servant be beaten for obeying her father's orders when they clashed with her own desires.

Agrippinus should have informed Hedia about what was happening, but that wouldn't have made any real difference. Besides, she'd been occupied with her bath and toilette; she wouldn't have welcomed an interruption.

She ran her fingertips over the vehicle's mother-of-pearl inlays; she couldn't feel the seam where it had been let into the ebony frame. And it wasn't as though Saxa would miss the money. . . .

"An excellent choice, my dear," she said, giving the girl a smile which was at least partly honest. "I'll congratulate Agrippinus on the skill with which he carried out your orders."

And she would have some other things to say to the majordomo. She understood his decision not to warn her, but it hadn't better happen again unless he wanted to sleep on his belly for a week or two until his back healed.

"Shall we go?" Hedia gestured with her left hand; her multiple rings caught the lamplight. Each was set with a pearl to match her three-strand necklace of large Indian stones hung on gold wire. "You should have the honor of seating yourself first, dear, since it was your idea."

Alphena had been angered at the way Hedia sequestered the boy—though Corylus had better sense than men twice his age, more was the pity—on the way back to the house. She'd bought the litter in order to show she was important—and very possibly, to provoke a quarrel with her stepmother.

Hedia had no intention of quarreling, not with so much in the balance. Her attempt to ally Corylus still more closely had been sensible rather than just a pleasurable whim, but it had been a little—well, provocative. If Alphena resented it, that showed the sort of spirit that the girl would need to find her own way in a world which men ruled.

Hedia seated herself on the rear-facing couch; the cushions were arranged so that the passengers faced one another as they reclined on their left elbows. Alphena had a guarded expression that could turn very quickly to petulance or anger, but there shouldn't be any need for that.

Hedia rapped her fan against the pillar behind her head. "You may go," she said in a tone that implied "And if you dawdle, you'll be whipped within an inch of your lives." Which was of course true.

The team lifted the vehicle smoothly and set off toward the Argiletum. There were lamps on the two forward corners of the canopy, and half a dozen additional linkmen trotted along behind the vehicle where Hedia could see them. Goodness knew how many there were in front.

"I'm doing this only to please you," Alphena said sullenly.

"I know, dear," Hedia said, "and I appreciate it. The whole family has to cooperate in the face of this"—she paused to choose the word—"this danger."

It would have been more honest to say that the women of the family had to cooperate because Saxa himself appeared to be part of the danger. And judging from what Hedia had heard about the reading, she wondered if Saxa's son wasn't also dangerous.

THE LINKMAN AND two under-stewards with cudgels in the lead suited their pace to the cautious rate that Lord Varus found comfortable. They were singing a current ditty, "The Girl from Andros," to warn others who were out tonight that they were sober and in good number.

Varus didn't like traveling in Carce at night. Well, nobody did, of course, but he thought he disliked it more than most. He wasn't exactly night blind, but he was sure that other people must see better than he did. Tonight there was a full moon, though, and they'd come most of the distance by the Sacred Way. That was the last street in the city where shadows might hide broken pavement or there'd be a dead ox blocking the road.

He no longer heard the Hyperboreans of his vision

chanting, but the rhythm of it was in his blood. He supposed that was why he was, well, more nervous than there was any reason to be. Even across the river in the worst part of Carce, a man with lanterns and twelve attendants wasn't going to be set upon by robbers.

There were men who used sedan chairs; Saxa himself occasionally did. Varus wasn't concerned about what Carce generally would think if he'd chosen to ride in a chair, but he cringed at the idea of Corylus seeing him arrive like a fine lady. Not that Corylus would say anything, or for that matter that he—being Corylus—would even think it.

"We've reached the base of the Capitoline, Lord Varus," said Candidus, the deputy steward in charge of the escort. He was competent enough but officious, and he talked far too much.

"Yes, I see the retaining wall," Varus said, though the irony probably went unnoticed. The small procession turned left toward the steps to the top.

He liked to spend time with his own thoughts, which was impossible in Candidus's company. The fellow would never behave this way with Hedia or even Alphena. The women would flay him with their tongues, and if he opened his mouth again at the wrong time, he'd lose the skin of his back in all truth. Varus didn't know how to do that, but—

"Candidus," Varus said, "if you interrupt my train of thought again, I'll have you assigned to my sister for a few days to correct your behavior. If you survive a few days, that is."

"Lord Varus, I never—," the steward began in horror. Varus stared at him; he shut his mouth and trotted forward to climb the steps to the hilltop with the leading trio.

Varus smiled as he too started up the staircase. He didn't suppose he'd ever be forceful, but he was learning ways to deal with the world on its own terms. The logical part of him didn't think that should be necessary, but the philosopher argued that the cosmos *must* be constructed correctly because it was, after all, the cosmos.

"The noble Alphenus Varus requires admittance!" Candidus announced to the guards at the top. The temple compound was walled and connected to the Citadel which covered the rest of the Capitoline, though at the moment the gate to the stairs from the Sacred Way was open.

In ancient times the hillcrest had been the last defense of the people of Carce. There hadn't been a serious threat to the city since Hannibal had marched to the walls almost three centuries before, but the guards weren't just a formality. The Temple of Jupiter Best and Greatest was the Republic's most sacred site, and the treasures dedicated in it by generations of conquerors were worth the attention of any thief.

Well, any thief who wasn't deeply religious. Varus didn't know criminals major enough to consider looting temples, but none of the family's pilfering servants had struck him as unusually religious.

"Pleased to see you, your lordship," the elder of the guards said. He wore a sword as well as a helmet and a leather cuirass; Corylus could probably say whether this pair were soldiers or at least ex-soldiers. "A fine, bright evening, isn't it?"

He'd noticed the broad stripe on Varus's toga and was probably hoping for a tip. Varus would see that the guards got a silver piece each; he wanted to be on good terms with them if he came back here.

He didn't know what was going to happen tonight, let alone in the future, but he could imagine things that *might* happen. Whenever possible he prepared for the most obvious possibilities. A silver piece—about a day's wage for a free workman—was a very modest investment to gain the goodwill of an armed man whom he might be seeing regularly.

"Is Master Pandareus here yet, sir?" Varus asked. *I'm being too deferential; I should say "my good man" or relay the question through Candidus even though we're standing only a few feet apart.*

"No, your lordship, though he's on our list," said the guard, lifting a shard of pottery with three names brushed on in ink.

"There's a fellow named Corylus, though," said the bucktoothed younger man. "A knight all alone, and no lantern either. But he's got a stick."

Varus smiled without comment and passed into the compound. Though his friend didn't brag, Varus had heard his stories of going out on patrol with the scout detachments. Corylus talked about the wildlife, the night birds, and especially the night-blooming flowers in the clearings—

But Varus knew the army wasn't patrolling on the east bank of the Danube just to view nature. He didn't think Corylus had much to worry about at night in Carce.

The Temple of Jupiter Best and Greatest was straight ahead at the top of the staircase. Varus had never been here before—he hadn't had any reason to be—but as he'd expected, the layout was the same as that of the temples nearer the town house where the family sacrificed on ordinary occasions.

An altar stood in front of the building. The temple itself was on a pedestal with steps—six of them—up from ground level in front. Six huge columns—Sulla had brought them as loot from Greece over a century ago—supported the great porch in front of the building proper. The full-height display doors were closed, but lamplight from inside gleamed from the edge of the pedestrian door set into the right-hand panel.

Candidus and the linkmen walked toward the building. Varus followed, supposing that Corylus had gone inside already.

A figure stepped out of the stand of cypress trees growing to the left of the temple; they'd shaded him from the moonlight. "Varus?" he called. "Is Master Pandareus with you?"

Varus turned to join his friend. "No," he said, grimacing. "I hoped he'd come with you and Pulto. I should've sent servants home with him so that they could escort him now."

"Pulto had other business," Corylus said. He was holding a wrist-thick staff as long as he was tall. It was a countryman's tool, not the sort of thing you saw in Carce; but Varus didn't think anybody would laugh at Corylus, at least to his face. "I should have thought of that too. The poor old fellow probably doesn't go out at night enough to realize how dangerous the city is."

"The poor old fellow, as you describe him," said Pandareus tartly as he joined them, "climbs to the Capitoline *every* clear night to observe the stars. Since I'm sober and keep an eye out for potential difficulties, I avoid problems."

"Master, I apologize," Corylus said, drawing himself up straight.

"It is my task to educate the young men who come to me," Pandareus said calmly. "You've provided me with a teaching opportunity, Master Corylus, for which I should thank you."

He smiled, though perhaps moonlight made the expression colder than he intended it to be. Corylus remained as stiff as a servant—or a soldier—being dressed down by a superior.

"It's best we go in, since tonight we're not here to observe the stars," Pandareus said, this time with his normal fusty precision. "Master Varus? Just the three of us, I think, though there may be temple servants present."

Varus turned to Candidus, who was standing fully ten feet away. *I should have thought of threatening him with my sister before.* Aloud he said, "Wait here in the compound. I don't know how long I'll be."

Corylus and the teacher were already walking toward the temple steps. Varus paused a moment longer and looked at the night sky.

All he had ever wanted to be was a poet and a scholar. He'd failed at poetry; he couldn't pretend otherwise after the reading. Tearing his manuscript to pieces had been the right thing to do with it, even if he wasn't aware of it when it happened.

Scholarship, learning about the world and organizing his knowledge, was all that remained to Varus. There too he was losing hope.

The constellations glittered in their familiar cold beauty, but now they danced a stately round in time with the rhythm in his blood.

WHEN HE REACHED the temple porch, Corylus looked over his shoulder to make sure his friend was with them. Varus had always been a little absentminded, and after what had happened during the reading even somebody solid could be excused for dropping the baton.

Though Varus had fallen behind, he was coming up the steps now. He smiled wanly at Corylus. He didn't look frightened, but there was something in his eyes that wasn't right. Maybe it was just the moonlight.

The pedestrian door opened. A servant in a tunic of bleached wool with a yellow linen sash stepped out, holding a lantern high for them.

"Good evening, Master Pandareus," he said, bowing to the teacher. "Lord Priscus is pleased to entertain you and your friends."

"Thank you, Balaton," Pandareus said, nodding as he entered. Corylus gestured Varus through before he followed, bringing up the rear. He'd felt uncomfortable having his friend behind him. Varus was perhaps the smartest person Corylus had ever met—even compared to Master Pandareus—but he just wasn't the man you wanted bringing up the rear if you thought like a soldier.

Despite the size of the sculptured porch and the rows of tall columns supporting it, the temple building itself was more modest. Half a dozen three-wick oil lamps on wall struts lit the interior adequately.

Though this temple was built when Carce held unrivaled power in the world, the platform on which it stood was that of the predecessor standing when the Gauls sacked Carce three centuries earlier. The statue of Jupiter was old also; the torso was terra-cotta, and the head and limbs were carved from wood. The painted skin and staring eyes made the god look like a shepherd who had gone mad from solitude and too much sun.

Near the front of the hall was a round table with a dining couch. A bulky man rose from the couch with the help of an attendant. A half-full cup of engraved glass sat with the mixing bowl on the table. Two more attendants stood alertly at a side table with a wine jar, a water pitcher, and additional cups. They were watching the newcomers.

"It's good to see you, Pandareus," said the man who'd been reclining. "Though from the tone of your note, you aren't here just to borrow a book from me, are you?"

"Indeed not, my friend," Pandareus said. "Priscus, may I present Gaius Alphenus Varus and Publius Cispius Corylus. Youths, this is Senator Marcus Atilius Priscus, a commissioner for the sacred rites and perhaps the most learned man in Carce."

"Possibly, old friend," Priscus said. "Except for yourself, of course."

He gestured to the side table. "Something to drink?" he said. "And you know that you and your friends were welcome to dine with me. The only blessing of my nights on duty here is that the temple cook is better than my own, and my own"—he gave his belly a jovial slap—"is extremely good, as you can see."

"These youths are my only present students who show signs of ability," Pandareus said, nodding toward them. Corylus and Varus stood stiffly, as though they were waiting to expound a literary passage. In a slightly warmer tone he added, "In fact they're the most talented students I've had since I came to Carce, though neither will make his name as an orator."

Priscus laughed. Looking from Corylus to Varus, he said, "Any associate of Pandareus of Athens can be expected to be a scholar and a gentleman. Boys, you're welcome indeed. Now you—"

He focused on Varus; Corylus felt himself relax minusculely. Priscus acted as though he were a jolly gourmand, but even without Pandareus's deference Corylus would have known that a keen mind directed the plump body.

"—would be Saxa's boy, would you not?"

"Yes, your lordship," Varus said; and said no more, just as he would have answered Pandareus in class.

"Your father collects facts the way a squirrel gathers nuts for the winter," Priscus said. "No rhyme or reason to them. But he knows things that not another man in Carce knows, boy. Not even me and Pandareus here. But don't you *be* like him, you hear?"

"No, your lordship," said Varus, his eyes focused on the three bronze lightning bolts in Jupiter's wooden hand.

"Come," Priscus said to the teacher, "we can at least sit. Some of us are fat old men, you know."

He gestured. "Seats for my guests, since they won't dine with me," he said. The servant who'd opened the door for them brought three folding stools—much like those which senators used, but with legs of walnut rather than ivory—from an alcove and set them around the table. Priscus sank back onto the couch—sitting rather than reclining, however—while the others seated themselves.

Corylus stroked the walnut with his fingertips and felt a sensation of great age. The silken seat must have been replaced many times, but the wooden legs could be as old as the original temple on this site.

Pandareus waved off the wine that a servant started to pour. "This isn't a social call, my friend," he said, "though perhaps I'll bring the youths another time and we can discuss Thucydides. We're here on a matter of the Republic's safety, and it may be the safety of the whole cosmos."

Priscus sniffed. "The cosmos can take care of itself," he said. "My duty is to the Republic. Go on."

"Although Varus and Corylus are well read," Pandareus said, "there are practical matters of which they may be ignorant. Would you explain to them why you're here tonight?"

"A rhetoric teacher talking about practicalities?" Priscus said with a chuckle. "But I'm happy to oblige."

He looked from Varus to Corylus. Corylus thought his friend sat even straighter than he did himself. The visions he'd seen yesterday—and the gods alone knew what Varus had seen!—had been disturbing, but what was happening now made him even more unsure.

All his life, Corylus had been steeped in the myth-shrouded history of Carce. That had been even more the case because he'd been raised on the frontier rather than in the civilized center of the empire. He felt in the core of his being that Carce was the village of bandits which by the favor of the immortal gods had risen into a city that dominated all the world which it didn't outright rule.

Now he was at the ancient center of the city, discussing its mysteries with two of the empire's most learned men. Corylus had never thought of himself as religious, but he shivered with awe.

"I'm one of the commissioners, as Pandareus told you," Priscus said. "There are ten of us now, but there were only two when Tarquin created the college. You know that?"

Varus lifted his chin in agreement; Corylus said, "Yes sir," as he'd been trained. A soldier who nodded in reply to a superior officer would be chewed out if the officer was a noble and knocked flat if he tried it with a centurion who'd come up through the ranks.

"We're not priests of Jupiter," Priscus went on, "but every night one of us dines and sleeps here in the Temple of Jupiter Best and Greatest. That's because we're responsible for the *Sibylline Books*, and they're kept here."

His silk-slippered foot tapped the floor, a mosaic of black, gray, and white chips. The design was geometric except for the four-by-five-foot rectangle in the center. There a monochrome portrait of Jupiter faced the god's statue as though it were a miniature reflecting pool.

"They're in a stone chest in the vault under this nave," Priscus said. "The opening is under the cartouche of Jupiter."

"Sir?" said Varus. "I knew that the Senate could order the commissioners for the sacred rites to examine the *Sibylline Books*. But that's for the whole Senate, after a major threat to the Republic. You don't have to wait by the *Books* in case a consul wants an instant response, do you? Unless the Emperor—"

"Not even the Emperor, my boy," agreed Priscus. "The whole Senate, as you say. But one of us, a senator—"

"Very senior and respected senators at that, Master Varus," Pandareus said with a nod of respectful approval toward his friend. "Vacancies are filled by vote, not lottery as they would be for judgeships."

"Yes, well, be that as it may," said Priscus. Despite his gruffness, he looked pleased. "Besides opening the books and examining them in a crisis, we commissioners are responsible for their safety. They're never left under the control of slaves and freedmen alone, like the temple itself is."

He looked beyond his visitors, toward—Corylus turned to follow his eyes—the servant who had admitted them. "Balaton?" he said. "Would you take a bribe from somebody who wanted to copy the *Books*?"

"I'm glad the responsibility is yours, Lord Priscus," the servant said with a smile. "I know my own frailty."

"Aye, so do I," Priscus grumbled. "He's as frail as that staff you came in with, boy. Cornelwood, isn't it?"

"Yes, sir," said Corylus, surprised out of his nervous discomfort. "You know trees, then?"

"I know how heavy that staff must be from the way it swings," Priscus said, "and I heard it when it rapped the floor. Cornelwood doesn't break and it doesn't give. I'd guess the man who carries it might be pretty much the same way."

"Sir, I—," Corylus said. He didn't know what to say. "Sir, thank you. I'll try to live up to the compliment."

"Well, Balaton's the same way, which is why I made sure he became chief of the commission's attendants," Priscus said. "I trust him a damned sight farther than I do some of my colleagues."

"And it's the *Sibylline Books* that bring us here tonight," said Pandareus. "Because of what I saw yesterday, I believe that a serious crisis faces the Republic; a crisis far worse than plagues and foreign armies and even the internal dissensions that caused the common people to march out and found their own city on the Esquiline, separate from the better classes."

"There's been an omen, you mean?" said Priscus. "Go on, then. I hadn't heard about it."

"My student Varus was giving a reading of his epic at his father's house," Pandareus said. "Corylus and I were present. There were various manifestations of a disturbing nature during the reading."

He turned toward Corylus and Varus on the stool beyond. "Tell the noble Priscus what you experienced, youths," he said. "Master Corylus?"

Corylus licked his lips. "Your lordship," he said, speaking directly to the commissioner, "I had a vision. I didn't see Varus. After the first, I mean. I drifted off and imagined I was in a snowy forest. I saw Senator Saxa and a man I didn't know. In the trees and snow, but really they were in the back garden of the house."

"The man was Nemastes the Hyperborean," Pandareus amplified in a dry voice. "He claims to be a wizard, and unfortunately I fear that he's telling the truth."

He leaned forward slightly to catch Varus's eye. "Lord Varus, now you."

Varus said nothing for a moment. Corylus squeezed his friend's right knee. Varus started and his eyes opened wide. He gave Corylus a shy smile, then said to the commissioner, "Sir, I remember starting to read but nothing more. I thought I saw men on an island, but I must have been dreaming."

He cleared his throat and looked down, then added, "Pandareus tells me I tore my manuscript up, but I don't remember that. I'm not sorry, though. I'm not a poet."

"Lord Varus, you had something in your hands after the reading," Pandareus said. "I don't believe it was a piece of your manuscript that I saw when your sister awakened you."

Corylus saw his friend's eyes open wide. His hands twitched together—only slightly, but toward the lump in the middle of his chest. It was barely visible beneath his toga.

"Sir, I don't remember anything," Varus said. The words might have been true, but they didn't respond to the question. "Please, won't you tell Lord Priscus what really happened, since Corylus and I can't."

Did Pandareus notice? Regardless, he nodded and said in his usual calm, precise fashion, "The room became dark. The walls vanished, but before that the designs painted on them seemed to come alive."

He quirked a smile at his friend. "The tiny figure of Apollo on the panel behind Lord Varus began to play his lyre, I think in the Myxolydian mode. I regret that I wasn't close enough to be sure, because I know music is a particular interest of yours."

"Perhaps we can repeat the experience with the two of us closer to the wall," Priscus said. He joked in an easy tone, but his expression was firm. "How long did the business last?"

"There was more," said Pandareus with a slight smile. "The floor appeared to become a pit. Figures crawled up the sides toward us."

"Figures?" Priscus repeated. "Not humans, then."

The teacher shrugged. "I would be very surprised if they were human," he said, "but they weren't clear enough for me to be sure. Spirits, let us say. Demons, to use the Greek word."

"Indeed," Priscus said softly. "And is there more?"

"My sister slapped me," Varus said, surprising Corylus and apparently the other men as well. "I didn't know that, but I felt it—"

He managed another shy smile and touched his left cheek with his index finger. Corylus had noticed when they met tonight that there still a little swelling.

"—when I woke up. The room was just like it was before I started reading. So that must have been the end. *I* was the cause."

"I don't imagine that Lord Varus was the cause," Pandareus said before anyone else—including Varus—could speak further. "That he was the primary target of magic is likely enough. But the important point is that the omen was real and threatening. The sort of threat that requires that the *Sibylline Books* be consulted."

Corylus let out his breath in a gasp; he hadn't known that he was holding it. Varus closed his eyes and rubbed his temples with both hands, then looked around at his companions again.

"This occurred in Saxa's dwelling," Priscus said. His face gave no hint of what he might be thinking. "Will he support a request to the full Senate? Because you already know, my friend, that I won't violate my oath." His smile was wry. "Even if Balaton would permit me to."

The servant stood against the east wall, motionless as a caryatid. His eyes were fixed on the light sconce across from him, and he didn't appear to have heard what was being said.

Men like Balaton—men like Pulto—trusted very few leaders, but they would follow those few into death or worse. Corylus was quite sure that Balaton trusted Priscus . . . as he should, because Priscus would always do his duty.

"I'm quite sure that Saxa will *not* support such a request," Pandareus said. "I fear that he has stepped into dangerous territory, under the sway of Nemastes the Hyperborean."

Priscus looked at Varus. Varus hung his head and muttered, "Yes sir, I'm afraid that's true. All of it."

"A Hyperborean," Priscus said in a musing tone. "A foreigner."

"Yes, my friend," Pandareus said; he wasn't agreeing. "A foreigner like myself."

Priscus snorted. "Not like you," he said. "But I won't even ask the Senate if Saxa would oppose the request. I trust you, but my colleagues would not." He shrugged. "More fools them," he added. "But that's not a new thought."

Priscus had been leaning forward slightly on the couch. He didn't stand, but his back straightened and he was suddenly a very different man. He looked at each of his three visitors in turn, then said, "Master Pandareus, my true friend: though the world should end, I will not violate my oath. I cannot unlock the chest until I am ordered to do so by the Senate."

"I understand," the teacher said, lifting his chin in agreement. "May I ask a favor, though? It's on behalf of the Republic of which I am a resident if not a citizen. May we enter the vault, all of us together? I don't intend that the chest be opened, but there are things which I believe we may learn in its presence."

Priscus remained still for a moment. Then he grinned and said, "I don't see why I shouldn't help three scholars with a matter of antiquarian research. Balaton, fetch the—"

But two servants were already bringing a ladder out of the alcove where the stools were kept; two others were walking toward the cartouche which covered the vault. Balaton's grin was even broader than his master's.

ALPHENA SCOWLED. BECAUSE she'd chosen the forward-facing seat, the lamps on the front corners of the litter lighted her face but left her stepmother in darkness. All she could see of Hedia was a slimly aristocratic shadow.

And Alphena had *picked* this seat. She'd done it to herself, as she always seemed to do. No wonder Corylus ignored her!

Agrippinus had claimed the bearers were a matched team of Cappadocians who had been working together for over a year. The majordomo had doubtless made a comfortable commission on the deal, but as with other business entrusted to him, it had been handled very well. Despite the size and bulk of this litter,

Alphena found the ride the smoothest of any chair she'd ridden on.

"Alphena," said Hedia, her teeth brief gleams in the shadow, "I'm worried that before long someone will inform the Emperor about Saxa's activities."

"Father's done nothing wrong!" Alphena said, shocked out of sad musings about cosmetics. She didn't know anything about making up her face, and she could scarcely ask Hedia. "My father would never plot against the Emperor!"

"Of course not," Hedia agreed, speaking calmly instead of raising her voice in response to Alphena's shrillness. "But I'm far less sure about what his friend Nemastes is doing. Nemastes is certainly acting to his own benefit, and I would be greatly surprised if his plans would benefit anybody else. Do you agree?"

Alphena felt fear wash everything else out of her mind, the way the surf swept over the battlements children built in beach sand. "Father could never be tricked into anything disloyal," she said. "He's a senator! No grubby foreigner is going to fool him!"

Even in her own ears, the words sounded dismal and silly. Saxa was a very learned man, but he had no common sense at all. And Nemastes might have bewitched him, stolen his soul with a poppet of wax or whatever Hyperboreans did!

"We're going to scotch Nemastes if we can, dear," Hedia said. "You and I and our friends. But if we don't succeed, I hope that you'll be able to escape the wreck under the protection of a powerful husband."

Alphena jerked upright. Her hair, in a bun to cushion the weight of a helmet, brushed the canopy. She opened her mouth to shout an objection . . . and closed it.

In a tiny voice, she said, "Hedia, I don't want to get married. But I'm afraid."

"Yes, dear," Hedia said. "We're both afraid, and so is

Anna. I suppose the men are afraid also, though no doubt being men they'd bluster and deny it. But we have to look ahead and prepare."

The litter bearers were singing a low-voiced chant that kept their pace even. Was it Cappadocian? But it might simply be nonsense syllables to fit a rhythm, not a language at all. It was hard to tell what was chance and what held real meaning in this world.

"I hope Father . . . ," Alphena said miserably, but she let her voice trail off instead of finishing the foolish sentence. Saxa wasn't going to come to his senses. He'd never shown good judgment in the past, and now that Nemastes had his claws in him there was even less chance. If Saxa was to be saved, the rest of them were going to have to do it.

The litter turned sharply; the bearers slowed to negotiate piles of building materials which spilled out from either side. Hedia leaned forward to see, giving Alphena a look at her profile in sharp silhouette.

Father didn't show good sense except perhaps when he married her, Alphena thought. Though she would *never* say those words aloud.

The bearers stopped, then lowered the vehicle to the pavement. "The Temple of Tellus, noble ladies," said the deputy steward in charge of the escort. "Your destination."

Alphena started to get out. Servants congealed about her, three or four of them.

"Get away!" she shouted. "Haven't I told you I'd have you whipped if you tried to hand me out of a vehicle again?"

There was a brief bustle. Servants stumbled into one another or over piles of construction supplies. Alphena got out and only then realized that the men she'd driven away weren't those who'd attended the litter: these had come from staff of the temple.

They were in front of the Temple of Tellus. It was a modest structure, but the grounds in which it stood were as extensive as those of more impressive, newer buildings. To make room for heavy wagons, the wall around the temple precinct had been knocked down to either side of the gate.

Alphena maneuvered away from a collection of stone cylinders, column barrels which would be fluted and set here at the site. They would replace the temple's four existing wooden columns. The originals couldn't possibly have survived three centuries, but until now the replacements had also been wooden. Those had been stuccoed to look like stone, but that had flaked off in the decades since they'd been placed; rot and wormholes now marked the bare wood remaining.

Farther back in the yard were heaps of bulk materials. On the other side of the vehicle were smaller piles of the tiny cut stones sorted by color; they would be laid into a floor mosaic. There were timbers, too, but in the shadows Alphena didn't know whether they were for scaffolding or were building materials.

"Good evening, noble ladies!" said a corpulent stranger who bowed to Hedia. Unlike the temple servants, he wore a toga. "The Temple of Tellus is honored to have you! I'm the chief priest, Gaius Julius Phidippides. I own the laundry three doors down on Sandalmakers' Street and the building next door to it besides."

Servants from Saxa's household were shoving the outnumbered temple personnel back. Alphena stepped to the other side of Phidippides to protect him from the same treatment. She shouldn't have shouted at the temple servants; that was what was making her escort so violently zealous.

"The temple is open?" Hedia said coldly. "And move away! I assure you that I could see quite enough of you from two paces distance."

The priest was a freedman. He must have been made a citizen by Augustus—formally Gaius Julius Caesar Octavianus Augustus—because he wasn't old enough for his patron to have been Augustus's adoptive father, the conqueror of Gaul. Alphena had already learned that these were the sort of people who made a point of their importance to the Republic. Hedia, a born aristocrat, treated Phidippides' fawning pomposity with contempt.

The priest backed off hurriedly, stumbling into a pile of clay and barely recovering. It would be fired into roofing tiles here on the site; that avoided the heavy breakage certain if tiles were transported by wagon through the streets of Carce.

"Yes, of course, your ladyship!" he said with nervous brightness. "Come right this way, please, right this way."

The household servants formed a double line to protect the women. Protect them from the temple personnel, as best Alphena could tell, but Phidippides' staff *had* been pushy at the start. They excluded the priest also, but he trotted on the other side of the deputy steward while continuing to chatter brightly toward Hedia.

Temple servants threw the double doors open. There were lighted lamps within, but attendants from both establishments brought in additional ones.

Alphena looked around. The Temple of Tellus was dingy. Of course the objects dedicated to it, particularly the pair of huge elephant teeth, had been removed to Saxa's house for safekeeping, but the floor was of bricks worn hollow, and the walls were coarse tuff which hadn't been sheathed with colored marble or polished limestone.

The ten-foot-tall wooden statue of Tellus had been repainted within the past few years, though not with any great skill. Her right forearm was lifted with the palm turned out; her left hung stiffly at her side. The whole figure—head, limbs, and torso—had probably been carved in one piece.

"I wonder, Lady Hedia?" said Phidippides in a wheedling voice that put Alphena's teeth on edge. "I discussed with your noble husband the Senator the idea of replacing this statue with a modern one of bronze. Do you know if he—"

"Take the matter up with someone who cares, Master Laundryman," Hedia snapped. "Now, leave my daughter and myself. At once!"

Household servants had hung additional lamps and placed a folding stool at the back of the room. "Your ladyship?" said the deputy steward. "Which of us would you like to remain inside with your noble selves?"

"None of you, Midas," Hedia said crisply. "Give Lady Alphena the prayer—"

A servant handed Alphena a tight roll; he bowed.

"—and wait for us in the courtyard."

Hedia followed the scurrying servants to the double doors. Midas closed them, and Hedia herself slotted the bar through its inside staples to lock the valves.

"Now . . . ," she said, gesturing Alphena to the center of the chamber. "Face the goddess, I think. We may as well get started."

She smiled as she sat on the stool. It wasn't an unfriendly expression, but it made Alphena again very glad not to be this woman's enemy.

CHAPTER VI

Hedia twisted her left hand behind her back to rub between her shoulder blades. Her stool was backless, and the rough stone doorjamb provided support but not comfort.

"Golden-throned Juno," Alphena chanted. She held the scroll open to the light from the lamp stand beside her, but by now she must be reciting from memory. "Queen of the immortals, surpassing all in beauty; sister and wife of loud-thundering Jupiter, goddess of marriage. Grant my prayer for a worthy mate, thou glorious one whom men and gods reverence and honor, even as they do your all-powerful husband."

The girl had straightened as she recited the prayer; now she slumped again. She turned to Hedia, her face twisted with tired despair.

"This isn't doing anything," she said, trying to raise her own spirits by getting angry. "We may as well go home!"

"Not yet, dear," Hedia said quietly. "It's not even the middle of the night. We can't set conditions of our own comfort on the will of the gods."

"Do you believe this?" Alphena demanded, waggling the scroll as if it were a baton. The layers of glued papyrus creaked in protest. "In Juno? In any religion?"

Hedia laughed. "Daughter, if you mean as an institution, I'm not sure I even believe in marriage," she said.

"But marriage exists, and it protected me at one time. Perhaps another marriage will protect you."

She got to her feet. Instead of going to Alphena, she bent backward and massaged the small of her back with both hands.

Hedia's fingers were slim but strong; even so, she half wished that she'd brought Balbo, the household masseur, in with her. He was a eunuch, so perhaps his presence wouldn't make the rites vain . . . but on the other hand, this business would be boring and uncomfortable even if her back didn't hurt, so there was no point in taking a needless risk for negligible gain.

"As for the gods existing," Hedia went on, "I have no idea. I know that if I strike steel on a flint in the correct fashion, though, I get sparks."

She crossed her hands before her and felt her expression tighten. "Generations of our ancestors have believed that this sort of divination is effective in bringing maidens into the state of marriage," she said. "Therefore you will continue to offer a prayer to Juno while standing in a sanctified building, and I will remain here with you."

Alphena stared at her for a moment. Hedia stood erect. She offered a pleasant smile, but she was ready for whatever the response was.

Instead of replying, the girl turned to face the goddess. "Golden-throned Juno," she said. "Queen of the immortals, surpassing all in beauty . . ."

As Alphena read, Hedia walked over to her and put a hand on her shoulder.

"Sister and wife of loud-thundering Jupiter," Alphena said, "goddess of marriage. Grant my prayer for a worthy marriage. . . ."

There was no response this time either. Shortly it would be the start of the third watch, midnight. Alphena would continue to pray till dawn if necessary, and Hedia would stay with the girl as a mother should.

Nemastes and his magic might destroy the whole house of Saxa and the gods knew what else. Regardless, Hedia would be fighting all the way with every tool at her disposal.

Hedia smiled and gave Alphena's shoulder a slight squeeze. She wouldn't have survived this long if she hadn't been willing to fight powerful men.

THE TEMPLE SERVANTS inserted iron cramps into slots in the floor on either side of the mosaic cartouche. The tools were similar to what Varus had seen workmen use at construction sites when they muscled heavy blocks into place.

"Ah—I can lend a hand," said Corylus, his eyes swiveling from the servants to Priscus. He started forward without waiting for an answer.

"Thank you, sir," said Balaton, stepping toward Corylus as though he were going to meet him. It took Varus a moment to understand what his friend doubtless had realized instantly: that the servant was blocking Corylus away from the task. "We're used to doing this, and it's probably safer that we handle it alone."

Corylus flashed a genuine smile. "Right," he said, stepping back with Varus and Pandareus. "If somebody slipped, the trapdoor might drop and be broken. Sorry."

Varus frowned in surprise. He asked quietly, "Corylus, would you have slipped?"

Corylus grinned. "No," he said, "and I wouldn't have forgotten to breathe either. But they don't know that; and anyway, they don't need my help."

Holding the cover up six inches above the floor, the servants walked it in unison toward the temple's great doors. When they set it down, it was completely clear of the four-by-six-foot rectangle. Another man lowered his ladder into the opening, then slid it a finger's breadth to the side so that the stringers locked into notches in the concrete subflooring.

Pandareus and the two youths stepped to the edge of the opening and looked down. The vault was of considerable size. In the middle was a chest about three feet long and a foot and a half wide, much like the ossuaries into which Varus recalled that Jews and other Oriental races gathered the bones of their dead after the flesh had decayed. The civilized folk of Carce, like the Greeks before them, cremated their dead and stored the ashes in jars.

This was something else, though. Varus shivered. He crossed his left arm over his chest; by doing that, he squeezed the ivory head against his breastbone beneath the toga.

Priscus shuffled up behind them. "Master Corylus," he said, "you look like a husky young fellow who wouldn't mind catching a weight of fat if it slipped off the ladder."

"Sir?" Corylus said.

Priscus chuckled like bubbles in hot grease. He said, "Go down into the vault and wait as I follow you."

"Here, I'll go down with the lantern first," Varus said to a servant with a light. It was actually a bronze oil lamp in the form of a three-headed dragon; each tongue was a blazing wick.

Without real objection, he took the short pole from which the lamp hung; turning, he backed down the ladder. The servant looked at Balaton for approval, but Balaton was instead frowning at his own superior.

"Lord Priscus," said Balaton, "perhaps your guests would prefer to enter the vault by themselves? There's no requirement that you go down with them, after all."

Varus reached the bottom of the ladder and stepped away so that Corylus could follow. When he raised the lamp, he saw that though the ceiling was low—it was no more than six feet above the floor—the vault extended ten feet on the short axis and twenty the long way. It was much larger than it needed to be to conceal the stone chest.

"Balaton," said Priscus, lowering himself carefully rung by rung on the ladder. "I'm a silly old man, but *you* are an old woman. I'll be perfectly all right. You won't let me fall, will you, Corylus my lad?"

"No *sir*," said Corylus, bracing himself to take the commissioner's weight if he slipped.

Varus smiled faintly, visualizing his friend, answering the legate of his legion as ranks of Germans prepared to charge. Whereas Gaius Varus would be wondering what the commotion was about and why those blond men with bull-hide shields were shouting so loudly.

Priscus wheezed coming down the short ladder, but the chief attendant's concern did seem overstated. Shrugging to settle his tunic—although the commissioner was on duty, he was dressed for dinner rather than to carry out official business—he said, "When we consult the *Books,* we do it down here: the *Books* never leave the vault. And you may think I'm fat and awkward"—he laughed again—"as well you might. But there are commissioners who are far more decrepit than I am, I assure you."

Pandareus was following Priscus into the vault with equal care. Varus bent to examine the stone chest, then thrust his left arm away so that he didn't burn himself on the lamps he held. Corylus took the staff from him and hung the lamp chain from one of the hooks placed for the purpose in the low ceiling.

Varus muttered thanks. He felt increasingly hot and uncomfortable. He doubted that was embarrassment: he was far too used to behaving in a fashion which those around him considered bumblingly incompetent.

As they had every right to do. *Priscus is old and fat, and I'm a bumbling incompetent. As well as being a bad poet.*

He squatted, keeping his shadow off the carvings on the side of the chest. It was limestone and not a particularly fine-grained variety at that, so the figures were necessarily crude. Nevertheless, they were powerful.

In the center was a chariot to which horses were hitched in parallel: four of them as best Varus could tell by the additional grooves shadowing the outline of the legs of the animal closest to the viewer. The figure driving the chariot had a woman's torso and breasts, but her head was that of a maned lion; bird wings sprouted from her back. A similar creature—sphinx? Gorgon?—ran on two bird legs in front of the team but looked back over her shoulder toward her fellow. The heads of all the figures were at the same height. Varus had seen similar bands of decoration painted on very old vases.

"Sir?" said Varus, looking up at Priscus. Suddenly realizing that he was speaking to a man who was far his superior in age, knowledge, and position, he wobbled upright as he would for his father. "Ah, Lord Priscus? Is this box Etruscan?"

"You've got a clever one there, Teacher," Priscus said to his friend. Pandareus didn't reply, but his smile was a trifle warmer than usual as it drifted toward Varus.

"And yes, boy," Priscus continued. "At any rate, it looks like Etruscan work to me, and early Etruscan besides. Which is just what I would expect, since I believe it's the chest in which Old Tarquin placed the books after he bought them from the Sibyl. Do you know the story?" He thrust his finger toward Varus. "You, I mean. Since you're a clever bugger."

I've been called worse, Varus thought.

"Sir!" he said as though he were in class. "An old woman approached Tarquin the First, an Etruscan and the fifth king of Carce. She offered to sell him nine books of prophecies by the Sibyl of Cumae at the price of three hundred didrachms. Tarquin refused to pay so much."

"So, boy . . . ," said Priscus, leaning slightly forward and scowling. "Was Tarquin a fool?"

This *was* like class! "Sir!" Varus said. "No, Tarquin was a tyrant and a foreigner, but he was reputed to be one of the wisest men of all time. The price, however, was enormous—particularly since Carce was then only a town and surrounded by powerful enemies."

He cleared his throat. Both Pandareus and Corylus were smiling smugly; they knew he wouldn't embarrass them.

And I won't. Varus continued. "The old woman threw three of the books on the fire in Tarquin's chamber. They were written on dry palm leaves and burned to ash. She then demanded the same price for the six books remaining."

"And?" said Priscus. He was smiling in satisfaction also.

Varus rested his left hand on the stone chest, feeling the carvings beneath his fingertips. He knew the story well, as he knew many stories. Until this moment it had been a myth, but now in this place he could see Tarquin, his stern face lighted by a sudden flare from the charcoal brazier which tried to warm the painted stone walls of his throne room.

"Tarquin again refused the offer," Varus said, "and the old woman threw three more books onto the fire. But when she offered him the final three books, Tarquin paid her the full price, three hundred didrachms. The *Sibylline Books* have been the most holy treasure of Carce from that day to this."

"Very good, boy," said Priscus softly, but he turned toward Pandareus. "A treasure too holy for me to display even to the scholar whose wisdom and knowledge I respect above those of any other man I know."

"If you don't mind, old friend," said Pandareus, "we'll stay in this vault while I tell you some of my history."

"Sir?" said Corylus. "Should Varus and I leave?"

"Not at all," Pandareus said. "You're welcome to hear, and for other reasons"—he turned his odd smile toward Varus—"I particularly want Lord Varus to be present."

"Sir," said Varus, lifting his head in acknowledgment. He wasn't sure he'd spoken loudly enough to be heard. He didn't suppose it mattered.

"I'm a Melian by birth," Pandareus said, facing Priscus and Corylus. His shoulder was to Varus, whom he seemed to be ignoring. "I went to Egypt, though, as a young man and spent a year in Alexandria."

"Melos?" said Priscus, frowning. He rubbed his chin with his knuckles. "I thought you were from Athens."

"Pandareus of Athens was a better name for a teacher," Pandareus said with a hard smile, "than Pandareus of Melos, an island which was a backwater when Cadmus founded Thebes and hasn't become any more important in the millennium since."

The others laughed. Varus felt warm and prickly on the inside of his skin. He no longer heard the chant that had been with him since the afternoon of his reading, but there was a keening at the edges of his mind. It could have been the wind, or perhaps a woman wailing in distant misery.

"The Egyptians are a dirty people," Pandareus continued, "and fond of superstition. But they're an old race, and their land is very old. In Alexandria I met an Egyptian whose name was Menre. He said he was a scholar of the Museum and had been a student of Demetrius of Phalerum."

"That's impossible, surely?" Priscus said. Corylus's sharp expression showed that he was thinking the same thing but hadn't wished to contradict his teacher. "Unless you misheard him?"

"I did not mishear him," Pandareus said, his smile slightly wider, "as you already knew. As for whether it was possible that Menre was a student of the man who advised Ptolemy to create the Museum three hundred years ago . . . I thought it very unlikely. I asked Menre to introduce me to his teacher, and he said he would when the time was right."

"And?" said Priscus.

"I didn't see Menre again while I was in Egypt," said Pandareus. "I left for Athens a few months later and gained a name there. Including the name Pandareus of Athens."

The others laughed. Varus remained in his warm, prickly cocoon. He saw and heard everything that was going on in the vault, but he was miles and ages away from his companions.

He reached beneath his toga and gripped the ivory head with his right hand; his left hand still rested on the stone box which held the *Sibylline Books*. He felt someone coming toward him through a tunnel of fog.

"I hadn't thought of Menre in decades," said Pandareus. "I was quite satisfied with my life in Athens. The students who attended my lectures were of reasonable quality, the range of books which were open to me there was wider even than here in Carce—they'd been brought into the city by men who loved learning, not soldiers in armor like those who gathered the libraries of Carce."

"But the pay, my friend?" Priscus said.

The teacher shrugged. His shadow quivered oddly, unpleasantly, on the wall of the vault.

"The only men in Athens who are as wealthy as a senator of Carce," Pandareus said, "are senators of Carce who've retired to Athens. Nonetheless some men of Carce send their sons to Athens still, as Cicero's father and Cicero himself did, even though there are teachers at home equal to the best in Greece. If only because we recently *were* the best in Greece."

Varus watched him grin in profile.

"And I will note," Pandareus said, holding the smile, "that the rich and powerful of Carce are no more punctual with their sons' school fees than their lesser brethren of Athens were. Your senatorial colleague Calpurnius Piso comes immediately to mind when I hear the words 'slow to pay.' "

An old woman hobbled toward Varus. He watched his own body standing with his friends in the vault while with another part of his mind he waited for the woman. She wore a cowled gray cloak over a long tunic—an Ionic chiton—of bleached linen; her face was wrinkled and ancient.

"But one night, in what must have been a dream," Pandareus was saying, "Menre visited me. He told me I must go to Carce so that I would be on hand when I was needed at a great crisis of the world. In support of his demand, he showed me astrological calculations which proved the necessity beyond any doubt. The stars didn't describe the *form* of the danger, however: only the fact that it was focused on Carce."

"All roads lead to Carce," Priscus said, quoting the old adage. He was smiling, but there was no laughter in his expression.

"Yes," said Pandareus simply. "Or at any rate, mine did."

He turned his hands up as if to show that they were empty, then said, "And lest you ask, I didn't remember a single one of the astrological alignments when I awakened—only that they had been convincing."

"Have you come far?" the old woman asked. Her voice was as thin and dry as the rustling wing cases of cicadas.

"Mistress," Varus said, "I'm in the Temple of Jupiter Best and Greatest. I haven't traveled at all."

She laughed like silver chimes in place of the cracked tittering he had expected. "Do you think so, Gaius Varus?" she said, reaching out with her right hand. "Come with me and we'll see what you say then."

Varus took the woman's hand in his left. Her skin was like thin vellum, and the bones within were as fine as a bat's. In the vault of the temple his body stood silently, touching the ancient stone box and gripping the ivory head beneath his toga.

"My wife, Claudia, is an estimable woman," Priscus said, "but she's more superstitious than a kitchen maid just up from the country with her love potions and beauty creams. This is the sort of thing I'd expect to hear from her."

No one spoke. Priscus sighed and went on. "And I suppose if Claudia does describe that sort of dream to me in the future, I'd better listen to her. Since I believe you, my friend."

The commissioner's voice trailed off, and the four figures in the vault faded into grayness. Varus and the old woman stood where they were, but fog rolled like a torrent beneath them. Low blue-gray hills on the horizon swept toward them. From the top of one boiled the fog which covered the world beneath.

"That's Vesuvius," Varus said. Who was the woman? Her fingers rested as lightly on his as a perching butterfly. "We visited Baiae when I was a child, my sister and I and our nurses."

He'd seen his father in Baiae one afternoon. He'd seen Saxa only rarely until he'd started secondary schooling when he was twelve.

"I remember Vesuvius, the smoke coming up all day," he said. "Just like that."

"Smoke, you say?" said the old woman. "Watch, Gaius Varus!"

The top of the cone lifted off with a shuddering roar.

Fireballs shot skyward, and a phalanx of lava gushed in all directions. The liquid rock was as orange as flame, but a sulfurous yellow haze hung over it.

"Watch!" the old woman repeated in her terrible voice.

Lava splashed and spread like water from a downspout. It reached an olive grove. The trunks of individual trees shattered as the rock lapped them. Severed branches fell onto the surface of the flow and were carried along by it. They blazed and dissolved until only black outlines remained, distorting slowly as the rock spread onward.

"Who are you?" Varus said. Though he shouted, no human voice could have been heard over the volcano's constant crashing thunder.

A flock of sheep grazed on the middle slope of the cone. They blatted at the oncoming lava; then, individually and in pairs, they turned and began trotting downhill. The shepherd and his two dogs stared in wonder for a further moment, then followed the sheep.

"Who?" Varus repeated.

The woman laughed. The cowl covered her face almost completely, but he saw the gleam of her eyes. "Who I am isn't important," she said. "I'm too old to be important. You're the only thing that's important, Gaius Varus, because you're the only one who can stop this."

The shepherd and his flock reached the edge of a knob, then froze in horror: bubbling lava had circled the knob to either side, racing ahead of man and sheep and closing to trap them. The shepherd threw up his hands. His dogs yapped and made short rushes but the glare of the rock drove them back each time.

"How do I stop it?" Varus shouted. "No one can stop it!"

The lava surged forward to cover the knob. The animals in its path, sheep and dogs and man, gouted steam an instant before their dried remnants burned in a bone-devouring fire.

"Only you, Varus!" the old woman cried. "And if not you, then no one!"

They had risen to a great height. The world was a globe, and fire was engulfing it. Varus saw the figures of squat demons with bodies of flame climbing from the pit of Vesuvius. They marched outward shoulder to shoulder, igniting animals and trees and the very soil itself into black ash which the blazing rock then covered.

Varus pointed to the fire demons. He was shouting, but he couldn't understand his own words.

"You or no one!" said the old woman, and Varus awakened. His friend Corylus was shaking him back to his senses.

CORYLUS FELT UNCOMFORTABLE. The air in the vault was still, but the lamp flames twisting at the corners of his eyes made it seem that the gryphon heads were moving. He clasped his hands behind his back to keep from twitching toward a spear or a sword hilt.

"I don't see that this brings us any closer to being able to examine the *Books*, though," Priscus said. "I already trusted you, and your dream visit from an Egyptian isn't going to help sway the Senate. I—"

"*And then a great river of blazing fire will flow outward,*" someone shrieked. The voice was that of an ancient woman, but it came from Varus's lips.

He stood with one hand spread on the stone casket and the other gripping the object he'd brought from where it hung on a thong beneath his toga. Corylus saw the wink of age-yellowed ivory within the cylinder of his friend's fingers.

"*It will devour every place, land and great ocean and gleaming sea,*" cried the voice. "*Lakes and rivers and springs, the implacable Underworld and the heavenly vault—all will be consumed!*"

Varus's stern, set expression reminded Corylus of a

statue of a young Stoic facing execution. His eyes blazed, and his throat swelled with the power of the voice that issued from it. Corylus hadn't seen him take a breath since he started his declamation.

Pandareus watched intently; Priscus stood transfixed, his face pale and without expression. Temple servants ringed the opening of the vault, staring down in a mixture of terror and confusion.

"All the souls of men will gnash their teeth, burning in a river," cried Varus's lips. "The world is brimstone and a rush of fire and a blazing plain, and ashes will cover all!"

Varus was swaying. Corylus made an instant decision—he didn't know what was happening, so he went to his friend. He took Varus by the left wrist and the right shoulder, shifting him back from the casket and the light.

"Varus!" he said. "Wake up!"

Varus slumped. His body had been rigid; now if Corylus hadn't had his arms around him, he would have fallen to the floor of fitted stone blocks. His flesh was icy despite the warmth of the vault.

"Lord Priscus!" called Balaton from the nave of the temple. "Should we come down?"

Corylus glanced up, caught the servant's eyes, and dipped his chin in negation. They didn't need more people down here at the moment.

Priscus took a deep breath. "Pandareus, you sly devil!" he said. "How did he do that? How did *you* do that?"

"Not me, old friend," said Pandareus. His smile was slight, but despite the pressure of events it was real. "And I don't know precisely what Lord Varus did either. But I thought that if I brought him near the *Books*, perhaps something would happen."

Varus straightened. "Thank you," he said hoarsely to Corylus. He squeezed his hand before they stepped apart.

Probably they both were a little embarrassed; Corylus certainly was.

They faced the older men. "Sirs," Varus said. "I dreamed the way I did during my reading, but it wasn't the same this time. I saw Vesuvius erupting."

He lowered his eyes and whispered, "It was terrible. Everything burned. People burned."

"So we gathered from what you recited to us, boy," Priscus said. He shook his head in wonder. "Do you remember that?"

"No sir," Varus said. "I didn't know what I was saying during the reading, either. What they tell me, what Corylus and Master Pandareus tell me I was saying."

"Sir?" said Corylus, holding the commissioner's eyes. He was angry at being kept in the dark, because that was what it amounted to. Though he tried to control it, his tone was marginally stiffer than he should have been using while speaking to a venerable and exceptionally learned senator. "Please? What is there about what Varus said that made you ask Master Pandareus how he did it?"

Priscus glanced at Pandareus, but before the teacher could respond he turned to the youths again. He gave them a crooked smile.

"I don't see any reason not to tell you," he said, "given what just happened. Master Corylus, your friend just quoted from the *Sibylline Books*. Which he's never seen and won't be permitted to see until he's been elected by the Senate to the Commission for the Sacred Rites. As I have no doubt he will be, in good time; but not till he's my age or close to it."

"I assumed you would recognize a passage from the *Books* if you heard it, my friend," Pandareus said. "I know and respect your memory."

Priscus sniffed, but he smiled also. "During consultations," he said—he wasn't whispering, but Corylus noticed that he pitched his voice a hair lower—"the *Books* are open. Any of the commissioners can read them. Most of my colleagues don't use the opportunity, so far as I've noticed, but I do, and"—he smiled more broadly at Pandareus—"as my friend suggested, I *do* have a good memory. I hope that I'm not generally a vain man, but I do pride myself on that point."

"Will you please explain to my students how consultations of the *Books* are usually made, Marcus Priscus?" Pandareus asked. He softened the formality of the request with a grin: the two old men really *were* friends. Their closeness went beyond mere respect and similarity of interests.

"Why me?" said Priscus. "You're their teacher, and you know the procedure as well as I do, don't you?"

"Perhaps," said Pandareus, "but you, most noble Senator, are a commissioner; whereas I am a foreigner, albeit a clever one."

It may be that the world is about to end, thought Corylus. *These men fear it is, at any rate. But they're quibbling over minutiae because they both love the details; and because nothing is going to make either of them show his fear by the way he acts.*

"It's simple enough, boys," Priscus said. "There are three books of prophecies, each made from sixty-one palm leaves—written on one side only. When the Commission is called to examine the *Books*, we open them a page at a time and drop a ball from a tumbler just like the ones they use in picking trial jurors from the general panel. There are one hundred eighty-two white balls and one black one. When the black ball drops, we have the page. Then"—he shrugged—"we draw lots again, the ten of us or however many arrived for the meeting. The one chosen points to a section of the page while blindfolded. We read that section aloud and decide what action the Republic must take in response."

Priscus looked at the three of them in turn. Corylus felt the weight of his glance: the commissioner was no longer a fat old man and something of a buffoon.

"I don't mind telling you that I'll be applying to the Senate for a formal opening of the *Books*," he said, "on the basis of Gaius Varus here reading a passage through a closed stone box. That's a greater prodigy than any calf speaking in the Forum, *I* think. And I witnessed it myself, so bugger what Saxa says—not meaning to be offensive about your father, boy."

"Sir?" said Corylus hesitantly.

"Well, spit it out, boy," Priscus said.

Everyone was looking at him: his immediate companions and the servants watching avidly from above. "Sir," Corylus said. "If you report to the Senate, they'll know that you let us into the vault."

"Well, that's what I did, isn't it?" Priscus snapped. "I thought it was proper. If my colleagues disagree, they can order me executed for treason. But my oath is to the Republic, and I'll report as is my duty even if that means being sewn in a leather sack and sunk in the Tiber. Do you doubt it?"

Corylus stood straight. His arms were at his sides and his eyes were focused on a ring bolt attached to the wall directly opposite him for some unguessed reason. "Sir!" he said. "No sir, I do not doubt you."

"Army, is he, Teacher?" the commissioner said to his friend.

"His father was, I believe," Pandareus said mildly. "I need hardly say that he's not what I expected from his background."

He coughed to clear his throat. "You may relax, Master Corylus," he said. "Your observation shows a commendable concern for the well-being of Commissioner Priscus. He does not hold it against you."

"Bloody impertinence is what it was!" Priscus said, but

then he looked at Corylus and grinned. "But you meant well, boy, and the fact that you realized that actions have consequences puts you ahead of most people. Puts you ahead of most of my senatorial colleagues, in fact."

He looked at Pandareus and said, "Are we done here, then? You've gotten what you came for, haven't you? There'll be a consultation of the *Sibylline Books* after all."

"We're certainly done from my viewpoint," Pandareus said, "but for my purposes there's no need that the *Books* be opened formally. Master Varus has directed us to the threat; now we must deal with it."

Priscus had looked relaxed for a moment. Now his face became wary if not quite hostile. "Aye," he said. "The Commission must deal with it, Teacher."

"The Commission will meet, will it not?" Pandareus said. Corylus and Varus stood still, pretending not to be present. The servants slipped back soundlessly so that they couldn't see or be seen by the nobles in the vault, though they were certainly still listening. "You'll consider the prophecy and carry out various divinations to determine the proper response to it."

"I suspect the procedure will be much as you describe, yes," Priscus said deliberately. "But though the methods by which the Commission reaches its recommendations aren't precisely a secret, neither are they matters which I will discuss with anyone who is not already a commissioner."

"Then we'll pass on from that," Pandareus agreed with a nod. "The recommendations themselves are matters of public record, however. In the past, the Commission has decreed sacrifices and public banquets, and occasionally it has summoned a foreign deity. I can imagine in this case that your colleagues might send a legation to the Brahmans of India and request that a company of them escort their fire god Agni to a new temple in Carce."

"Your description of past history is of course accurate," Priscus said. His words were clipped and careful. "I won't speculate as to what the Commission might recommend in this or any other case."

"Of course," said Pandareus. "You will work in your fashion, my friend, and I will work in mine. I'll tell you frankly that I hope your method succeeds. Indeed, I hope that the Republic and the world have as much time as it would take for a senatorial delegation to reach Barracucha on the Indus. I dearly hope that."

He thrust out his hand. After a delay of a heartbeat or perhaps two heartbeats, Priscus clasped it. The two old men hugged one another as fiercely as Corylus and Varus had done minutes earlier, then stepped apart.

"Time to leave, then," said Pandareus. "It must be close to midnight."

Priscus gestured him to the ladder. "Go on, and I'll follow you," he said. "Varus, you bring the lamp, and Corylus? I'll want you ready to catch me if I fall, all right?"

"Yes sir," said the youths in unison. Corylus added, "But you won't fall, sir. You're not so decrepit as you pretend."

"Cheeky one, isn't he, Teacher?" Priscus said as Pandareus carefully climbed toward the servants waiting to assist him. "And clever. They're both clever, as I knew from the fact that you vouched for them."

"Master Pandareus?" Corylus said as Priscus mounted the ladder in turn. Pandareus tilted his head to look down.

Corylus stiffened formally. "Now we know why you were sent to Carce," he said. "If you hadn't been, the prophecy wouldn't have been heard in time."

If it is in time, he thought. *May the gods grant that it is in time.*

"—EVEN-AS-THEY-DO-YOUR-ALL-POWERFUL-HUSBAND!" ALPHENA SAID, racing through the last phrase because her throat was hoarse. She didn't want to choke and fail to complete the prayer after she'd gone to the effort of speaking the first part.

She turned to her stepmother, seated again. "Do you have more wine?" she said harshly. That was the only way she could say *anything* with her throat so raw, but she was tired and angry and she hurt.

Hedia walked over, exchanging the vellum sheet for a different skin of wine than the one they'd drunk from earlier in the evening. Alphena took it gingerly and worked out the wooden stopper. She wasn't used to drinking from a skin, and she'd managed to squirt her tunic once already.

"I've found that success in life requires less brilliance than most people think," Hedia said. "And a great deal more persistence. Tonight is an example for persistence, I'm afraid."

Alphena squirted wine onto the back of her throat, then swallowed—and coughed. "This is unmixed!" she said, and immediately felt embarrassed. She knew she'd sounded accusatory, as though she were the kind of prude who would *never* drink unmixed wine.

"Yes," said Hedia with her usual cold smile, "and so is the third wineskin I had Agrippinus send along. I decided that if we had to stay the night through, we were going to need something to warm us. As well as soothing your throat."

"Thank you, Stepmother," Alphena said quietly. She took another mouthful, this time with greater care, and stoppered the mouthpiece. "I, ah, usually drink wine mixed. But this is good."

"By this time in the evening," Hedia said, her smile broader and knowing, "the older heads will have left the dinner party, and those of us who remain will be drinking the vintage without water to thin it. I'll take you with me in a year or two. After you're properly married, of course."

Alphena felt her face twist into a grimace of disgust. *I know the kind of party you mean!*

Hedia's expression softened from the smirk of lust it had worn the moment before. "Here, dear, let me have some of that wine," she said. She stepped close, but instead of taking the skin, she waited till Alphena handed it to her.

She drank, watching the girl over the sack. The goatskin had been sheared and painted with a zigzag design that reminded Alphena of Moorish fabrics.

When Hedia lowered it, she said, "I'm sorry, dear; I shouldn't joke like that. Probably I've had too much to drink already."

Alphena turned her face away. She said, "It doesn't matter."

Her cheeks were hot; with anger, she'd like to have said, but she knew that much of what she felt was embarrassment. *I'm such a child! And she's—she's everything I'm not!*

"It matters quite a lot," Hedia said. She set the wineskin on the floor, then put her hand on Alphena's wrist. "Listen to me, dear. Don't let anybody tell you how you must behave. Not your father, not me; and not your husband either, when you have one. You behave the way that's right for you. However that is."

"I won't have a choice when I'm married, will I?" Alphena said, hearing her voice rise. "And that's what you want for me, isn't it? A husband to take care of me and tell me how to behave?"

"Look at me, girl," Hedia said. She didn't raise her voice, but it snapped like a drover's whip. Alphena jerked her head around.

"I'm proof that being married doesn't turn you into

a basin for your husband to wash his feet in," Hedia said in the same harsh, demanding tone. "You father doesn't treat me like a servant, and Calpurnius Latus didn't either. Decide how you want to live your life and *live* it."

She unexpectedly hugged Alphena and stepped away. "Just remember," she said, "that everything comes with a cost. Don't cry to me if the cost of what you want is a high one."

In a still lower voice she added, "I hope for your sake that the price isn't as high as what I pay."

Alphena shivered. The air was warm, but she had goose bumps on her arms for a moment. She held the prayer, but she wasn't ready to resume the litany yet. She glanced at the stool.

Hedia followed her eyes and said, "I should have had the servants bring another one, shouldn't I? I said that we might have to spend the whole night here, but I suppose I didn't really believe my own words."

"Hedia?" said Alphena, looking down at the floor of worn bricks in a herringbone pattern. Would her father be replacing this too? "What's going to happen about Nemastes? About all of it?"

Hedia's face went hard, then softened. "I'm not sure," she said. "I hope we'll learn enough to avoid problems. Perhaps Nemastes will go back to Hyperborea or wherever he really comes from. From the Underworld, I shouldn't wonder."

Alphena looked up, surprised at the note of bitterness in the last phrase. The older woman ordinarily sounded cool and detached, even when her eyes said she was considering murder.

Hedia laughed and gestured with her left hand, sweeping away the mood of a moment. "I've even thought of hiring a couple of your gladiator friends to deal with our wizard, dear," she went on. "The trouble is, he seems to vanish into thin air except when he's with your father, and I don't want to risk an attack with Saxa present."

"Because he'd know it was you behind it?" Alphena said. Her lips were suddenly dry.

"No," said Hedia. "Because it wouldn't be safe. Violence isn't something you can control, not when it starts. I won't chance Saxa having his head bashed in or taking a dagger through the ribs because of a mistake by some animal who can barely mumble his own name in Thracian."

She turned abruptly. "I need some wine," she muttered. "Do you?"

"I'll drink some more," Alphena said in a little voice. The night was pressing down on her. Not the darkness outside, but something much wider and much deeper than that.

Hedia passed her the wineskin. Instead of removing the stopper immediately, Alphena said, "M-Mother? What if Nemastes attacks you? He knows you're his enemy, surely? He wouldn't even have to hire somebody."

"You think he might try to strangle me with his own hands?" Hedia said. She chuckled. "Well, dear, this would be one answer to the problem."

She lifted the front fold of her chiton and drew a finger-length dagger. Its sheath must have been sewn into her cloth-of-gold girdle, where it was completely concealed by the loose linen gathered over her bosom.

She slipped the knife back and let the chiton hide it again. Giving Alphena a cold smile, she continued. "But since Nemastes appears to be a man, there may be a simpler way to make him less threatening."

"Ooh!" said Alphena. "You would with *him*?"

She'd spoken before she took time to reflect; and besides, she didn't feel like pretending to be sophisticated. It was pointless with this woman. And the thought of that bald *creature* putting his, well, hands, on her was disgusting.

Alphena thought that the response might be a peal of laughter; instead Hedia gave her a lopsided grin. "You're young, dear," she said in a soft voice and a tone of what seemed to be affection. "If the gods are good to you, perhaps you'll never have to learn more about the world than you already know. I hope that's the case."

Alphena made a moue with her lips, then offered the wineskin to Hedia again. "Here," she said. "I may as well say the prayer. Since we're here anyway."

Hedia gave her the vellum, but she waved away the skin. "Just set the skin on the floor," she said. "I'll hold the lamp. This stand is too high for you."

She rose onto her toes to lift the lamp chain from the hook. Alphena's body was turned toward the statue of Tellus, but she was looking back over her shoulder at her stepmother.

A tremor shook the building. Dirt from the roof showered the interior. A body, either a cat or a large rat, fell from the rafters with a *splop*. Chittering, the creature scuttled into the shadows and vanished. Hedia kept hold of the lamp, but the bronze stand lost its balance and hit the floor with a clang.

"We should get out before—," Alphena started to say.

"Alphena, daughter of Gaius Saxa!" a voice boomed.

Alphena turned. The statue of Tellus was staring at her. Its painted lips moved as it said, "Joyous news, Alphena! You are fated to wed Spurius Cassius and to reign with him forever in the Underworld!"

Alphena dropped the page of vellum she was holding. She felt as though she'd been caught in a winter storm and covered with ice.

"No!" she cried.

A second tremor struck. A crack zigzagged across the brick floor. Roof tiles rattled hard together, shaking down chips of broken terra-cotta. The statue of Tellus toppled toward Alphena like a ten-foot club.

Hedia gave a shout and leaped at the frozen girl. The statue smashed itself into dust and splinters on the floor beside them.

"Come on!" Hedia wheezed. The women scrambled toward the door, holding each other's hands.

Together they slid the bar from its staples and shoved the door open. Alphena glanced over her shoulder as she stumbled into the babbling servants. Oil which had spilled when the lamp smashed began to burn on the bricks. The flames gave off a hungry yellow light.

CHAPTER VII

Y ou're sure you wouldn't like a lantern bearer?" Varus called to Corylus. His friend waved his free hand in response, then trotted eastward toward his home.

"He's a very sturdy young man," said Pandareus gently. "I would judge that the staff in his hand would be more than a match for a footpad's dagger."

Varus sighed. "Yes sir," he said. "That's just what I was thinking earlier this evening, when we met at the temple. But since what happened, I'm. . . ."

He didn't know how to conclude the sentence. He looked up the escarpment. The Temple of Jupiter was set too far back for him to see it at this angle, but the memories of what had happened there weren't going to fade soon. Probably they would still be clear on his deathbed.

He looked at his teacher and managed a smile. "Sir," he said, "nothing seems certain anymore. I feel as though that cliff could slump down like the Tiber bank in a flood. Though"—Varus really grinned—"I think the Citadel will fail before Corylus does. I offered him an escort because I was afraid, not because I thought he needed one."

He cleared his throat. Two linkmen stood close with their lanterns, but Candidus was remaining at a discreet distance.

"I hope, sir," Varus said diffidently, "that you'll permit me to send you home with attendants?"

"I'll certainly walk partway with you," said Pandareus. "And then we'll see, but I have to admit that I'm feeling less sure of myself than a good philosopher should be."

He looked at the moon, now at zenith, before lowering his eyes to Varus again. He continued. "I've been preparing for tonight's events, you might say, during my whole life. But when it came—when I found myself in the midst of the wonder and the mystery that I've been seeking—I found it rather disconcerting. I *find* it disconcerting."

Varus smiled faintly. *At least it's not just me. Though it would be better for Carce and the world if I were being foolishly concerned.*

Aloud he said, "We'll proceed now, Candidus. We'll go through the Forum, then by the Sacred Way."

That wasn't the most direct route toward Saxa's town house, but it would take them closer to Pandareus's apartment. Varus tended not to think much about money. Every once in a while, something like the discussion between his teacher and Atilius about school fees reminded him that others might not have the luxury of ignoring money, and that a learned scholar might be in actual want.

To Pandareus he said, "I'm not frightened, really, but I'm lost."

He thought for a moment and went on: "What I'm frightened about is that I'll do something terribly wrong. That I'll"—he lifted his hands as though he were flinging out a heap of possibilities—"destroy the world in fire or, well, anything."

"It sounds as though someone else is already working to destroy the world in fire," Pandareus said. They were walking past the back of the Temple of Concord. The sheer stone wall was blank and forbidding in a way that the Capitoline Hill, broken up with bushes and vines all the way to the top, was not. "Perhaps you can cause the waters to rise. Deucalion's Flood was a very long time ago, after all."

Varus blinked. "Sir?" he said. Only then did he realize that his teacher had been joking. Or rather, poking fun at his student's dour seriousness.

Varus cleared his throat and said, "The reasoning portion of my mind doesn't think that the earth and heavens rotate around me, sir. I'll try to keep that reasoning portion more generally in control than my previous comment may imply."

"I think it's quite reasonable for you to feel lost," Pandareus said. "I certainly do. My friend Priscus is more fortunate in that respect. He knows exactly how to deal with the crisis."

"Through the Commission, you mean?" said Varus. "As you said in the vault, with a banquet for the gods or a new temple?"

"Priscus believes that the gods have spoken," Pandareus said. "He and his colleagues on the Commission have the duty of determining the Republic's proper response to the gods' warning. Whereas I—"

He paused in midphrase, waiting till Varus looked up and met his eyes by starlight. They were ambling along at Varus's usual pace. That was probably slower than the teacher would be walking on his own, but it was a better rate for talking anyway.

"—am not sure that the Sibyl is speaking the words of the gods. Indeed, I'm not sure that the gods exist, Gaius Varus. Which is not an admission that I would make generally, even in so large and sophisticated a city as Carce."

"No sir," said Varus. It wasn't likely that Pandareus would be executed for blasphemy the way Socrates had been in Athens centuries before, but if there was a loud to-do about the matter, he would lose students. Whatever they might think privately, very few politically inclined fathers would want themselves and their sons to be associated with someone who denied that the gods fought for Carce.

Varus met his teacher's eyes again. "And sir?" he said. "Thank you. I appreciate the compliment. Though I do believe in the gods."

The more so after what I saw tonight. But those words caught in his throat when he considered speaking them aloud.

"I was praising your ability to consider all sides of a question," Pandareus said. "Not your opinions themselves. Though I hope"—his voice lost some of its lightness—"that you don't think I'm saying that I'm smarter or wiser than my friend Priscus. We're in disagreement on the point at issue, as we are on a number of points. Whether the authorship of the *Nicomachian Ethics* can really be ascribed to Aristotle, for example. One or both of us must be in error on many issues, but I will say"—Pandareus smiled much more broadly than he usually did—"that my friend and I make far more subtle and intelligent blunders than the ordinary run of men do."

Varus pondered for a moment. His hesitation wasn't over what question to ask but rather whether he should speak at all.

"Ask, my student," said Pandareus in the tone of dry pedantry that he generally employed in class. "You needn't fear that I will consider you stupid; and as for ignorance: all men are ignorant, are we not?"

"Sir," Varus said, keeping his eyes for now on the pair of linkmen two paces ahead. They were the closest servants. He doubted they could hear the conversation, and if they did, there was no one they could repeat it to that would matter.

"What do you think the solution to the . . . ," Varus said. *Threat? Danger?* "To the situation, that is, will be? Since you don't have confidence in the sort of response that the Commission will recommend."

"I think, Lord Varus . . . ," Pandareus said, subtly changing the dynamics of the discussion. Heretofore they had been teacher and scholar. Now he was addressing Varus with the formality owed by a foreigner to a senator's son. "The answer will come from you. You have twice demonstrated knowledge which goes beyond where scholarship and logic have taken me."

"Me?" said Varus, so startled that he managed to kick the heel of his right foot with his left toe. He almost went sprawling. "Sir, I don't *know* anything. I didn't even hear myself speaking when you say I did. I mean, I believe you, but I can't guide you."

"Perhaps," said Pandareus, but his tone didn't suggest that he agreed with Varus. "In that case, someone or something is guiding you. I hope that we—that all of us, that the Republic—can benefit from that guidance through you."

"Sir, I . . . ," Varus said. He didn't know what to say next. The servants leading the entourage had slowed to a loiter at the intersection ahead, where the street which led east toward Pandareus's apartment branched from the Sacred Way. Varus needed to go north to get home.

"Ah, Master Pandareus?" Varus said. "Would you like us to escort you the rest of the way to your suite?"

"It's scarcely a suite, young man," said the teacher drily. "And no, I'll be fine from here."

"Candidus?" Varus said on a rising inflection. He felt relieved that the conversation was ending. He didn't want to terminate it formally, but he didn't see any good direction to go from where it was now. "Send a linkman and another servant home with Master Pandareus. Men who won't have problems at this time of night."

"Hey, send me, Candidus!" a burly servant called. Varus didn't know his name, but he'd noticed his accent in the past. He was from the northern border of Britain—or from across it. "I wouldn't mind knocking some heads again."

To Varus, learning was the primary goal, and he knew that exalted rank didn't guarantee exceptional learning. Therefore he didn't have the concern for rank that his sister and stepmother did. The servant from North Britain was obviously no scholar, but his enthusiasm for keeping the old man safe shouldn't become cause for punishment.

"Candidus," Varus said before the under-steward could react, "send the Pict. And Master Pandareus, you *will* take an escort tonight. I wouldn't sleep if you didn't."

"You're a fine student," Pandareus said. "I would be remiss as your teacher if I did anything to interfere with your getting necessary rest." He winked, undercutting the deadpan delivery. "And besides, I'm not at my sharpest and most observant tonight, Lord Varus. I don't want to have my head knocked in because I failed to notice somebody with a brick who was looking for the price of a jar of wine."

To the servants Candidus had chosen—the Pict and a tall man who carried his lantern hanging from the tip of an iron rod—Pandareus said, "Come along, my good fellows. Which chariot teams do you fancy? I confess to a liking for the Whites, as they represent the epitome of purity. Unfortunately, I find that they almost never win races."

The three men headed south at a more rapid pace than they'd been keeping in Varus's presence. And no doubt Corylus was trotting along as blithely as he would have done by daylight. Well, individuals had different skills; and the noble Gaius Varus had never claimed to be an enthusiastic pedestrian.

"Home, Candidus," he ordered. They set off again.

Varus found himself smiling. Ever since Homer, poets

had been describing men as pawns in a game of the gods. He had done the same himself in his abortive epic of the First Punic War.

He'd never expected to be one of those men whom the gods were playing with, however.

HEDIA STAGGERED ACROSS the yard of the temple. Alphena tried to stop as soon as they were under the open sky again. Hedia dragged the girl with her, snarling, "Come on! If the building collapses, stones will come bouncing out for Hercules *knows* how far!"

The servants babbled like a flock of geese; they even fluttered their arms in the air. *All they have to do is to begin spraying green shit all over the landscape to complete the resemblance!*

With servants dancing attendance but afraid to touch the noble ladies even to help, Hedia reached the gap where the gate had been. They could go into the street and get behind what was left of the perimeter wall, but she doubted blocks would roll this far through the piles of building materials. Besides, the earthquake seemed to be over for now.

She released Alphena. The girl drew herself up with returning dignity. From the look on her face, she was wondering whether to scream at her stepmother for treating her like a child or to hold her peace, since Hedia had, after all, done the right thing. Even if she hadn't been polite in the way she did it.

"Your ladyship!" cried Phidippides. Fear and confusion made the priest of Tellus sweat like the pig he so greatly resembled. "Whatever's the matter? What did you do?"

"We didn't do anything, you fool," Hedia said. "The earthquake knocked over the lamp stand and the statue too. Midas."

The deputy steward was standing close, ready to move

the priest away if requested to. He wore a troubled expression.

"Get some of your men to put out the oil that spilled from the lamp. Smother it with the sand piled over there, I suppose."

Midas turned, relaying the order with a bellow. The workmen's tools were stacked in the shelter of the roofed colonnade to the left of the temple proper. One of the servants had noticed that along with the shovels, trowels, and cramps, there were tightly woven baskets for carrying loose materials. He shouted to get his fellows' attention and started tossing baskets down.

"But your ladyship?" Phidippides said in horrified wonder. "There wasn't a—"

He paused. He'd apparently heard the words that had just come out of his mouth and decided instantly to change the tenor of his comment.

"Ah, that is," he said, "we were waiting here in the street as you directed. With your men. We heard, ah, rattling, but we didn't feel an earthquake. Your own man Midas can tell you that, can't you, dear fellow?"

"Don't you contradict her ladyship, you Milesian toad!" said Midas, grabbing a handful of Phidippides' tunic and shoving him backward.

"Enough of that, Midas," Hedia said. The priest edged away, ready to run if Midas reached for him again. "Now, listen to me: *did* you feel an earthquake?" She gave an angry flick of her hands. "And *don't* just say you did because you think that's what I want to hear," she said. "Tell me the truth or I swear I'll have you flayed."

The deputy steward's face went blank. He bowed low and said, "Your ladyship, I heard tiles breaking and I thought there'd been a gust of wind. But I didn't feel anything through my sandals. Or feel wind. Your ladyship."

"There had to have been an earthquake," Alphena

said. She was hugging herself. "The statue fell. And I heard it *speak*."

"Midas," Hedia snapped, "leave us. And make sure this temple rabble keeps clear also! Lady Alphena and I have matters regarding the divination to discuss in private."

"At once, your ladyship!" the steward said. In a voice that could be heard in neighboring apartment buildings, he went on, "Ferox and Mensus? Break the legs of anybody who comes within twenty feet of their ladyships!"

As people sprang away from them—the household servants dragged or pummeled temple personnel, who were afraid to defend themselves in the presence of the great ladies—Alphena said, "It said I was going to marry Spurius Cassius. It's *horrible*. I don't even know who Spurius Cassius is!"

Hedia doubted that the girl had consciously waited until the servants were out of earshot before she started talking about what had happened. If Hedia hadn't acted quickly, all the hundreds of household servants—and all the thousands they talked to or who talked to somebody who talked to them—would have been chattering about the terrible omen during the marriage divination. *Try to arrange a decent marriage for Alphena then!*

"I don't think you should take the voice you thought you heard too seriously," Hedia lied. The girl was distraught. Besides, they were both tired and they'd drunk quite a lot of wine. "I suspect it was the wood squealing when the statue of Tellus fell over, don't you?"

"It wasn't," Alphena said. She bent over, bracing her buttocks against the wall as she pressed the knuckles of both hands against her mouth. "The goddess spoke to me. I saw her *mouth* moving!"

Is she about to begin screaming? That could be passed off as a reaction to almost being crushed by the toppling statue, of course. In fact it might go some way to balanc-

ing the stories about the girl's unnatural interest in masculine pursuits.

"I'm not going to marry Spurius Cassius," Alphena said through her fists. "I've never heard of Spurius Cassius. I won't!"

"Get yourself together, Daughter," Hedia said without raising her voice. "Venus, girl! Don't put on a show for the servants."

Alphena straightened with a wide-eyed stare, as though Hedia had slapped her—which was more or less what she had done, though with words. The girl looked around, aware of her surroundings for the first time since they'd stumbled from the temple.

When she saw that the nearest people, Ferox and Mensus, were over twenty feet away, she relaxed. With their backs to the noblewomen, they brandished cudgels threateningly toward other servants and the gawkers who'd come from neighboring residences.

"And even if what you thought you heard really was a spirit speaking to you . . . ," Hedia continued. The edge that had been in her voice a moment before had vanished; she was now the soothing mother—or perhaps the older sister. "Just remember that bad marriages are like bad colds: they're unpleasant, but they're too common to bother talking about. And they don't have to last long."

"Do you know Spurius Cassius?" Alphena said.

"No," said Hedia. "Perhaps your father does. Don't worry, we'll learn who the fellow is—if he even exists, as I said."

The lantern bearers were all outside the five-pace circle she'd decreed, but she and Alphena stood in full moonlight. Everyone was staring at them. They would have to do something before long. The girl seemed to have settled down adequately.

Alphena looked up suddenly. She'd gathered herself together, but Hedia now saw anger in her expression.

"Mother," she said. "Did my father do this?"

"Saxa?" Hedia repeated. The question had taken her aback; she could scarcely imagine anything that would have seemed more improbable. "No, dear, I can't imagine him doing anything of the sort. I know he's not—"

She turned her palms upward; she supposed that was in subconscious hope that a softer phrasing would drop out of the sky into them.

It didn't. She went on baldly, "Saxa doesn't pay much attention to anyone but himself. But dear? Insofar as it's in him, he does love you and your brother. He wouldn't deliberately harm you."

"But Father told you to bring me to the Temple of Tellus, didn't he?" Alphena said fiercely. "And that's the goddess who spoke to me!"

Hedia frowned in frustration. "He was renovating this temple," she said. "And it's close to the house; it's the natural choice. Believe me, dear, your father doesn't have it in him to hurt or frighten you in any way."

Alphena was wavering. *She accused her father because she needs someone to be angry at. Otherwise she can only be afraid.*

Hedia put her arms around the younger woman. "Be strong for me, Daughter," she lied. "This business frightens me terribly; I need you to cling to. But"—she straightened and leaned back to look Alphena in the eyes—"we mustn't attack people who aren't our enemies just because we're afraid. And Saxa isn't our enemy."

"I'm sorry," the girl muttered to the ground. "I wasn't . . ."

"Come, dear," Hedia said brightly. "Let's get back to our own beds. Tomorrow we can start asking about this Spurius Cassius."

She led the girl out to the litter. "Midas, we're returning to the house," she called.

The priest hovered beside the deputy steward, dancing from one foot to the other as though the stone pavers were too hot for the soles of his feet. While Alphena got into the litter, Hedia paused with a hard smile.

"Master Phidippides?" she said. "I'll talk to my husband tomorrow. It appears that your goddess will have a new statue after all."

Hedia settled herself onto the seat and gave Alphena a pleasant smile. No one seeing her composed face would guess that she was thinking that while Saxa certainly hadn't done this, his friend Nemastes probably had. In that case, the danger to Alphena was much worse than merely a bad marriage.

CORYLUS WALKED AT a leisurely pace, thinking about what had just happened in the temple. Unlike his friend's prophecy during the reading yesterday, this one didn't seem to come from a malevolent spirit. Neither time had Varus himself been speaking, though.

The moon gave good enough illumination that Corylus could have gone much faster—even trotted, if he'd felt like it. He wasn't in a hurry, and moving fast at night in Carce called attention to you. He was ready for trouble, but he wasn't looking for it.

A double line of heavy wagons pulled by four oxen each was rumbling down the center of the boulevard, carrying storage jars of wine. They were outbound, like him, but the only time the pace of an ox rose above a crawl was if the beast was lightly loaded and smelled water at the end of the day.

They shouldn't have been abreast. The wagoneers who properly would have been at the back didn't want to wait extra hours to unload.

They were hauling Greek wine landed at Ostia and brought up the Tiber on barges. These wagons were hauling it to taverns on the outskirts of the city. Because of the expense of land transport, it was cheaper to do this than it would be to bring wine overland even as little as twenty miles from vineyards in the Sabine Hills.

The wagon wheels were iron-shod, spitting sparks from the paving stones and ringing like Vulcan's workshop. Corylus didn't want to follow the wagons all the way to his apartment, but getting around them even on a street as wide as the Argiletum was tricky. If he misjudged, he took the risk of being squeezed between two wagons or even slipping under a wheel. The weight would take off whatever body part was between iron and the paving stones as thoroughly as a German's sword could do.

Somebody shouted from ahead. A drover's whip whacked over the sudden frustrated lowing of oxen. The leading wagons had met an equally large vehicle coming the other way.

A narrow alley led off to the left. Corylus ducked into it rather than thread his way through the mess ahead. Neither the teamsters nor the draft animals were going to notice a slim youth if he happened to be in the place they intended to pass through.

He heard something scuttle in front of him. He guessed it was a dog or a drunk—it was too big for a cat. He didn't suppose it mattered so long as it was going away. He'd lost the light. The moon was behind buildings, he thought at first, but he didn't see the outline of the roofs against the lighter sky.

He looked back toward the Argiletum. He didn't hear the wagons anymore. Instead, an owl called. The sound was familiar—but not in Carce.

Corylus moved forward, walking on the balls of his feet and holding his staff at a slant before him. *I'm having another spell like I did during the reading. My body is in Carce, but my mind has gone somewhere else.*

The air was cold, and the wind carried a hint of snow with it. There were trees around him in this dream, towering conifers whose needles matted the ground. This time he seemed to have a body, though. He kept moving, taking long strides as he'd learned to do with the scouts when they had to cover ground quickly before daylight caught them.

The ground had been rising almost imperceptibly. Corylus came into a clearing and at last saw the moon again: it was in its first quarter and just above the horizon. In Carce the full moon had been at zenith when he left his friends at the base of the Capitoline Hill.

He heard wolves to his left and behind: one and two, then many. They filled the night with their harmony. They had picked up a scent.

They howled again, noticeably closer. Corylus was pretty sure whose scent they had.

Corylus turned to his right and broke into a trot, dropping his toga as he ran. He'd worn his best to meet Atilius Priscus tonight, but he could replace it for money. If he survived.

There were no paths in this forest, but the trees smothered the undergrowth between their mighty trunks. He should be heading in the direction of his apartment, if he ever fell back out of this dream into the world where his apartment existed.

The wolves continued to howl. Two were noticeably ahead of the remainder of the pack. Corylus knew he could outrun them; but if he did that, their ten or a dozen fellows who were loping comfortably behind would bring him down exhausted not long thereafter.

At the edge of his consciousness, Corylus sometimes caught glimpses of streets and buildings. He didn't recognize anywhere in Carce for certain; he couldn't even swear that what he thought he saw was the city in which he had started this night.

He would trade this forest for passage to the shadow city, though, no matter what might be waiting for him there. He'd seen the bodies of wounded men whose friends hadn't found them before the wolves did.

The leading wolves yipped in excitement. Corylus didn't dare look over his shoulder—a slip would be fatal—but he knew that the pair had him in sight.

He lengthened his stride, knowing it was just a matter of time. No matter what he did, the result would be fatal.

A hundred feet ahead, a rock the size of a twenty-oared ship humped from a clearing. The soil nearby was too thin for firs to grow into giants, but a mix of small cedars standing shoulder to shoulder with dogwoods surrounded it instead.

A tangle of multiflora roses covered half the outcrop. A figure hunched on top—a wolf? But better to deal with a single enemy in front than to have a dozen tear you down from behind. The roses would keep even wolves from coming at him through them.

The figure stood. It was a woman clad in a shift as thin as the moonlight.

Corylus sprinted, ducking to crash through the band of small trees. He supposed losing an eye to a cedar twig would be a cheap price if it got him to the relative safety of the outcrop; he'd still avoid it if he could.

He staggered to the base of the sandstone outcrop. It was six feet high and nearly sheer on this face. After his run he would have had trouble vaulting to the top if he'd been barehanded, but he thrust the staff behind him and pivoted himself up.

The wolves who'd been on his heels wormed out of the thicket an instant later. They were young males, best fitted to push the quarry's pace while the more experienced members of the pack saved their energy for the kill.

One of them leaped. Corylus had his footing. He gave the wolf a two-handed blow over the head with his staff. The wolf yelped, thumped into the side of the rock instead of landing on top, and sat down on the ground whimpering. His companion thought better of attacking directly and instead circled the injured animal.

Corylus's hands stung. The thick cornelwood staff had gotten home perfectly. It should have dashed the animal's brains out instead of just stunning it. These beasts looked like wolves and they weren't much bigger than the wolves he was familiar with on the frontier, but they were much heavier built. A skull that could absorb a blow like the one he'd just dealt must be as thick as a wild bull's.

"You're a strong one, aren't you?" a throaty voice said. "Your mother would be proud of you."

Corylus glanced at the woman; he'd almost forgotten her. He supposed she could knife him or simply shove him off the outcrop, but even so she would have been a lesser evil. "My mother?" he said, feeling a little silly when he heard the words come out of his mouth.

The rest of the pack slipped through the undergrowth, appearing on all sides of the rock simultaneously. They'd waited till they had him ringed to close in. They were silent now, save for an older female who whined as she sniffed the injured animal, then licked the bloody pressure cut in the middle of his forehead.

The bone hadn't been broken, though. The young male got to his feet, wobbly but apparently alert.

"I knew her, yes," the woman said. "Frankly, I thought she was too skinny to be as full of herself as she was, but I suppose I shouldn't speak ill of her now."

Even the brief glance Corylus had given her was enough to show that this woman was beautiful in a lush, full-breasted fashion. He thought that her garment was pastel, not white, but by moonlight he couldn't guess the hue.

"Ma'am?" he said. "Am I dreaming?"

She laughed like a brook gurgling. "Goodness," she

said, "I don't think much of your taste in dreams if that's what you believe this is!"

A wolf on his left sprang. It hadn't snarled, but Corylus had seen its haunches quiver. He slammed it in the throat, this time using the staff as a spear instead of a club. It was like punching a bullock, but the wolf spun hard into the ground.

Corylus pivoted. The wolf which had poised to jump from the other side instead circled and whined, looking up at him sidelong.

"Ma'am!" he said. "Keep behind me. I'll hold them off as long as I can."

The pack's leader was huge, with the bulk of a big man. He must easily weigh two hundred pounds. He had scars on both shoulders, and his left ear had been chewed to tatters. He stared at Corylus from beneath bony brow ridges, calm and murderously determined.

"I don't see that there's much 'behind' when they're on all sides," she said, "but they won't bother me. Normally I wouldn't interfere with them either, but for your mother's sake—"

A wolf leaped from the right. Corylus batted it on the nose, throwing it back with a yelp of pain. He'd stopped trying to deliver killing blows: that risked him losing his balance to no particular end, given how rugged the animals were.

As expected, the leader with two younger males behind him was already coming up the less abrupt slope to the left. Corylus stabbed at the big wolf's shoulder with the end of the staff, then swiped sideways to shove the wolf on that side off in a cartwheel. It was like lifting a wagon one-handed, but Corylus's muscles were up to the job under the goad of fear.

The third wolf slammed its teeth into the fluttering hem of his tunic. Corylus punched, this time with the short end of the staff. He heard the beast's lower jaw crack, but he fell to one knee and the leader was on him again.

A coil of rosebush looped the big wolf's hindquarters and pulled him away. He snarled and bit at it. A cane slapped him across the muzzle; the thorns drew bloody furrows like the nails of an angry woman.

The bush dragged the wolf back and released him, sending him tumbling. He scrambled to his feet, snapping and growling, but he didn't rush in again. The other wolves backed off also.

Corylus stood, using his staff to brace himself upright. His mouth was open, and gasping in air. He tasted blood; he must have bitten his lip. His whole body was trembling and he was queasy with exertion.

"You shouldn't be here, you know," the woman said.

He could barely hear her over the roar of his own blood in his ears. He bent forward slightly to help him breathe better.

"I didn't mean to come," Corylus wheezed. "I don't know why I'm here."

He'd banged his right knee hard on the rock. It was already swelling, and the skin was torn; he'd have a bruise for a week.

The wolf leader had been sitting on his haunches, licking the shoulder where Corylus had stuck him. Now he got to his feet, growled, and barked curtly. The pack vanished into the undergrowth much as they'd appeared, though he heard the male with the broken jaw whining long after he had disappeared from sight.

"Here, let me smell you," the woman said, kneading her fingers through Corylus's hair and drawing his head down to sniff his dark curls. Out of reflex he resisted, but she was unexpectedly strong; he got the impression he would pull his hair out by the roots before he broke her grip on it.

She laughed, kissed him on the tip of his ear, and

released him. "It was a man named Nemastes," she said. "At least he calls himself a man. Here, I'll send you back if that's what you want."

"Ma'am?" Corylus said. He was dizzy from reaction and wasn't really sure what he was hearing. "Yes ma'am, I really want to go back to Carce. Can you do that?"

"Of course I can," the woman snapped. Behind her, the tangle of rose canes quivered. "Why else would I have said I could?"

Corylus didn't see her move or speak, but a flash of white light enveloped him. Needles dug momentarily into his bones. He stumbled forward.

People were shouting at him. He saw lanterns and men with cudgels coming from both sides. He raised his staff, trying to back away but aware that his right knee was stiff with the bruise. He wouldn't be able to escape this time.

"Wait!" cried a woman's clear voice. "That's Corylus!"

THE LEADING LITTER bearers shouted, "Wau!" and stopped together, rocking Alphena forward in her seat. The team was so well matched that the bearers on the back of the poles didn't slam the heavy vehicle into the thighs of their fellows in front.

Escorting servants ran past the litter, some of them brandishing their cudgels. Alphena leaned out to see what was happening. In the light of bobbing lanterns she saw a hunched man with a heavy stick confronting the entourage.

The litter bobbed: Hedia had gotten out. "Wait!" she called in a voice of command. "That's Corylus!"

Is it? The fellow was stumbling backward. He had his stick up, though, and the servants weren't pressing him too hard.

"Get back, you ninnies!" Hedia said, striding into the middle of the ruck. "Midas, if any of these blind fools strikes Master Corylus, he'll spend the rest of his life in a lead mine in Spain!"

Alphena got out, caught her long tunic on the door latch, and almost fell on her face. She blushed, furious at herself though she doubted anybody had seen her clumsiness. They were all too interested in Corylus and the bustle of people around him.

The litter bearers alone hadn't joined the tight circle. The on-duty team had set the vehicle down but then waited, each man with his replacement, for orders.

"Get out of my way!" Alphena demanded, pushing at servants with both hands. Her female voice drove an immediate passage where a man might have met reflexive resistance. "Let me through!"

Corylus's right knee looked like raw meat, and his eyes were wild. His linen tunic was torn and bloody. The garment was too light for the evening, but there was no sign of a cloak or toga. Blood-matted fur clung to both ends of his stout staff.

"Corylus, what's happened?" Alphena said in horror.

Hedia put her left hand over his on the staff and said, "Careful with your stick, dear boy. You're with friends now."

"Is this Carce?" Corylus said in a savage rumble. He sounded like a beast claiming his territory.

"Yes," said Hedia crisply. "We're very close to our house, Lady Alphena and I. Are you able to walk? We have a litter."

"I can . . . ," Corylus said. "I don't need a litter, I'm all right."

Hedia knelt, gripping the youth's right thigh and calf. "Bring a lantern close, someone!" she said. "And don't wriggle, my dear. I want to look at this knee."

"Corylus, I can hold your staff," Alphena said. He wasn't flailing with it anymore, but Hedia had been right to worry that he might. "I'll be careful with it."

"What?" he said, but his voice had settled toward normal instead of showing the spiky challenge when he first staggered toward them. "Oh, yes. Sorry, Lady Alphena, I didn't . . ."

His voice trailed off. Her lips pursed, but she didn't blurt something that she would regret later. He gave her the staff, looking down as Hedia probed his leg.

He didn't have to finish the sentence. She could finish it for him: "I didn't notice you because I was mooning over your beautiful stepmother."

The staff was heavier than Alphena expected; she wondered if an iron rod had been set into its core. Also it was sticky where she held it.

"You," she said in an undertone to one of the linkmen; she had to tap his shoulder to get his attention. "Bring your light here."

He obediently turned with his short staff. It had a grip on one end and an oil lamp in a cage of bronze wire attached to the other on a short chain. When Alphena examined the smooth wood in the haze of light, she saw bloody handprints on it.

Hedia rose. Corylus started to rub his eyes. She took his right wrist and said, "No, your palm is all over blood. Is it yours?"

He looked at his hand with a puzzled expression, flexing it. "Maybe," he said. "I, when I fell on the rock I probably put it down. When I hit my knee. But I don't remember."

"Well, let's get you to our house," Hedia said in a tone that didn't so much compel agreement as rightly assume it. "We can put you on the servant's bed in Varus's room, that way you'll have your privacy. And speaking of Varus—"

She turned, looking down the boulevard. The lights of a large party were flickering toward them; Alphena heard men singing, "Hermes! The Money Rolls In." Somebody called, "Who's that in front of us? Announce yourself or it'll be the worse for you!"

"Candidus, you fool!" boomed Midas. Alphena wasn't sure which of the deputy stewards was the more senior. From the rancor in Midas's voice, it wasn't a certain thing between the men themselves. "What do you mean by threatening their ladyships!"

"Corylus?" Varus called, rushing to his friend's side. Hedia straightened and took a half step sideways. "What happened to you? And how did you get here?"

"I don't know how I got here exactly," Corylus said, clasping arms with Varus. "But I much prefer it to the place I was before. Wherever that was."

Corylus straightened and looked around the growing circle of attendants. "I was attacked by dogs!" he said loudly. "I took a shortcut through an alley and dogs attacked me; there's fur on my staff, you see. But I'm all right now, and I can make my own way home."

"You will not," said Hedia. "Varus, dear, Master Corylus will sleep in the servant's alcove in your suite tonight. Does that suit you?"

"Why . . . ," Varus said. "Of course. Corylus, you're welcome anytime. Or you can have a guest suite."

"But before he does that, Lenatus will look him over and put ointment on that knee," Hedia continued. She was perfectly calm and perfectly in control of the situation. "Now, my young friend, are you sure you can walk? Because the litter's right here."

Corylus grimaced. "Ma'am," he said, "I think I'm better off to walk on it for a bit. If I let it set up, I, well—it's not a problem now, but it could turn into one easy enough if I let it."

"Very good," Hedia said. "Midas, send a man ahead to wake Lenatus and have him ready. And let's go, all. The sooner we get Master Corylus to the house, the better off he'll be."

She turned. "Alphena dear, that goes for us also. Into the litter now, if you please."

Seething inside, Alphena obeyed. Having to hold the staff made her clumsy, but she'd promised Corylus to take care of it, so she couldn't very well pass it off now to a servant.

Hedia got in with the supple ease of a snake. She snapped her fingers and the bearers took the weight of the litter again. They started forward.

Alphena squeezed the wooden staff hard. The blood was tacky and gave her a good grip. It would be very satisfying to smash it into her stepmother's fine features and end her effortless flow of commands.

But because Alphena had more self-awareness than she was comfortable with, she also knew that Hedia's quick, concise decisions had been correct from first to last. *That* was what made her so irritating.

CHAPTER VIII

U sing a stylus on a wax tablet, Hedia wrote,

> My dear Anna, if you are well it is good; I also am well.
>
> Corylus is staying tonight with my son.
>
> Matters have occurred which have bearing on our discussion this morning. Please visit me tomorrow at the seventh hour—not earlier, though I might wish it, because I will be attending the rites involved with my husband taking up the consulship.
>
> I will have a litter waiting at your building at midday. The attendants will help you down the staircase.

Sighing with relief, Hedia set the bronze stylus in its holder and motioned to her secretary, Praxos, who waited silently on the other side of the small writing desk in her reception room. The gesture was unnecessary: Praxos was already closing the tablet. Red wax warmed over the desk lamp, ready to pour on the ribbon closures when the secretary had tied them. He would press in the seal also, a piece of wood in which worm tunnels formed an H.

Well, Hedia told herself, it was an H. It was as good an H as she could have made herself.

Writing notes to friends with her own hand was a polite accomplishment for a woman with any pretense to social status, so of course Hedia could do it, but if any more had been required than a few lines, Praxos would have written it to her dictation. The result would have been quicker and clearer; one of the reasons Hedia used wax instead of brushing ink on papyrus or thin board was that corrections were easier to make. Treating Anna as an equal was both polite and politic, however, since they were allies in this business with Nemastes.

"When it's sealed, give it to a courier to take to the apartment of Master Corylus off the Argiletum," Hedia said. "Give it to Iberus, now that I think of it; he already knows the way. And he's to wait if Anna and her husband aren't home when he arrives."

It was possible that they would be working—digging—in the old cemetery until nearly dawn.

"Yes, your ladyship," said the secretary, bending over the sealed tablet with an ink brush. He was writing Anna's name on the thin sheet of elm which covered the written surface of the wax.

Anna wouldn't be able to read it herself, but her husband, Pulto, would. He'd been a watch stander in the army, so he had to be able to read a guard roster and basic orders. Poor as Hedia knew her handwriting to be, it was probably better than that of many centurions.

Hedia rose to her feet and stretched. She could use some exercise to get rid of tonight's tension, but it didn't seem likely that events would fall that way. Still, an optimistic outlook had brought her more than one unexpected reward. Sometimes even more than one reward at a time.

She smiled. She wasn't sure how the expression read to the servants with her in the room; from the fact that they all went determinedly blank-faced, they probably didn't take it as involving humor. It did, but that might bother them even more—particularly the straitlaced Praxos.

"I'm going to see my husband," Hedia said in quick decision. "Syra, wait up, though I hope I'll not need you. The rest of you can go to bed."

The servants waited like statues until Hedia had swept regally through the door of the suite, which one of them was holding open. They were afraid that if they called attention to themselves, their mistress might find additional tasks for them.

In fact Hedia was neither petty nor the flighty-minded sort of person who changed her mind often. The servants might prefer to think of her that way, though, than to dwell on the fact that if she threatened to have them flogged—or flayed—she wouldn't change her mind then either.

According to Agrippinus, her husband had come home—without Nemastes—not long before she and Alphena arrived. He wouldn't be asleep yet; and anyway, she was willing to wake him up for this.

Saxa's suite had its own doorman. He didn't attempt to stop her, but he turned his head and called loudly, "Her noble ladyship Hedia, your lordship."

She brushed past him. Saxa was sitting up in bed, attended by six servants. One was reading a poem, apparently on astrology in epic stanzas, while another was carefully tilting a cup of mulled wine so that his master could drink without using his hands. The wine warmer was a bronze basin with a water bath between its charcoal brazier and the mixture of wine and herbs; two servants tended it. The remaining pair were ready to fluff pillows, adjust the covers, or do anything else that the Senator wished.

"You lot may leave," said Hedia, emphasizing with a curt gesture that they *would* take her offer. The reader continued, though he wasn't ignoring her. His eyes sought his master in terror for acquiescence or argument, so that he wouldn't have to decide whom to obey on his own.

Saxa hunched a little and pretended not to be aware of his wife's presence. Hedia felt a degree of pity for the reader; the gods knew that she'd had a lot of frustrating experience with trying to get her husband to make a reasonable decision.

Nonetheless, the servants had to learn that Lady Hedia was the person to obey because *she* wasn't going to brook any alternative. She plucked the scroll from the reader's hands—he gasped but didn't try to fight her for it—and deposited it in the charcoal glowing under the wine warmer.

"Out," she repeated, gesturing again.

The reader squealed in despair. He started for the door, then froze for a moment—and snatched the scroll back before finally scrambling out of the room. The papyrus was beginning to char, but it hadn't caught fire yet.

Hedia watched him go with a mixture of contempt and admiration. He was risking death by torture for a book which could be replaced for a few silver pieces. That was simply stupid—and it wasn't even his book.

On the other hand, the servant believed in something greater than his own life. That too was probably stupid . . . but it nonetheless made Hedia feel small about herself and her sophistication.

She and her husband were alone in the room; the doorman latched the panel behind the reader, the last of the attendants. Saxa looked up and grimaced.

"Hedia, dear," he said. "I can't talk tonight, I'm very upset. I was just trying to settle my mind before I went to sleep, and now I think I'm ready."

Hedia didn't bother calling her husband a liar. "This is about your daughter," she said. "Who is Spurius Cassius?"

"What?" said Saxa. He no more could act convincingly than he could fly, so he really was at a loss. "I don't know any Spurius Cassius. And what has he to do with Alphena?"

He fluttered his hands in agitation; it was just as well that the servant had put the cup down on a side table instead of leaving it with his master. "Anyway, I *can't* talk now, dear, I'm just not up to it!"

Hedia sat down on the bed beside her husband. She felt tired and sad, but she wasn't angry anymore. Saxa looked helpless. His fists were clenched on the bedspread, but he looked more like he was going to try to rub tears of desperation out of his eyes than to hit anything.

He certainly wouldn't hit her. There'd been a number of men in Hedia's life who had—and had lived to regret it—but Saxa wasn't like that. He was a *decent* man, and because of that she loved him.

"Dear heart," she said, "tonight the statue of Tellus told your daughter that she would marry Spurius Cassius and reign in the Underworld. The voice was male, so I don't imagine that the goddess was really speaking; it must have been a trick, but a very clever trick."

She took a deep breath and went on: "I saw the statue's lips move. I thought I did."

"Really?" said Saxa, sitting up straighter. "Why, that's very interesting, my dear! I've read of similar prodigies, but to have one occur now and in my own family—why, this is amazing!"

"Saxa," Hedia said, knowing that she was letting her exasperation show. "This is your daughter, Alphena. Your *daughter*."

"She wasn't harmed, was she?" Saxa said in sudden concern. "I know I've been distracted, dear, but it would be terrible if anything happened to Alphena. Or to Varus, of course."

"Varus is fine," Hedia said, wondering why she'd bothered to start this conversation, "and nothing happened to Alphena tonight except that she was badly frightened."

The girl would certainly object to being characterized as frightened, but it was true. Hedia would have said the same thing even if it weren't true: she had to get her husband to open up to her. Making him afraid for his children's safety was one of the few tools she had to do that.

"It's what's *going* to happen to Alphena that worries me," she continued harshly. "She has to be dead to be in the Underworld, whether queen or not. Doesn't she?"

"Yes, I quite see what you mean," Saxa said, but the brief personal note was gone from his voice. "And you're quite sure you saw the statue's lips move?"

"I'm sure," Hedia said curtly, though by now she *wasn't* really sure that her eyes hadn't been tricking her in the dim light. And she'd drunk quite a lot of wine. "My lord husband, is Nemastes behind this?"

"What?" said Saxa. He stiffened and leaned his upper body away from Hedia, though of course he wasn't going anywhere until he disentangled his legs from the bedclothes on which she was sitting. "Why do you say that? What *could* Nemastes have to do with it?"

I don't know, Hedia thought, *but you must at least have an idea or you wouldn't find the question so disturbing.* Saxa really shouldn't try to lie or even to conceal the truth.

She got to her feet. Staring down at him, she said, "My lord Saxa, this is your daughter's life—or worse. What is Nemastes doing to her?"

"Nothing!" Saxa said. He closed his eyes in misery. "Nothing, nothing, nothing! Not that I know of, Hedia. But"—his voice became a wail—"I know so little, and the dangers are so great!"

Instead of a gush of frustrated anger, Hedia felt her heart melt toward the poor man. He was completely out of his depth, and he knew it. She was out of her depth also, but that made her the more determined to fight; her own strength was all she had left.

Saxa, dear kindly Saxa, didn't have any inner strength.

Well, he had her; she would supply the backbone that nature had not.

Hedia sat on the bed again and tousled his hair with her left hand. For a moment she massaged his bald spot with her fingertips; she knew he liked that.

Then she unpinned one shoulder of her chiton and tugged it down to her waist. "Come, dear husband," she said, lifting her right breast and holding it out to him. The nipple hardened in anticipation. "Come, you know you'll feel better. You always do."

"No, Hedia, not now, *please*!" Saxa said. His face scrunched up and he looked even more as though he were about to burst into tears. "In the morning I'll look into the prodigy. There have been similar ones, but none that I recall that involve private persons."

He must have seen the way the planes of her face had hardened. With a flare of his own anger, he snapped, "I said I would look. That's all I can do!"

Before she could decide how to respond, Saxa sank back into misery and desperation. "Hedia, Hedia," he said. He *was* crying now. "You say it's my daughter. It's not. It's the whole world. Unless we stop them, they'll destroy the whole world!"

Saxa buried his face in the pillows. Hedia, her mind wrestling with questions she couldn't properly form, left his bedroom.

She was almost back to her own suite before she remembered to cover her breasts again.

ALPHENA HAD FOUND Lenatus waiting in the street when she and the others arrived. Varus had helped along the limping Corylus. Most or all of the thirty-odd attendants were better suited to supporting the injured youth than Varus was, but he'd insisted on being the one his friend leaned on.

Alphena had taken time to change into a short tunic

and comfortable shoes in place of the high buskins that formality required. Now she was ready to join the men.

She'd heard Lenatus say that he'd look at Corylus in the bathhouse, a small affair attached to the exercise ground. Occasionally Hedia used it, but normally the family went to the large public bathhouse on the corner of the Argiletum, where the facilities were much more extensive and comfortable. The private one was intended for members of the household who had just exercised in the gymnasium. That meant Alphena herself—and recently Corylus.

Servants were gathered outside the closed door. There must be fifty of them, squeezing together so that each could claim to have been present. They couldn't possibly have been overhearing what was said inside: their breathing alone would smother words that penetrated the thick panel.

Alphena felt her anger blaze. She'd been threatened by a spectral voice and bullied by her stepmother; now she had a legitimate target for her temper.

"Get out of here!" she shouted. "I'll have you flogged! By Hercules, I'll flog you myself! Where's a whip? I want a whip!"

The crowd burst like a melon dropped onto a stone pavement. Servants ran in all directions except straight at the young mistress—and, blinking, Alphena realized that with the way they were shoving each other, it was perfectly possible that one of them *would* lose his balance and knock her down.

A scullery maid slipped and was trampled by several of her fellows. She squealed in terror every time someone stepped on her. Tear-blinded, she was still squirming on the hallway floor after the rest of the servants had vanished either into the back garden or toward the front of the house.

Alphena felt queasy. *She's no older than me!* She bent

and took the girl's hand. The maid rose to her knees; she wasn't really hurt. When she wiped her eyes and saw who had helped her, however, she gave a muffled shriek and ran into the garden.

Alphena pulled open the bathhouse door. In the light of a pair of three-wick lamps, Corylus reclined on the table while Lenatus applied ointment to his knee. Varus was refilling a basin from the large boiler in the corner. This facility was too small to have a proper heated bath, but servants could sponge you with hot water before a massage.

Now that the torn skin had been cleaned, the scrapes didn't look too serious. His right knee had swollen to half again the size of the left, however. Unless it went down under the trainer's ministrations, it would be as stiff as if it had been splinted.

The three men stared at Alphena. She had assumed that she'd announced her presence when she shouted at the servants, but the trio had obviously been too involved with their own business to pay any attention.

Lenatus had a napkin draped over his knees to wipe his hands as he applied the ointment. He tossed it over Corylus's manhood and rose to face her, standing between Alphena and his patient. The pot of ointment smelled like sheep.

"Your ladyship, you shouldn't be here," Lenatus said. His expression was one of cold misery, like that of a brave man who has just been sentenced to death. "Please leave now."

"Who are you to tell me where I can go in my father's house, you *servant*?" Alphena said. She heard her voice rising to a scream and hated it, but she could no more control the tone than she could stop breathing. "Don't you *dare* give me orders!"

Lenatus flinched, but he didn't move. In a quiet voice without inflection he said, "Your ladyship." It wasn't a plea or a complaint, just the simplest acknowledgment he could make of the fact that the young mistress was shouting at him.

Alphena gasped, appalled at herself. She thought of the look on the scullery maid's face when she recognized her mistress.

The trainer knew that no matter what he did in the present situation, there was a good chance that he would be dismissed and possibly crucified. All the servants knew what it meant to anger their ladyships, Alphena as surely as Hedia.

If Lenatus let her stay while he worked on Corylus's injuries, however, her father's social position meant he would *have* to take action if he learned about it. The trainer was bound to have at least one enemy among the hundreds of servants in the town house, so Saxa would surely learn.

Varus stepped forward. He'd put down the basin, but his hands were still wet from wringing out the bloody sponge.

"Sister," he said with a dignity that Alphena didn't recall him displaying in the past. "Please show courtesy to our guest, Master Corylus. He isn't an exotic animal on display at the Games."

Alphena stepped back into the corridor, but she kept hold of the door. "Yes," she said. "Master Corylus, I apologize. I'm, I . . . tonight was upsetting. And to you too, Lenatus."

"Thank you, Sister," said Varus, reaching out to take the door from her.

"A moment, please," Alphena said sharply. Speaking as though the trainer were a curtain, she said, "Master Corylus, you won't be going to the auguries for my father's consulship tomorrow morning, will you?"

Lenatus had given a sigh of relief when Alphena backed

from the bathhouse. He stiffened again, though this time he looked wary instead of doomed.

"Ah, no, your ladyship," Corylus said. If she could have seen his expression, it probably would have been as careful as the trainer's was. "It's a nonbusiness day so we don't have class, but I thought I'd go home and . . . well, to be honest, I'd reassure Anna. She fusses over me, you know."

"I'll leave you with Lenatus now," Alphena said. "But promise you'll train with me tomorrow before you leave."

There was frozen silence from the bathhouse. Alphena added, "At the fourth hour. And I understand, we won't be sparring."

"Yes, your ladyship," Corylus said.

Alphena grimaced. She wanted to hit something. She wanted to hit Corylus.

Unexpectedly, Corylus—still hidden behind the trainer—went on, "Sure, Alphena. And it would probably be good for my knee. I'd like that."

Mother Juno, thank you, Alphena thought reflexively. She kept the words from reaching her tongue. Aloud she said, "But Brother, you have to come with me now. They don't need you here, and I do."

"Surely there's no impropriety in my remaining with my good friend!" Varus said in surprise. The dignity was there again, but this time it was offended.

"It's not that," Alphena said peevishly. "I need to talk to you. You know history, don't you?"

"Well, yes . . . ," he said doubtfully. He looked over his shoulder.

Lenatus bowed slightly. "We'll be all right, your lordship," he said. His relief at getting Alphena out of the way was obvious.

Alphena's renewed irritation turned to a grin when another thought occurred to her. It could be that Lenatus was just as glad not to be present while the two youths discussed things that might be dangerous for a servant to know.

"What do you want to know?" Varus said as he came outside and firmly closed the bathhouse door behind him. He paused, then said, "Corylus is well-read too, of course; but I'm, well, probably the right person to ask."

"Let's go out into the garden," Alphena said, thinking of the crowd of servants who were probably clustering close to where she and Varus stood in the short hallway. The garden wasn't large, but it would give them more privacy.

With her brother following obediently, Alphena walked past the gymnasium and through the open door into the garden. As she'd expected, half a dozen of the servants she'd rousted from the bathhouse entrance were there, talking in muted voices with the night doorman. They stared in concern as she and Varus entered.

"Leave now," Alphena said. To the doorman she added, "You too, Maximus. Stand outside the gate until I call you."

She spoke calmly, but after her recent rage the servants fled through the back gate as though she were chasing them with branding irons. They'd reenter the house by the front entrance, as many of their fellows must have done already.

As the doorman pulled the iron-strapped gate closed behind him, Varus slid the heavy bar through its staples. He walked back to face Alphena as she stood between the two fruit trees.

"Now, Sister," he said. "What is it you want to know in such secrecy? Not history, surely."

Maximus had taken his lantern outside with him, but the moon's cool light was full on Varus's face. He looked like the marble statue of a philosopher.

Whatever happened tonight changed him, Alphena thought. *Into a man, I think.*

"It is history," she said. She swallowed. "At least I think it is. Have you ever heard of a man named Spurius Cassius? I think he must be dead."

Varus didn't speak for a moment. Then he said, "I can check the lists of magistrates which some of the temples keep, and perhaps the Cassius family has records which they would let me see." He smiled with quiet pride. "I dare say they would show me whatever they have," he added. "For Father's name, but they will have heard of my interest as well, I believe."

"But you don't know of anybody yourself?" Alphena said in frustration. She had so hoped for an answer!

Her brother raised his hand in curt negation. "I didn't say that," he said. "In fact the only man of that name whom I do recall has been dead for over five hundred years. He was one of the earliest consuls of the Republic, a great general who led our armies to several victories. But when he tried to become king, he was captured and executed in his own home. The house was pulled down over him and a temple was built on the site."

"Brother," Alphena said. She wrapped her arms around herself as though she were cold. "Which temple was it? Do you know?"

Varus frowned. "I'd have to check," he said. "Does it matter to you? I think Cicero may mention it in the oration he gave when the Senate voted to rebuild his house. I'm sure I can find it somewhere."

"Was it the Temple of Tellus?" Alphena said, looking at the ground. "Tell me, *was* it?"

"Why yes, I believe you're right," said Varus. "That's the one Father is renovating, isn't it? The dedicated gifts were brought right here to the garden, in fact. See the tusks? It happened while I was, ah, reading here."

"Tonight the statue told me I was going to marry

Spurius Cassius," Alphena said. She felt tears welling up in her eyes. She went on, knowing that she was blubbering. "And he's dead! He's *dead*!"

"Ah . . . ," said Varus. "I . . ."

He put his arms around Alphena as she cried. He was very awkward, but she appreciated what her brother was trying to do.

But in her heart, Alphena wished he were Corylus instead.

A CELTIC FOOTMAN, one of the three waiting at the door to Varus's bedroom suite, said, "Your lordship, Master Corylus is already inside. We told him you were in the library, but he said he preferred to go to bed."

"Very good, Asterix," Varus said, more polite in his acknowledgment than most people would have thought necessary. Politeness, even to a slave, cost nothing. He'd heard philosophers say, "A man has as many enemies as he has slaves," and during riots and other unrest, a servant's hostility could be fatal to his master.

The Republic was at peace now, though of course that might change when the Emperor—not a young man—died. Even so, Varus was polite simply because he preferred to be. As a general rule he didn't care much about other people, but he found life more pleasant when those nearby weren't angry with him.

Another footman inside the suite whisked the door open and bowed as deeply as if he were welcoming an imperial delegation. "Your lordship!" he said.

Varus forced a smile. The fellow was new and apparently hadn't been told—or didn't believe—that pomp made the young master uncomfortable. *I'll speak to Agrippinus in the morning,* he thought.

"You may leave the suite now," he said aloud. "Are there any more of you here?"

There were, of course: three male servants and the

maid who was responsible for straightening the bed-clothes stepped forward to call attention to themselves. Corylus, beside what would ordinarily be the night servant's alcove, smiled a greeting standing.

Varus gestured. "You may all leave, please," he said. "If we need anything during the night, we'll call for it."

The servants bustled from the room, though the new footman seemed so confused that he was on the edge of arguing. The maid slapped him on the back of the head and hissed a warning. Two servants fought to slam the door behind them.

"Perhaps we could go out in the courtyard?" Corylus said, raising an eyebrow.

"And have spectators on the balcony as well as at ground level?" Varus said, smiling at his friend. "Here, sit on your bed and I'll draw up this"—he picked up a square wicker stool; its legs were only four inches tall, but it would keep his buttocks off the floor—"seat."

Corylus liked to be outdoors; so did Varus, for that matter. But Corylus thought of "outdoors" as the great forests flanking the Rhine and the Danube. Here in Carce it meant an open space surrounded by people listening.

"Did you find anything useful in the library?" Corylus asked politely, seating himself when Varus did. He was being extremely cautious. That was natural after what had been happening, but it saddened Varus to see his friend—his only friend—feeling that he too might be a danger.

"In a manner of speaking," said Varus, smiling at the thought. "I read Vergil to calm down; as you probably guessed, since you courteously chose not to disturb me."

Corylus laughed. "Well," he said, "I *hoped* that was what you were doing. Though I might have suggested somebody lighter than Vergil."

"The *Aeneid* not only has structure, it *is* a structured universe all by itself," Varus said, letting his mind slip back for a moment into the great epic's measured cadences. "The structure of our world seems to be melting away like ice in the sunshine."

He shrugged and realized that the gesture had been more violent than he'd intended. "I didn't try to find anything dealing with our problem. I wouldn't know where to start. Even Pandareus didn't know where to start!"

"We'll deal with things as they come up, my friend," Corylus said gently. "I've had the advantage of being with soldiers in the field. You learn fast there that you can't plan for the worst things, but that doesn't mean you can't survive them. At least you and I can trust our leaders."

"Pandareus and Atilius, you mean?" Varus said. "Yes, you're right. And this Menre who spoke to Pandareus—he must be on our side too. Perhaps he'll appear shortly and give us some direction more useful than simply telling our teacher to come to Carce."

They chuckled together. Varus felt better just for being with his friend. Corylus was in his way just as solid as Vergil's perfectly constructed epic.

The wooden staff leaned against the wall of the alcove, beside the headrest where Corylus could snatch it instantly if an alarm awakened him in the night. It had been wiped clean of fur and blood, then apparently waxed. Alphena must have told a servant to polish it before returning it to its owner.

Which forced Varus to think about his sister. And about his friend.

"Alphena was holding a marriage divination in the Temple of Tellus tonight," he said, looking at the mosaic floor. In the center were Neptune and his bride Amphitrite, while all manner of sea creatures swam in the border running along the walls. By sheer effort of will, he raised his eyes to meet those of Corylus.

"She—and my stepmother—heard a voice saying that

she was going to marry Spurius Cassius," he continued, keeping his voice calm. "I think that must mean the would-be tyrant of five hundred years ago. The temple was built where his house was."

Corylus smiled. "And here I was wondering if our rhetorical training would ever be useful in normal life," he said. "Cassius is the rhetorical model of a man who reached the highest level in the Republic, consul and even dictator, and then fell to the depths of ignominy to be executed for treason. He was so perfect"—his grin grew playful—"that I wondered if he was real or just the creation of orators who weren't above improving history for a really good example."

"I recall mention of him in the Chronicles of the Claudian Family," Varus said. "I believe he was real. A very clever, dynamic man, but unfortunately a man who wouldn't stop at anything to gain the power he wanted."

He thought back to the week he'd spent in the library of one of his father's senatorial colleagues. He'd been looking for information on the First Punic War for his epic, but he'd found a great deal of other interesting information also. The oldest scrolls had been written on leather, not papyrus.

"That he was executed," Varus continued, looking into his friend's calm eyes, "was both the law and common sense: the Republic would be in danger for as long as he lived. But the particular savagery of his execution and the fact that his house was pulled down over him—I think that must have been because the other senators were terrified of him."

Varus made a deprecating gesture, turning his palms up and then down again before him. "That's how I would have described him," he said, "if I'd written an epic on the early Republic as I considered doing: an enemy as great as Hannibal, but growing in the heart of the Carce instead of attacking us from the outside."

A pang of embarrassment twisted his face. *I was such a fool to think that I could be a poet!*

"Varus?" Corylus said. His voice was perfectly calm, but a hint of worry pinched the corners of his eyes.

"Sorry," Varus said. "It wasn't anything important; I was thinking about my poetry. And that's *certainly*"—he didn't even try to hide the bitterness and embarrassment— "not important."

Corylus cocked his head to the side. "I think you're wrong," he said. "Poetry mattered to you, and you were willing to put in the effort to do it. Not many people really try to do anything." He smiled and added, "I'm proud to know you."

Varus opened his mouth to snap, "And did you like my epic?" His mind caught the reflexive sourness before it reached his tongue, though.

He smiled broadly and said, "Thank you. I put in enough effort to prove beyond the shadow of a doubt that I have no talent for poetry. Perhaps I should have concentrated my efforts on swordsmanship like my sister."

Corylus's face became completely blank. Varus winced at the expression and said, "I was *joking*. Yes, I know you've seen me doing sword exercises. Although it could be that I'd still make a better gladiator than I would a poet."

"If you put in the effort, Lenatus and I could turn you into a passable swordsman," Corylus said carefully. "It would take a *lot* of effort."

"Whereas Alphena is pretty good, isn't she?" Varus said. The conversation was where he needed it to be. He'd vainly hoped that his pause in the library would show him the way to broach the difficult topic; sitting down and talking to his friend had been the right answer.

"Yes," said Corylus simply. He looked directly at Varus, but his face wasn't giving anything away. "Not as good as she thinks, but good. If she were sparring instead of hitting the post, she'd learn she lacks strength. She's got lots of stamina, though."

"You're not going to be sparring with her tomorrow, though," Varus said. He didn't make the words a command, but he wasn't asking a question either.

"Not tomorrow or any other time, Varus," Corylus said. He stood up, but that was just to make him less uncomfortable. To show he wasn't trying to threaten his friend with his height and strength, he turned sideways. His hand squeezed the corner of the alcove. "I wouldn't do that, and Lenatus wouldn't let me if I tried. And"—he grinned again, but from his tone this wasn't a joke—"if he needed Pulto's help to convince me, he'd have it."

Varus stood also. "She's my sister," he said to the wall fresco of a Cyclops standing on a rocky cliff. "After she's married, she's her husband's concern. But for now she's my sister."

Corylus put his arm over his friend's shoulder. "Varus," he said, "believe me, it never crossed my mind. And I don't mean just because of the difference in our stations. Alphena doesn't interest me."

Neither of them was mentioning Alphena's father. Varus grimaced. *With me the closest thing in the family to a man, no wonder Alphena behaves the way she does!*

"I do believe you," Varus said. "But it's pretty obvious, even to me, that she's interested in you."

Corylus said, "Well, she's going to have to put a lot more snap into her backhand cuts before *I'll* give her more than a peck on the cheek."

Varus felt his torso turn to ice. He stared at his friend's perfectly straight face—then burst out laughing. "I'm sorry, Corylus," he gasped. "You told me, so I should have just shut up. As I'm doing now."

"Do you believe that Cassius is behind . . . ," Corylus said, as though Alphena's name hadn't come up at all.

He gestured with his right hand. "That Cassius sent your visions and all the other things? Because I still think Nemastes is involved."

He paused as though wondering whether to speak further, then went on. "A woman I met when the dogs attacked me said Nemastes was responsible. And I don't think they were dogs. They were wolves."

He sighed. "Also," he said to the mosaic of Neptune and Amphitrite, "I was in a forest, not Carce. I just ducked into an alley and I was. I don't know how that could have happened either."

"You had sap and pine needles on your tunic," Varus said. Corylus was wearing a tunic borrowed from a footman of roughly the right size. Varus was too stocky to loan his friend any garment but a toga, all of which were cut to a standard size. "Along with the blood. I suppose you could have gotten them in Carce, but if you say you were somewhere else, I don't have a problem believing it."

He waited till his friend raised his face, and added, "If you say you were dancing with nymphs in the moonlight, Corylus, I believe that too. I don't know what's going on, but I know I trust you."

"We weren't dancing," Corylus said steadily, "and there wasn't much moon. But I think she was a nymph. A rose nymph. In the forest. Though it was firs, not pines."

"Well, I was happy to have a three-hundred-year-old Egyptian as an ally," Varus said. "I'm not going to turn down nymphs and dryads. We need all the help we can get, it seems to me."

He was still at a loss about what was happening, but it didn't bother him as much as it had before he and Corylus began to talk. Some of the things hiding in his ignorance were *good*; and as for the bad surprises—he and his friends had survived them so far. Though—

"I hope nobody sends a wolf after me," Varus said aloud.

Corylus grinned, but the expression wasn't entirely one of humor. "It was a pack of wolves," he said. "And the only thing that saved me was the woman, mainly because she sent me back to Carce."

He cleared his throat while looking at the wall, then faced Varus again. "Your father knows Nemastes," he said. "And your father is the one who's rebuilding the temple where this Cassius spoke to your sister. Varus, is Saxa . . . ?"

Varus swallowed, appreciative of the way his friend had let the question trail off. He said, keeping his voice calm, "My father isn't a conspirator, Corylus. He isn't capable of conspiring, even if he were willing to. I can imagine him weeping in his bed for days, but he wouldn't have sent Alphena and Hedia into a trap if he'd known what he was doing. And he certainly couldn't have set a pack of wolves on you."

The thought amused him, though he knew his smile was a poor excuse for one. "Like as not," he said, "he would have fallen into the wolf pen if he'd tried."

"Sorry," Corylus muttered. "It was a silly thing to say."

"No, it was a question that had to be asked," said Varus, feeling stronger as he spoke. "My father has gathered more information than any other person I know. None of it's connected, though. I don't think he could use it to do anything, either good *or* bad. He isn't disciplined. But"—he felt his face stiffen, and looked toward the frescoed Cyclops again—"he has a superstitious streak. And that might make it possible for someone who *is* disciplined to lead him in bad directions."

Corylus clasped Varus's hand. "We'll deal with Nemastes," he said. "And if Spurius Cassius is with Nemastes, we'll deal with him too. We *will*, friend."

It made no logical sense, but the confidence in Corylus's voice made Varus hopeful again.

"And now," Varus said, "we'll sleep."

CORYLUS WAS DREAMING. He knew that, but the wind through the forest was chill and the ground felt cold beneath his bare feet. There were patches of snow between the spruce trees.

He was wearing the tunic he'd borrowed to sleep in; it wasn't sufficient clothing here. The sun was well below zenith, but he suspected that meant he was looking south. He must be dreaming of the far north: farther than his physical body had ever been.

A bird jeered angrily, then flew through the straggling branches to another hidden perch. It looked like a jay, but the rusty brown color was wrong, and its tail seemed too long.

Corylus listened intently. There were distant birds and a chatter which might have been a bird or a squirrel. Over everything else came the rustle and creak of wind through the branches.

He didn't hear wolves. If he didn't find food and shelter soon, wolves wouldn't be necessary to dispose of him.

He grinned at the thought. Apparently he'd stopped pretending that he believed he was dreaming.

A pair of ravens curved through the trees. One landed on a sandstone boulder the size of a man's chest; the other gripped the trunk of a spruce for a moment, then croaked harshly and hopped to the ground.

The birds stared at him, cocking their heads sideways. Neither was more than ten feet away. *I'm not hungry enough to try to eat a raven. I'll never be that hungry.*

"You see?" said one raven to the other. "I told you he was injured."

"Not seriously, though," said the other. "He'll still be able to accompany us."

The second raven looked at Corylus, twitching its head slightly side to side so that one eye or the other was always looking at him. "You can walk, can't you?" it said.

They were huge birds, even on the ground with their wings folded. Overhead they had a black majesty more impressive than that of most hawks.

Corylus flexed his right leg. The knee felt constricted as though he were wearing heavy breeches, but it bent and there wasn't even as much pain as he had expected.

"Yes," he said. "If I want to go."

"Want!" said the second raven. It gave another croak, scarcely less harsh than its normal speaking voice. "Do you want to stay and freeze to death, is that it? You have that choice surely, but no other choice."

Corylus wished he had sandals. He would have liked to have a heavy cloak and a woolen scarf to wrap around his head, but sandals were what he would have described as necessary if he'd had the slightest hope of getting them. There wasn't, and he wasn't about to give up.

"All right," he said. "Where do we go?"

The ravens hopped twice to turn, then lifted with powerful wing beats. They didn't answer. *It* was *a silly question, I suppose.*

Corylus started at a trot, though he wasn't sure how long he could keep it up. The birds curved to the ground only fifty feet away, their black plumage gleaming against the snow.

Despite their being willing to wait for him, Corylus decided to continue trotting for as long as he could. The exercise warmed him, though his feet would lose feeling before very long. "How far are we going?" he called.

"Not far," said a raven. They looked back at him over their shoulders.

"It will seem far to him the first time," said the other raven. "But no, not very far."

The birds flapped off but again landed within sight.

Their beaks were deep black chisels. Ravens would eat carrion, but they also killed their own prey when opportunity sent them a lemming or a young rabbit.

If these are really birds.

"Friend ravens?" Corylus said as he approached the waiting birds again. "What are your names?"

The ravens hopped to face him. "You ask a great thing, youth," one said.

"A greater thing than you know," said the other. "A greater thing than you have any right to know!"

Corylus stopped, still-faced. "I am Publius, son of Publius, Cispius Corylus," he said, raising his voice so that it rang through the silent trees. "I am a citizen of Carce, born in the province of Upper Germany. What are your names, fellow creatures?"

Their croaks rattled like stones bouncing down a cliff face. Corylus thought they might be laughing.

"You may regret it later," said the one to the other.

"Regret, regret," replied the other. "And yet I will still speak my name. Corylus, I am Wisdom, and my companion who worries about what might have been—"

"I am Memory," said the second raven. "Others may forget the past if they wish to or must, but the past will not forget them."

"Are you content, Corylus?" said Wisdom.

"Yes sir," said Corylus. *How do you tell the sex of a raven?* But the birds were already airborne, curving toward him to gain height and then swooping off in the direction they had been going before.

The ground rose as they went on. The whole surface glittered, as if the crust of snow had grown thicker. It didn't feel cold, though, and Corylus didn't crunch through it as he had initially.

He wondered if his feet were growing numb. He could still feel the shock of each stride, though.

The ravens arced up and down, often crossing in the

air. When they landed they took a hop or two; they were heavy birds and didn't stop where they first touched. Their eyes gleamed like polished coal when they looked back.

The rhythm of the run numbed Corylus's mind. His consciousness blurred into a tunnel directly ahead of him; the edges were at first white and gleaming like ice, then gray, and finally a pastel aura that shifted as his heart beat.

The trees were shapes that he avoided. The snow on their crinkled bark sparkled like diamond dust. The trunks became crystalline pillars, then columns of light. Eventually their light merged with greater light and vanished.

Corylus jogged on. He would run until he dropped. He would run forever.

The ravens were no longer flying; they appeared ahead of him, then were gone and reappeared. "Once the Midworld ended in ice," said one. "Stopping all, burying all. Ice could rule forever."

"But not this time," said the other raven. "The Midworld will burn. Fire will lick the heavens, fire will drink the seas. Everything will burn."

"Unless Corylus prevents it," said the first. "But he won't. His memories of friendship will prevent him from saving the future."

"And the fire will rule all," said the ravens together in croaking laughter. "All things, forever!"

Corylus saved his breath for running. He didn't have anything to say, not really; until he knew more.

He knew nothing. And he had to run.

The ground had become a surface of pastels that wobbled into one another so subtly that Corylus was never sure when one color became another. He thought he was still climbing. His legs throbbed and his breath rasped through his mouth like drafts of fire.

The fire will rule all . . . , he heard, but that might have been memory.

Ahead was a white haze, unguessably distant. The ravens flickered present and gone, barely distinguishable from the black spots that fatigue sent dancing across his vision.

Corylus glanced over his shoulder, careful not to lose his stride and trip. *How far could I fall?*

At first he saw nothing behind him but stars and the blackness of night. When he blinked, he noticed the blue dot—no bigger than a lentil but still larger than the hard spikes of the constellations.

Corylus faced the bright haze before him again and ran on. The ravens were just ahead, close enough for him to call to. He had nothing to say, and he had no breath to say it with.

His legs were logs of wood. He was afraid to slow to a walk, afraid that he would think about where he was and what he was doing. There were no answers, but he was a citizen of Carce, a soldier of the Republic, and he would go on until he died.

Corylus burst through the whiteness into a forest of larches. The twigs had their spring buds, but the air was chill and melting traceries of ice overlay the leaf litter.

Before him was a hillside whose thin soil had slipped in gray patches from the rock beneath. A cave entered it. The ravens waited to either side of the opening.

"I told you he could follow," said the bird on the right to its companion.

"Enter the cave now, Corylus," said the other. "You won't come so far and not go the last of the way, will you?"

"He might be wiser if he did," said the first. "But he will go in, and the future will come. The fire will come!"

"The fire will come!" repeated both birds together, then slipped into croaking laughter.

Corylus strode forward. He had to keep moving or his legs would stiffen into agonizing knots. He *had* to move.

The cave opened about him. Its walls were so full of light that the interior was brighter than the forest outside. The ceiling was higher than the hill outside.

The only furniture within the cavern was a high-backed chair in the far distance; on it sat a figure in a gray cloak. His features were largely hidden by his wide-brimmed traveler's hat, but the spill of his full gray beard left no doubt of his gender.

The ravens flew past Corylus, rising on a flurry of strong wing beats before gliding in interwoven curves toward the distant throne. They croaked, the sound diminishing as their black shapes faded against the light. When they croaked again, it was in a harsh whisper.

Corylus had paused in shock when he passed the entrance. He sighed and started forward, wondering how long it would take him to reach the seated figure. The air of the cavern had a bluish tinge as though the light were passing through thick ice as Corylus had occasionally seen on the Rhine, but he no longer felt cold. Perhaps that was a sign that he was freezing to death, though—he smiled grimly—he didn't feel sleepy, and his lungs still burned with the effort they'd just expended. He wouldn't mind a little numbness there, and in the throbbing muscles of his thighs as well. Then—

Corylus was standing at the foot of the throne. There hadn't been a transition: in the middle of a step he was facing the seated man, who glared from his one visible eye.

He was tall but not a giant. He gripped the crossguards of a long sword, still in the scabbard; its round point rested on the floor between his feet. Though the cloak hid his body, his fingers suggested gnarled tree roots rather than the bulging muscles of a bull.

Wisdom and Memory perched on the chair-back to

either side of the man's head. They opened their beaks as though they were ready to laugh, but neither words nor croaking issued. Their tongues were black.

"Sir!" said Corylus, bracing himself at parade rest. "Why have you brought me here?"

The bearded man laughed. The sound boomed like surf during a winter storm and there was no more humor in it than that.

"I haven't brought you, boy," he said. "You came of your own choice. If you want to go back without hearing me, I'll let you do so now."

"You asked *our* names, Publius Corylus," said Memory. "Other guests have asked the name of our lord, and he has told them."

"But he put a forfeit on them in exchange for answering their question," said Wisdom from the other finial of the chair-back.

"They paid the forfeit and rued every moment of their lives to come," said Memory, cocking one eye and then the other toward Corylus.

The birds laughed. The sound reminded Corylus of the croaking he had heard one winter when he'd found ravens feasting on the carcass of a deer.

"Your lordship," he said in a clear voice to the bearded man. He didn't bow. "I am Publius Corylus. What is it that you can tell me about the danger facing the Republic?"

"A wise youth," the fellow rumbled. He smiled, but the expression was one that might have better fitted a wolf met on a forest trail. "How wise are you really, though? Will you take my advice?"

"Your lordship," said Corylus. "I will do whatever I believe most benefits the Republic."

The man laughed again, but with even less humor than before. "I thought I had summoned a warrior," he said, his voice growing louder. "But here it seems I have a lawyer instead. Is that true, boy? Are you warrior or lawyer?"

"Your lordship," said Corylus, swallowing, "I'm both. Or—trained as both. I will not take a stranger's judgment over my own and the judgment of those whom I have learned to trust."

"If he weren't a warrior, One-Eye," said Wisdom, "he would not have dared be a lawyer to your face."

"Offer him the mead," said Memory. "Men sometimes find fellowship in drink."

"And sometimes drink brings death," said Wisdom. The ravens laughed together.

The bearded man shrugged with a grim smile. He reached to his side with his left hand; a drinking horn, gold-banded and studded with smoothly polished jewels, suddenly rested on it. He drank from the horn, then held it out.

"Take it, warrior," he said to Corylus. "Drink your fill. Drink it all, if you can."

The horn was twisted and heavy in Corylus's hands. If it came from a ram, it had been bigger than any sheep he'd ever seen.

He sipped. The liquor was dry and very strong, carrying the aroma of the herbs it had been brewed with. It and the word which the raven had called it by, mead, were unfamiliar.

Corylus found it difficult to handle the drinking horn without spilling. He'd seen such forms before—and had also seen human skulls mounted as cups by German chieftains—but he'd never tried to use one before.

"A sip for fellowship," he said as he handed the liquor back. Being drunk wouldn't help him in this situation, whatever the situation was. "Your lordship, why are these things happening to me? I'm no magician or priest."

The bearded man lifted the horn and turned his hand, sending the mead out of the present. He bent forward slightly and said, "Twelve wizards of Hyperborea plan to loose the Sons of Muspelheim on Midworld, smothering you and all men in fire."

"Nemastes!" Corylus blurted.

"When the Band was thirteen, Nemastes was among them," said the bearded man. "Now they are the Twelve and Nemastes fights to block their plans."

Corylus rocked back on his heels. "Sir," he said, "then Nemastes isn't our enemy? He wants to save us?"

The bearded man grinned. "Save you for cattle," said Wisdom.

"Oh, he's *your* enemy, Publius Corylus," said Memory. "He believes that you're the agent the Twelve have sent to stop him, as their bodies cannot leave the Horn."

"But why would he think that?" said Corylus in puzzlement. "Why would any man want to stop him? That would mean to spread Vulcan's fires across the earth."

"Why indeed, Corylus," said Wisdom. "And yet your friend Varus is the tool of the Twelve."

"You are active and resourceful," said Memory. "So long as Nemastes thinks that the wizards whom he deserted are working through you, he will not pay attention to your friend. Until too late, while your world burns."

There was no transition. As the words rang in his ears, Corylus stood over a sea of bubbling lava, orange and red and licked with the blue flames of sulfur. In every direction, fire lapped the horizon. The rock roared deafeningly, and the sky was a pall of black destruction.

Corylus was back in the cave again, staggered by the vision. *Was this what Varus saw in the temple?*

"Midworld will burn," said the bearded man, leaning back on his throne. "All who worship me in all times will burn. So, lawyer who is a warrior, you must act now: you must kill this Varus, for your own sake and your world's."

"I won't kill my friend!" Corylus said. "I won't kill anybody because you say to!"

"Then you'll watch Midworld die!" the bearded man said. "You'll watch *your* world die. And your friend will burn with you, you fool!"

The walls of frozen light shivered to his booming voice, their color changing from bluish through green and yellow to red. When he fell silent, they trembled back to their cool resting state.

Fear made Corylus want to run or to strike, but it was his duty to learn how to save his world. Not by killing his friend, though.

"Your lordship," he said. "I'll talk to Varus. He must not realize what he's doing. When he does he, well, he *won't*."

"Will he believe you?" Wisdom asked. The ravens laughed.

The bearded man didn't speak for a moment, but thunder boomed within the great cavern. The eye Corylus could see beneath the hat's broad brim glittered like a light-struck sapphire.

"The Twelve have caught your friend, boy!" the bearded man said. "He won't listen to you. He *can't*."

"If Gaius Varus dies now, the Twelve will not have time to find another cat's-paw . . . ," said Wisdom. The bird's tone was musing, not imperative. "Nemastes will shift the fire onto them instead."

"Many men have died," said Memory. "Throughout all time, every man born on Midworld has died—"

"—or will die," Wisdom concluded.

"This Varus will destroy Nemastes," the bearded man said, "and the Twelve will destroy Midworld. Unless you act, warrior!"

"Your lordship," said Corylus. He swallowed; his mouth was very dry. "I will not."

"Fool!" said the bearded man.

"And yet," said Memory, "you have not always acted on the knowledge that you yourself bought at such a price, One-Eye."

"The regret of a friend's murder would be a terrible thing," said Wisdom. "Better perhaps that Midworld should die; in fire this time."

"As before it died in ice," agreed Memory. "Better by far."

"Fool!" repeated the bearded man, rising from the throne. He was greater than the cavern; its ceiling split in thunder, and the starry universe above burst more loudly still.

Corylus was falling. He would have shouted, but he had no breath in his lungs. He flailed in nothingness—

And shot upright. He was in the servant's alcove of Varus's suite. Moonlight streamed through the clerestory windows in the outside wall.

Corylus's legs were cold. When he rubbed them, he found that his bare feet were wet with crystals of melting ice. He took a deep breath.

He'd thrown the coverlet off in the night; he hadn't needed it in this weather. Smiling grimly, he tugged it up to cover his legs, then lay back on the couch and twitched shut the curtain.

He didn't remember when he'd been so tired. He was asleep in moments, and he didn't dream.

CHAPTER IX

Hedia turned with regal care, looking south over the sprawling city. Her maids had teased her hair high and held it in place with silver-chased ebony combs. Her coiffure included a lace mantilla also, which wasn't as good an idea on top of the Capitoline Hill as it had seemed in her bedroom: the stiff breeze whipped it violently.

She didn't want to look a fool by having her hair rearranged in public—in front of the chief temple in Carce, as a matter of fact. On the other hand, she'd look even more of a fool if the *damned* lace tore or tugged the combs loose to go clattering across the pavement.

Hedia minded less that her tunics and the short purple cloak she wore over them were being pressed hard against her body. It was quite a good body, and—she smiled—there were several very presentable men among the hundreds of spectators here for her husband's auguries. Hedia wasn't actively hunting, but she'd found that it never hurt to keep her options open.

Saxa was talking with the priest of Jupiter—the *Flamen Dialis*—who would officiate over the ceremony. He was Gnaeus Naevius, Hedia's cousin by her first marriage.

Like all the other relatives of Calpurnius Latus, Naevius had blamed Hedia for the problems of the marriage. She hadn't expected the family to take her side—they were bound by blood to support her husband—but the venomous attacks on her had seemed extremely unjust. They of all people knew what kind of a man Latus really was.

Still, she knew not to expect justice in this world. In fact, she knew her own sins too well to *want* justice. She smiled coolly as Naevius, feeling her eyes on him, looked up. He flushed and resumed his conversation with Saxa with loud enthusiasm.

Varus stood at the grove of cypresses, writing in a notebook while his servants chatted among themselves. Nearby were the half a dozen senators who had come to watch Saxa take the auguries and then swear the oath to defend the Republic during the period of his consulate.

Which would be a few weeks or perhaps a month, unless the Emperor decided to shorten the period still further. It had always been possible to appoint a temporary consul to replace one who had died. Now that the Emperor was guiding the Republic, it had become the practice of consuls to resign after a brief term to make way for more of their fellow senators in the office.

There were several hundred general spectators also, held at a proper distance by temple servants stretching a plush rope. Many seemed to be either urban idlers or countrymen here for the show, but among them Hedia noticed Varus's teacher, Pandareus. She'd seen him declaiming in the Forum, but they'd never been introduced. Given that there was a delay in the ceremony—Venus knew why, but the reason didn't matter any more than the rest of the completely empty spectacle—it was a good time to rectify that omission from her duties as mother.

Hedia strode toward her son, followed by her train of servants. They had learned to jump when she moved. She didn't care much whether they followed her, but woe betide anybody who got in her way because he hadn't been paying attention.

Varus looked up, saw her, and straightened. He'd been bracing his right foot against the tree behind him and resting the wax-leafed notebook on his raised thigh. His expression as she approached was reserved rather than welcoming.

"Are you working on your poem, Son?" Hedia said brightly. Perhaps if she showed some interest in his activities, he might stop viewing her as a potential enemy.

The boy's careful expression became glacial. "I must have risen in your estimation to be worth mocking," he said. "I suppose I should feel honored."

He put his foot against the tree bole again and reopened his notebook. He pulled the bronze stylus from its clip on the spine and poised to resume writing.

Hedia stepped forward and snatched the notebook away. Varus looked up in amazement. Hedia *clack*ed the leaves shut under his nose.

"Listen, young man!" she said. "I said nothing that I thought would be offensive to you; but if I had, that is my *right* as the mother of a son who has not been emancipated."

Hedia had been leaning toward him. Now she straightened and offered him the notebook. "If you'll courteously explain my mistake," she said, "I won't make it again."

She took a deep breath and urged herself to relax. Her anger hadn't been a pretense, though she knew the boy's silliness wasn't the real cause.

Varus blinked; it was a moment before he noticed the notebook and took it back with embarrassment. "Mother," he said. "You weren't present at my reading, of course."

"I've never pretended to know anything about poetry," Hedia said quietly, slightly regretful of her outburst. Still, with men it was never a bad idea to go with honest passion if you could manage it. "If you'd wanted me at your reading, Varus, I would have attended."

That probably wasn't true. Not only did she know nothing about poetry, but listening to it struck her as only slightly less boring than watching plaster set. It was the politic thing to say now, however.

"I'm sorry, of course you needn't have done that," Varus said, looking down but then forcing himself to meet her eyes again. "I was terrible. My poem was terrible. There was, there were the other things too, but I mean the poem. And I won't make a fool of myself that way anymore."

He was a *very* nice boy, though what he really needed was something his mother couldn't provide him with. Hedia smiled and gestured with her index finger toward the notebook. "If not verse . . . ?" she said.

"Ah!" said Varus, brightening visibly. "Well, you see, I realized that many of the rites of the Republic have never been written down. They're passed on orally in the priestly colleges when a new man is inducted. But I thought, there should be a formal record of the rites and procedures for scholars who don't happen to be priests to consult."

He gestured to the crowd. "It isn't secret, after all," he said. "And I thought, well, *I* could be the person who collects the information!"

Hedia's gaze followed the line of his arm. The senators were becoming restive, and the rural folk were beginning to drift away. Perhaps they were getting something to eat and drink, because hawkers weren't allowed within the walled precincts.

"For instance," Varus burbled, "they haven't been able to begin the auguries yet because all the birds which have flown over the temple have come from the left side. The priest's left, of course."

"I thought they were using chickens," Hedia said in puzzlement. "And if they eat the grain, then my lord's consulate will be auspicious."

The grain would be the first food the birds had seen in a full day. The consuls who'd been in command when Hannibal wiped out the Republic's army at Cannae had performed the same ceremony; so had every other consul presiding over a disaster. Hedia wouldn't have had a great deal of faith in the auguries even if she'd believed in *any* supernatural power.

"Yes, but before that rite can be held, there has to be a bird flying from the right, the side of good fortune," Varus said. "Usually that's no problem, the temple staff tells me: there's always a pigeon or a crow or something. But today, all the birds have been coming from the sinister side."

"I see," said Hedia politely. She thought that some of the men she'd met had no more sense than a pigeon, but that still didn't mean she believed it was a good idea to hand the conduct of public business off to birds.

She cleared her throat. "I noticed your teacher in the crowd there," she resumed. "Would you introduce me, please?"

"Pandareus came?" Varus said in surprise. "Oh, by Hercules, I didn't know that! Please come, I'll do that right now!"

Hedia strode along beside him, smiling faintly. She was pleased not only to have gotten out of the lion pit she'd innocently fallen into, but apparently to have improved her relationship with her stepson in the process.

The attendants, more than a score of them together, initially followed her and Varus. When they realized that their noble principals were walking toward the crowd of spectators, the burlier males rushed ahead with cudgels lifted to drive a path through the commoners.

"Midas, stop!" Hedia said. She could too easily imagine Pandareus being laid bleeding on the ground because some flunky wanted to impress his mistress with how zealous he was.

"Balaton," said Varus unexpectedly. He gestured to the older man wearing an embroidered sash over his tunic, apparently the ranking member of the temple staff. "Tell your men to pass the learned Master Pandareus through their cordon, if you please."

"At once, Lord Varus," Balaton said. He knelt instead of passing on the order, but two servants were already performing the difficult feat of lifting the rope high while bowing the teacher through.

"Thank you very much, Lord Varus," Pandareus said. He nodded to Varus but turned his attention to Hedia. "The family crowding around me were eating the cabbage rolls they'd brought from their home in Tusculum. I fear that the cabbages had been off even before they were cooked yesterday morning."

Hedia returned the teacher's stare. He was small and very trim—clean-shaven instead of favoring the full beard which a certain type of learned man thought gave him greater credibility as a thinker.

Pandareus's tunics and sandals were simple and not new, but he didn't look poor. He wasn't young and he might in fact be seventy, but the bright interest in his expression kept him from seeming old. In all, Hedia decided that the word "neat" seemed to best describe him.

"Master Pandareus?" said Varus. "Allow me to present my mother, the noble Lady Hedia."

"Mother?" said Pandareus, raising an eyebrow. "Surely stepmother, is it not?"

"I prefer 'mother,'" Hedia said, "which is my legal

status so long as Lord Varus lives under my husband's roof."

She hadn't expected the teacher to be anything like so *sharp*. She'd wanted to meet the man from whom Varus and Corylus were getting advice on the trouble with Nemastes, but she hadn't expected to be impressed by him.

Very few men impressed Hedia, intellectually at least; Pandareus did. She'd been looked at—occasionally—as knowingly before, but never with such profound neutrality.

"Thank you, Varus," she said with a crisp nod. "I believe your teacher and I have matters to discuss before the pigeons get their orders straight. Master Pandareus?"

"Yes, thank you," said the teacher. With a polite nod to Varus—the boy looked startled but not angry at suddenly being excluded—Pandareus and Hedia walked in the direction of the Temple of Juno on the other knob of the hill.

"I heard you in the Forum three weeks ago," she said when they were out of general earshot. Her entourage kept at a distance of several paces and made sure no one got any closer than that to their mistress. "You argued that altruism was better than self-interest. I thought it was a very persuasive lecture."

"Thank you, your ladyship," Pandareus said. "But?"

A very *clever* man. "But," she said with a nod, "most lecturers would have followed that speech with another the next day which proved self-interest was better than altruism. Couldn't you have done that?"

Pandareus shrugged. "Certainly I could have," he said. "I teach young men the skills needed by a lawyer, and I would be a very poor teacher if I lacked those skills myself. The problem, you see, is that I regard myself as a teacher rather than as an entertainer. My school fees keep me in bread and vegetables, suitable fare for a philosopher. I prefer"—he stopped and met her eyes directly instead of chatting with side-glances as they walked along—"that diet to pork sausage bought at the price of my honor. Because I really believe what I said about altruism, you see."

"I see," said Hedia. She wasn't used to people being quite so blunt about the choices they were making.

"I thought you might," said Pandareus. "Seeing that you're of the same opinion. A rare one, I'm afraid."

Hedia was glad they'd stopped, because if they'd still been walking, she would have frozen in her tracks. "I don't think you'd find many people to agree with that judgment of me, Master Pandareus," she said.

Then, in part because she wanted to change the subject, she went on quickly, "Why have you come to view the ceremony, if I may ask? Are you of a religious inclination?"

"No more than they are, your ladyship," Pandareus said. He gestured toward the squad of the Praetorian Guard posted in front of the Temple of Juno; the Republic's mint was housed in the precincts of that temple. "But I thought Master Nemastes might make an appearance—"

"I'm glad he didn't!" said Hedia.

"I understand that," said the teacher, "but I fear Nemastes could be more of a problem when we don't see what he's doing than he'd be if we did."

He cleared his throat. "Regardless," he went on, "I wanted to observe what happened to Lord Varus at an event as charged with spiritual power as this one is. Odd things have been happening in your son's presence recently."

"You mean what happened last night?" Hedia said. "At this temple, I believe. Though Varus wasn't very forthcoming when we met him on the way home. Corylus had been attacked by a pack of dogs, he said."

"I won't be very forthcoming either, your ladyship,"

Pandareus said drily. "Though for what it's worth, I don't have any great insights to offer anyway. Nor did I know anything about the . . . dogs, you say?"

"*He* said dogs," Hedia corrected with mild emphasis.

Saxa and Naevius had been talking with a number of temple functionaries. One of the latter trotted toward an outbuilding. Even before he reached it, a man with triple chins and the double-striped toga of a knight waddled out, followed by four servants. Two carried a rectangular wicker cage, while the others had a baton and a small grain jar respectively.

"I gather the noble Gaius Naevius has found the omens favorable," Pandareus said. "Shall we move closer, since you have very kindly brought me through the barrier?"

"Naevius couldn't find his ass with both hands," Hedia said, letting her opinion of her former cousin by marriage show more directly than she usually would have done in front of a near stranger. She must trust the teacher more than she had any reason to do. "And I don't have much more confidence in the chickens."

Pandareus smiled faintly as they walked to where Saxa stood with the priest. "I'm sure that they'll eat," he said. "Certainly I never found any difficulty in eating after I'd fasted for a day."

"A religious rite?" Hedia said.

"No, a rite of poverty," the teacher said in the same dry deadpan as before. "Many philosophers claim that it strengthens the soul, but I don't believe my own soul would have been seriously weakened by a scrap of bread or an onion in season."

"My noble lords!" said the fat chickenkeeper. "I am Sextus Claudius Herennianus, a knight of Carce, and honored to hold the office of overseer of the sacred fowl!"

His speech would have been more impressive if he

hadn't paused to cough after the word "honored." Not very impressive, but more so.

Seeing him beside the two senators, neither of whom was exceptionally tall, Hedia realized that Herennianus would barely come up to her own ear. Not that she had any intention of letting him get that close.

"Yes, yes, man," growled Naevius. "Get on with it, won't you? We've wasted enough time already!"

Saxa looked a trifle put out by the priest's attitude. This was, after all, his moment in the highest formal position in the Republic of Carce. To Naevius, of course, it was simply a tiresome exercise that he had to perform a dozen or more times a year in exchange for his reserved box at the Games and other public events.

Hedia's smile grew harder. Naevius had never attempted to see things from any viewpoint other than his own. The fact that this nonsense was important to Saxa wouldn't cross the priest's mind—or affect his behavior if it did. She wanted to walk over and caress her husband, but this wasn't the time for it.

"Your noble lordships!" Herennianus repeated, bowing as low as his ample girth permitted. He straightened and took the baton from the servant, then used its tip to scribe a circle about three feet across in the dirt. The ground was hard, but his ragged line in the dust was adequately visible.

The chickenkeeper handed back the baton and took a small scoop in exchange. The servant with the grain jar came forward, tilting its open top toward his master. Varus had moved closer too; he was continuing to jot notes.

"I will now sprinkle the sacred—"

"Yes, you fool, get *on* with it," Naevius said.

Herennianus withdrew a scoopful of meal from the jar, but the priest's brusqueness had flustered him. He scattered half the contents onto the ground before he got

the scoop over the circle he'd drawn. He stared transfixed at the spill, then reached for the jar again.

"By Hercules, you fool!" said Naevius. "That's enough.
Just get back."

The priest paused for a moment to compose himself.
Then he pulled up a fold of his toga to cover his head
and lifted the curved rod in his right hand.

"I pray to you, Jupiter, the chief and best among the
gods, all-seeing and lord of all!" he chanted. "You are
the fulfiller who whispers into the ears of the prophets.
Be gracious, all-seeing lord of the heavens, most excellent
and great! Bless these undertakings with your wisdom!"

Naevius lowered his staff and stepped back. He looked
ready to snarl at Herennianus, but the chickenkeeper
had already gestured frantically to the servants with the
basket. They lifted off the wicker top and tipped the
opening down to decant the sacred hens into the circle.

Three birds spilled out. Their feathers were completely white; Hedia presumed that was a requirement
for the post.

But one hen had blood in her neck where another had
pecked her. There was a collective gasp from the spectators. Even Hedia, who knew little and believed nothing
about this business, felt a stab of cold to see the blotch.

"Catch that chicken!" cried the priest, swinging his
staff at the chicken. "Don't let it eat!"

All three birds turned and ran toward the grove of
cypresses, squawking and flapping their wings. The birds
took increasingly long hops. Their wings had been
clipped but not recently enough, and when the breeze
gusted all three managed to get airborne. Herennianus
ran after them bawling in horror, but his servants remained transfixed.

Varus shrugged out of his toga and ran after the
chickenkeeper. Hedia saw him drop his notebook down
the neck of his tunic so that the sash would hold it at his

waist. Pandareus jumped from her side and sprinted through the circle; his feet scattered the uneaten meal.

Like the escorts of the other nobles, the boy's servants had been keeping well back from the ceremony. They must not have realized what was happening immediately, because Varus had dropped his toga. When Candidus recognized the youth in a tunic as his master, he started after him with a shout as horrified as that of Herennianus a moment before.

The chickens vanished among the cypresses. *They flew into the branches,* Hedia thought; but their white feathers should have showed up vividly against the sparse foliage.

The chickenkeeper, Varus, and Pandareus followed—and vanished. There were only six trees in the grove, but Hedia couldn't see the men among them.

And from the increasingly desperate shouts of Candidus and the rest of Varus's escort, neither could they.

CORYLUS AWAKENED IN broad daylight and slid open the curtain of the alcove. Though the shutters were closed, the suite was so bright that he had to squint.

"Good morning, Master Corylus," said an oily understeward who'd been part of Varus's escort at the Temple of Jupiter. He bowed deeply. Three footmen stood with him against the outside wall of the bedroom proper. "His young lordship instructed us to provide you with whatever you wished upon rising."

That's typically thoughtful of Varus, Corylus thought. The fact that his friend had been able to get up and dress without waking his guest was remarkable, though. *I must have been sleeping the sleep of the dead.*

"A little bread and wine for breakfast, if you please," he said aloud. His stomach rumbled. He thought of porridge but decided he didn't want the weight. *But perhaps some cheese? No, not that either.*

A footman scurried off in silent obedience. Corylus thought of the dream he'd had, then looked down. His feet were splashed with mud, and a half-rotted birch leaf, one cast the previous fall, stuck to the inside of his left arch.

He peeled it off, thinking. The servants watched, silent and probably uninterested. The leaf was a matter of concern only because of the dream—of which they knew nothing.

Corylus swallowed. "What time is it?" he asked, suddenly remembering that he'd promised Alphena to exercise with her.

"Almost half past the third hour, sir," said the steward, bowing again. *His name's Manetho, isn't it?* Not that it mattered. "The young master has gone with his father and mother to the Temple of Jupiter to take auspices for the noble Lord Saxa's consulate."

The steward coughed delicately into his palm. "The young master directed that we show you every courtesy until his return, which he expected would be not long after midday."

The footman reentered the suite. Instead of bringing a quarter loaf of bread and a cup of wine lees to dip it in—Corylus's normal breakfast, perhaps with fruit or (out of season) dried fruit—he was accompanied by four members of the kitchen staff. The first held a platter with six styles of breads and buns; a silver mixing bowl and cup were on the second man's tray; and the maids carried a jar of wine and a jar of water respectively.

Corylus stared at them in a mixture of frustration and horror. *They* knew *I just wanted a simple breakfast!* But maybe they didn't know; and anyway if they brought this panoply, they couldn't be accused of not carrying out the young master's orders. Varus wouldn't play that sort of game. His sister might if she was in a bad mood, though; and Alphena seemed to have more than her share of bad moods.

"Right," he said. He was *still* frustrated and more than a little horrified. He wouldn't take it out on the servants, but neither was he going to be bound by their standards of propriety.

Corylus took the wine jar from the girl—she *eep*ed but didn't object—and the cup from its tray, then poured a few ounces of unmixed wine into the cup. He returned the jar, then took what he hoped was a wheat bun from the other tray while the servants watched in concern.

He'd expected Manetho to protest aloud. He seemed to have become less officiously garrulous than Corylus remembered him being in the past.

"I'm going into the back garden to eat my breakfast," Corylus said in what could easily have been taken as a challenging tone. "I do not wish to be attended while I do so."

He turned toward the door to the suite. Manetho bent to whisper in the ear of a footman. As soon as Corylus was out of the door, the footman sprinted past him.

Nothing is simple, Corylus thought with a grimace. But in this case, the footman was probably going to clear the garden for him.

That *was* an advantage to being extremely rich. You certainly couldn't get everybody out of the central courtyard of the apartment block Corylus lived in, not unless you were willing to deploy most of a cohort for the job.

Corylus sauntered past the gymnasium on one side and the summer dining room on the other. A miscellaneous group of servants was leaving the garden as he approached; they hastened to get out of his way. Mostly they turned their faces away when they saw him, but the footman who'd brought the warning made a short bow of acknowledgment.

The gate onto the alley banged closed as Corylus entered by the inside door. Apparently Manetho's order had applied—or been applied—to the guard on duty as well as to loitering members of the household staff. Corylus didn't imagine that he had real privacy, but at least he wouldn't find himself listening to a watchman's reminiscences about service in the army . . . or the city watch . . . or the bodyguard of some Lycian chieftain.

Corylus really wanted to relax and think about last night's dream or whatever it was, before he had to deal with Alphena. That wasn't going to be relaxing.

There were two trees in the garden, a pear and a peach, but the pear was leafless and the bark was scaling off its dead trunk. Munching a bite of bun which he'd dipped in the wine, Corylus walked over to examine it.

His frown deepened. Several of the branches had split along the grain. Corylus had seen that happen in Germany, when a hard frost had struck early and sap still in the limbs of fruit trees had split them. There'd been no such frost in Carce, not in the past few nights—or ever, he suspected.

"Well, hello!" someone behind him said in a throaty voice.

Corylus spun, choking on the last bite of what had turned out to be a currant bun. A young woman was seated on the curb of the spring in the corner beyond the peach tree. He'd never seen her before. She had red-gold hair and wore a silk synthesis dyed to a perfectly matching color.

Whoever the woman was, she hadn't come far. She was barefoot, and her garment was so thin that Corylus could be certain that she didn't wear anything beneath it.

"I'm Persica," she said, patting the ancient stone. "Come sit with me, why don't you? I'm more fun than she was, even before the Hyperborean killed her two days ago."

Corylus coughed his throat clear, then swallowed to dispose of the last of the crumbs. "Ma'am?" he said. "You say that the Hyperborean killed this tree? Nemastes, you mean?"

"Come!" she repeated in a sharper tone, patting the curb again. She pouted and said, "I don't know about their names. He and his kind hate anything that's alive."

Her expression became petulant. Before she could repeat her command, Corylus walked toward her with the care he'd have shown if he were on point for a patrol on the east bank of the river.

Smiling again, Persica—Peaches, a name she'd probably adopted because of her hair and rosy complexion— went on. "I don't know why this one left the Band. They should all stay on the Horn, where there's nothing but themselves and the demons."

Corylus seated himself on the woman's right, keeping the wine cup—now almost empty—in his left hand. She shifted closer and took the cup, setting it on the curb on the side opposite him, where it didn't get in her way. She snuggled closer still.

He didn't know who Persica was, but she was obviously at home in the town house and she wasn't a kitchen maid. She might be Hedia's sister, come to stay with them. Her behavior was, well, even more blatant than Hedia's.

Or she might be Saxa's mistress. Corylus didn't know much about how nobles conducted their private lives, but he suspected that any household with Hedia in it would be conducted loosely by any standards.

"Ah, do you know why Nemastes killed the tree, ah, Persica?" Corylus asked. He didn't move from where he was sitting, but he leaned his body as much to the right as he could without being *too* obvious about it.

She put her arm around his waist. "My," she said as he tensed. "You're hard all over, aren't you? You don't have *any* fat."

Corylus stood up abruptly. "I was wondering about Nemastes?" he said, giving her a weak smile. He gestured to the pear. "Why he killed this tree?"

Servants would be listening to everything that was going on. Regardless of whether Persica was a senator's mistress or a senator's sister-in-law, the best thing that could result from Corylus getting involved with her would be that he'd be barred from the house immediately.

And though his father was a native-born citizen and a substantial businessman in his own right, there was a real possibility of much worse results. The gap between Corylus and the urban riffraff wasn't nearly as wide as the gap between Corylus and a senator.

Corylus grinned despite himself. Nor was he naive enough to imagine that the fact that the woman had made advances to him would have any effect, except possibly to enrage Saxa even more.

The girl pouted. "You're as cold as a Hyperborean yourself!" she said. "And anyway, he killed pear"—she didn't say "the pear"—"by accident anyway. Not that he would have cared. He was doing a divination and something went wrong."

She looked up with a cruel grin. "Maybe his friends back on the Horn have found him," she said. "They're pretty mad, I shouldn't wonder."

Her pique turned to anger. Glaring at Corylus, she said, "Do you ignore me because of that little girl? Why, she'll *never* be able to do the things for you that I could!"

"Hercules!" Corylus said. "No, that's—well, I'm not interested in Alphena. Hercules! You shouldn't suggest such a thing in her own father's house!"

"Him?" sneered Persica. "Why should I care about that soft old man? Though you're not much more interesting than he is, it seems."

That doesn't mean she's not Saxa's mistress, Corylus thought with a grimace. In fact, given what he'd seen of the girl's personality, it was even more likely that she was.

He glanced at the sundial. He was sure that Alphena would come to find him if he wasn't in the gymnasium when he'd promised to be, but that would be at least another ten minutes. For once the girl's presence—and the scene she would probably throw—would be welcome.

"Mercurial" seemed far too mild a word for Persica's moods. He didn't want to learn what would happen if he tried to leave the garden without a rear guard, so to speak. . . .

"Where did Saxa get these elephant teeth?" he said, walking carefully toward the portico on the south side of the garden. "I've never seen any so large. Or curved like this either."

"That's more of the Hyperborean's doing," Persica said with obvious disinterest. "He brought them here because a foreigner wouldn't be allowed in the temple they came from. He wanted them for a focus. I listened to him and the old man talk."

Corylus touched the ivory with his fingertips. Though the tusk was faintly yellow, age hadn't begun to craze its surface. The distance between the tip, worn by digging, and the base was as much as he could span with both arms, but the length along its deep curve was much greater.

They were nothing like the tusks of the elephants he'd seen in the arena, trapped on the Mediterranean coast of Libya. Carthaginian explorers had claimed that the elephants living far to the south, beyond the great desert, were bigger—but not this big, and anyway, Corylus didn't take everything he read as true beyond question. The giant serpent that attacked Regulus in Varus's epic was described by historians also—though without the poisonous breath.

He ran his fingers along the ivory. What these reminded him of were the tusks of the shaggy elephants that he'd seen in the vision which ended with Saxa and Nemastes chanting over a brazier.

They'd seen Corylus, also. No wonder the wizard thought that the youth intended to attack him!

He turned. The girl was staring at his back with an unpleasant expression.

"Ah, Lady Persica?" he said. Even if he was overstating her rank, it was safer than making the opposite mistake. "Do you know where these teeth came from originally? That is, are they from . . . well, Hyperborea?"

"How would I know what there might be in Hyperborea?" Persica snapped. "But yes, I suppose they were. The wizard said something like that."

She got up and walked into the southeast corner of the portico. Corylus was glad to see that she wasn't joining him but wary about what she *was* doing. She touched the oscillum, the disk of polished marble, there. It was in full sun. As it quivered, it threw highlights across the shaded interior.

"You find the bones of dead *animals* more interesting than me, I see," the girl said. She didn't raise her voice, but the inflection she gave "animals" was nothing short of poisonous. "Well, would you like to see why he wanted to use them?"

She gave the oscillum a hard flip, making it spin more quickly than a breeze would have done. The reflections licking across Corylus were alternately bright and diffuse: one side of the disk was smooth, while the other bore a low relief of Priapus holding his outsized penis in both hands. The curved side scattered the sunlight more.

"Ah, yes, thank you, I would," Corylus said. He doubted that he would learn anything useful, but perhaps there'd be something he could describe to Pandareus. Anyway, it would occupy the girl for a time; a long enough time, he hoped, for Alphena to arrive to save him.

"Stand where you are, then," Persica said. She brushed the bottom of the oscillum to slow it, then gave the edge a tap with her finger to adjust the speed at which it rotated. "The Hyperborean used an incantation too, but he didn't understand light. None of you do."

She sounded sourly irritated. She was obviously angry that he'd rejected her advances. But what had she expected, here in Saxa's own house?

"What should I do now?" Corylus asked quietly. In Persica's present mood, she was likely to scream at him whether he spoke or kept silence, but he was going to try to be pleasantly attentive even though he didn't expect it to work.

"Stand where you are!" the girl said. "Are you deaf as well as being a eunuch?"

The reflected light made Corylus slit his eyes to watch through his lashes. It wasn't so bright that it dazzled him, but the rhythm was beginning to be bothersome. Persica continued to tap the disk, never hard but minusculely faster each time.

Corylus was becoming dizzy. "Lady Persica—," he said, about to end the demonstration—or at least his part in it.

Light glinted on snowfields. "Stop this!" he said.

Corylus took a step toward Persica and fell onto a stony beach. His skin prickled, and his eyes throbbed with the flashing pattern of the oscillum. He heard the triumphant trill of the girl's laughter; then that too was gone.

Corylus was alone beside a river, facing a distant shore on which a snow-covered volcano smoked. Blocks of ice wobbled in the slow current, and in the cold white sky a seagull shrieked.

ALPHENA STORMED INTO the back garden. She'd left her helmet behind in the exercise yard, but she carried her shield because she hadn't bothered to unfasten the strap from the stud on her breastplate. Lenatus had chosen not to follow her.

She was furious: with Corylus, who hadn't kept their appointment, and also (though she couldn't have given a reason for it) with her stepmother. All Lenatus could tell her—or would tell her—was that he hadn't seen Master Corylus this morning and that the boy hadn't changed in the dressing room.

Alphena had caught a pair of footmen near the door to the gym before they could scatter. They had exchanged glances before one admitted hearing a maid mention that the young man was taking his breakfast to the garden, "—though I haven't seen him myself, your ladyship."

If Corylus was here, reading a book and forgetting the time they'd set to meet, Alphena would let it pass. Well, let it pass mostly.

But in her heart she was *sure* that Corylus had gone out the back gate to meet her stepmother and go off somewhere together. Hedia was supposed to be at Father's ceremony, but Alphena knew that she could have gotten out of that with no more than a bland excuse that Saxa would never question. She was *awful*!

Corylus wasn't in the garden. Neither was Hedia, but the blond woman who sat on the well curb was even more, well, brazen. She wore a synthesis you could see through, and not so much as a girdle or bandeau under it. None of the servants should *dare* to dress like that!

"Who are you?" Alphena said, goggling. "I've never seen you before!"

"If it's any of your business, Miss Snip," said the woman, rising to her feet as smoothly as oil flowing, "I'm Persica. And as for what you've seen or haven't, I doubt you look very hard."

Persica smiled. She was the physical opposite of

Hedia, but that expression was one Alphena had seen on her stepmother's face. It had nothing to do with humor.

"I suppose," she went on with the same catlike softness, "it was the spell that the Hyperborean worked here that lets you see me now. Though I must say, Pirus was a stuck-up bitch but at least she wasn't an ugly little *boy* like you. I'd rather have her back."

"Why, you—," Alphena said. She stopped because she didn't know how to continue. Who *was* this woman?

"You're a whore, aren't you?" she said in a shrill voice. "You're just a whore that one of the servants brought in! Why, I'll have you flogged! I'll flog you myself!"

"Do you think so?" said Persica, standing hipshot and thrusting her groin out against the thin silk. "And do you think that will bring Corylus to you, little boy?"

"I don't—," Alphena said and stopped again. "What do you know about Corylus?"

"I know you're mooning over him like a lovesick heifer." Persica sneered. Alphena bridled, but the blond woman went on. "And I know where he's gone."

Alphena gasped, then swallowed. She gripped the ivory hilt of her sword, though she didn't draw it from the scabbard.

"You hussy," she said, her voice shaking. "You tell me where Corylus is this minute or I, I'll *punish* you myself."

Persica looked at Alphena's shield where it covered the sword. She must have known what the girl's hand was doing behind it, but she curled her lip nonetheless.

"Poor little boy," she said, walking to the portico. She touched an oscillum with two fingers of her left hand. "Well, the truth is, Corylus was here in the garden with me. Alone. And after we were done—"

Persica's smile grew broader. She obviously didn't intend to complete the thought until she'd forced Alphena to ask her again.

"Tell me where he went or I'll slap your face!" Alphena said, raising her empty right hand.

"You can't give me orders, child," Persica said, but her smile had slipped. She stared at Alphena for a moment, rotating the hanging marble disk with gentle touches of her fingers. "I'll tell you what he might have done, though. He *might* have stood on the well curb there."

"What?" said Alphena, looking at the coping where the other woman had been sitting when she entered the garden. "Why would he do that? The water has weed in it; it's no good for anything but watering the plants."

"You little fool," Persica said contemptuously. "You ask me a question and then you tell me you already know the answer!"

Alphena didn't respond. She walked to the coping and touched it with her fingertips. The porous volcanic rock stayed rough even where it was worn.

"All right," Alphena said, facing the woman again. "What did Corylus do then?"

"I'm telling you what he *might* have done," Persica repeated, continuing to turn the polished disk. One side was carved with the image of a sphinx, its human face toward the viewer and one clawed forepaw raised. "That spring is older than Carce, older than mankind, even. Since the Hyperborean opened a door here into the cosmos, many other things were opened as well."

"But what did Corylus do?" Alphena asked, no longer in a tone of hectoring rage. She blinked instinctively at the bright reflection of the disk's smooth side, then slitted her eyes so that the woman wouldn't make her blink again.

"What he might have done . . . ," said Persica, "is to stand on the ancient stones, and when the rhythm of the light—" She broke off, then snapped, "Stand on the curb, child. You won't learn unless you stand on—yes, that's right."

Alphena wore cleated military sandals. They scrunched on the stone, but she didn't slip as she turned to stare at Persica; her balance was perfect. She wished now that she'd taken the shield off before she left the gymnasium, though.

"Does the spring lead somewhere?" she said. "Did Corylus go through it?"

"No, nothing like that," said the other woman. She spun the oscillum just a hair faster now. "Stand where you are until the rhythm is—"

The world blurred. Alphena felt herself falling *somewhere*. She tried to throw herself forward, but she was standing on emptiness.

"You're done with your Corylus now, child!" Persica shrieked in triumph.

The last thing she saw before the blur became darkness was Hedia entering the garden. Alphena felt a surge of joy in her despair. *She'll take care of that bitch Persica!*

WHEN VARUS HAD first read *The Gallic Wars*, he'd envied Caesar so much that he'd ached. It wasn't that loot had made Caesar rich, nor that he'd used his victories to become in all but name the sole ruler of Carce. What Varus had longed for was the personal experience of great events. No historian since Thucydides had been so lucky. If only Gaius Varus could have been at Caesar's side while the great man conquered Gaul!

Though in truth, Varus knew that he wouldn't have been able to write as clearly and effectively as Caesar had. But oh! for the chance.

He had the chance now. Varus knew something was happening, even before the light in which the chickens and Herennianus plunged took on a yellow-green cast.

He sprinted faster, feeling the notebook and loose stylus jounce wildly against his chest. He hoped he wouldn't lose them, but there hadn't been time to pack them safely in a satchel.

Varus grinned despite himself. He wasn't used to carrying a satchel either: one of his servants would normally do that. He wondered if any of those servants would have been willing to follow him into this hazy light. More likely, they'd have grabbed the young master and dragged him back if they'd realized what he was about—and Saxa would have rewarded them for their good judgment.

I wish Corylus were here, he thought. But this was a chance for Gaius Varus to report on a unique and marvelous event. He wasn't going to pass it up just because he had to do it alone.

Well, almost alone. The fat chickenkeeper had halted thirty feet ahead and was looking around in horror. He bleated, "Where are you? Isis help me, birds, come back! You're ruining me!"

Varus finally took stock of his surroundings. He couldn't see the chickens, but that had become minor. He couldn't see the temple, the crowd, or anything else that had been on the top of the Capitoline.

On the stony ground about him, brush and occasional birches grew at the bottom of a steep-sided crater. Varus thought he glimpsed the mouth of a tunnel with an arched roof a hundred feet away in the wall of black rock, though the slender white trunks obscured it. Perhaps something fluttered there. Herennianus started toward the tunnel, calling, "Birds? Come, birds, I'll feed you! Birds!"

Varus turned, instinctively looking backward to see if he'd somehow missed the Temple of Jupiter frowning down on him from the edge of the cliff. Instead he found Pandareus coming toward him, breathing hard.

"Master!" Varus said. He felt enormously relieved at his teacher's presence. It probably didn't make any practical difference, but he was no longer alone. "Do you understand what's happened, sir? Why the light has this yellow color?"

"I didn't know that it was yellow," Pandareus said, stopping beside Varus. He didn't wheeze, but that was through an obvious effort of will. "I do see that the trees have changed, and"—he smiled and looked over one shoulder, then the other—"so has everything else. Except for you and the knight Herennianus. Do you have any additional knowledge yourself, Varus?"

"I just followed the chickenkeeper," Varus said. He tried to reach down the front of his tunic to retrieve the notebook, then pulled his sash out and let book and stylus both fall to the ground. He picked them up. "I, ah, wanted to be able to record the event. As though I'd been at Caesar's side."

"I see," said Pandareus. "I might point out that while Caesar doesn't dwell on the matter, quite a number of those at his side must have been killed because of where they were standing. Though here I am with you, so I can't object to your logic."

"Come, chickens!" Herennianus called. He wasn't trying to run anymore. Though he continued toward the tunnel, he kept turning his head in hope of seeing his birds.

A chicken squawked. "Oh, bless you, Isis!" Herennianus cried, stumbling forward again. The chickenkeeper was a hundred feet ahead of Pandareus and Varus and by now very close to the mouth.

Varus started to follow. Pandareus touched his arm and said, "Let's wait here. We have an adequate view of Caesar, I would say."

Varus frowned slightly, but by reflex he deferred to his teacher. Besides, Pandareus had made his point before the fact when he mentioned how dangerous it must have been to be close to Caesar in a battle.

A chicken rushed out of the tunnel with raucous determination. The bird's flapping wings no longer had enough strength to lift it, but it was certainly running as fast as it could.

"Blessed Queen Isis, I'll sacrifice a bull to you!" said the chickenkeeper as he tried to grab the bird. His religion appeared to be Egyptian, like his accent.

Varus frowned more deeply. The worship of Isis and Sarapis was legal for a citizen of Carce, but calling on a foreign god was in poor taste for a senior functionary of Jupiter.

The hen dodged to the right. Herennianus stumbled as he tried to follow it. A forked tongue as thick as a man's thigh licked out of the tunnel and licked back with the bird. White feathers floated behind it, drifting toward the ground.

Herennianus screamed. He stumbled again as he tried to get to his feet, then began scrambling away on all fours like a child playing a game.

"Come, sir!" Varus said, tossing the notebook down. If he'd been alone, he might not have known what to do. Now his first thought was to save his teacher. The slope behind them was climbable for at least some distance upward.

The snout of something lizardlike thrust out of the tunnel and kept coming. The head alone was at least six feet long. The skin was wrinkled and had a pebbled gray surface. Fangs from the upper and lower jaws of the lipless mouth crossed one another.

Pandareus jogged, but he must have spent himself in following Varus to this place. He dodged around a low bush that Varus would have jumped over and Corylus might have dashed through. His foot turned on a slick rock; he would have fallen if Varus hadn't caught his arm and kept him upright.

Varus glanced over his shoulder. Herennianus had

gotten to his feet and was running. His eyes were open, but fear had blinded him.

The creature watched Herennianus from the tunnel mouth, its head cocked slightly to the left. When he was twenty feet away and starting to find his stride, it lunged forward like a snake striking. Its splayed forelegs were short for the length of the body, but they still raised the creature's chest six feet above the ground. It was a lizard, but a lizard that could prey on elephants.

The jaws clopped shut on the chickenkeeper's hips. Herennianus screamed like a mother in despair.

"Come *along,* master!" Varus said. He wished he could pick the old man up and run with him. Corylus could have done that.

The lizard tossed Herennianus in the air like a spinning doll. As he fell, he shrieked, "Isis help me!"

The upturned jaws closed again, this time with the victim's head and torso within them. The lizard's throat sac bulged and squeezed. The creature cocked an eye toward the two men.

Pandareus had reached the crater wall and started up, grasping the stems of brush that had sprouted from the cracked black lava. The slope grew steeper near the top, but even here at the base it was a stiff climb for an old man.

Varus wasn't an athlete, but he threw the ball well and hard. He picked up a fist-sized rock and hurled it. His missile hit the brow ridge protruding over the lizard's left eye and bounced away.

The lizard's head didn't move, though its tongue licked out. A glittering inner lid slid sideways across the visible eye, then withdrew as the creature's throat continued to work.

Varus considered the choices—and giggled, a sound that his intellect found distressing. Under the circumstances neither fighting nor fleeing was a very practical option. Still, if the lizard stayed where it was for long enough, he and Pandareus might be able to get to safety. Perhaps there was a crack in the rock too narrow for the creature to follow them into.

Varus climbed. *Since it had to happen, it's a good thing that Herennianus was so fat. He'll take a while to digest, even for a monster as big as this.*

Pandareus had reached a ledge some seventy feet up the lava wall and turned. He hunched to aid his breathing as he watched Varus climbing toward him.

"Lord Varus," Pandareus rasped through harsh sobs, "you must go on without me. I am bony, I'll admit, but between me and the late knight of Carce, we may sate the creature until you've reached the crater rim."

Varus climbed onto the ledge. Slabs had cracked off the walls at various spots within eyesight, leaving black patches against the deep gray of rock that had weathered longer. It would be harder and maybe impossible for them to climb higher; perhaps that was why Pandareus had stopped.

"I don't think so," Varus said, trying to catch his own breath. "And anyway, I'm not going to leave you."

The lizard started forward again, finally bringing its full length out of the tunnel. Its even more powerful hind legs were the same sprawling length as the forelegs; its back swayed slightly and the great belly almost rubbed the ground. With the long, stiff tail the creature was the length of a five-banked warship, over 150 feet.

"Come, Master Varus," Pandareus said tartly. "A student must leave his teacher someday if he's to amount to anything. Present circumstances are merely a special instance of a general truth."

"If you want to climb further, I'll brace you," said Varus. "And then you can give me a hand up."

The lizard came toward them in the sinuous curves of a fish swimming. It cocked its head up; its eyes glittered beneath the prominent brow ridges as one, then the other, considered its next victims. Brush cracked to its passage, and the rock trembled when each clawed foot came down.

"I think not," said Pandareus. He cleared his throat. "There are philosophers who would claim it's a blessing if you never know the pains and weakness of old age, Lord Varus, though I suspect they would be trying just as hard as I am to extend that old age for themselves. I regret if my presence costs you your life."

He turned to the wall behind them. "However," he said, "I noticed before you reached me that the rock"—he patted it—"appears to have cracked, like the slab that slipped downhill to create this ledge. If you'd been willing to continue climbing, I'd have tried to work it loose. I doubt I would have succeeded alone, but since I'm *not* alone—"

"Yes!" said Varus. The lava had flowed out and cooled in layers over months or centuries.

He touched the vertical crack behind him, then bent down and found a pebble to work into it. "Sir?" he said. "If you'll do the same, then if it goes wrong we at least won't crush our fingers."

"It's commendable that you're thinking of the future after our escape," said Pandareus drily. He blocked his side of the crack, though.

The lizard started upward, its claws scrabbling like battering rams against the side of the crater. Bits broke off and clattered down.

The fractured slab behind their ledge was about three feet wide and the height of the layer of rock—a little taller than Varus or the teacher. He couldn't tell exactly how thick it was, but it was so massive that it barely wriggled when he strained with the fingertips of both hands.

"Sir?" he said. "If you can pull from your side too, then maybe . . ."

"Wait," Pandareus said sharply. He'd removed the sash of his tunic and held one end out to Varus. "Help me work this over the top, just far enough to catch. That will give us the most leverage to tip it forward. Ideally without following it ourselves, but I don't think we'll survive long anyway if we don't drop the stone on that creature."

The lizard had gotten half its body up the side before sliding back in a storm of dust and gravel. It started to climb again, making a deep hooting sound.

Arms stretched upward, Varus worked the sash as far back as he could over the slab. The wool was tightly woven, but it wasn't what he'd have chosen for heavy pulling. A pity that he and Pandareus hadn't attended the ceremony carrying pry bars and a length of ship's cable. . . .

Pleased not so much at the weak joke as at the fact that he could make one under the circumstances, Varus wrapped his hands in the sash and began to pull; Pandareus did the same on the other end. The fabric stretched but didn't break.

Varus lifted his right foot to waist height and pushed on the rock beside the slab they were trying to move. He strained, knowing his whole torso was leaning out into the crater. His eyes bulged. All he could see was black spots floating through a red haze. The blood roaring in his ears covered the grunts of the lizard climbing toward them.

Pandareus shouted. Varus felt the slab start to go over and twisted his body away, using his grip on the sash as a fulcrum. He slammed the rock wall so hard that he almost rebounded off the cliff after all. He was dizzy and couldn't get his breath. He could see Pandareus was kneeling on the other end of the ledge.

The slab tore downward in a spray of lesser fragments; the sound of its jouncing progress was literally earthshaking. Varus got a mouthful of dust and began sneezing violently. He looked over the ledge, splaying his left fingers over his eyes to stop some of the flying chips.

The six-foot slab hit the lizard fifty feet below with a sharp *crack!* and bounced. The shock drove the lizard back to the bottom of the crater.

It writhed to its feet and shook itself. Its gray hide showed no sign of injury. It placed its right forefoot on the crater wall and began to claw upward again.

"I suppose," Pandareus croaked, "that we should not be surprised that a creature we meet under these circumstances would not be of a wholly natural sort. I wonder what Aristotle would say?"

The ivory talisman throbbed against Varus's chest; he felt the prickly white haze close over him as it had in the vault of the Temple of Jupiter. He thought he saw figures moving in the shadows, but they made no sign when he raised his hand to gesture.

The fog felt cool. It soothed his burning lungs.

"Greetings, Lord Varus," said the wizened old woman he'd met when he was in the temple vault. She held a closed scroll in her right hand and a clear glass ampoule in her left. Something moved within the jar, but it was too small for Varus to tell what it was.

"Mistress?" he said. "Can you help me?"

"Help you, Lord Varus?" said the old woman. "No, not I. But you can help yourself if you like."

Her lips moved as though she were speaking, but from Varus's own throat piped the words *"Out I go at once, flinging wide the doors! I have no fear—"*

The fog dissipated into bright light and cries of wonder.

"—as I welcome my kinsmen!" Varus said.

He staggered forward as his legs crumpled. His stepmother caught him and kept him from falling.

He was back beneath the cypresses of the Capitoline

Hill. Servants clustered around him; Midas was supporting Pandareus, whose knees and even cheek had been scraped by the rock.

Mine too, I suppose, Varus thought as he took his weight on his own legs again. Hedia was surprisingly strong.

He looked at his teacher and grinned. *Not even Caesar had* this *to write about,* he thought. But he was already sure that he wouldn't be discussing what had happened with anyone but Pandareus and Corylus.

CHAPTER X

The breeze that fluttered the hem of Corylus's borrowed tunic had come from the north, across the river beside him in which blocks of ice bobbed. He knew he'd be extremely cold—maybe dangerously cold—shortly, but for the moment his blood was too hot with emotion for him to feel it.

He was on a strand of dark gravel—broken basalt, he thought. The river was turbid, roiled to a pale gray from silt; in the near distance to the north was a tall cone from which a line of steam drifted westward. Lupine and magenta fireweed grew down into the shingle, while a little higher up the slope were scattered spruce trees and the little white flowers of bunchberry.

There was no sign of wolves or, for that matter, any animal life. Corylus hunched and walked up the gravel margin, then raised his head cautiously. Stands of birches and alders were darker blotches on a plain covered with coarse grass. A straggling line of brush a quarter mile to the east probably marked a lesser stream flowing into the river on whose bank he stood.

Or was it an inlet of the sea? Corylus returned to the edge and dipped two fingers of his left hand, then licked them. The water was fresh, but it had a gritty texture.

Floating near the shore was a brown, spindle-shaped object almost ten feet long. Corylus started back, thinking it was a sea animal; after an instant he realized it must be an overturned leather boat. It had apparently caught on something.

He thought for a moment, then pulled off his tunic and tossed it onto a carpet of ferns and fireweed to keep it off the ground. He didn't know how deep the water was. Stepping into it would be unpleasant regardless, but his skin would dry more quickly than the woolen fabric would.

Corylus stepped into the water. His right leg found bottom at knee level, but his left followed it to midthigh.

He grabbed the prow of the boat and pulled with both hands. It resisted. Wondering what it could be caught on, Corylus tried lifting it. The boat was much heavier than it should be. Finally he braced himself on the smooth rocks of the bottom and strained until he managed to turn the boat onto its keel again.

It bobbed free and came to shore with him then. It was a kayak. The occupant was still laced tightly into the cockpit. He was a stocky man with coarse black hair and a flat face. He'd been dead about three days, as best Corylus could judge.

Corylus pulled the kayak far enough up on the shingle to be stable, then looked at the man. He wore skin garments skillfully sewn with the fur side in. He was probably in his midtwenties, but Corylus couldn't be sure. The corpse had been hanging upside down in the straps, so its face was mottled and swollen.

The wind was beginning to bite. Exertion had kept Corylus warm while he struggled with the boat, but his body was cooling quickly now.

The dead man wore a shoulder belt to which a number of tools were tied with lengths of sinew. Corylus drew a knife from a sheath which covered half the bone hilt. The blade was grayish green and translucent: obsidian, not metal, and sharp enough to shave sunlight. He used it to cut the straps, which had swollen from their long immersion.

Having sheathed the knife carefully—it was a godsend to him under the circumstances—Corylus was able to lift the corpse. Its legs had stiffened at a right angle to the body, but he was able to work them out through the opening. He set the body on the strand and stripped off the tool belt and the long, soft boots. Then he paused to consider the situation.

The fur coat and trousers would be very useful, even though the dead man had been at least a handbreadth shorter than Corylus was. He wasn't bothered by the notion of stripping the garments from a corpse, but to remove them he'd have to break the stiffened arms and legs. That wasn't the way to treat a benefactor, even an unwitting one.

Corylus sighed. He could cut himself a wrap from the boat, he supposed, if he didn't decide to paddle somewhere himself.

The situation came home to him like someone piling bricks on his shoulders: he didn't have anyplace to go. Carce—or even the German provinces—must be unimaginably far south of here. He'd try, of course, but the thought robbed him of strength and hope.

A pair of ravens flew overhead, turned, and banked to land on the shingle some fifty feet away. For a moment Corylus imagined that they might be Wisdom and Memory from his vision, but these seemed to be ordinary birds. They croaked angrily, then hopped closer while keeping their eyes on him.

Which brought up another problem: what to do with the body? He could simply leave it where it was, of course; or he could shove it back into the water where he'd found it. He didn't really owe the dead man anything, after all.

He heard plaintive yipping; it was probably foxes, though it might even have been birds. The sound couldn't have been far away, since it was coming from downwind of where he stood with his dilemma.

He sighed. Well, he'd already decided when he didn't take the garments, he supposed.

Feeling like a fool but with no doubt in his mind, Corylus carried the corpse to the top of the floodway and set it among the ferns. Without pausing to think the matter over—his skin had dried off, and his tunic would feel very good against the breeze—Corylus strode into the water again and began picking up rocks from the channel.

The dead man's equipment had included a basket woven from finely split willow withies. Though it folded into a package no bigger than a man's paired fists, it was capacious and tough—the perfect tool for carrying five or six head-sized rocks at a time from the river bottom to the corpse.

Corylus kept working at the cairn without allowing himself to think about what he was doing. He had many pressing tasks to accomplish if he was to survive; but he had to complete the tomb immediately if it was to be of any purpose. A half-raised cairn would be simply a dining hall for the birds and beasts.

The ravens were angry. They hopped and even flew short distances to one side or the other, but they didn't come within twenty feet of the corpse.

There were egg-sized rocks among the gravel which Corylus could have thrown with hard accuracy, but he wouldn't bother unless the birds tested him a little closer. Till then—and the ravens seemed to understand the unspoken rules—Corylus could concentrate on building the cairn.

He'd started by dumping rocks on the ground nearby, then setting them on the corpse. As the job wore on—and wore Corylus—he began decanting the stones directly onto the body. He was as gentle as he could be, but it simply wasn't practical to pretend to the niceness that leisured civilians could indulge in.

The dead man hadn't been coddled in life. He would understand.

It wasn't until Corylus started to place the last basket of rocks that he understood that it *was* the last basket. The corpse was hidden beneath a mound that was at least two layers thick. The individual rocks were too big for birds or foxes to move, and they'd give pause even to wolves.

Voles could creep in, he supposed, but they could tunnel through the soil as well. Besides, voles weren't interested in the flesh, though they'd gnaw the bones when decomposition had freed them.

Corylus shrugged into his tunic, then hung the tool belt over his own shoulder. He looked at the mound and quirked a smile at it.

"May the stones lie light on you, my friend," he said. He didn't have a better prayer to offer; and maybe there wasn't a better one.

Cold, tired, but surprisingly satisfied with himself, Corylus started off westward. It was time to think about his own meal, because he'd definitely worked up an appetite.

ALPHENA FOUND HERSELF standing on turf instead of the stone coping. She flailed her arms instinctively as her cleats dug into the sod. The weight of her shield nearly pulled her over.

It was night instead of noon as it had been in the garden. Besides that, the moon was in its first quarter instead of being a day past full as it would be when it rose tonight in Carce. The warm air was scented with unfamiliar spices, and the trees were nothing like anything Alphena had ever seen.

Something very close by screamed in metallic rage. Alphena turned toward the sound and drew her sword. She didn't know what was happening, but it obviously wasn't happening in the garden of the noble Senator Gaius Alphenus Saxa.

The shriek sounded again. Alphena sidled toward it carefully, looking over the top of her rectangular shield. Three layers of birch had been laminated into a sheet so that the grain crossed and then recrossed. The whole was about two inches thick, bulky as well as heavy.

Alphena suddenly didn't mind the shield's awkwardness. At the moment it gave her more confidence than the double-edged short sword in her other hand, though that too was of army pattern.

She worked her way around a line of leaves which were each the size of a blanket. Twenty feet away, a cat the size of an ox was clawing at the thin trunk of a tree topped not with branches but rather with what looked like a single dock leaf.

A man in a full cloak balanced precariously on the leaf. His broad-brimmed traveler's hat lay near the base of the tree where the cat must have surprised him. He met Alphena's eyes, then looked away. The leaf concealed him from the beast's vantage, but out of sight obviously didn't take him out of the creature's mind.

The cat stretched to its full height, then ripped both forepaws down. Strips and fragments flew from the trunk; the top wobbled, causing the man to adjust his position. The cat couldn't reach to within fifteen feet of him, but in a few minutes the severed trunk would topple him to the ground.

The cat moved back slightly and paced, its eyes always upward. Alphena had thought it was a cat beyond the size of any lion she'd seen in the arena. When it moved out from the shadow of the leaf, she saw that its head was human—or almost human.

The creature's long, narrow face wouldn't have aroused comment on the streets of Carce so long as it kept its mouth shut. When it opened its jaws for another high-pitched, terrible scream, Alphena saw teeth like the points of javelins.

She recognized the creature then: it was a sphinx. Had Persica transported her to the lands below Egypt where such monsters might live?

The sphinx leaped at the tree, slashing furiously with both forepaws. The top swayed, tipping toward the creature despite the attempts of the man hiding there to shift his weight to the back.

His only chance of survival was to distract the beast long enough for him to get away or at least to a more secure refuge. *He could have called its attention to me easily enough, then run the other way. He didn't do that.*

The sphinx's back was toward her as it ripped into the tree trunk. Alphena sprinted toward it. The short sword wasn't the best weapon for the job, but if she had her choice she wouldn't be here at all.

The beast must have gotten an inkling of her presence just before she reached it, because it twisted down at her with astonishing speed. She thrust toward its kidneys, but the tip of her sword skidded across its ribs instead of biting into the vitals.

The sphinx's paw batted the shield like a stone from a siege catapult. Alphena skidded backward to the edge of the leaf from which she'd charged. Her left arm was numb, and the creature's claws had ripped through the wood in three places. She braced her legs under the long shield, knowing that she couldn't get up yet.

The sphinx poised. Its tail stood straight up like a bulrush with a bristly tip; it waggled twice, side to side. Alphena saw the stranger leap down from his trembling vantage, cloak fluttering. *At least this is going to work out well for somebody.*

The creature leaped onto Alphena. Her thighbones stood like pillars to take the strain, but the pain on her knees and hips was incandescent. She stabbed upward, too blind with agony to have a target.

The weight came off instantly. The sphinx tumbled sideways with a querulous shriek and backed a few feet away. Blood dripped from its side; the turf sizzled where drops fell.

Alphena rolled to her feet. The tatters of her shield hung from the strap; her left arm couldn't hold it out from her body. She hadn't been sure her legs would support her either, but they did: she guessed the emotions surging in her blood masked the pain for now. She didn't suppose she would live long enough to feel the hurt.

The sphinx gave her a look of savage rage. Its jaws opened silently; moonlight glinted on its fangs. The tail tuft twitched once, twice—

The cloaked man grabbed the tail and twisted it to the side. The sphinx shrieked and pivoted toward him. Alphena lunged with a strength she didn't know she had remaining and stabbed the creature through the neck.

The cloaked man ducked to avoid a swipe of the creature's forepaw. When Alphena's sword drove home, the sphinx tried to twist back. Its left hind leg folded and the creature fell on its side. The man sprang away, barely avoiding having it roll over him.

Alphena clung to the sword's ivory grip with her right hand and as much support as her left could add now that she'd given up trying to hold on to the shattered shield. The blade withdrew more easily than she'd been afraid it would. Blood gouted from the wound and from the creature's mouth.

The sphinx bunched its legs to leap—but sprawled forward instead. Alphena tried to step back but her left leg buckled; she went down on that knee. It took all her concentration to keep the sword lifted.

The sphinx struggled to its feet and turned toward Alphena; she couldn't read the expression on its human face.

The creature collapsed onto its left side and began to thrash. The fountain of blood from the wound suddenly faltered. Though the violence of its spasms lessened, as long as Alphena remained where she knelt, trying to gather strength, there was always a limb or a knot of muscles under the moonlit hide twitching.

Sod smoldered over a wide area. Places where blood had poured out in quantity were burned into craters.

The stranger had picked up his hat; he came toward Alphena. She fought to her feet and stayed there, though she wavered for a moment. She managed to thumb the support strap off the rivet in the belly of the shield and let the debris fall away. The broken layers had begun to separate.

The stranger stopped a polite six feet away. He was tall and, despite the cover of the cloak, seemed thin.

"I am Deriades, mistress, and I owe you my life," he said. "I believe I owe you a sword as well. If you'll come with me, I'll discharge the latter debt at once. Our home isn't far."

Alphena looked at her sword for the first time since the fight began. Half the blade had wasted away. As she stared, another blob of steel dripped onto the ground, where it continued to sizzle slightly.

Alphena flung the hilt away in horror. "If you could find me something to drink," she croaked, "I'd like that even more."

HEDIA TURNED AS one of the chairmen came into the back garden holding Anna's two walking sticks. The second chairman followed the first, carrying the arthritic woman herself.

Between them, the servants set Anna down. One held

her upright until the other had put the canes in her hands and made sure her feet were firmly on a path of marble chips. Only then did they step back.

Anna glared at one, then the other, pivoting her head like a screech owl. "There was no need for that!" she snapped. "I could have walked through the house!"

Hedia gestured the chairmen toward the door to remove their irritating presence from her guest's sight. She and her maid were now alone with Pulto's wife.

"I regret that my servants were overzealous, Anna," Hedia said, touching the older woman's hands on the heads of her canes. "Still, it was well meant, so I won't punish them too seriously. Will you care to sit down? And I can send Syra here to bring whatever refreshment you'd like after your journey."

In fact she'd make sure the chairmen got a silver piece each for their initiative. The chair itself wouldn't fit through the doors and turns of the town house, but the servants had judged that Anna wouldn't be a problem simply to carry—and had done so, ignoring her false insistence that she didn't need the help.

"No, I don't want anything to drink," said Anna, softening slightly. "And I won't sit down either, not just yet. What is it you saw?"

"My daughter was standing over here," Hedia said, walking to the spring. "On the coping. She was wearing that armor she practices in; Lenatus said she left the gymnasium looking for Corylus. And I think I saw a blond woman, quite pretty in a common fashion, right there in the portico. But then they both vanished."

She touched her lips with her tongue and went on. "No one has seen Master Corylus either, since he came into this garden to eat his breakfast. He wasn't here when I entered."

Anna stumped over to the coping and looked at the stones without speaking. She raised her head and said,

"No wonder my boy stank of magic when he came home from your house after the reading. This place—"

She gestured around her with one cane.

"There were altars in the woods," she said, "when I was a girl in Marruvium. There'd been sacrifices on those altars when my grandmother was a child, and probably back to her grandmother's grandmother. But they didn't have the *reek* that this garden does."

"We knew Nemastes was a wizard," Hedia said calmly.

"Aye," said the older woman. "And now we know how much of a wizard he is. I don't like it, your ladyship. I truly do not like it."

There was a moment of gray silence as Hedia and Anna looked from the well curb to the corner of the portico, then back again. "Omphale saw the woman with Lady Alphena," said the maid unexpectedly.

Hedia snapped around. She composed herself in the space of three heartbeats before she said, "Syra, who is Omphale and where did she see the woman?"

"Omphale is a downstairs maid," Syra said in a little voice. Her eyes wandered in a nervous circle, never quite meeting her mistress's cold gaze. "A new one, she was only bought a month ago. She fancies Master Corylus, your ladyship, and she was peeking through the door"— Syra gestured without moving her hand any distance from her body—"to see if he was still here. She saw Lady Alphena and the woman in the yellow shift before she ducked back again. She was afraid because they were arguing."

Anna had walked from the well to the portico, moving more easily than she had when she entered the garden. The emotions the old woman felt—and Hedia suspected that the thrill of a challenge was as significant as the fear she'd confessed to—were making her joints more flexible.

"Bring her here," Hedia said without raising her voice. "Tell her I want her immediately."

Instead of disappearing into the house proper, Syra tapped three times on the door. It opened and a pert girl entered the garden with an abruptness that suggested she had been pushed. Obviously the servants had decided among themselves how to handle a business that might be very dangerous for them.

"Your ladyship," said Syra, pinching the girl's left ear and drawing her toward Hedia with that grip. "This is Omphale. Tell her ladyship the story, and *don't* lie."

"They're all against me," the girl whined to the ground; she was afraid to meet Hedia's eyes. "They dragged me here, your ladyship, and they said you'll boil me *alive* if I don't tell the truth!"

"Then you'd best tell the truth, hadn't you, Omphale?" Hedia said calmly. "What was my daughter and the other woman arguing about? And do please look at me, child."

She'd seen the girl before, but she couldn't have put a name to her. The enthusiasm with which the other servants had turned on her suggested that Omphale hadn't made herself well liked during her short tenure; she was pretty, and she was too young to have learned that pretty alone didn't last.

Omphale raised her eyes with trepidation. "The young ladyship wanted to know who the other girl was and what she was doing in the garden," she said.

When Hedia nodded encouragingly instead of doing something violent, the maid went on. "She said she was Persica. She wasn't a servant, anyhow; she wasn't taking nothing from her young ladyship, just like she was a great lady herself."

"And what happened then, child?" Hedia said. She thought of patting the girl encouragingly, but she was afraid that in her present state Omphale would burst into tears of terror.

"Your ladyship, I ran away!" Omphale whimpered, lowering her face into her hands and speaking through her whimpers. "The ladies were really angry and I was afraid that if anything happened I'd have to testify in court and I'd be *tortured*! I didn't see anything, your ladyship, I didn't see anything!"

"I'm sure you didn't, child," Hedia said. Her voice was calm, though her mind was filled with doubt and darkness. *None of this helped!* "When I saw this Persica and my daughter, they were both unharmed."

A slave's testimony against a citizen was permitted only under torture. This girl had obviously feared that Persica and Alphena were going to come to blows or worse. Her fear proved that the discussion really was angry—not just a girl dramatizing an ordinary conversation for the servants' quarters.

"Send her away, your ladyship," said Anna, standing near the peach tree. She lifted one cane to indicate Syra. "The other girl might better go as well. We have private things, you and me."

"I'll call you when I need you, Syra," Hedia said. She appreciated Anna's discretion. Syra knew quite a lot about her mistress's personal affairs, but this business involved magic. Sometimes that affected people in ways that something as ordinary as sex did not.

The door closed behind the two servants. Hedia turned to Anna, who grimaced and tapped the peach tree with a cane.

"Persica is the spirit of this tree," the older woman said. "A wood nymph. I don't suppose it's a surprise that she might appear, with as much magic as Nemastes let loose in this garden."

Anna stared glumly at the tree. "She must know what happened to your daughter," she said. "Likely she had something to do with it, and maybe with my young master disappearing besides. But I can't make her come out to answer questions."

"Perhaps I can, then," Hedia said, taking the small dagger from the folds of her girdle. She stepped to the tree, thrust the point into the trunk, and peeled a strip of bark down.

A shrieking blond woman appeared beside them. The thin silk of her synthesis couldn't absorb the blood welling from the long wound on her right thigh. She clapped her hand over the injury. Glaring at Hedia, she cried, "You bitch! How would you—"

Hedia backhanded her across the mouth. She wore rings on all four fingers; two of them cut the skin of the nymph's cheek.

"You would be Persica, I assume," Hedia said, smiling. "Watch your tongue, girlie, or you won't have it anymore."

"Not her tongue," Anna objected calmly. "We need her to talk."

If we'd rehearsed this, Anna couldn't have responded better, Hedia thought with a rush of appreciation. *Of course neither of us is joking.*

Aloud she said, "I saw you with my daughter Alphena, so don't bother telling me that you don't know where she's gone. I want you to bring her back *now.*"

"How am I supposed to do—," the nymph began. Hedia stepped toward her, bringing her left hand back for another swipe.

Persica cowered down, crossing her forearms before her face. "Don't!" she said.

"Listen, girlie," Hedia said, hearing her voice rasp like a stone saw. "I could find an axe somewhere in the house, I'm sure, but I won't do that: I'll have the scullery maids peel your bark off with paring knives, working down from the thinnest branches. *Or,* you can tell me where Alphena is and how to get her back."

Persica straightened warily. She looked at her palm, then the silk shift. The wound was no longer bleeding, but it had stained the fabric in a broad wedge.

She glanced at Anna, then looked away quickly. The old soldier's wife was at least as determined as Hedia herself.

You're not dealing with little girls, now, Hedia thought.

"She's in the spirit world," the nymph said in a chastened voice. "But she could be anywhere. She—"

She gestured toward the spring enclosure and saw the blood on her palm again. She clenched her fist.

"I sent her from there," Persica said; she dropped her eyes during the admission, but she raised them again. "She wanted to find Corylus, and I said the stones are a gateway and he might have used them to go to another world."

"Did he?" said Anna. "*Is* that what my boy did?"

"I don't think so," the nymph whispered. "I think he might have used the mammoth tusks instead."

She nodded briefly to the great curves of ivory sheltered under the portico.

"That Hyperborean might have been responsible, don't you think?" Persica said.

No, I do not *think Nemastes was responsible,* Hedia thought. *Not when you were here and we know what you did to my daughter.*

But first things first. However much Hedia liked young Corylus, Alphena was family.

"All right," she said. "You sent my daughter into this spirit world, so you can now go bring her back."

Persica opened her mouth to protest. Before she got a word out, Hedia added, "Otherwise, you're of no use to us."

"But I *can't,*" the nymph said in a tone of desperation. "I can't leave my tree, don't you see?"

A man might feel sorry for you, missy, Hedia thought.

Aloud she said, "If you can't bring her yourself, how do we return Lady Alphena to this world?"

She didn't bother to add a threat. Persica certainly understood by now that if Hedia couldn't get her daughter back, the nymph and her tree would die after several days of agony.

Persica turned her head so that she looked at Hedia through the corners of her eyes. "I can send you after her," she said in a small voice. "But I can't send you exactly where, I *can't*. You'll need a guide when you get there, and I can't help with that either."

Hedia looked at Anna and raised an eyebrow in question. The old woman shrugged. "She can't leave her tree, that's true," she said. "Which doesn't mean we shouldn't have her turned into firewood, but that won't help with either of the children. I wouldn't be much use in the dreamworld myself"—she lifted a cane to waggle it, then planted it firmly on the ground again—"which leaves you, milady. Unless you think perhaps Lord Varus . . . ?"

"No," said Hedia more curtly than she had intended. "How will I find Alphena after I've done this, gone to this dreamworld?"

"I can send you there!" Persica said. "No one else can!"

Hedia looked at Anna again. The older woman gave her a slight smile and said, "I might manage, but it'll be easier if she's helping. If anything goes wrong, I have my own paring knife. I won't need your maids to help me."

"I didn't hurt the girl," the nymph said, hugging herself. "I didn't hurt anybody. I just did what she wanted!"

Both women looked at her. Anna said to Hedia, "You'll need your own guide, your ladyship; it requires the help of the spirit of somebody close to you. Do you have a lock of your mother's hair, perhaps, or a ring that your father always wore? Something like that?"

Hedia thought for a moment, then laughed like ice tinkling down onto a tile roof. "Not hair," she said. "And not a parent. But yes, I have a part of someone who owes me more than he can ever repay. I'll have my husband's ashes brought from his tomb."

VARUS LOOKED AT the Spring of Egeria, flowing through rock at the base of the Aventine Hill. A century or two ago it had been ornamented with a semicircular curb of polished limestone, but graffiti defaced the stones and trash choked the pool.

When Carce was young, the region was rural, and according to legend the nymph Egeria lived in the spring. She had become the mistress of Numa Pompilius, the second king of Carce, and had whispered her wisdom to him on their couch.

The Appian Way entered the city here, and now two huge aqueducts crossed just to the north and brought water to the southern half of the city. Traffic was heavy and constant, and nobody had time for legends.

Varus sighed. He wished that someone would whisper wisdom to him. The rhythm pounding in his mind was—

He shied away from the word "maddening." But he was very much afraid that the beat was driving him mad.

The spring was adjacent to the Temple of the Muses, a simple structure where ordinarily no one was present except a caretaker. Varus had come frequently to sit on the temple steps and write when he was fooling himself that he was a poet. It wasn't peaceful, not alongside the busiest highway in the empire, but he enjoyed the association not only of the Muses but also with Carce's legendary history.

A troop of gladiators swaggered through the Capenan Gate, up from their training school to the south. Sea bathing was part of their regimen, so many of the schools were on the Bay of Puteoli, where Corylus's father had his perfume factories.

They were singing a bawdy song about the king of

Syria in what was meant to be Latin. Each of the dozen gladiators had a different accent. Apart from the fact that the king's private parts were improbably large, Varus couldn't understand much of the burden.

The gladiators wore richly embroidered tunics, and a small army of servants attended them with food, drink, and shades against the sun. A stranger might have mistaken them for foreign royalty. In the minds of the crowd which would cheer them in the arena, that's what they were.

Varus thought about his sister and her sword practice. He grimaced, but he'd been wasting his time just as thoroughly with his poetry. At least Alphena hadn't made a fool of herself in public!

A bareheaded man with white hair had left the highway and was coming toward him. Varus frowned in surprise; then he remembered that he was alone. Ordinarily when he came to the temple, he had a dozen servants. He directed them to keep well away while he was writing, but they nonetheless made sure that beggars and hawkers stayed at a distance also.

After the living vision on the Capitoline Hill, Varus wanted to be *really* alone. There were people passing by constantly here, but nobody knew him and nobody would pay him any attention. He'd even insisted that Pandareus not join him. He wanted to think.

He smiled faintly. He hadn't been doing much thinking, at least not in any useful fashion. He wondered if he'd expected Egeria to pop out and speak to him. She would have to struggle to get through the potsherds, the broken wheel, and assorted other rubbish which people had tossed into the pool over the years.

Varus turned to the white-haired man and said, "I haven't a coin to give you, even if I wanted to do that. And if the servant who normally would accompany me with my purse were present, I fear that he'd have cracked you over the head before you got this close to me. Go your way, sir, and leave me to my thoughts."

"I'm not a beggar, Lord Varus," said the stranger. "I shouldn't have thought that I looked like one. Certainly not as much as you do in your present state of disrepair, if you'll permit me to say so."

He paused. The smile that quirked his lips had more of sadness than humor in it. "My name is Oannes," he said.

Varus looked down at himself. He'd been so lost in his mind that he hadn't paid any attention to his physical presence.

He had left his broad-striped toga with the servants at the temple because he didn't want the wool rubbing on his various injuries. Balaton had sponged off the blood with a mixture of water and sour wine. The temple stores also provided a very soothing ointment made from herbs crushed into the grease of raw wool: apparently it wasn't uncommon for suppliants to manage to burn themselves while tossing pinches of frankincense on the altar.

"As you say, Master Oannes," he said with a smile, "I *don't* look like an obvious person from whom to solicit alms."

He coughed to indicate the delicacy of what came next, then said, "My name is Gaius Varus, which you already knew, and I apologize for my insulting presumption about your motives. But I really don't want company now."

"I suspect you came here for answers," Oannes said. "It would be natural for a man of your antiquarian bent to wish that Egeria would speak to you as she is said to have done to your ancient king."

He stood beside Varus, just over an arm's length away. He was facing the spring, but he turned his head slightly as he spoke. His knee-length tunic was simple; over it was a short cape with a fringe of leather tassels, a fashion Varus had never seen before. He wore a leather satchel on a shoulder strap as though he were a traveler, but he had neither hat nor staff.

Smiling at Varus, he said, "Do you believe that Egeria was real, your lordship?"

Since he knows who I am, this isn't a chance meeting.

Aloud Varus said, "I believe that my ancient ancestors had divine guidance, yes. I find that less improbable than that a gang of shepherds and bandits founded the city that became Carce *without* divine guidance. But—"

Oannes watched with the detached calm of a man observing a beehive.

"—I don't know if one of those divine spirits was named Egeria. Or for that matter, if one of the men was named Numa."

Oannes smiled faintly. "If she—whatever her name might have been—had ever been here," he said, nodding toward the pool, "then I fear she's long gone. Even so, I think it would be polite to clear her precincts. Perhaps I'll do so after I've finished the business that brought me here."

Varus faced the stranger. The traffic on the Appian Way flowed back and forth, more people in an hour than there were in most country towns; singing, jabbering, praying. None of them paid any attention to him and Oannes. Every traveler or group of travelers was a separate world, sufficient to itself.

All Carce was like that. All the *earth* was like that, a gathering of elements each as discrete as a grain of sand. Gaius Varus was alone, except for the maddening drumming in his mind.

"What is your business, Master Oannes?" he said stiffly. "And what do you see as my part in it?"

"I'm a magician," Oannes said, looking toward the pool. "Of a sort—I don't want you to mistake me for your Nemastes."

Varus straightened in surprise. "Why do you say that?" he demanded. He tried to be commanding, but he noticed with embarrassment that his voice wavered on the last syllable.

"I was told by the stars," Oannes said simply. "I saw your need, and I know my own capabilities. So I came to you."

He faced Varus again with a slight smile. "My abilities differ from those of Nemastes, you see, but they're real nonetheless. You need a guide to bring you to the Legions of Surtr, which you're to lead. My wife is in the spirit world, and she will supply you with that guide."

What are the legions of Surtr? Varus thought. *And who would want me to lead anything?*

Aloud he said, "What am I to pay you for this?"

"For me, nothing," Oannes said. He grimaced and turned toward the pool again. In a changed voice he continued, "You will pay my wife in the coin she requests. The charge will not be exorbitant."

"Why am *I* to lead legions?" Varus said, hoping to find wisdom if he worked the words around in his mind for a while. "Why should I lead anybody? Not me!"

But as he spoke, he felt the insistent rhythm in his mind. He knew that the stranger was right.

"I don't know the purpose," Oannes said. "I don't know if anything has purpose, Varus. I know only the means."

He looked directly at the younger man. "I love my wife more than life itself," he said, "but I cannot go to her. When I die, no one will send her visitors. She will wear away to hunger; nothing but hunger. Therefore—"

Oannes smiled. Varus looked into his eyes; for an instant he saw a skull, but only for a flash of time.

"—I must live even longer than I have lived already."

"What if I don't want to go?" Varus said.

Oannes shrugged. "I was told you needed my help,"

he said. "If the stars were wrong, shall I protest to them? But the stars are never wrong."

The rhythm pressed and pressed harder. Varus felt his mind strain, trying to squeeze out of his eye sockets and through his ear canals.

"All right," he said. "What am I to do?"

"Stand where you are," Oannes said quietly. He opened his satchel and took from it what looked like a handful of ground millet. He walked around Varus, dropping pinches of the dust on the ground as he went.

Oannes seemed to be chanting under his breath, but Varus couldn't be sure that he wasn't hearing the dancers in his mind instead. There was a haze between him and the traffic of the busy highway. No one was looking at him and Oannes, but no one had looked at them earlier either.

The fog grew thicker and enveloped Varus.

CORYLUS EYED THE creek with satisfaction. It was only about a dozen feet across, but it had undercut its banks and carried a considerable flow. The water had the same milky opacity as that of the river it would join in a few hundred yards; that was ideal for his present business: catching trout for his dinner.

He set his gear a safe distance up on dry ground and took a three-point stance on the bank, facing downstream. Any silt that he stirred up would drift onto the fish he was approaching, dulling their senses; though as cloudy as this stream was, it probably didn't matter.

Corylus stretched his right arm toward the far bank, then bent it at the elbow with his hand pointing back at him. Only then did he lower his hand and forearm into the water. He couldn't touch the bottom, though he judged the back of his hand must be close. Slowly, controlling not only his breathing but his heart, he brought his hand toward the bank.

A Batavian scout on the Danube had taught Corylus to tickle fish. He'd done it often before his father had retired to Italy, but then it had been an amusement—like learning to throw the javelin accurately. Now his life depended on the technique.

He smiled faintly. It was possible that javelin throwing would turn out to be another necessary survival skill.

When Corylus didn't find a fish on the first attempt, he edged a few feet downstream and repeated the process. The stream was literally icy, but that couldn't be helped. While he was concentrating on the task, nothing else mattered.

As his second pull neared the bank, Corylus realized that his forearm was touching a fish. He did nothing for long moments, calming his heart. The pulse in his arteries was enough to spook the trout if he wasn't careful.

The trout felt the warmth as well as the minute pressure, but it didn't move except for flicks of its fins to keep it in place. The current this close to the bank was scarcely noticeable.

Corylus lifted his hand—or perhaps his hand rose; he wasn't really conscious of making it happen—until his fingertips touched the trout's belly. He didn't move farther. The creek burbled past; sometimes the swirls showed patterns, or seemed to. The surface was as white and opaque as a sheet of marble.

The ravens had followed; they croaked now with quizzical interest. Corylus smiled faintly. He'd have something for them before long. But he wouldn't let them eat a man's eyes.

Corylus might have moved in a moment, but the fish took the initiative: it began to undulate, rubbing itself against his fingertips. The contact was scarcely more than the brush of a butterfly's wing.

Corylus let his fingers slide down the length of the trout's belly, then back toward its throat. It writhed slowly against his touch. He gradually increased his contact with the fish, but he remained very gentle.

The fish relaxed. Was it asleep? He didn't know if fish ever slept. He continued to stroke its belly, but he began to curl his fingers around it as well. He didn't really plan for the next step, but when his hand was close to the trout's balance point—not far behind its gill covers—his fingers closed and jerked the fish straight up.

The fish thrashed, but its powerful tail had only air to flap against. Corylus swung his arm back over the bank and brought it down fast and firmly, as though he were using the trout's head to club the rock he'd placed there, ready for the moment of need. The trout went limp after a spasm.

Corylus laid it on a bed of damp moss in the basket—it made an excellent creel—and moved a little farther downstream. The ravens were excited, but they could wait. Patience was the essence of fishing, after all.

By the time Corylus had worked his way down to the river, his basket held three trout running two or three pounds apiece. He kept an eye on them as he dragged driftwood to the spot just above the strand which he'd chosen for his fire.

The ravens were watchful, but they appeared to accept the situation. Occasionally one uttered a peevish *cluck*, but a glance was enough to move them back if they hopped within twenty feet of the basket.

Corylus smiled. He was starting to appreciate the birds' company: he'd never been so completely alone before. The dead man's presence meant there must be living humans nearby, though. The kayak wasn't something you could make long voyages in, and the man's equipment had been well made and sophisticated in design. He hadn't been an outcast living alone.

Among those items of equipment was a sealskin case with an elderberry rod, a round elm knob with a socket, a short cedar board, and a leather strap about the length of his outstretched arm. At first Corylus hadn't been sure what the packet was, but as he handled the wooden pieces their use came to him the way objects become visible when sunlight burns the fog away.

He held a strap drill for starting fires. It would be very nearly as valuable as the obsidian knife.

Corylus built a fireset with shavings from a birch which a collapsing bank had dropped into the stream several years before. He placed the cedar board on the ground and held it down with a branch which he kneeled on. Setting the elderberry rod on the board with about half the strap wrapped around it, he fitted the elm socket on top, then bent to grip it with his jaws.

Corylus had to keep his head in the direction of the creel, since he couldn't watch the ravens themselves while holding the top piece. He took one end of the strap in either hand and began to spin the rod back and forth.

The mouthpiece filled Corylus with a sort of motherly sadness. He felt an urge to comfort a spirit that he felt as a blurred presence, but the elm was beyond anything except regret. The same was true of the man who'd fashioned the socket, of course. It was the way of life.

The elderberry began to smolder. Corylus decanted the coal into dried willow catkins from a separate pouch. When they were burning well, he placed them on the shavings and bark pith at the center of his fireset and breathed gently on the flames. As the fire grew, he added fuel until branches the thickness of his wrists were starting to burn.

When the fire was going, Corylus cleaned and gutted the fish. He dumped the heads, tails, and guts at a point midway between himself and the ravens. The birds were on the offal, croaking grumpily, by the time he'd seated himself to cook the filleted trout on a grill he'd tied together from stems of rye grass, last year's crop.

"You're eating before I am, my friends," he reminded them. The ravens grumbled anyway.

Corylus smiled. *There are people like that too.*

His face sobered as he wondered how long it would be before he saw people again. With nothing else appearing, he'd start walking south in the morning. Perhaps he'd wait to catch more trout and smoke them into jerky; tonight's grilled leftovers would do for tomorrow, but fish wouldn't keep long without proper drying. That would take eight hours over a slow fire, and Corylus wasn't sure he wanted to wait. Perhaps he could deal with that after a day of walking, but now—

Now he felt as though ants were crawling under his skin.

The trout were delicious, even without salt. He wouldn't have as much remaining for tomorrow as he'd thought. This was early in the year for berries, but likely enough he'd find cattails or other edible roots. He didn't think he'd starve.

Corylus looked over his shoulder at the smoking volcano. It was bigger by far than the daily presence of Vesuvius, which he'd viewed from his father's perfume factory on the Bay of Puteoli. Vesuvius had an air of menace, but this stark cone was far worse. Well, he'd be far to the south by tomorrow evening and farther yet in succeeding days.

With his stomach full, Corylus cut a trench in the lee of a hummock and lifted out the turfs to raise walls for his shelter. He floored it with a layer of ferns—still green, but some protection from the clay ground—and settled himself into it without a coverlet. Tomorrow he'd fashion something, but tonight he was too tired.

Though the sun had finally set, the twilight lingered. Corylus fell asleep anyway.

A figure strode toward him out of the darkness of his sleep; its features were those of the man he had buried.

"Well met, Corylus," the figure said. "I'm Odd's Vengeance. We have business, you and I."

CHAPTER XI

Corylus thought he was dreaming, but he'd thought that in the forest also. Indeed, maybe he *had* been dreaming—but he was pretty sure that if the wolves had gotten their teeth in him, he wouldn't have returned alive to Carce.

"You're the man in the kayak?" he said. This fellow was fully dressed including boots, but he *had* to be the same man.

"No, that was Odd," the figure said. "He's at peace now, thanks to you. I'm his vengeance."

The sky was light enough to show the visitor's features. He looked younger than the man Corylus had buried, nearer twenty than thirty, but the blood congested in the face of the corpse had probably aged its features.

Corylus rose to his feet. He hesitated a moment before stepping up from the trench he'd dug, because he didn't want it to seem that he was trying to use his greater height to dominate his visitor.

This man—if he was a man—wasn't going to be dominated that way or any way, Corylus decided. He preferred to stand on turf rather than moss cuttings laid over clay, so he stepped out.

"Sir," he said. "You're a ghost?"

"If you wish," the figure said. "I'm Odd's Vengeance, as I told you, but it doesn't matter if you prefer to call me a ghost."

Corylus laughed, because he might as well. "All right," he said. "Have I done something that requires vengeance? If I was wrong in taking your tools for my own use, I apologize; and if an apology isn't enough, then you have me here to settle it in such fashion as you choose."

I fought wolves, he thought. *I suppose I can fight a ghost.*

Vengeance laughed. "You're a castaway yourself," he said. "You honored Odd as you could, and you took nothing he needs where he is now. He's at peace, as I told you."

He turned to the river and gestured. "There's an island in midchannel," he said. "Do you see it?"

"Yes," Corylus said. Now it was a flat, dark line against the white water, but he'd noticed it before sunset. It was treeless, but some brush grew among the rocks.

"That's the Isle of Dreams," said the figure. "Odd went to the island three days past, to sleep under a spell and enter the spirit world. But while he slept, his brother Frothi, the chief, and Frothi's wizard, Nemastes, followed him to the island also. While Odd dreamed and could not waken, they laced him into his kayak and held it upside down until Odd was drowned."

Vengeance laughed again. The sound was harsher than the ravens' croaking.

"Odd went to the island to learn secrets known only to the dead," he said. "Now he knows all those secrets. And he is at peace."

He smiled. "Frothi thought the overturned kayak would float to sea," he said, "until Odd rotted and fell to the bottom where the eels would eat him. And so it might have happened, had it not been for Odd's knowledge and your help, friend Corylus."

"Did Odd bring me here?" said Corylus. "He was a wizard too?" He'd been assuming—

"Nemastes sent you here," said the ghost. His smile

was one that Corylus had seen before, on the faces of soldiers talking about the grim butchery that a victory on the border meant. "And your own good nature led you to give Odd the only help he was still able to receive."

"I'd thought Nemastes was responsible," Corylus said. "I don't know why he did it, though. Sent me to this place."

"It was his mistake, one of many that wizard has made," said the ghost. "As he will learn in time. But you will help me repay Frothi, Corylus, and I will help you return home."

Corylus didn't speak for a moment. The ravens had flown north over the river after they'd finished the scraps of trout. He wondered whether they were roosting in the tall trees at the base of the volcano or if they'd simply settled for the night on the island. He doubted that a fox could swim across to attack them in their sleep.

He looked at Vengeance. "How is it that you speak Latin?" he said abruptly. "Do Odd and the other people here speak Latin?"

"Vengeance can speak any language, Publius Corylus," the ghost said, "but we are not speaking Latin now. The whisper of the breeze is the same to birches in the heart of Carce as to the birches here in Thule, and all languages have become the same to you. You may think of it as Nemastes' gift, though he didn't intend it."

"Master Odd didn't intend to save my life when he put on his tool belt for the last time," Corylus said, grinning wider in his mind than he allowed to reach his lips. "I'll admit that I feel better disposed to Odd than to Nemastes, but perhaps I'm being unjust to the wizard."

"You may feel any way you please toward Nemastes," the ghost said, perfectly matching the youth's grin. "But you will do as I direct regarding Frothi. Say the words: the words will bind you."

"My word *always* binds me," said Corylus. "I will help you repay Frothi as you wish. A man who drowns his sleeping brother is no friend to me."

He cleared his throat as he considered the situation. The sky had finally become fully dark; the constellations were subtly distorted from what he expected.

"Sir?" he said. "Vengeance? What do I do next?"

"What you would do anyway," the ghost said. "Walk south. By midday you'll meet the tribe. Tell them that Odd is dead, drowned in the Ice River, and that you buried him."

"Will they accept me?" Corylus said, frowning.

"If they respect you," said the ghost. "Do you think you can make them respect you, Corylus?"

"Yes sir," he said. He flexed his hands, feeling suddenly warm. He grinned. "Or I'll die trying."

Man and ghost laughed together at the joke.

"And one thing more," Vengeance said. "You will say to Frothi that he must give you Odd's flute because you buried Odd's body. When you have the flute, you will be able to return home."

Again Corylus pondered the situation. "Will he give it to me?" he said. "Frothi, I mean."

"Eventually," said the ghost. "If you force him to. Will you be able to force him?"

"Or die trying," Corylus repeated, and again they both laughed.

The figure of Vengeance was fading. Corylus didn't remember lying down on the moss and going to sleep; but suddenly he was dreaming, and after that his sleep was dreamless.

HEDIA STIRRED THE mixture again, then set the whisk on the garden bench she was using as a worktable. The supplies she'd used were lined up on the ground beside her: the urn holding the remainder of the ashes of Calpurnius Latus; the mortar and pestle with which she'd ground a spoonful of them; the carafe of wine she'd mixed the powdered ashes with; and the small jar of honey which she'd just finished adding to the wine and ashes.

She didn't know whether ashes had any taste: they might well be as bland as charcoal or rock dust. Since they were part of her late husband, however, Hedia expected them to be bitter.

She gave the contents of the cup a doubtful glance, then looked up at Anna. She asked, "Is it ready?"

The older woman was leaning on one cane; the other lay on the bench. She'd become noticeably more limber since she undertook to help Hedia in this business.

Anna gestured over the northeast wall of the garden. She said, "The moon's up. That's the only thing that matters to me. Are *you* ready, Lady Hedia?"

"Yes," said Hedia, "I suppose I am. Where do I stand?"

They were in the back garden of the town house; Anna had said that it would be easier to enter the spirit world here because of the rupture which Nemastes had forced. Hedia felt uncomfortable, but she imagined that she would be uncomfortable anywhere doing what she was now.

"Here, I think," Anna said, pointing to the ground near the frost-blasted pear tree. "It's where the Hyperborean had his brazier."

She glanced at the peach and added, "Unless you'd prefer to be farther from Persica?"

Hedia sniffed. "Persica said she'd help," she said. "If she tries to interfere, I'll build a fire over her roots and we'll go on with our business while she cooks."

Anna laughed. "You'd have made a good soldier," she said. "Face the moon, then, and I'll tell you when to down the draft."

Hedia paused. "Anna?" she said. "If we're successful tonight, there'll be questions asked and I won't be here to protect you. I've left a note for my husband—"

Saxa had gone out in the early morning and hadn't returned yet. He was almost certainly with Nemastes.

"—telling him I'm going to Baiae, but he'll question the servants. This may become very difficult for you, especially with Master Corylus missing as well."

"You take care of your part, your ladyship," the older woman said. "Don't worry about me."

She began to chant in a harsh falsetto. The language wasn't Latin, though the rhythms were similar, nor Greek.

Hedia vaguely recalled that the Marsians still spoke Oscan in their hill villages. She wasn't much interested in any of the rural louts south of Carce. They had no culture as she understood the word. They merely provided the Republic with shepherds and soldiers; and with witches, of course.

From where Hedia stood the moon, still full at least to the eye, was caught in the branches of the peach tree. Were any of the servants listening from behind the walls? Probably not; they'd be afraid that whatever the witch was doing would affect them also. And indeed, it might.

Hedia thought about Anna's comment—that she'd have made a good soldier. No. Soldiers had to endure a great deal of physical discomfort, which Hedia disliked; and they had to obey orders that other people gave, which she couldn't seem to do.

Drink the wine now, your ladyship.

Hedia blinked. *That's Anna, and she's speaking to me!*

Embarrassed by her woolgathering, Hedia lifted the cup—it was silver, chased with dolphins and sea nymphs—and gulped the mixture. She noticed first the cloying touch of the honey, then the gritty aftertaste.

Latus. Not bitter, but coarse and unpleasant.

She sipped, then drank down the remainder of the cup without pausing. She'd decided to do this thing, so there wasn't any question but that she would go through with it.

The moon blurred and expanded as Hedia stared through the branches. She blinked, but that didn't clear her eyes. Anna continued to chant; her voice had the timbre of an angry night bird calling. Hedia thought she heard Persica also.

Will I see Latus's face in the moon? she thought; and as the words crossed her mind, the bright glow of the moon became a cave before her. She set the silver cup on the ground and walked forward.

I said I would do this thing.

For a moment Hedia continued to hear the harsh cadence of Anna's voice. Then she was striding into the earth, following a path which was a slightly lighter gray than that of the black mouths branching out from it. She was wearing a long tunic and simple house slippers. They were leather dyed red and a little sturdier than silken dress shoes, but they still weren't what she would have chosen for exploring caves.

Hedia smiled coldly. Ordinarily she would choose to leave cave exploration to other people, but she'd do whatever was required to get Alphena back where she belonged.

Something in a left-branching tunnel screamed. Hedia put her hand on her girdle, but she didn't take out the little dagger. She'd first thought the cry was angry; after consideration she decided it was probably desperate misery instead.

It didn't matter. Her business was with whatever lay at the end of the path she was following. *Assuming there's an end.* But she would keep walking until she dropped.

The path blurred into a jungle of trees with snaky branches. Their leaves variously resembled ribbons and spikes and blankets. They were a thousand shades of gray, and the sky was lighter gray. There were no stars and no moon.

Out of curiosity—not fear—Hedia looked back the way she had come. The jungle surrounded her. Fruit the size and shape of tight leather handballs hung from a branch that she should have walked under. She doubted anything in this place would be edible, but she supposed she would try if she had to.

Lightning flashed across the sky, briefly silhouetting the foliage. She thought she saw branches move, but that was probably an illusion. There was no thunder.

There was no longer a lighted path. Hedia stepped forward, using her left arm to swing aside a bunch of fruit so heavy that it bent the top of the stalk it grew from. Beyond was a clearing, and in it stood her late husband, Marcus Calpurnius Latus.

"Greetings, dearest Wife," Latus said. He giggled. "I won't say I'm surprised that you would join me here, but I'll admit that I didn't expect you to seek me out while you were still alive. Am I so dear to you that you can't live without me?"

The silent lightning rippled and rippled again across the gray heavens.

Latus looked as she remembered him. He wore a tunic with the broad stripe of a senator. He had wanted all those who met him to be reminded of his rank, even when he was relaxing at home without a toga.

"I've come to ask you to do something decent for a change, Latus," Hedia said. "A girl, the daughter of my husband, has been lured into the spirit world. I need a guide to find her and bring her back. I'm told—a witch tells me—that you can show me to such a guide."

Latus threw back his head and laughed; lightning trembled above the treetops in time with his merriment. He had been a short man and sensitive about it; in this place he retained the thick-soled buskins that he'd worn in life. He tended toward fleshiness, and though he'd died at age twenty-five his hairline had already begun to recede. Even so he had the face of a young god.

He sobered with the suddenness of a switch being thrown. "Why should I do that for you, *dear* Wife?" he said. "How can you even *imagine* I would do that for you?"

"I was always a better wife than you deserved, Latus," Hedia said. "But no, I don't expect you to do anything for me. The girl is innocent, though. I ask your help for Alphena."

She kept her voice steady and her eyes on his. She wanted either to flounce off or to slap him, but those things wouldn't help. Slapping him *probably* wouldn't help.

Hedia saw movement in the treetops. At first she thought small animals were scurrying in line; then she realized a large snake was crawling along the branch.

"Will you give yourself to me, dear Hedia?" Latus asked archly. His voice trailed up into a titter.

"You know I never refused you, Husband," Hedia said, trying to keep the tone of disgust out of her voice. She opened her cloth-of-gold girdle and hung it over a bush whose leaves looked black—they were probably dark red—but which sent up spikes with large white flowers. "Though it was obvious that you preferred boys."

The broach fastening the left shoulder of her tunic was in the form of a serpent with ruby eyes, swallowing its tail. She unpinned it and let the garment shimmer to her feet. She hoped the ground wasn't damp, but there was no help for that. She stepped forward, out of it.

"Where do you want me?" she asked.

Latus reached out to embrace her, but his arms passed through her body without contact. Laughing with a bitterness she hadn't heard from him this night, he stepped back.

"Put your clothes on, Hedia," he said harshly. "I'm no good to you now. I'm no good to anybody, and myself the least of all."

Hedia half knelt to retrieve her shift. Lightning had been constant in the sky a moment before; now it had stopped. She let the garment fall over her head rather than pulling it up. As she repinned the tunic while watching Latus, she said, "Will you send me a guide, Husband?"

"I've already done that," Latus said. He'd backed to where Hedia had first seen him, almost engulfed by a plant. Its leaves shot almost straight up from the ground; they had pale edges and darker cores. "Go find your girl and bring her back—if you have the strength."

Hedia sniffed. "Indeed, if I have the strength," she said.

The girdle fastened behind her. Ordinarily a maid would buckle it, but there was no one to help her here. She wasn't sure that she would have asked Latus even if he'd had a physical presence.

Fully dressed again, she raised her face to him. "Where do I find the guide?" she said.

Latus gestured to what Hedia had taken for a boulder part-shrouded by saplings whose leaves drooped like wax ornaments. "There," he said. "It looks like darkness, doesn't it? I assure you that it's not nearly as dark as the place I'm in, dear Wife."

Hedia nodded curtly. "Thank you, Husband," she said.

She stepped toward the place he indicated. Up close she saw that it was an absence rather than a presence: it was emptiness made manifest in the heart of lush gray jungle.

"Hedia?" Latus said.

She looked over her shoulder. The plant was even more closely about the figure of her husband.

"I'm not doing this for some fool girl," he said. His voice sounded muffled. "Now go!"

Hedia nodded. Head high, she walked into darkness.

ALPHENA FOLLOWED DERIADES through the strange forest. The light was vaguely green, as though it were straining through a canopy of leaves. If there was such a canopy, it must be unthinkably far above them: the trees through which she and Deriades walked swiftly were only twenty feet high—or at most thirty—and didn't block sight of what she thought was the sky.

Something hooted above her, then burst into a cackle. She looked up. A bird sailed away, dipping out of sight into the forest beyond. It looked like an owl, but Alphena had never known an owl to make a sound like what she had just heard. It carried something in its beak.

Deriades said, "Here we are." He touched a globe the size of a thatched hut. Except for size, it looked like a spiny puffball. Darkness spun open in the side, a motion like that of water swirling down a hole in the bottom of a bucket.

Deriades glanced back. Then, instead of offering Alphena politely to precede him, he stepped into the opening with a sweep of his long robe. He had to duck to clear the lintel.

Alphena bent forward also, though intellectually she knew she needn't have. Many puffballs grew near the threshold, but they were no more than the familiar inch or two in diameter.

The interior of the hut was pitch dark until the opening reversed itself and spun shut. Light, a brighter version of the green tinge outside, flooded them.

The room was huge. Alphena stopped in wonderment.

There were no straight lines; it was more like imagining the fibrous insides of a squash with all the seeds removed. There was furniture, but like the walls it appeared to have grown rather than been built; the pieces didn't seem to be intended for human beings.

"I have brought a guest, children," Deriades called. A chorus of high-pitched cries responded. Only then did Alphena realize that what her light-struck eyes had taken for shadows were actually smaller versions of Deriades, all caped and hooded in gray. They streamed out of the great room, disappearing around partitions and into niches which might until then have been crinkled portions of a wall.

"Children, you are being discourteous to our guest!" Deriades said in a tone of reproof but not anger. "Alphena has saved me from a sphinx at great risk to herself. Greet her with the honor her selfless courage deserves."

Gray figures, some of them as tall as Alphena herself, crept back into view. After a moment, the taller ones began to edge closer with their heads bowed. The others followed carefully, apparently in order of height.

"That's better, children," Deriades said with satisfaction. He turned to Alphena and said, "You're more than our guest, Alphena: you are our friend. We will send you on your way better for the meeting, as we are certainly better for having met you."

This was the first time Alphena had seen her host face-to-face in good light. Though Deriades remained hooded, she should have been able to make out his features; instead, she was looking into a gray fog in which two red coals glowed.

She restrained herself from jumping back. She was already disquieted because he knew her name, though she hadn't spoken it.

"I don't know what my way is," Alphena said honestly. "I—I just want to get back to Carce. I don't know where I am."

She tried to avoid sounding terrified, but she knew she hadn't been completely successful.

"We will put you on the way to your home, Alphena," Deriades said with quiet assurance. "Through your skills and with the help of your friends, you have a very good chance of reaching it."

Alphena's smile was wry. She supposed she should appreciate the candor, but at the moment she would have preferred some unfettered optimism. "Thank you," she said. "I hope you're right."

On the walls were what seemed to be washes of light when she looked straight at them, but out of the corners of her eyes she saw complex pictures: castles and rocky landscapes. Among them were figures too elongated to be human. When each time by reflex she turned to get a better view, the image vanished into flooding color.

The children, if that's what they were, came closer. Alphena heard them whisper among themselves, but the sounds were too faint for her to catch words. It was more like passing close to a hedge after sunset and rousing the birds nervously from their repose.

"We'd normally have dinner as soon as I returned home," Deriades said. "Would you care to join us, Alphena? You'll find the meal nutritious; and I hope tasty as well."

I am hungry, she thought. She'd had only a few figs when she got up; she hadn't wanted her stomach full before a heavy workout in the gym.

She'd had a workout, certainly; and the tension of the past several hours had probably taken even more out of her than fighting the sphinx had. But to eat here—

"Yes, thank you," she said. She had to eat somewhere unless she got back to her home very quickly. Deriades and his home were very strange, but the sphinx proved that there were stranger things in this—this dreamworld?—and that some of them were openly hostile.

"Children," her host said, "lead our friend to the dining area."

The family streamed out of the large hall with its members cheeping and chittering among themselves. The tallest led, but the smaller members—some barely came up to Alphena's knees—clustered around her like doves in hooded garments, urging her forward.

The children's touch was as light as that of leaves fluttering in a zephyr. Alphena went along with them, wondering what would have happened if she'd refused.

Nothing, she guessed. Some people would say that she couldn't afford to trust anybody in her present situation, but since she couldn't get out of this place—whatever it was—by herself, she couldn't afford *not* to trust others who weren't openly hostile.

She grinned. Deriades, walking at her side, noticed the expression. "Our dwelling pleases you?" he asked.

"Yes," Alphena said truthfully. "But I smiled because I was wondering whether the sphinx might not have had the secret which would return me to Carce."

"She may indeed have known that secret," said Deriades solemnly. "But she would have imparted it only after she ate you."

He paused, then added, "I can find another sphinx if you care to make the trial, Alphena. Though you'll pardon me if I keep my distance during the interaction. Since you won't be around to save me afterward."

Alphena giggled. She felt better than she had since Persica tricked her into this place.

They entered a room paneled with glittering brightness. Here the furnishings were of precious metals. The low tables were shaped like clumps of algae in eddies;

their tops were silver and their legs gold. The couches followed the sinuous curves of the tabletops. The cushions looked like bark but were firmly resilient to Alphena's touch, and the frames had a fiery luster like no metal she had ever seen before.

"That's orichalch," Deriades said with quiet pride. "Not the brass that some folk in your world call by the name of the metal their ancient ancestors saw on the walls of Atlantis."

"Atlantis was real?" she said.

"Yes, Alphena," said her host. She was sure that if she could have seen his face, he would have been smiling. "As real as I am."

Some of the taller figures had vanished into rooms beyond. Deriades gestured her to a bench. When she hesitated, he twisted onto one himself. Though he sat upright, she suspected that they were really intended to be curled up on.

Regardless, Alphena seated herself as decorously as she could at the other end of Deriades' bench. Four—at first she thought five—of the smallest offspring crowded opposite them, and the remainder took places around the room.

Immediately those who had bustled off initially reappeared with platters of food and drink, and place settings made of the brilliant orichalch that she'd remarked already. The plates were only slightly concave; their rims had the same organic outlines as the tabletops against which they blazed.

Alphena looked at the sole utensil she had been offered, seemingly an elongated spoon. "The back edge is sharp," Deriades warned. "Though"—he broke a rounded cake on the platter between them and placed part of it before Alphena—"the nut loaf we're having this evening doesn't require cutting."

He raised his portion to the blur within his cowl and

lowered it with a bite gone. The little figures across the table began gobbling smaller chunks with enthusiasm.

Alphena, embarrassed at her hesitation but hesitant nonetheless, took a bite of hers. It was nut loaf, or she supposed it was; and it *was* delicious.

Deriades raised his mug and drank. Pausing, he said, "Would you care to finish this cupful, Alphena?"

"No, not at all," she said. She snatched up her own mug and drank deeply. The liquid was water with a slight tang, as though a slice of lime or lemon had been rubbed on the rim of the vessel. She wondered if she was tasting the orichalch itself.

One of the little figures placed another chunk of loaf on her plate. It—he, she?—started back when she glanced toward it. *I don't need that much,* she thought; but she took a bite, and before she was done, she'd finished the loaf. The nut loaf was very good, and she'd been hungrier than she had realized.

"If you're ready," her host said, poised to get up, "we can take care of the other matter now. A sword to replace the one you lost, I mean."

"Yes sir," said Alphena, rising. She was uneasy at every suggestion, though each was reasonable and everything had gone exactly as she would have wished. *I have to trust somebody!*

She left with Deriades through a doorway that she hadn't noticed when she came in. The offspring stayed behind, cleaning the dining room with the chirping bustle of a wave of birds browsing among dry leaves.

Her host stopped before a patterned wall and gestured. It swirled into darkness and vanished, opening as the dwelling itself had. Racks and piles of arms filled the interior; they seemed to be as tight as the catch in the hold of a fisherman's boat. At a glance, every sort of personal weapon was present, from a stone tied with rawhide onto the end of a branch, to a suit of silvery armor articulated at each joint and fully engraved.

"Where did all these come from?" Alphena asked in amazement. As she spoke, she realized that though the question was innocent, the answer might not be. She looked toward her host in concern.

Deriades stepped into the armory. She hadn't thought there was room for anything bigger than a dormouse to enter, but he slipped between stacks without touching the delicately balanced equipment.

"Not all our visitors are as polite as you, Alphena," he said. "Indeed, over the years many have thought they could become wealthy beyond their dreams if they succeeded in robbing us . . . which would have been true, had they succeeded."

Deriades reached the middle of the room. His head turned from one side to the other; then he stepped to his left with amazing aplomb.

"You found me in difficulties with a creature of great magical power, Alphena," he said. "You mustn't imagine that my children and I are without resources in our own dwelling, however."

He bent. Alphena couldn't see exactly what his long-fingered hand did, but it came up with a gold-hilted sword. Its scabbard seemed to have been washed by a rainbow.

"There," he said in satisfaction. He displayed the short, leaf-shaped blade, then sheathed it and wormed his way back to her. The sword looked as delicate as an iris, and equally useless as a weapon.

"Ah," said Alphena. "Sir, that sword seems very beautiful, but perhaps it's too valuable for me. I'd be happy with a simpler weapon, like the one that killed the sphinx."

Deriades balanced the sheathed sword on the tips of two fingers of his left hand. For an instant his palm seemed abnormally long, but a fold of the cloak quickly covered it again. "This blade is sturdier than it looks, Alphena," he said. "It could cut through a boulder and perhaps shave sunlight . . . if there were sunlight in this world."

He advanced his hand slightly to emphasize the offer. "I have other reasons for saying that this is the sword you need now, however," he said.

I have to trust somebody.

"Thank you, sir," Alphena said. Instead of reaching for the lustrous weapon, she unfastened the empty scabbard she'd brought to this place. The sheath of her military-pattern sword had hung from studs on the equipment belt; the new one had ribbons of some gleaming metal as flexible as linen. She tied them directly to the belt, then straightened.

"Alphena," Deriades said. "You are very welcome to remain with us as long as you wish, but if you really want to return to your home despite the dangers that entail . . . ?"

"I do," Alphena said. It suddenly struck her that she'd fought and killed a sphinx. *She* had.

Deriades nodded. "Then I will show you the first step of the way," he said. "Your friend Hedia is searching for you—"

Alphena stiffened in surprise. *Hedia is?* She didn't speak aloud.

"—and she won't find you if you remain here. Others who are not your friends search for you also, but your sword will take care of them."

The surge of pride at having killed the sphinx was ebbing away, but it left Alphena's spirit warmer nonetheless. "Thank you, sir," she said. "I'm ready to go."

"Then step forward, Alphena," Deriades said. "And if you worship gods, may they be with you, my friend."

I'll walk straight into him if I step forward, Alphena

thought. But she'd correctly trusted Deriades in the past, and she had nothing to complain about the result.

She stepped off with her right foot like a soldier and found herself in the strange forest outside. Deriades' dwelling was nowhere to be seen.

THE GLOWING FOG which closed Varus off from the Appian Way and the rest of Carce abruptly shrank in upon itself the way fog vanishes when the air warms. He was in a chamber like the cell of a great sponge.

The structure was opaque though faintly yellow with internal light. A wall resisted Varus when he pressed it with his hand, but even so he wasn't sure that it was solid. The floor was of the same substance and felt faintly resilient.

There was a hole a few feet across in the ceiling and another hole in one of the walls. Varus crawled through the latter, into another cell of the same sort as the first. He didn't see other people or even other life. The wind sighed as though it were blowing through a funnel in rocks, and he felt the distant throb of dancers in his mind.

This cell was smaller than the first, but it had three holes at a level which Varus could reach without jumping and trying to pull himself upward. If there'd been reason to hope for something better at the higher level, Varus would have climbed, but he saw no hope for anything better *anywhere*.

He hesitated, wondering whether to keep moving blindly from cell to cell until he starved or to stay where he was and starve in one place. *I may as well keep moving. That way I can at least* feel *as though I'm accomplishing something*.

Varus started toward the hole he happened to be facing. As he did so, a woman wriggled through the opening to his right and stood.

"I was afraid you weren't going to come," she said. He couldn't read the look on her face. "I was so afraid. . . . I'm Urash. You are welcome. You are so welcome."

Varus felt a wash of relief, not because of what the woman said but simply because he wasn't alone after all. "I . . . ," he said. "I'm Gaius Varus. I—your husband sent me to you. Oannes? He said you could guide me to . . ."

He paused. His tongue was reluctant to frame the words, but the pounding in his mind increased.

"I'm to lead the Legions of Surtr," he blurted. "You can guide me to them."

Urash smiled and ran her fingertips along his right arm. "I guide you?" she said. "No, not me; I can't leave this place, Varus. But I will send you to a guide, and in exchange you will pay me."

Urash was short and dark, with Levantine features and straight black hair. Her linen tunic was appliquéd with bands of leather cutwork: a repeated pattern of trees of life and horned goats licking the outspread hands of a female figure on a dais. When she first entered this cell, Varus had thought her complexion was pale and her hair mousy, but that was clearly wrong. Perhaps it had been a trick of the light which bled through the walls.

"I have nothing to pay you with," Varus said. Had Oannes misunderstood? But he'd *told* the man that he didn't have even his purse. "After I return to my world, I'll give you what you ask; but I have nothing now."

Urash turned so that they stood side by side instead of facing each other, but she moved closer. Her hip bumped his gently, and her left hand traced from his waist to his shoulder.

"I should have died," she said so softly that Varus wasn't sure she was speaking to him. "Oannes wouldn't allow that to happen. He has great knowledge, knowledge of all things, but even Oannes makes mistakes. He can turn every answer into a question and find each next answer, but this time he stopped when he found the answer which suited his desires."

Varus would have edged away, but he was almost against a wall. He didn't like the feel of whatever this place was made of, and he didn't want to offend the woman whose help he needed.

"So I am here," Urash whispered. "By my husband's choice and by his power. And then he asked the next question, but it was too late. Even for Oannes, it was too late."

"Mistress Urash?" Varus said. "Where is this place?"

There was more sorrow in the woman's laughter than there could have been in all Niobe's tears for her murdered children. "This is no place, Varus," Urash said. "This is the place between, and I am here forever."

Varus's mouth was dry; he licked his lips. He didn't know what to say. After a moment, he said, "I'm sorry, mistress."

"You came to me," Urash said. He could barely hear her. "That's as much as anyone can do, and you did it."

She turned to her right and gestured. The cell structure was that of spheres of varied size pressing against one another. One of the irregular walls brightened, then became a window onto a high knoll. It was night, but a full moon lighted an open cairn. Beyond, a forest stretched to the horizon in all directions.

Men with torches stood outside the cairn. They were clad in furs, and their bearded faces were as solemn as the cairn itself. Their eyes were on the open entrance.

Urash gestured again. The plane through which Varus watched swept toward the side of the cairn. For an instant he saw turf layered over a core of stones fitted into a corbeled arch; then he saw the inside, where two men held the arms of a tall woman with blond hair.

"She is Sigyn," Urash said. "She will guide you."

The men—one had a torch in his free hand, holding it out to the side because of the low ceiling—had forced the woman onto a bench made from a single large slab. She strained hopelessly to rise, but she kept her lips closed over her fury.

"Should we help her?" Varus said. He squeezed his hands together, trying to work out their sudden chill. "How do I help her?"

Sigyn wore a shift of thin wool. A third man stepped to her from the side, avoiding her barefoot attempts to kick him. In his hand was an iron dagger with a rounded tip.

She first pressed her chin against her chest, then tried to bite the man as he reached over her to grab a handful of her long hair. Forcing her head back, he cut her throat with a single powerful stroke. The blade sparked where it rubbed the stone.

A fountain of blood splashed the roof and all three men. Instead of trying to jump out of the way, they continued to hold the woman until she stopped thrashing.

The man with the dagger wiped its blade on her shift. All three left the tomb, ducking to clear the low opening. They didn't look back at their victim. Stones laid from outside began to close the entrance.

Varus took a deep breath. He looked at Urash and said, "You told me she would be my guide."

"She must die to guide you to your destiny, Varus," Urash said. She tugged the talisman out from beneath his tunic and stared for a moment. Her fingers caressed the ivory.

"She will guide you," Urash said, "because you will compel her. Your verses have power in this place."

In a whisper she added, "You have the power of Botrug in this amulet."

"What do I do now?" Varus said. His mouth was so

dry that he could barely speak. He already knew the answer. His back was pressed against the wall of the cell, and Urash was untying his sash.

"Now," Urash said as she drew his tunic up over his head, "you pay me, Varus."

CHAPTER XII

Short though the night had been, Corylus awakened at dawn. To his surprise, the sun was rising in the constellation Gemini, not Pisces as it should have.

He'd known that he was far to the north even of Germany. According to the astronomer Manilius, whom he'd heard lecture in the Forum, the sun moved through the zodiac at the rate of a house in 1,950 years. That meant Corylus was many thousands of years distant in time from his home. That didn't seem possible, but much that was happening would have been impossible in the world in which he had lived a week ago.

Odd's Vengeance was nowhere to be seen. Had Corylus really met him in the night? His memory was very clear, but that didn't mean he hadn't been dreaming.

He smiled, working his limbs to take out the stiffness of the chill night. Even if it was a dream, the ghost—or whatever—could have been real. Corylus simply couldn't rationally judge possibilities in the present world.

Rather than eat the remaining trout immediately, Corylus started hiking south, generally paralleling the creek. He would have a better appetite for breakfast after he'd warmed his muscles back to suppleness.

He left the tumbling river of ice and meltwater behind almost immediately; after a half mile, there wasn't so much as a faint rumble to remind him of its existence. The volcano, though, would remain unchanged for a long time yet. Every time Corylus glanced over his shoulder, the cone and the plume of smoke were fixed against the pale sky.

Groves of small trees punctuated the rolling grassland. Corylus decided to eat his trout in a stand of rowans on a hump too small to be honestly described as a hill. It was slightly out of his way—it stood above the creek, which had borne east while Corylus decided to walk straight south—but not so much that it mattered.

As he approached the rowan copse, a woman with reddish hair stepped out from behind a trunk and smiled. He half stumbled. More women appeared.

They couldn't have hidden behind trees whose boles were no thicker than his forearm. Corylus swallowed but continued walking toward them.

"Hello, Corylus!" called the first woman he'd seen. They were all of a type, slender and russet-haired, but he thought he could tell them apart. There were six of them, just as there were six rowan trees.

"You have the advantage of me, mistresses," Corylus said. Then, because he decided that he really wanted to know and asking was the best way to learn, he said, "Mistress? Are you dryads?"

"Of course we are, silly," said the first woman. "I'm Sorba and these are my sisters."

The women smiled and murmured. Though young— they seemed young—they were poised and their manners were courteous.

"I, ah, I'm Publius Corylus," he said. He shook his head at his own words. "But of course, you knew that. I, ah, didn't expect to meet you."

"And why not?" said Sorba cheerfully. "Since you were coming straight toward us. We're glad of your company, Corylus."

"And you should be glad of ours too," another tree

nymph said. "If you keep going in the direction you're headed . . . ?"

She raised an eyebrow in question. Corylus swallowed again and said, "Yes, I want to meet a chief named Frothi. I'm told I will if I keep going south."

"Frothi doesn't matter," said Sorba. "But he has Nemastes with him, and Nemastes will serve you out the way he did Odd, Frothi's brother."

"Frothi and Nemastes murdered Odd," said a nymph.

"We saw them go past," said another. "And when they returned, they boasted about it."

"Nemastes urged Frothi to kill his brother," said a fourth. "Odd had a flute, which he would not give to Nemastes."

Corylus set his slight gear down and stood among the rowans and the dryads. He placed his right hand on the trunk of the nearest tree, simply to have something to do. A nymph giggled.

Blushing, Corylus jerked his hand away. *All* the nymphs giggled. He continued to blush.

The dryads were the sort of girls that Saxa wished his daughter would be: pretty, pleasant, and above all *proper*. Even gladiators' equipment couldn't prevent Alphena from being pretty, but she seemed to make a point of being unpleasantly improper.

Corylus cleared his throat. "I, ah, come from a long way away—," he began.

He stopped because the nymphs broke into peals of laughter.

"We know where you came from, Corylus!" a girl laughed.

"There are rowans then too, silly!" said another.

They seemed to be trying to compose themselves, but every time they allowed their eyes to rest on his stricken expression, they began to laugh again. Finally Sorba turned to her sisters and raised her hands. The nymphs quieted, though with the occasional gurgle of amusement.

Sorba faced him again and said contritely, "You'll have to pardon us, Corylus. Mostly we have only our own company; and that of the animals, of course. We ought to behave better when a gentleman like you visits."

"I was at fault," Corylus said. He supposed that was only half true—he hadn't had any way of knowing how much information the dryads had—but it was how he always felt when things went wrong. "What I was going to say, though, is that there's a wizard named Nemastes where I come from also."

"The same man," said a nymph.

"If he's a man," objected another.

"Well," said a third. "As much as Corylus is a man, don't you think?"

"Only not nearly so nice!" objected two together.

"Nemastes was one of the Band," said Sorba, who seemed to have a leading if not dominating position among her sisters. She pointed behind them to the cone smoking on the northern horizon. "They live there, on what the nomads in Thule call the Horn."

"They're Hyperboreans, like Nemastes?" said Corylus.

The nymphs tittered behind raised hands. Even Sorba smiled. She said, "We're all Hyperboreans to your people, dear Corylus. We live above the north wind. But Nemastes and his siblings live on the Horn, and that is true of them alone."

"No one can go onto the Horn," said a nymph. "And the Twelve can't leave it now, though their souls do sometimes."

"Nemastes left it," said another nymph. "He left, and he took the talisman of Botrug with him."

"Nemastes left to rule the world alone," Sorba said, nodding in agreement, "for all time."

"The Twelve remain on the Horn," said a nymph, "but not really in it."

"They have a connection," said a sister. "A close connection to this world."

"But they aren't not *in* it," chorused three together, nodding as they spoke. "Not in this world."

"Or in your world either, Corylus," said one of the two who'd spoken before.

"Though your world is this world now," said the other with a giggle.

"Nemastes may destroy his siblings," said Sorba, "or the Twelve may destroy Nemastes. But either would destroy you if they got the opportunity, dear Corylus."

"They'll destroy the world between them, like as not," said a nymph.

"This world and your world," said another.

"And perhaps the Horn as well," said a third. "Even the Horn, where there's nothing but rock, and the wizards dance with demons."

"Nothing but rock and fire," a nymph agreed with sad finality.

"We'll help you, though, Corylus," Sorba said. "For kinship's sake."

"And because you're so handsome," tittered a nymph behind her raised hand.

"So very handsome!" said another. "And so *strong*."

"Here, I'll borrow your knife," said Sorba. Corylus nodded permission, but the nymph had already reached to the hilt and drawn it from its sealskin case. The blade of gray-green glass winked like the eye of a cat.

"Oh, use me!" said a nymph, clapping her hands together.

"*Me!*" the whole troop chorused. "*Me, oh me!*"

"Hush, Sisters!" Sorba said sternly. "*Me,* of course."

She lifted a lock of hair between her left thumb and forefinger and sawed it off close to the roots with the obsidian blade. She slipped the knife back into its sheath while she tucked the pinch of hair into the upturned peak of the hat Corylus had taken from Odd's corpse.

Sorba kissed him lightly on the lips, then hopped back and grinned. Her sisters giggled like reed chimes.

"Now," said Sorba, "you need to be on your way."

She pointed her arm southward. Corylus turned. On the horizon several miles away were six humped forms. A herd of pony-sized creatures spread widely across the landscape to east and west of the larger animals.

"The elephants?" he said. They seemed to be carrying burdens.

"The mammoths," said/corrected Sorba. "And the reindeer. The Tribe is camping, dear Corylus. There you will find Frothi and Nemastes. Be careful."

"Do be careful, Corylus," other voices said, fading as they spoke.

"Thank you—," Corylus said as he turned toward the dryads, but they had vanished. "Well, thank you anyway."

He still hadn't eaten. He shouldered his light pack anyway and resumed his trek southward.

"Frothi and Nemastes," whispered a voice that was only in his mind. "And the bone flute, Corylus; and vengeance."

THOUGH ALPHENA STEPPED from Deriades' dwelling into the same forest where she'd fought the sphinx, the sky now was bright as day. Bright *as* day, but it wasn't really daylight because there wasn't any sun that she could see.

She looked carefully, but she couldn't see the dwelling she'd been in a moment before. At her feet was an arc of spiky puffballs, but they were all small.

Alphena didn't quite hug herself, but she rubbed her biceps with the opposite hands. It was comforting to remember that her stepmother was searching for her. That her *mother* was searching for her. Hedia would figure something out.

Alphena didn't know what to do, but she walked—strolled, really; she had no destination—along what was probably a chance aisle among the trees rather than a path. Most of the vegetation looked *wrong*, but she wasn't some gardener who knew the names of plants and how they were supposed to look.

Corylus was a gardener, or anyway his father was. She wished he were here. But in a way she couldn't have explained, the fact that Hedia was coming to find her was more comforting than the youth's presence would have been.

Alphena drew the sword and looked at its curved delicacy. It didn't seem to weigh any more than a dandelion stalk, but the more she examined it, the less of a toy it seemed.

What on earth is the blade made of? It certainly isn't steel, not with that rainbow luster.

But maybe that was the wrong question to ask. Wherever this place was, it wasn't on earth.

Alphena sheathed the sword and resumed her amble through the forest. Just ahead was what looked like an ordinary oak, standing out from trees which seemed to have snakes or even seaweed in their ancestry. On an outstretched limb sat a brunette who could have modeled for a statue of Athena: hard, beautiful, and sneeringly superior.

Alphena stopped in consternation. *How long has this woman been watching?*

"I am Alphena," she called, her voice commanding. "Daughter of Senator Gaius Alphenus Saxa. Who are you?"

"I'm Dryope," said the woman, "if it's any of your business."

The limb was ten feet up the heavy trunk, but Dryope slid easily from it to the ground. Her knees flexed as she landed, but she instantly straightened.

"And you didn't need to tell me your name, girl," she continued, "because I already knew it, and because it doesn't matter. *You* don't matter."

Alphena started toward the older woman, flexing her right hand. She wouldn't use the sword, but if this bitch thought she could get away with being openly insulting—

"You're the one who Nemastes marked out," said Dryope. "You're a piece in his game."

Nemastes is back in Carce. "How do you know about Nemastes in this place?" Alphena said, pleased that her voice didn't tremble as it rose into a question.

"And what better place is there to know about Nemastes?" Dryope said with a laugh of cultured scorn. "I know that he's a mistake, dearie. Which is more than you know—but you don't know much of anything, do you?"

To Alphena's surprise, that sneer cooled her mind instead of driving her into a fury. She looked with detachment at what was going on. Dryope was being pointlessly nasty because she felt weak and ignored; which, if she lived alone here in the forest, she probably was.

Alphena smiled. She had a sword; Dryope didn't have any weapon or armor. The power was in the hands of Alphena, daughter of Gaius, who therefore could afford to be magnanimous.

"Then tell me about Nemastes, Lady Dryope," she said. "So that I can see for myself how wise you are."

Dryope's eyes narrowed. How old was she, anyway? Her skin and hair were too fine for someone even thirty, but despite that she gave the impression of age if not of wisdom.

"The shaman Botrug summoned Nemastes and his

siblings, the Band, from far away," Dryope said, her gaze watchful as though expecting Alphena to use the words to trap her. "Botrug thought he could control them and use their power."

"They're all Hyperboreans?" Alphena said. As she spoke she realized that she might better have stayed silent, but it was too late once the first syllable was out.

"None of them are Hyperboreans," Dryope said; the sneer had returned. "Botrug was a Hyperborean, but the Band came from a distance you can't fathom, girl. They're not Indians or even the Serians who weave your silk. They're from much farther away."

"You're very wise, milady," Alphena said submissively. In this place she could *use* a sword on someone if she wanted to. That's what she'd done to the sphinx, in fact. Alphena had as much power as she wanted to take. Knowing that sluiced away her frustration.

"Wiser than you," the older woman sniffed. "Wiser than Botrug too. The Band couldn't touch him, but they could enter the dreams of Botrug's brother. The brother made an image of Botrug, and the shaman is trapped in it."

A line of gleaming birds twittered into the clearing, curved around the oak, and vanished again. Alphena could hear their high-pitched cries for a moment longer.

Her tongue touched her lips. They hadn't been birds. They were green dragonflies, seven of them, and each bore a tiny human rider in bright clothing. One had waved and called Alphena's name as he zipped past.

"Nemastes is in Carce," Alphena said, forcing her mind away from the procession of insects. "But his brothers are here?"

Dryope laughed. She was delighted at the chance to use her knowledge—*not* wisdom, but the silly cow thought it was—to toy with Alphena.

"No, of *course* not, little child," she said. "Nemastes

is in the waking world, which he hopes to rule, while the Twelve are on the Horn. The Twelve will destroy Nemastes' world, your world, to protect themselves."

The woman's laughter wasn't forced, but Alphena heard more madness than humor in it. "The Legions of Surtr will race over the waking world, dearie, leaving nothing in their wake except the smoking rock. Nothing but the Horn, where the Twelve have walled themselves behind spells that not even they can break!"

Alphena licked her lips again. Most of the vegetation around her had sharp outlines, as though it were a painted stage set. She imagined it curling at the touch of flames, turning to heat and blackness and terror.

She'd seen great fires. Anyone who lived in Carce was likely to have, since the buildings were close together and the top floors of even the most modern had walls of wicker under a thin coat of plaster. It was easy to imagine flames lapping the whole horizon, sweeping down on Carce, over Carce—

She swallowed. Over Alphena, daughter of Gaius.

"But the *real* joke, little girl," Dryope said, her voice rising into a shriek. "The real joke is who will lead the fire that destroys you, all of you! Your brother will lead the legions, dearie, with the talisman of Botrug!"

Alphena drew the sword and stepped forward. Dryope blinked in sudden awareness, then slipped backward and vanished. *Into* the oak, but maybe that was an illusion.

Alphena was breathing hard. She raised her sword to slash the trunk—Deriades had claimed the blade would cut even rock. Instead she sheathed it again.

However sharp and strong the blade was, it wasn't an axe and it wasn't meant for felling trees. In this place she might need the sword for a sphinx or something worse than a sphinx. And besides . . .

Alphena got control of her breathing. She hugged

herself for a moment, then continued on through the forest.

And besides, there was enough destruction already, in this world as well as her own. She wouldn't create more unless she had to.

HEDIA STEPPED INTO color and warmth, which would have been a pleasant change from her late husband's dank gray world even if—she smiled at the thought, but it wasn't really a joke—it involved the hot breath of an orange tiger from India. Now that she was out of that cave, she wasn't sure that she could bring herself to re-enter it if that was required.

Latus said he expects me to join him eventually. I'll die first. She clamped her lips over peals of hysterical laughter.

Hedia was in a forest of beech and . . . she looked at the ground and found as she expected the quartered black husks that had covered hickory nuts . . . yes, hickories. Waving immediately overhead, however, was a near blanket of what looked like giant dock leaves. They filtered the light to a yellowish green.

She stopped, frowning. Her husband had promised her a guide. The gods and Hedia too knew that Latus would lie, had lied, on almost any subject, but there hadn't been any reason for him to lie about this. Was she looking in the wrong place?

Something chirped from the top of a hickory. The call ended in a metallic *cling-cling-cling* that made her wonder if it was really a bird.

Hedia began walking. The dock stems were fuzzy; she kept her distance from them, wondering if they would make her itch if her arm brushed them. The call sounded again, and she walked more quickly.

A mass of blackberry canes with white flowers mounded a fallen log. In the heart of the brambles Hedia noticed a bird's nest. As she glanced away, tiny human faces peeped from the nest and giggled. She stopped and jerked her attention back.

They vanished. There was nothing in the nest but down from the parent birds, worked with cobwebs into a lining for the structure of woven twigs.

Hedia stopped and squinted. Her gaze wanted to glance off to one side or another, but she forced herself to concentrate on the interior of the nest.

And there they were: human figures, tiny but perfectly formed, smiling back at her. "Good morning, missie!" called one. He looked at his companion and said, "She can see us, Arga."

"She's very pretty, Grattus," the little female said. Then, doubtfully, "Is she prettier than me, do you think?"

Probably not, thought Hedia. The sprite's features were perfect beyond what anything human could attain to.

Smiling coldly, Hedia continued on into what became open woodland. There was a person's appearance, which was an asset that came from the gods and a good team of cosmeticians; and then there was the way a person used her assets. Hedia wasn't afraid to compete with any woman she'd met. If she included tiny, lovely sprites now, well, she still wasn't afraid.

To the left, lines of great linden trees framed an alley. In it danced . . . men and women, she thought, some of them holding wands high in one hand or the other. At first she thought they wore tunics or kirtles of thin fabric. As they dipped and spun, their garments shifted place and color: they were made of light itself.

The whirling figures closest to Hedia smiled and beckoned. She turned and walked on more swiftly.

The dancers' skin had a faint reddish cast, and their figures were too regular for Hedia to be confident that they and she were the same species. Besides that, she heard enough of the faint music to which they danced that she feared if she joined them she would never be able to leave.

Three purple herons, familiar to Hedia from the marshes near Baiae, strode from the heavy brush and trotted past her in the other direction, their necks stretching out and curving back with each step. Riding each bird was a chipmunk wearing a yellow cap, red vest, and blue trousers. They watched Hedia silently, their heads turning till they were almost looking back between their own shoulders.

The herons vanished into the undergrowth. The black feathers in the riders' caps mimicked the birds' crests.

Hedia walked on. Would her guide be a chipmunk? Not one of *those* chipmunks, at least . . . but she glanced back to be sure.

She wasn't afraid, exactly, but she was frustrated because she didn't know what was happening. Rather, she didn't know what was supposed to happen: nothing *was* happening.

Hedia trusted her late husband within the limits of their bargain, but he'd never been communicative. Death hadn't changed that for the better, though . . . she remembered the way Latus had seemed to be sinking into the foliage of that horrible forest when she left him. It might be that learning more wouldn't have made her easier in her mind.

To Hedia's left was a grove of maples. She glimpsed a patch of tawny hide within the undergrowth of evening olive and spiky, brittle viburnum bushes.

A deer, she thought. The animal turned and looked at her with human eyes, then crashed out of sight deeper in the thicket.

The forest to her right had grown deeper and much darker. Sheets of gray lichen hung from the branches of great trees. Hoots from far in the distance could have been birds, but she didn't think they were.

Something large splashed into an unseen body of water. Hedia wondered for an instant if it or another behemoth would shortly burst out of the screen of willows and mimosas, but nothing did. She took her hand off the little dagger.

Someone was playing a lyre among the oaks ahead. The shade was deep enough to thin the undergrowth, but saplings whose trunks were only the diameter of Hedia's finger nonetheless impeded the way. She held the spindly branches to keep them from snagging her garments as she walked by.

Occasionally she broke one off, but that was accidental. She had the feeling that it would be better not to leave more trace of her passage than she had to.

The music was coming closer—well, she was approaching it; the source hadn't moved. She didn't recall ever hearing a lyre played more beautifully. She stepped carefully past a holly tree and looked into a clearing without seeing the musician.

Drawn by the plangent tune, Hedia looked up. A web spread from the top of a hickory to a huge white oak. A spider whose body was the size of a pony hung from the silk by her back legs; with the three pairs remaining, she played the lyre.

The spider's multiple eyes followed as Hedia walked on at a measured pace, carefully avoiding any hint that she was frightened. She looked over her shoulder as soon as she was out of the clearing, but only the music followed her. It slowly faded, and even more slowly, Hedia brought her thudding heartbeat under control.

She was approaching a garden. It hadn't been hacked out of the forest; rather, the forest was encroaching into it. The wall of fieldstones laid without mortar was collapsing in the embrace of tree roots, and the plantings were bushy and overgrown.

A statue of Priapus, the traditional protector of gardens, stood at one end. His torso and bearded head had been crudely hacked from a length of tree trunk; his phallus was a separate branch of cedar as long and thick as a man's thigh. The wood still had a realistically ruddy tinge.

Hedia walked past. Out of the corner of her eye, she saw the statue wink and waggle its enormous penis. She didn't turn and stare, but she smiled as she went on. She had enough experience to associate a *really* impressive partner—she'd known one or two—with pain, not a thrill.

A man stepped out of the forest. He was nude; his deep chest was covered with flat, distinct sheets of muscle. Black curls covered his head, and over his right shoulder he carried a stout wooden club.

His legs from midthigh were hairy, and the knees bent the wrong way; he walked on split hooves. *He's not a man after all.*

"My name is Maron, woman," said the faun. "I am compelled to be your guide."

VARUS TURNED HIS back as he pulled on his tunic. He didn't know what to say, so for the moment he pretended that Urash didn't exist.

"Varus?" she said.

He looked over his shoulder, embarrassed by his own behavior. He hadn't even unlaced his sandals! "M-mis . . . ," he said. "Yes, Urash?"

She'd lifted herself onto her right elbow and was watching him. She was noticeably more solid than she had been when he first entered this . . . place between places.

"When will another come to me?" Urash said. Her

need, her *longing*, were so vivid that Varus blushed with the memory of her body writhing under his.

"I don't know!" he said harshly, and hated himself as the words came out. The pulse in his mind was strong and growing stronger as he delayed in this place.

Varus knelt beside the woman and took her hands, then met her eyes. "Urash," he said, "I don't know about, well, anything. I don't even know what I'm supposed to do, just that they say I have to do it or the world will die. I met your h-h-hus . . . I met Oannes this afternoon and he sent me here, but he didn't tell me anything."

His face scrunched with misery. He wished he could make the truth something else than he knew it was. If this had been a poem, he could change his scheme and bring consolation to this ordinary, *nice* woman and her perfectly decent husband who had made a mistake out of love alone.

Homer had brought the goddess Athena out of the heavens to end the feud between Odysseus and the families of the suitors whom he'd killed. But Varus couldn't summon gods; and he wouldn't lie.

"Urash," he said, "I'm sure that Oannes will do all that he can for you, as he has in the past. But I can't tell you any more than that."

"I'm sorry," Urash said softly. She got to her feet, bringing him up with her. She didn't put her clothing on. "You've been very kind. I know that it isn't anything you could control, but I needed, I need . . ."

Her voice broke off and she began to cry silently.

Shriveling inside, Varus stepped close to Urash and kissed her, tasting the salt. "Dear?" he said. "How do I reach my guide?"

Urash lifted her face and looked toward the window into the sacrificial mound. Though the men had taken the torches with them when they left and the entrance was blocked up, the corpse was still visible in a faint blue aura. Sigyn's blood was a deeper blackness on the stone.

"Open the way, Varus," Urash said. She stroked his tunic where it lumped over the ivory talisman. "You have the power of Botrug. You have the powers of a god, Varus dear."

Varus turned his head slightly to the side. "Urash?" he said. "Can I help you?"

He felt himself coloring again. "Can I help you leave this place, I mean?"

"Not even a god can do that, Varus," she said. She touched his shoulders and gently turned him to face the barrow. "You have your duty."

Varus drew the ivory head from beneath his tunic and cleared his throat. He didn't know how to proceed. *Do I just . . .*

As Varus hesitated, the now-familiar fog swept in to enclose him. He couldn't see Urash anymore. Either she'd taken her hands away from his shoulders, or he was no longer in the place where she must stay for eternity.

Varus walked into the mist. Was there really anything beneath his feet? Did he have feet or any material existence here, or was it a trick his mind was playing on him?

He came out in brightness. The old woman sat cross-legged on a stone plinth. Beside her was a brazier from which licked thin violet flames as long as a man's forearm. She smiled, forming new creases in her wrinkled face.

"Lady," he said, making a slight bow. "I have to come to you when I need power. Magic, I guess I mean."

They were on top of a bare sandstone knob. Below them—thousands of feet below—a brilliantly white cloudscape humped from horizon to horizon. The wind was thin and very cold, and it didn't appear to affect the lambent flames from the brazier.

"*I* don't exist, Lord Varus," the woman said, smiling still more widely. "All power, all knowledge, are yours. I'm just the way you choose to assert your power."

Varus narrowed his eyes. He started to say that he didn't believe what she had just said, but that would be discourteous. Besides, the mechanism didn't matter. If his mind told him that he had to come to this plane, this cloud-world, that was perfectly all right so long as it permitted him to do what was necessary.

Which in this case . . .

"Lady," he said, "I need to go to a woman in a tomb, Sigyn. She's . . . she will guide me."

"Then go, Varus," the woman said. "Open the portal. You know how."

Her face worked over silent words. "*Out I go at once,*" Varus squeaked, "*flinging wide the doors! I have no fear—*"

Varus felt his soul swoop into the ocean of clouds. He was blind and felt as though he were spinning. He was suddenly afraid that he was going to vomit. *At least that would prove I have a body,* he thought.

Varus was laughing as he stepped into the dank blue interior of the tomb. The stones were slick from moisture that had sweated through the cairn and frozen, but the worst of the chill was spiritual. The chamber stank of blood and death.

Sigyn lay on the slab, face upward. Her eyes were open, and her throat gaped raggedly; the knife had been dull, though the killer's strength and nervousness had made quick work of the task.

Sigyn was younger than Varus had realized. *She couldn't be any older than Alphena!* He swallowed.

How do I . . . ? Varus thought, gripping the talisman with his left hand. The ivory felt warm.

"Awake, good maiden!" he called in his own voice, surprising himself. "Awake, Sister Sigyn!"

The corpse stirred, but as mindlessly as a grapevine touched by a breeze.

"Awake, my friend!" Varus said. "You sleep in a cave of darkest night, but we must go forth together."

The corpse's eyes were already open; now they focused on Varus. Her head lifted slightly. In a rusty voice she said, "Who is it that calls Sigyn? Sigyn is dead. Now there is only the Bride."

Varus squeezed the ivory talisman with his left hand. His brow was sweating, and the hair on the back of his neck prickled. "Awake, Sigyn," he said, "and we will go forth together—or I will hedge you with fire and compel you!"

Sigyn sat up with the creaking deliberation of a wagon turning and fingered her throat with her left hand. Dried blood had matted her flowing hair.

"Who are you to command me, poet?" she said, eyeing him now with comprehension. Her voice was stronger, and her features were beginning to show animation.

"I am Gaius Varus," he said, choosing the words consciously for the first time since he had entered the tomb. "I have the power"—he held out the talisman to the length of the thong around his neck—"and the need. I must lead the Legions of Surtr or the world will die, so you must guide me to them."

The woman got off the slab, moving stiffly but without wasted motion. "You have the power," she said. "You cannot compel Sigyn, but the Bride will guide you on your way."

She looked at Varus; his hand tightened on the talisman. When he realized he was keeping it in front of him as a barrier against the woman's cold gaze, he let it fall and stood with both arms at his sides.

"You have a great task, Varus," she said; her voice

seemed without emotion. "Do you have the strength to complete it?"

"I have to try," Varus said, trying to keep his tone calm. "Otherwise the world will end."

The woman laughed like pebbles rattling. She took him by the right hand. Her flesh was cold, and he almost gagged on the stench of her fresh blood.

"Come, Varus," she said. They walked together toward the end of the chamber, and the stones dissolved before them.

CHAPTER XIII

The back wall of the cairn had been a blur. It cleared, and Varus stepped onto a trail along a mountainside. To his left was a cloud-filled gorge, and above, the sky showed the smooth pearl of high overcast. A patch near zenith was brighter than the remainder, but the sun wasn't visible.

The woman released his hand. "Come," she said, starting along the trail. The fog beside them swirled and eddied in the direction they were walking.

"Sigyn?" Varus said, his head turned slightly toward the gorge. The mist moved as swiftly as a millrace. Occasionally he saw the top of a pine tree, and once something in a treetop stared back with unwinking eyes.

"There is no Sigyn, Varus," the woman said. "Sigyn died in a far place and at another time. If you want an answer, you must ask the Bride."

Varus didn't speak for a moment. He hadn't been a good poet, but he'd been a meticulous one. He understood the importance of words.

"Sigyn," he said firmly. "Where are you taking me?"

The woman raised her left hand and traced her fingertips along the line of the cut. She began to laugh; flakes of blood cracked off the skin of her throat.

"We go to pick the fruit of the First Tree, Varus," she said. "The Tree is on an island in a sea which cannot be crossed. When you have picked the fruit, then we will go to the entrance to the Underworld, where the Guardian waits. You have already met the Guardian."

Varus thought. "The lizard that Pandareus and I had to run from?" he said.

"The dragon that you ran from," said the woman. "The Guardian cannot be harmed. We must pass the Guardian to enter the Underworld, where we will meet my destined husband. My husband will direct you to the end of your route, Varus."

Varus said nothing for a time. The path was broad enough for two, but he found himself lagging a half step behind his guide. The upward slope to the right was just short of a sheer wall. He saw a few birches and once a squat, gnarled conifer, but all those trees grew from cracks in the rock. Other than that, only lichen provided patches of color.

There was a dot in the sky. Varus stared at it for a moment. It didn't seem to move, but when he closed first one eye, then the other, the touch of blackness remained. It wasn't a speck in his eye.

Now and then a whorl of mist cleared on the left. The glimpses through those eddies showed that the descent into the gorge was equally steep. *What would happen if I fell?*

Varus opened his mouth to ask the question aloud, then swallowed the words unsaid. Nothing good would happen. He would die, or he would cripple himself— could he die in this place? Sigyn hadn't—or perhaps he would spend eternity in a dank gray abyss whose walls he certainly couldn't climb. It was better that he not fall.

The path didn't seem to have been cut, but it couldn't be natural given the slope above and below it. It was free of debris. No pebbles had weathered out and fallen onto it from above, nor had slabs cracked into the gorge to narrow the path into a ledge down which Varus would have to sidle with his heart in his mouth.

If I can concentrate on the small puzzles, Varus thought, *then I don't have to think about the great ones. The latter mean life or death for the world—and I can't solve them either.*

He grinned. His logic was impeccable even though the situation was completely irrational. *Pandareus would be proud of me.*

At first Varus had thought he could see the opposite wall of the gorge, but now the sea of mist spread into the unguessable distance. There was a howl from below. It could have been the wind, but he didn't think it was.

"Sigyn?" he said. "What made the sound I just heard? From down in the valley."

The woman glanced back at him. She laughed, making the edges of her severed throat wobble.

"Are you afraid, Varus?" she said. "Nothing here can stand against the wizard who dared to steal the Bride of Loki."

"I'm not afraid," Varus said. The sudden anger warmed him. "Not about that, anyway—I'm afraid I'll fail, of course. But I want to know what that animal is because I like to know things!"

The woman's mocking smile faded. "It is not an animal," she said. "Once it was a spirit, but that was long ago. Now it is a hunger and a memory, but it cannot climb to where we are."

"Thank you, Sigyn," Varus said. He coughed for an excuse to lower his eyes.

I shouldn't have spoken so harshly. She's been murdered, after all; she has an excuse for being, well, negative.

"Sigyn knew little and feared much," the woman said, facing the path again. "All the folk of Thule did. When the Horn, the mountain on the shore, rumbled, they were frightened. The Horn belched smoke that burned our throats and bleached the leaves, so the men of the

Tribe gathered in council. They vowed Sigyn to Loki in the Underworld."

She looked at Varus again; he met her eyes by an effort of will. Her smile this time was different from the cold cruelty he'd seen in it before.

"Now I am the Bride," she said. "I know all things; but I do not fear, and I do not care."

Varus had a sudden vision of what for him would be Hell . . . and perhaps was Hell for Sigyn also. He swallowed, then wiped his stinging eyes. She was too young to have done anything that deserved this. Perhaps no one deserved it.

"Where is Thule, Sigyn?" he asked. His throat unclogged as he spoke, as he had hoped it would.

"You speak to one who is dead," the woman said petulantly; but after a moment she went on. "Thule is in the north. I cannot describe the location in a form you would understand."

Varus chewed cautiously on the inside of his cheeks to work the dryness out of them. Sigyn might be past fear, but he wasn't. It wouldn't prevent him from going forward, though.

"Sigyn?" he said. "This volcano, the Horn?" She'd described it as a mountain that rumbled and blew out sulfurous smoke. "Do Hyperboreans live on it? Wizards, I think?"

The woman laughed horribly again. "You mean the Twelve," she said. "They went to the Horn and walled it off from the waking world when Nemastes left them. But they do not live, Varus, they exist; just as the Bride exists."

For a moment, the pulse of the dancers in Varus's mind was so strong that he staggered. He dipped to one knee and pressed the fingertips of both hands against the rocky path.

The pressure drained as suddenly as it had begun.

Varus got to his feet and said, "I'm sorry. I'm all right now. We'll go on."

The woman had waited for him; now she resumed her measured pace. In the distance ahead were touches of red and yellow instead of the omnipresent cold white that Varus had seen thus far in the sky here.

"The spells protecting the Horn are stronger than the cosmos itself," she said, her eyes on the horizon. "So long as the Twelve exist, the spells cannot be breached. Not even the Legions of Surtr can pass them, though they march across the whole waking world besides."

"*I'm* going to lead the legions," Varus said. He heard his voice rising. Furious with his weakness, he grimaced.

The woman laughed. After a moment, she pointed ahead of them. She said, "We are nearing the First Tree, wizard."

The thing in the gorge howled again. In a moment, another of its kind answered in keening despair.

ALPHENA FORCED HER way through a clump of plants whose sword-shaped leaves stood vertically. The edges weren't sharp enough to cut, but the underside of her forearms tingled after the contact. She wondered if the soft skin there was going to break out in a rash.

As she'd hoped, she'd reached a clearing. The ground was covered with grass whose blades were as fine as a cat's fur. It was an immediate relief that foliage wasn't touching her as it had done for all the past hour or more. The track had been worn by animals—pigs, perhaps?—whose shoulders came no higher than Alphena's knees. Above that, leaves hung close on both sides.

Round orange fruit dangled from a tree growing from the wall of vegetation across the clearing twenty feet away. Alphena doubted they were really oranges— the tree trunk twisted like the body of a snake, and its branches were lesser snakes writhing from it—but the fruit was certainly edible: scraps of rind, some of them whole half-spheres, lay scattered on the grass below. The pulp was pallid with a faintly blue cast.

A bird with a long tail flew off with a cry that was more like a cat than anything with wings. Alphena hadn't seen the creature till it moved, which disturbed her. *I have to be more careful. What if it was a snake?*

To the right of the fruit tree grew a stand of saplings; their leaves drooped in ribbonlike tassels. In the foliage dangled blue flowers, each as big as a man's head. Alphena couldn't tell whether the blooms hung from the saplings like the leaves did or if their stems dropped from the limbs of trees deeper in the forest.

A Cyclops twelve feet tall stepped through the curtain of leaves; his passage made only a faint rustle. He was clad in skins that had been knotted together, not sewn; they were raw and stank of sour death.

The giant's face was a shaggy mass with only the nose and brow clear of tangling hair. When he opened his mouth in what was either a grin or a silent snarl, his breath was foul as a tannery.

Alphena shouted, "Wau!" and jumped backward. When she was five years old and playing in the garden of the family villa in the Sabine Hills, a large grasshopper had lighted on the back of her neck. That was the only time she could remember having been equally startled.

The Cyclops stepped toward her. Despite his size, he moved gracefully. In vegetation as thick as that around her, Alphena was sure that the monster's weight and strength would allow him to catch her in a few strides if she turned and ran.

She had been startled, not frightened. She drew her sword. Well, she was frightened too, but she was going to fight.

The Cyclops's eye was red and bloodshot around a

black iris; each lash was as thick as a tiger's bristle. It focused on the rainbow beauty of Alphena's sword. She waggled the blade, wondering if it was long enough to reach the creature's body if he stretched out a hand for her neck.

With a bellow like a bullock in the jaws of a bear, the Cyclops spun and leaped back the way he had come. He was looking over his shoulder toward Alphena—or at least toward her sword—so he collided with the fruit tree instead of vanishing through the hanging leaves which had hidden his presence. The tree was six inches thick where his shoulder struck it, but the trunk cracked and a split ran down it almost to the roots.

The impact jolted the Cyclops to his right and half turned his massive body. He didn't lose his footing, however. Pivoting like a dancer, he crashed through the screen of saplings and into the forest beyond. Alphena heard the sound of smashing vegetation and the Cyclops's cries of wild terror.

She straightened from the crouch she'd dropped into when the monster came at her. She was gasping for breath, though the only effort she'd expended was to draw a sword that seemed as light as a willow withy.

Alphena looked at the blade, shimmering more like a piece of jewelry than a weapon. It was so highly polished that she had difficulty seeing the metal. The reflections from its rounded surface seemed to be brighter than the light filtering through the treetops which woke them.

Is it magical? The Cyclops had certainly seemed to be afraid of something more than a sharp point in the hand of a girl. Maybe that was what Deriades had meant when he'd given her this weapon in particular.

Alphena had her breath back. She started to sheathe the sword again, but her hand was trembling with reaction. There hadn't been fighting to burn the emotions out of her. She didn't want to stab herself in the thigh, and besides . . . well, after the surprise she'd just survived, keeping the sword in her hand didn't seem like such a bad idea. It didn't weigh much, after all.

The giant had proved when he appeared that he could slip through the forest without leaving a trail, but in the panic of his flight he was tearing a path that a blind man could follow. Some of the more supple trees had merely been pushed down and were springing up again, but anything more than an inch in diameter had been either snapped off or torn out and cast aside.

Alphena eyed the pig track she'd been following, then looked at the gap the Cyclops had made. In a way it seemed foolish to go in the same direction as a monster she'd been only too glad to see the back of, but he hadn't been willing to face her sword before, so there was every reason to expect he'd flee again if they met. Besides, she was tired of having to almost swim through the foliage. She set off on the Cyclops's trail.

That curved slightly to the left, through an understory of small hardwoods. Many of the saplings had been pulled out of the soft ground. Tiny movements—Alphena saw colors rather than shapes—shifted about the dying trees. She thought of Dryope, then remembered Persica. *Yes, of course! Persica!*

In anger she squeezed the sword hilt harder—but Persica had been a jealous bitch, not a monster. Alphena had met plenty of girls who behaved as badly as Persica, but she wouldn't think of killing them. Well, she wouldn't *really* have killed them, though she might have said something like that.

When the sphinx poised to rip Alphena's throat out, she had gotten a better understanding of what killing meant—and of death.

She might have the servants cane Persica when she

got back, though. Or bruise the bark of the peach tree, if they couldn't find Persica in the garden.

Right now Alphena was feeling sorry for the flecks of light hovering around the uprooted trees, just as she would for kittens she found drowned in the gutter. She hadn't been responsible, except that she'd frightened a monster that was otherwise prepared to eat her alive. She wasn't so sorry that she would die to save sprites, if they were what she was seeing.

The trampled path jerked to the right as though the Cyclops had run into a stone wall and caromed off. Alphena paused in surprise, then used her left arm to part the line of sedges which the giant had been tall enough to look over. She kept a tight grip on her sword.

Beyond was a clearing surrounded by palms whose fronds sprang from squat, coarse trunks like earthenware tubs. On the grass was a pair of small boards tied together along one edge: a notebook. It looked very like the notebook her brother always carried.

"Varus!" Alphena called, filled with sudden hope. *I'm not alone!*

She sprang into the clearing and snatched up the notebook. The boards were plain wood and blank on both sides. They could have been written on with a brush of ink, but her brother normally used a stylus on a wax coating.

A pair of wraiths larger than a man stepped from the palm fronds. The creatures' surface had a liquescent slickness, as though they were made of pink mucus. They made no sound.

Alphena dropped the notebook and stepped backward, keeping her eyes on the wraiths. A third creature grasped her from behind; its grip was cold and clammy, like that of a giant toad.

Alphena spun. The wraith was inhumanly strong, but

she could twist her forearm enough to slash through the creature's thigh. The edge met no more resistance than a cobweb would have given it, but the limb flowed together unchanged behind the stroke. The dank paws didn't slacken their hold.

The first two glided across the clearing, as silent as slime molds. Alphena again cut the creature holding her, but the wound—this time across its chest—closed like water over the gleaming blade. A wraith held Alphena's wrist and plucked the sword from her with its free paw. It stepped aside while the others stretched her arms out to either side.

As if they're about to crucify me. And perhaps they were.

Alphena kicked, but she couldn't reach the creatures holding her. It wouldn't have mattered if her blows had landed.

A man stepped into view, smiling. He was in his late fifties, but he looked as fit as someone half his age. He had iron gray hair and a full beard that gave his features an archaic aspect.

He wore a toga with a broad purple stripe. He was a senator of Carce.

"Help me!" Alphena cried.

He laughed. "Oh, indeed, I'll help you, Lady Alphena," he said in a deep, melodious voice. "I'll make you a queen, just as I promised. Have you forgotten?"

"I don't know you, sir," Alphena said, hoping desperately that she'd managed to control the tremble that wanted to get out through her throat.

"You will, Alphena," said the man. "I'm Spurius Cassius, and you are the queen who will rule the Underworld at my side!"

HEDIA EYED THE faun with the detached interest she gave any well-set-up man. Any well-set-up *male*, she supposed she should say, but in regard to Maron she thought that was a distinction without a difference.

The faun's truculence faded as he felt—and obviously understood—her gaze. He stood a good six inches over six feet, even taller than the new German doorkeeper; his chest was a broad wedge tapering from his collarbone to a waist that looked narrow only by contrast to his shoulders and massive thighs.

That those thighs were shaggy, or that the two hinted bumps in Maron's curly hair might be the tips of horns, really weren't important. As he grinned back at Hedia's inspection, the pink tip of his phallus began to extend from its sheath. That *might* become important . . . though not now.

Hedia unwrapped the bandage of crimson silk which she had worn wrapped around the back of her own cloth-of-gold girdle. "Maron," she said, "you are to take me to my daughter. Is that correct?"

"To take you to the girl," the faun said. He spoke in a nasal tenor. "To protect you from harm, and to take you to the passage by which you will depart this place for the waking world from which you came. By a will stronger than my own, I am compelled to do these things."

Hedia nodded and tossed him the red cloth. "This is the sash Alphena—my daughter—wore last night," she said. "I am told"—Anna had told her—"that you will need some object of the girl's in order to locate her. This should do for the purpose."

Maron turned the garment over in his hands, examining it from all angles. Then to Hedia's surprise, he lifted the silk to his nose and snuffled it.

Like a beast! she thought; and of course that was true.

He tossed the sash onto an ordinary-looking bush whose leaves immediately writhed upward to nuzzle the cloth. Hedia frowned and reflexively reached for it. The faun noticed her movement and said, "Did you want it back? Take it, then."

"No, there's no need," Hedia said, irritated with herself. She'd brought the garment for her guide's use; if he was done with it, then he was right to throw it away. She didn't like the thought of leaving anything in this place, however.

She smiled without humor. That was probably because she was afraid that she would end her days here also. Well, she'd known the risks when she decided to do whatever was necessary to bring Alphena back.

Maron lifted his nose high and this time sniffed the air itself. The hairs on the tips of his pointed ears twitched minusculely; perhaps he was aware of currents in what seemed to Hedia to be dead calm.

"All right," he said, dropping back into his normal posture with his split hooves flat on the turf. His legs had springy angles at knee and ankle, quite unlike those of a man standing upright. "She's some hours away if we travel at my speed—or a few days, if we don't go any faster than you can run."

Instead of bridling at the challenge, Hedia gave the faun a superior smile and drawled, "I don't suppose you're suggesting that I send you off to rescue my daughter by yourself, dear boy. Why don't you just tell me what you do have in mind?"

Maron snorted angrily; his ears snapped sideways and then back to vertical. Calming himself, he said, "I'll carry you. On my back—you don't look like you weigh very much. If you dare."

Again Hedia smiled faintly. "Yes, if you're capable of that, it would be the best way," she said.

She suspected that she weighed more than the faun thought she did. She kept herself very fit, though without the silly masculine trappings that Alphena affected, and muscle was a good deal heavier than fat. Still, men like Maron would burst their hearts with the effort before they'd fail to make good on a boast to an attractive woman.

"Here, then," the faun said, turning his back to her and squatting. He curled his arms at his sides, though he still held the sturdy wooden club in his right hand.

Actually, the woman doesn't have to be terribly pretty for most men, Hedia thought, smiling more broadly. *Just interested, or possibly interested; and I am.*

She put her hand's on Maron's shoulders and stepped through his arms, then hiked her skirts up to clamp his waist between her thighs. He rose without noticeable effort and immediately started off through a wall of cowslips the size of wine bowls.

The faun's pace was more like a canter than the pounding trot which Hedia had feared. She didn't especially like riding, but she'd done a certain amount of it during her first marriage. Calpurnius Musca, a cousin of Latus, had managed her husband's villa in the Campania. Musca liked to ride, so he'd taught her when she visited the estate.

Musca had been one of the most rabidly hostile members of the family after Latus died. Well, he knew better than most that she hadn't been faithful to her husband. Musca wasn't the only man she'd met who had the knack of limiting his vision to the part of a situation that suited him.

Hedia held close to Maron as he paced along. A saddle rubbing between her legs had been interesting; the faun's back was . . . more interesting. The play of his muscles was like physical lute music, each movement distinct and perfect. It felt like wires shifting under the skin. *He must not carry any fat at all. . . .*

She could look only to the side unless she wanted to risk being slapped in the face by a passing limb, so she pressed one cheek or the other alternately to the faun's back. They were loping by a thorn tree when she turned her head to the right.

What's the bright foliage? she thought. The colors—thousands of tiny figures, winged like butterflies but wearing clothing—flew from the tree in enormous waves, dipping and spiraling in the light.

"What was that!" Hedia blurted.

"Ah, don't worry about them," the faun growled. "They can't hurt you."

For an instant she thought that the strain of running had deepened his voice. Then he added, "The wolf who's following us, he'd gobble you down bones and all if I let him, though."

Maron angled slightly to the right, taking them through brush that clawed Hedia's legs. She would have cried out if she hadn't been so worried about the wolf.

The faun burst through the spiky brush and stopped. They were in a grassy clearing bounded by four huge oaks. The trees' foliage was thick, but that shouldn't have shaded out all the undergrowth.

"Wait here," Maron said, dropping his club and shifting to grip her hipbones from behind. Without further explanation, he pitched Hedia up and forward. Ten feet in the air, she fell across a broad limb which thrust out horizontally from the trunk.

Hedia yelped, but she managed to clamber onto the limb and sit normally. She looked down to object, but instead remained silent. Maron wouldn't pay any attention, and she didn't want him to now. The wolf had followed them into the clearing.

It was the size of a pony with pure white fur. It looked up at Hedia, then toward the faun. Its tongue lolled from its long jaws as though it were laughing.

"Go on your way, halfling," the wolf said in a rumble from deep in its throat. For all its seeming assurance, the beast's posture showed it was as ready to dodge as to rush in. "I'm not interested in you this time."

"You're far from your snowfields, wolf," said the faun. He'd picked up his club and was tossing it from hand to hand as he hunched forward, facing his opponent. "This is my world. I'm not going to be chased out of it by a furball from the north."

The wolf paced the edge of the clearing, then twisted like a snake to go back the other way when he'd covered a quarter of the arc. His shaggy head always faced Maron. The faun sidled, keeping himself between the beast and Hedia on the tree limb.

"Is a woman so important to you, halfling?" the wolf said. His words were losing definition, breaking into a saw-toothed growl. "I suggest you masturbate while you still have your male member to do it with. Otherwise I'll swallow it down like a sausage before I tear your liver out."

"I'm under a compulsion, puppy," the faun said, his voice lilting. "But that wouldn't matter, you see, because I'd run you back to your snow wastes regardless. The cold hides your stink, so you should stay—"

This time the wolf only half turned. In midmotion, it leaped for Maron. Its mouth opened in a terrible snarl.

Maron's club took the wolf at the base of the jaw, snapping its head up and to the right. The beast twisted in the air.

Maron stepped forward, both legs off the ground and scissoring. As the wolf slammed to the ground, the faun's hooves sliced pairs of parallel gouges across its left shoulder and the left side of its muzzle.

The wolf rolled to its feet as part of the same motion that had sent it tumbling. Blood matted the fur of its shoulder and mixed with the froth it sprayed when it shook its head. Hedia would have sworn its eyes glowed with internal light.

Maron screamed and leaped the twenty feet separating him from the wolf. It sprang to meet him in the air. Their bodies crashed together. Maron managed to avoid the wolf's jaws, but the beast's greater weight drove him back and put him on the bottom as they thumped to the ground still linked.

The wolf twisted down, jaws open to finish the fight. Maron forced his club into them. The wolf worried the wood, jerking its head side to side. Of a sudden it hopped sideways, spitting out splinters. Something pink clung to its belly.

Maron was on his feet again, his mouth in a snarl and his arms spread like those of a wrestler waiting the next fall. The fur of both legs was bloody from hoof to knee. The dangling pinkness was a coil of the wolf's intestine.

The beast growled, then looked back and nuzzled its belly. Maron screamed and grabbed a young tree growing at the edge of the clearing. Most of the undergrowth was autumn olive, a brittle shrub whose stems spread from a common base, but this was an oak sapling sprung from one of the four giants.

The wolf growled like sliding rocks. It crouched low, then yelped and bounced onto its toes. More intestine had spilled through the hole the faun's hooves had sliced. Dirt and dead leaves clung to the glistening surface.

Maron's legs were spread and his hands were linked around the sapling's trunk. *He* can't *tear that out of the ground!* Hedia thought.

Maron gave another high-pitched cry. He sounded more like a cat than a man, let alone a goat. His back muscles stood out like waves on a frozen pond. The sapling came up, scattering dirt in all directions. The taproot had broken a foot below the ground.

Maron brandished his new club. The wolf turned and shambled back through the undergrowth. Crackling brush and the beast's pitiable yowls continued for some while.

The faun knelt, using the sapling as a pole to support him. Hedia considered for a moment, then turned on the bough and let herself fall to arm's length. She held there for a moment until her legs had begun to swing back, then dropped to the ground. She wasn't a rope dancer, but more than one man had commented on how supple she was.

Maron turned his head to watch as she approached. He rose with a convulsive motion, using the strength of his shoulders; the sapling flexed but didn't break.

He grinned. "You saw it?" he demanded. "You saw me rip that furball? I ripped his guts out!"

"Yes, you did," Hedia said. Her voice was husky. "I saw you, and you ripped him like a cobweb!"

The gore on the faun's legs was drying, but there was a cut on his right biceps. He was spattered with bloody foam, not necessarily all from the wolf.

He reeked of maleness. The odor was familiar to her, but Hedia had never smelled it so powerfully.

"My beast," she said. "My great, bloody *beast*."

She released her girdle and tossed it on the ground. She was dizzy with desire.

"I cannot harm you!" Maron said in alarm. "I'm under compulsion never to harm you!"

"Silly beast," Hedia whispered, lifting her tunic over her head. "It's never harmed me before."

She dropped the garment over the girdle and stepped toward the faun. His phallus was fully erect.

"*My* beast," Hedia said as she felt his mighty arms encircle her.

CORYLUS FIGURED THE tribe must have seen him almost as quickly as he saw them. Faces, pale though too distant to have features, turned in his direction. He waved his left hand high, showing them it was empty.

The closest thing Corylus had to a weapon was Odd's obsidian knife. That bothered him emotionally, but the lucid part of his mind knew that he couldn't fight that many opponents even if he were wearing full infantry kit. Looking friendly and harmless was his best chance of survival.

The tribe was in the process of setting up camp on the rim of a vast grassy crater. Domed leather tents were rising on frames of willow saplings. There were nearly forty dwellings and, at a quick estimate, around two hundred folk all told. Presumably every head of house was a warrior, and there would be grown sons as well. No, this wasn't a time when force was the best option for a lone stranger.

Corylus still wished he had his staff with him. *If I can get a message to Persica, perhaps she'll send it on.* He grinned at his silent joke.

Three men started toward him, holding what looked like bundles of short spears. They stayed close together, which was actually good news: it meant they were concerned with mutual support if he attacked them. Had one moved out on either flank, they would be preparing to hunt him down if he ran.

Before the trio got close, a fourth man called them back. Corylus heard the tone of command in the shout, though the meaning was only to be guessed.

That will be Frothi. He was no taller than the others, but his beard was blond and spread like a flag across his chest.

Corylus waved again. He was smiling. In part his determined good humor was a way to convince himself that everything was going to be fine.

Two birds circled overhead. Anything at that height would look black against the pale sky, but the exceptionally deep wings meant Corylus was probably right in guessing they were ravens.

That didn't mean Wisdom and Memory were escorting him, however. They or two of their kin might simply be hoping for a meal.

Corylus quickened his pace, the way any lone traveler might do when he sighted companionship ahead of him. Tribesmen came from their previous occupations, some of them running, but nobody pushed beyond the point where Frothi stood.

They stood in a hierarchy of place: the sturdiest men were to the chieftain's either side; older men were right and left of that central core; then boys; and finally the women with the children. All the men were armed, though their light javelins had heads of stone or sharpened bone.

The tribesmen had no swords for lack of metal, but Corylus didn't see stone axes or edged clubs either. These were hunters, not warriors. To be sure they could kill a man easily enough, but the question of intent was important.

Their herd animals were squat deer whose antlers swept back over their necks. They seemed as tame as sheep, but they were spreading across the plain now that the herdsmen had gone to look at Corylus. The six hairy elephants, the mammoths as the tree nymph had named them, were grazing in a loose group. They'd been unloaded, but two still wore net harnesses of leather and grass rope in which the tents had been packed.

The space immediately to the chief's right had been empty. Nemastes stepped into it. He wore leather clothing, but nobody would have mistaken the tall, bald man for one of the tribesmen.

The figure behind Nemastes was taller even than the wizard. It had a low forehead, a long jaw, and massive brow ridges that prevented Corylus from thinking of it as human even though it stood erect on two legs. What seemed at first glance to be a shaggy coat was the creature's pelt. It smiled, showing powerful canine teeth in both the upper and lower jaws.

Corylus was within thirty feet. He'd expected that Frothi would address him, but the chief kept haughtily silent. The other men let their eyes shift from him to the stranger and back again, but Nemastes stared fixedly at Corylus. *You'd almost expect him to have a membrane that flicked sideways across his eyes, the way a snake does.*

"Hail, Chief Frothi!" Corylus said, stopping where he was. He raised his left arm again, keeping his empty right hand ostentatiously in sight. "We are well met. And hail to you also, Nemastes."

Odd's Vengeance had warned Corylus to expect Nemastes, but the ivory figurine hanging around the wizard's neck from a thong was a surprise. It was the miniature head which Varus had worn since his public reading.

Nemastes didn't move, but the sudden stillness of his face was as good as another man's shout of surprise. The creature behind him hunched and gave an angry "Hoo!" It bared its teeth, this time clearly as a threat: it had felt its master react.

"Who are you?" Nemastes said. "And why have you come to us?"

Corylus hadn't heard him speak in Carce. His voice was high pitched and rough.

"I'm Publius Corylus," he said, sauntering forward. He held his hands at waist level, palms open and turned upward. "And I'm here as a friend."

As he approached, the tribe circled behind him. If there was going to be real trouble, it would be with Frothi and the men beside him. It still made Corylus uneasy to know that he was surrounded.

More uneasy, I mean. He smiled to himself. The gods alone knew what the tribesmen made of the expression.

"That's Odd's dagger," a woman said in a harsh, accusatory voice. She was close enough to the left of Corylus to touch him. "And that's his basket: I wove it myself."

"Yes," said Corylus, turning to her. She was young and as trim as any of these folk; they were all on the stocky side. She wore a cape woven from the mammoths' black guard hairs, picked out with geometric designs from the beast's russet underfur. "I found Odd's body in the river—"

He gestured with his left hand, but didn't turn away from the woman. So long as he faced her, he could keep Frothi and the wizard in the corner of his eyes.

"—and buried him on the shore. Odd's spirit came to me in the night and ordered me to tell his brother Frothi what had happened."

"Odd went seal hunting!" Frothi said, his voice rising. It was the first time he'd spoken to Corylus.

"Odd went searching for wisdom!" said the young woman, wheeling to face the chief. "As you knew, Frothi!"

"Shut your mouth, Sith," Frothi said in a harsh, frightened whisper. "This is no business of yours."

"Odd went to the Isle of Dreams to search for wisdom," Corylus said. He spoke directly at the chief and his wizard, but he pitched his voice so that most of the people crowding close about them could hear his words. "He found death instead. What can you tell us about your brother's death, Frothi?"

Frothi opened his mouth to snarl, then flinched. He was looking at Corylus, but there had been a flicker in the air between them. *Maybe he saw something more clearly than I did.*

Nemastes lifted the ivory talisman in both hands and began chanting what sounded like nonsense syllables; his eyes glazed. The tribesmen to his right jumped back as though he had suddenly burst into flames, and even Frothi edged aside.

Corylus tried to step forward. He couldn't move. The atmosphere took on the faintly yellow-green hue of rotting urine, blurring the shapes of those watching.

The figure of an ancient man clambered out of the talisman and swelled to full size. His features were those of the ivory carving. He started toward Corylus with a grim black smile.

Corylus felt a sudden tingle. Sorba stood at his right side. She stepped between him and the spirit of the talisman.

"Go back, Botrug," said the nymph. "Go back or I'll send you back."

"You know who I am, rowan," Botrug said in a rasping voice. He sounded old and very tired, but also certain. "You know too that you can't protect the youth against me. I'll break you if I must."

This is the wizard who brought Nemastes and his brothers here, wherever here *is,* Corylus realized. If Botrug had been powerful enough to control the Band for any length of time, it didn't seem probable that Sorba was going to stop him. Corylus strained, but his muscles simply wouldn't move.

"I can protect this youth, Botrug," the nymph said. "His mother was one of us."

Nemastes and the members of the tribe had faded from Corylus's vision, but he saw twelve other figures watching avidly from the edge of the yellow-green haze. They were tall and thin, and their features were indistinguishable from those of Nemastes.

"Even so," Botrug said. He raised his right arm toward Corylus.

Sorba slapped him like the crash of lightning. Botrug's head spun sideways; he stumbled to one knee. "*This* youth," she repeated in a voice like a silver flute.

Botrug looked up. Without sound or warning, his

form dissolved into a net of sparks. They flowed back into the talisman in Nemastes' hands.

Sorba had stepped into the blow. Now she shifted onto her heels again, rubbing the fingers of her right hand with her left.

She glared at the watching Twelve. She hadn't changed in any way Corylus could describe, but only with effort could he remember the giggling nymph he'd met in the rowan grove.

"Do you want to try?" Sorba shrilled to the wizards. *"Do you?"*

The circle of wizards vanished as swiftly and imperceptibly as rainbows fade. The haze of foul light disappeared and Sorba with it.

Corylus stumbled with the effort of moments before, now released. He felt light-headed.

The present came back to him in a rush. His eyes focused on Nemastes, staring at his talisman with a stunned expression. The wizard looked at Corylus. He gave a harsh croak like a heron, turned, and collided with his even taller servant. Nemastes swung around the giant as if it were an awkwardly planted tree; he ran into the encampment.

Corylus stumbled again. He'd been off-balance from his paralysis, and he hadn't had the presence of mind to plant himself firmly before he tried to chase the wizard.

Many people were shouting. Corylus got to his feet. The tall servant was shambling after his master, occasionally looking over his shoulder. It moved gracelessly, but it covered ground quickly because its legs were so long. Corylus started after it.

"Stop," said Sith, trotting at his elbow. "You can't fight the Stolo, Publius Corylus. You can hardly stand upright!"

"Get out of my way, fool!" Corylus said.

Sith wasn't in his way. And if Nemastes' seven-foot-tall servant was the Stolo, she was right that Corylus couldn't fight it. Couldn't fight it and win, anyway. So why was he chasing Nemastes when he knew he couldn't reach the wizard without getting through the Stolo first?

Corylus tripped on a tent peg. He would have sprawled onto his face if Sith hadn't taken his weight.

He let himself relax. His vision was clearing. "I'm sorry," he said to Sith. "I was being foolish."

"You're exhausted," the woman said. He was squarely on his own feet again, but she continued to touch his arm. "You need to rest. How far have you come?"

Sith had proved unexpectedly strong, but her face was smooth and girlish. Corylus wondered how old she really was. Her clothing was decorated with designs made by working splinters of dyed bone through the leather.

Corylus rubbed his eyes and looked around. They were in the middle of the encampment. Nemastes—and his Stolo—had vanished, but the rest of the tribe was watching him.

Everybody gave Nemastes a wide berth when he started working magic, Corylus thought. He managed a slight grin. *I wish I could have kept clear too; though thanks to Sorba, it turned out all right.*

"I'm not tired," he said. He spoke to Sith, but he kept his eyes on Frothi and the three or four men who appeared to be accompanying him. "Not my body, that is. Nemastes did something that left me feeling as though I'd had a fever, but I've shaken it off now."

He cleared his throat. "I really do apologize, Sith," he said. "I was delirious, I guess. I knew what I was saying—but I shouldn't have been saying it."

"Nemastes is a great wizard," Sith said. She spoke loudly, challenging Frothi. "You're a greater wizard yet, Corylus. You defeated Nemastes and made him flee!"

"I'm not a wizard," Corylus said. He wasn't sure what—or how much—he should say. "But I have friends."

The huts were low. Corylus was a few inches taller than the tribesmen, but even they would have to hunch if they tried to stand in the domes. Some of the deer were used as pack animals, carrying light loads. Paired satchels lay where they'd been dropped at the stranger's approach, but there were no obvious weapons among them.

A meat-drying rack had been partially assembled between the huts nearest Corylus. The staves of the frame were hardwood, six feet long and an inch in diameter. One of those would do. . . .

Frothi stopped well short of Corylus. He said, "Sith, go to your hut!"

"Yes," the woman said in a clear voice. "We owe hospitality to a stranger. I will feed Corylus in my hut."

The man to Frothi's left barked a surprised laugh, then bent his head away from the chief and pretended to be coughing. Corylus took a deep breath. He thought he was fully recovered from the wizard's spell. *I'd better be.*

"Sith, you're my wife!" Frothi shouted.

"Third wife," a woman called. The men of the tribe formed an arc behind the chief and his three henchmen, but the women and children crowded close behind them.

"Aye," said another in a feigned aside to her neighbor. "Maybe he should have stopped at two, do you think, Fiolswitha?"

"I sewed the case for Odd's knife myself," Sith said, touching the scabbard. Like her garments, it was decorated with a pattern in bone needles dyed rose and saffron. "It's right that it return to the dwelling where I made it!"

"Slut!" said the chief. Like most of the men, he carried a spear thrower and three light javelins in his right hand. He lunged toward Sith, raising the bundle to flog her with.

Corylus picked up the staff and stepped between them. It was hornbeam, strong and supple. When as well cured as this, it became hard enough to dull iron tools quickly.

"No," he said. He didn't raise his voice, but it rasped like the growl of a stiff-legged dog.

Frothi jumped back. "Bearn!" he said, looking at the men with him. "Todinn, Gram—hold this insolent puppy!"

The men looked away. Somebody back in the crowd sniggered.

Frothi grabbed the man on his right and shouted, "Bearn, didn't you hear me?"

Bearn had been slouching, looking at the ground. He straightened and met the chief's angry glare. He said, "I guess I figure a man's wives are his own business, Frothi."

"Sure," called someone behind them. "But that's if he's a man."

For a moment, Corylus thought that Frothi was going to come for him after all. Instead the chief turned on his heel and strode back through the spectators. A young boy didn't get out of the way in time; Frothi batted him wailing to the ground with the sheaf of javelins.

"It looks to me," said a woman archly to no one in particular, "that maybe Odd isn't dead after all."

There was general laughter. Even Frothi's henchmen smiled, though their expressions turned back to concern when they eyed Corylus again.

"Come," said Sith, taking Corylus by the left wrist. "My hut is the one with the stars woven into it."

She tugged; she was very strong. Besides, Corylus couldn't see any reason not to do as Sith directed.

CHAPTER XIV

Varus paused, staring at the new world. The woman took a few steps farther, then stopped and looked back at him. She said, "You said you wanted to gather fruit from the First Tree. Have you changed your mind?"

"I'm just looking around," Varus said defensively. "I've never seen a place like this."

The woman laughed. "Stay as long as you like," she said. "I have only time."

They stood in a rolling meadow. The fog and escarpment had vanished. The ankle-high vegetation seemed sun-drenched, but there was no sun in the bright sky to cast the illumination. A single tree with drooping branches stood silhouetted against the horizon.

Varus squatted to examine the ground cover. It wasn't grass or ivy. In fact it seemed to be—

He stood up abruptly. "Sigyn!" he said. "These are trees—little trees. Where are we?"

The woman shrugged. "On another world than that from which you came," she said. "From another world than mine as well. We are not part of this place, though we exist in it for the present. Does that matter to you, wizard?"

Varus considered the question. He suspected that it *did* matter, though he wasn't sure how.

So far as Sigyn was concerned, all that mattered were the things that affected his present quest. He had a life beyond the quest, or he hoped he did. It would be point-less to ask the woman questions which she couldn't understand, let alone answer.

"We'll go on," Varus said, starting forward again. Sigyn fell in beside him, since their goal was obvious.

The vegetation underfoot crackled slightly. Varus wondered what he was trampling besides tiny trees, but he had no choice. Carce and mankind depended on him.

The horizon was farther away than Varus had at first thought. After a time he looked over his shoulder and saw their footsteps stretching into the distance beyond where he could see. The Tree seemed little closer than it had been when they started, though now he saw that it was on an island. A strip of water separated it from the forest over which he and the woman walked.

"Sigyn?" he said. "How can we cross the water? Is it shallow?"

"Sigyn cannot answer your questions, wizard," the woman said, looking at him with a smile that he couldn't read. "You must cross by your own powers . . . but the depth of the channel will not matter to you."

That isn't as hopeful a statement as I might wish, Varus thought.

He met the woman's eyes, then after a moment managed to smile. *I've always liked puzzles. Poetry writing is just a puzzle in words, after all; at least the way I did it. I'll figure out the puzzle of the water when we reach it; and if that means swimming, I'll hope that I swim well enough.*

Though any creatures that lived on the ground were too tiny for Varus to see without him putting his face down into the miniature trees, things like birds fluttered about the forest, lighting and pecking into the foliage. They kept at a distance from Varus and his guide, but even so he could tell that they didn't have feathers and their tails were serpentine. When they called to one another, they shrieked like angry mice.

Varus cleared his throat. "Sigyn?" he said. "What do they eat, those birds?"

"Birds?" said the woman. He thought she sounded amused. "They eat whatever they catch, wizard. Is it any different in your world?"

"I suppose not," Varus said. He swallowed, hoping to work the feeling of discomfort out of his throat.

But it *was* true. He thought of his epic, of the dragon swallowing down the soldiers of Regulus in the wastes of Libya. That was a fantasy. In the waking world, his own world, it was generally men who devoured other men. Here, perhaps, the greatest danger was dragons. For those folk whom Gaius Varus and his guide didn't step on.

The woman stopped; they were at the edge of the water. Varus wondered how long he'd been musing. It hadn't seemed long enough for them to have come this far, he would have said.

The water was gray and speckled with flotsam. It rose and fell heavily, like the chest of a sleeping giant. There was no current that Varus could see.

He looked at the woman. He knew that distances were deceptive here, but he was sure that the strait couldn't be more than a few hundred yards across. At his father's villa near Baiae, he'd swum a full mile and been sure he could have gone twice that distance if he'd had to.

Perhaps if I call her "Bride," she'll give me a real answer.

But Varus wouldn't do that. That would put him in league with the barbarians who'd murdered her. He *wouldn't*.

"Sigyn?" Varus said. "Should I swim across the channel?"

She had been staring into the distance. Now she turned and focused on him; and smiled again. "The Bride cannot tell a wizard of your power what to do," she said.

She extended her finger, pointing toward a bird rising from the stunted forest thirty feet away. It squealed angrily, dropping something from its beak. The woman's finger gave a flick; the bird snapped toward the island, tumbling over and over as its wings beat in an attempt to regain control.

A tentacle slashed from the turgid water, looped the leathery bird, and vanished below the surface again. Bubbles swirled briefly, then dissipated. The sea returned to its previous appearance of gelid calm.

Varus closed his eyes and rubbed them, trying to erase the memory of what he'd just seen. "Thank you," he said softly.

The woman laughed. "I did nothing," she said. "All the power is yours, wizard."

Varus opened his eyes and stared at the water, his face going hard as he concentrated. Words swirled just beyond the boundaries of his mind, but they wouldn't come clear. He strained and, straining, slipped into the fog of his memory again. He forced his way forward, willing himself to have a body.

Abruptly Varus stood in a cave which echoed with the sound of waves. The old woman sat on a bench carved into the stone wall, reading by the light of a single oil lamp. She lowered the palm-leaf book in her hand and smiled at Varus.

"Greetings, Lord Varus," she said. "I didn't think you would come back to see me again."

"I have to," he said uncomfortably. "I tried to cross the water without your help, but I need you. Please, help me. For the world's sake."

"Will you tell me about the world, wizard?" the old woman said. Her smile was a thin line within the wrinkles of her face. "But I said to you before: the power is yours to use or not use."

Varus screwed his face into a grimace. "I would—" he said. He broke off.

The old woman's mouth worked, but he heard the words coming up through his throat: *"The heavens split! Sweeps down the great wind—"*

Lightning ripped into a crown of thorns hanging in the sky. Varus was back on the edge of the strait, his hands raised and Sigyn beside him. A wind from nowhere howled over the water without ruffling the First Tree or the miniature forest.

"—and with it the frost!" quavered from Varus's lips.

The strait rocked like a kettle coming to a boil. Varus felt a gush of unexpected warmth; the water turned dazzlingly white.

The sky cleared like moisture wiped from a sheet of silver. What had been gray water was now an ice waste lifted into hummocks by the pressure of its creation and shattered into brilliant crystals.

Is that a tree? Varus thought when he saw the twisted lump a hundred feet away. The strands weren't branches but tentacles like the one which had snatched the bird moments before; they had frozen as the strait itself had. They issued from an elephantine conch shell which projected just about the surface of the ice. At the base of the tentacles was an eye, huge and filled with icy hatred.

"How long . . . ?" Varus said, but he didn't finish the question. Even if Sigyn told him how long the strait would remain frozen—which she probably wouldn't—the answer didn't matter. He needed to cross to the Tree. Even if he became next to certain that the ice would give way before he started back, he had to try.

"Let's go," he said, stepping onto the ice with the care so slick a surface deserved. He grinned. It was liberating to be in a situation where he had to go forward to succeed. It didn't matter if he was afraid of being hurt or even of dying: he had to go on.

He looked at the woman. "Thank you for guiding me, Sigyn," he said.

She turned her head, but she didn't smile as he'd thought she might. "I have the time, wizard," she said. "I have all eternity."

She didn't mention the compulsion he'd used to force her from the cairn. Varus wondered if he would do that again, now that he'd, well, spent time with her. She'd saved his life when he was about to try swimming to the island. She hadn't had to do that.

He tried to peer into the ice, but the fractured crystal was as opaque as a similar thickness of marble. How many tentacled creatures were hidden in it? Though one would have been enough.

The surface wasn't smooth, but its irregular humps and sheared angles were slick. Varus spread his feet wide and took small steps so that his weight generally came straight down onto the surface.

Corylus must have a lot of experience walking on ice. He'd do better here.

Varus grinned. His friend lacked one necessary attribute for success in this situation: he wasn't a poet, and Varus was. Varus was an extremely *bad* poet, granted; but his mind had the trick of looking at things which poetry required. It didn't matter in this world that he executed his understanding so poorly.

Varus had to watch where he was putting his feet; even so he almost fell several times. He risked a glance toward Sigyn. Despite being barefoot, she walked with the same poised nonchalance as she had when crossing the miniature forest.

She's probably used to ice, Varus thought. In his heart

he suspected that the fact she was dead had more to do with her aplomb, but that thought made him uncomfortable.

Varus stepped onto grass. That was so unexpected that he almost fell. They'd reached the island.

He looked up and stared in wonder at the Tree. "Oh," he said.

It wasn't a tree from this angle. Instead, it mounted stage by stage like a mural of an impossible landscape. Each level was perfectly clear to Varus, a mass of distinct branches merging in a curved surface which mounted to the next level.

The twigs were heavy with fruit. No bunch was the same as any other that Varus could see. Those hanging closest to him ranged from something that looked like a hairy plum the size of a man's head, to a cluster of tiny glistening seeds which he saw as points of light instead of being distinct surfaces.

"You have reached your goal, wizard," the woman said. "Your first goal. Take a sprig of the fruit and we will go on."

Varus reached out, paused, and lowered his hand again. "Sigyn?" he said. "Does it matter which fruit I take? There are so many."

She looked at him with a smile as cold as the frozen strait they had crossed. "Eventually, wizard," she said, "you will learn that nothing at all matters. But because the Bride is under your compulsion—"

"I'm not compelling you!" Varus said. "I'm asking you a question as a friend!"

"Do the living have friends among the dead, wizard?" the woman said, her smile twisting oddly. "Nevertheless, all fruits are the same for your purpose. This is the First Tree."

"Thank you, Sigyn," Varus said, bowing formally. He considered for a moment, then twisted off a twig with a spray of berries. They looked like holly, but they were colored the purple-blue of juniper instead of being bright red.

Turning to her again, he said, "What do we do now, if you please?"

"Now," said the woman, giving him the familiar cold smile, "we go to the Guardian of the Underworld. And you pass him, if you can."

THE FOREST MARON led Hedia into was more open than what they'd been plunging through before the wolf attacked them. It was hard for her to keep up, even though the faun wasn't striding along as quickly as she knew he was capable of doing. It would have been hard for her even if her groin didn't ache.

Trotting on her own legs was still a better choice than continuing to ride the faun piggyback, putting much of her weight on the same aching groin. What had been a delightful titillation earlier in their association would now be screamingly painful. Maron was—Hedia smiled with memory—quite an enthusiastic fellow.

The faun muttered what she thought was a curse— the words were indistinct, but the tone seemed clear— and paused. He started off again, bearing to the left around a mass of broken boughs and splintered tree boles. The grapevines which had used the trees for support wove the whole into a tangle impenetrable even to someone of Maron's strength and agility.

Hedia heard the sound of women crying. All she could see were flutterings like ghosts of the winged minims who'd flown from the thorn tree as she and the faun had passed earlier. Sometimes the movements seemed clearer in shadows than in the light which flooded the jumbled wreckage now that there was no canopy of leaves to block it.

"Maron?" she said. They were skirting the wrack at a

slight distance, avoiding the tops of trees which had been thrown to the ground. "What happened here? A windstorm?"

"Watch out!" the faun said, sweeping her behind him with his right arm. He gripped his new club in both hands and advanced slowly. He'd broken off the thin end of the sapling and all the foliage.

Hedia hunched to see forward beneath his right elbow. Ahead was a waist-high wall of polished stone or metal. It trembled as if—

It has legs! "Maron, that's a centipede!" Hedia said. "But it's huge!"

"It's pinned where it is," the faun said in a grating voice. He prodded the leaf mold with the butt of his club, then bent and came up with a fist-sized rock in his left hand.

"What are you doing?" Hedia said, trying to hide the concern in her voice. She'd been bitten by a centipede when she was a child; her little toe had turned white and lost all feeling for a week. This creature was the length of a warship. . . .

"Hey, Manylegs!" Maron shouted. "Want to chase me now?"

The centipede twisted, shoving a crackling mass of branches with its head in a vain effort to reach the faun. Its eye-clusters glittered like huge topazes.

Maron's rock cracked off the headplate between them, denting the iridescent surface. A pair of scythelike pincers ripped foliage and squirted orange venom as they scissored shut.

"Maron!" Hedia said. "Why are you wasting time with this? We have to find Alphena."

"Faugh, she could keep," said the faun, but he started through the forest again. "It's not often you find one of these where it can't get at you."

He looked back at Hedia with an angry frown. "Don't think I'm afraid, though!" he said. "I'm not."

"All right," she said in a neutral tone. Of course he was afraid. Any sane person would be afraid of that creature! But that didn't mean it was a good use of time to torture an enemy simply because you could.

"Besides," Maron said gloatingly, "it'll take days to die. It'll die of thirst, I shouldn't wonder."

Hedia sniffed. Cruelty had always seemed a waste of effort to her. Ruthlessness was quite another thing. She could give lessons in ruthlessness.

"What smashed the forest like this?" Hedia said. She didn't bother mentioning that she'd asked him the same question before. "Was it a windstorm?"

The faun laughed. "How could wind crush trees into the ground, woman?" he said. "No, that was someone from the waking world walking past. Your world."

"*My* world?" Hedia repeated. "How could that be?"

"They were in this world but not of it the way you are," Maron said. "As a matter of fact—"

He didn't stop, but he raised his nose to sniff the air again. He looked back at her and said, "Does this girl of yours have a sibling, a male?"

"Yes. Varus," Hedia said in puzzlement. "Her brother. My son, but not by blood."

"Well, it was the brother who did that," the faun said. "Be thankful that you weren't there when it happened."

"And you?" she said, letting her irritation show. "Aren't you thankful too?"

"Aye," Maron admitted sourly. "There wouldn't have been time for me to save you, but I'd have been compelled to try nonetheless, no matter how pointlessly. So yes, I'm thankful."

"Is Varus searching for Alphena also?" Hedia asked

after a moment. Then, regretfully, "Though I don't suppose you can tell that by sniffing the air."

Maron looked at her again. She couldn't read his expression. After a time he said, "Not by sniffing the air, no; but I don't suppose there's any reason you shouldn't know the answer. There will be great disruption in your world, but"—he swept their surroundings with his right arm—"nothing here, so it doesn't matter. Nothing but the occasional passerby like this boy you call your son."

Maron had obviously meant the gesture figuratively, but Hedia looked to the right as she framed her question. The trees here were poles without branches; stiff leaves slanted from the tops all the way to the ground, forming cones. Nearby grew brush with stiff stems and magenta foliage.

"What sort of disruption will this be?" she said, keeping her tone mild. *At least I'm no longer thinking about how much it hurts to walk.*

"It doesn't matter," Maron repeated. "You can stay here."

"But?" Hedia said, keeping her temper in check. She was by no means sure that the control her husband had given her over the faun would extend to demanding information that didn't conduce to finding Alphena.

"There was the Band," Maron said equably. "Then there were the Twelve and one, who was Nemastes. The fire god of the Hyperboreans will shortly loose his legions on the waking world. Nemastes and the Twelve who were his siblings are battling over whether the fire will burst through at the Horn or at Vesuvius."

He looked at Hedia, grinning with a cruelty that seemed as natural to his face as lust was.

"Your son acts for the Twelve, woman," he said. "He will succeed, so all your world save the Horn will end in fire. And the Horn is no longer of your world."

Hedia licked her dry lips. Maron continued to pace forward, using his hooves to break off stems that would otherwise snap back at her. He was an excellent escort, but she was coming to understand the degree to which he wasn't human.

"The lava will reach Carce?" she said, forcing the words out.

"Are you deaf, woman?" the faun snapped. "Your *world*, your whole world, will die because the Twelve wish it. They'll be safe then, from Nemastes and from all interruption save that of time."

"How . . . ," said Hedia. "How can these Twelve be stopped, Maron?"

He shrugged and smirked at her again. "Don't worry," he said. "Time will end even the Twelve. And the First Tree will cover the waking world again, as it has twice in the past. I will keep you occupied, woman."

All the world, Hedia thought. She didn't have anything to say, and her throat was too dry for words anyway.

"We're close by the girl, now," Maron said. "I'm compelled to take you both safely to the passage to the waking world, but don't worry. You don't have to go."

All the world . . .

CASSIUS TOOK ALPHENA'S sword from the wraith, then grinned at her. She tried not to react. *I am a proud daughter of Carce.*

With the hilt in his right hand, Cassius flicked the blade with the nail of his left index finger. It rang like a golden chime, a sound as musical as the call of a linnet.

Is he going to stab me? Or will he rape me so that I have to stab myself like Lucretia?

Alphena choked down a hysterical giggle. *I don't have to be* that *proud a daughter of Carce.* Though Cassius was disgustingly old; he must be sixty! Perhaps she could close her eyes and pretend that somebody younger, somebody attractive—

She blushed. She'd been thinking about a certain somebody. And it hadn't been disgusting at all.

"This is a remarkably fine sword, my dear," Cassius said. "Where did you get it?"

He eyed her speculatively, the way Alphena had seen her brother view a well-made book. Varus looked at books more lustfully than anything she read in this man's expression, however.

"None of your business!" Alphena said. She was trying to be haughty, but she knew she sounded more like an ill-tempered six-year-old.

"The sheath," Cassius said.

She looked down in puzzlement, wondering what he was talking about. There was nothing special about it, though it glittered a little more than the ordinary tin-and-enamel scabbard which it replaced.

He hadn't been talking to her. The third wraith unfastened the belt and handed it to Cassius.

The creatures looked like men who had begun to dissolve. Their flesh was slightly translucent, and their faces had no features.

Cassius snugged the belt around his own waist and sheathed the sword with a faint *ching*. He grinned at her. He wasn't a young man, but he was fitter than her father or any of Saxa's senatorial friends. The reflexive way he slid the sword home proved that he knew how to handle weapons too.

"Now, my queen . . . ," Cassius said. He was of average size, but his presence dominated the scene. "We will go to our kingdom. A return on my part, while you have before you the excitement of the first view of your new domains."

"I don't want to be your queen," Alphena said. She

was afraid that she sounded like a pettish child about to cry. "I don't want to be anybody's queen!"

"No?" said Cassius with an arched eyebrow. She could *feel* the man's passion, but he gave no outward sign of it. She was sure that if he pulled the limbs off flies—or broke the bones of men, one rib at a time—he would do it with an appearance of complete detachment. "I don't really believe that, dear, but you already realize that it doesn't matter. Now, will you come with us on your own legs, or shall my servants carry you?"

She'd put the wraiths out of her mind. Now she shuddered, feeling the clammy grip on both her arms. It was like being stuck in cold mud.

"I'll walk," she said to the ground. Then, trying to hide the desperation: "Make them let go of me."

"Lady Alphena," Cassius said, as sternly as a judge pronouncing sentence. "Look at me."

"I said I'd walk!" Alphena said, raising her eyes to his. She caught movement in the background. At first she thought something was rustling the bushes from which sprays of white, bell-shaped flowers hung; then she realized that the bushes themselves were crawling away.

"If you give your word," Cassius continued inexorably, "to me, in this place, you will keep it. Do you understand?"

"I will walk with you," Alphena said, sounding each word distinctly. Voice rising she added, "Make them let me go!"

"Release her," Cassius said mildly. The hands came off her wrists. She wasn't sure that the creatures had distinct fingers; it had been like being wrapped with blankets soaked in sewage.

"Now, my queen," Cassius continued, "we will go to our kingdom."

They set off along a trail which led out the back of

the clearing. Had the whole business, including the Cyclops's apparently aimless flight, been planned to trap her?

"You made the statue of Tellus speak, didn't you?" Alphena said. She tried hanging back; a wraith's touch on the back of her neck made her scramble up alongside Cassius.

"I?" he said. "Not I, my dear. I have no power in the overworld, not since I was executed." He laughed without humor. "In the courtyard of my own house," he said. "As my colleagues of the Senate thought fitting."

Cassius looked at her. Alphena had seen more merciful expressions on lions rending victims in the arena. He said, "I will not have colleagues now, Alphena. I will reign alone—but you will have all power under me."

"All power over the dead!" Alphena said. She was afraid she would start crying out of anger and frustration. Not fear, not now; she was too angry to be afraid.

"All men die, my dear," Cassius said. His voice sank into a soft rattle. For an instant she thought she saw the skull beneath the strong features of his face.

They walked down an avenue of trees whose huge purple leaves had magenta veins. They arched overhead, coloring the light of the pale sky. Alphena saw the shadow of a huge caterpillar through a leaf. When they were past, she glanced over her shoulder. The worm was looking back at her. The segments of its body were mottled blue on yellow, but its head was that of a dark-skinned woman.

They were now among trees that looked like pines except that their bark was the bright green of verdigris. A squirrel ran up one just ahead of them. Each time it curled out of sight on the other side of the trunk, Alphena saw something other than the flick of a bushy gray tail, but the creature was always a squirrel when it reappeared.

Cassius looked up at the squirrel. It ran out on a branch and called, "Dead man! You don't belong here! You shouldn't have come!"

"Silence, animal!" Cassius shouted, anger blazing out for the first time. *"Silence!"*

"You're going to regret it, dead man," said the squirrel. He gave a chattering laugh.

Cassius whipped out the sword and rushed toward the pine. The squirrel made a standing leap of at least twenty feet to the next tree, then leaped again deeper into the forest. Alphena heard its laughter long after the flag of its tail had disappeared.

She had frozen where she was; the wraiths had stopped also. Cassius returned, his face blotched with rage. They walked on, for some way in silence.

"I bought you from the wizard Nemastes, dear lady," Cassius said suddenly. "Do you know him?"

"What?" said Alphena. "*Bought* me?"

"When I was in the waking world," Cassius said instead of answering directly, "I had a talisman of great power—a flute of bone made by Odd the wizard. If I could have learned to use Odd's flute, I would rule the world from Carce to this day. The whole world!"

He's insane, Alphena realized. But that didn't mean that what he said wasn't true.

"But before I could learn," Cassius said, "they united against me and cut off my head. In the courtyard of my own house. And at last Nemastes came to me in the darkness where my soul dwelt. He offered me kingship in the Underworld, while he would rule forever in the waking world. Nemastes brought me out of the darkness, my queen!"

"He couldn't sell me," Alphena whispered. "He doesn't own me."

"I gave Nemastes the secret of where I hid the flute," Cassius said. "In the Temple of Jupiter but not of it. And

Nemastes has given you to me, to be my queen forever. He will rule the waking world, but with you at my side I shall be king of the Underworld!"

Once I'm there, I'm there forever, Alphena thought. Not even in myth did anyone return from the Underworld. *Forever.*

They stepped onto a plain unlike anything Alphena had seen in this world. Cassius stopped and looked around with a dumbfounded expression.

Alphena followed the sweep of his eyes. The forest behind them was gone also. Instead they stood in tawny grass no higher than their ankles. The wraiths shifted uneasily, looking more than ever like statues of pink aspic.

Cassius drew his sword. "How did you do this?" he snarled.

Alphena felt her lips quiver. "I?" she said. "I didn't do anything. I couldn't!"

A trio of pillars appeared around them. They were of golden light so vivid that Alphena slitted her eyes and looked between two. There may have been shapes within their brilliance, but she couldn't tell.

"*You do not belong here, Spurius Cassius,*" said a voice in Alphena's mind.

"I don't want trouble with you!" Cassius said, speaking toward one of the figures in light. "Let us pass and you'll never see us again!"

His head moved slightly, back and forth; just enough to keep the other two creatures alternately at the corners of his eyes. The sword in his right hand pointed out at waist height, as though he were ready to stab up from around the shield he would have carried in battle.

"*Our prince is missing, Spurius Cassius,*" the voice said. Alphena heard/felt/thought a slight tremolo; perhaps it was three voices, or many. "*You have his sword.*"

Then, staggering Alphena with its intensity, *"Where is our prince, Spurius Cassius?"*

"I don't know your prince!" Cassius said. His left hand fumbled with the buckle of the sword belt. "I've never seen him. Here"—he sheathed the sword with a quick motion, then held it with its accouterments out at arm's length—"take the sword. We'll go our separate ways!"

"We will have our prince, Spurius Cassius," said the voices, *"or we will have you."*

"Destroy them!" Cassius said.

The wraiths started to move. The light brightened. Alphena threw her arm across her eyes and felt the skin on the underside prickle.

There was a noise like hogs being gripped by the snouts for slaughter—a drove of hogs. She fell to her knees, sick with the horror of the sound.

The prickling stopped. Alphena eased a careful glance, then lowered her arm. Where the wraiths had stood, scraps of gelatin soaked into the loam. The grass glistened, but it was already drying.

The pillars of light drifted toward Cassius. Effort made his muscles swell like hawsers, but he could not move. The lights merged with him. There was a golden flash and a scream, then nothing.

Alphena sprawled on her face in the forest. A bird that might have been a long-tailed hawk screamed at her, then glided from its high branch. It disappeared through a screen of yellow irises as tall as cherry trees.

Hedia came toward her at the side of a tall, nude man with hairy legs—and hooves.

Hedia's with a faun!

"I HAVE SOME trout," Corylus said, squatting beside the doorway to offer Sith his basket. The basket she had woven. "It's, ah . . . I caught them after I built the cairn."

"You don't have a line or net," the woman said,

making a fireset with wood from a bundle and tinder from one of her two packs. She'd brought them over from where the reindeer had been unharnessed before the stranger appeared on the horizon. "Did you catch them with your hands?"

Ten feet away, an arc of children sat on their haunches and stared at Corylus. The adult members of the tribe were more circumspect, but he was clearly a matter of interest to all. The tribe must not meet many strangers, and a man in a linen tunic was probably unique to the experience of even the oldest.

"Ah, yes," said Corylus. There had been plenty of time for the woman to inventory his belongings, most of which had been Odd's to begin with; but he was impressed that she'd done so and had drawn the correct conclusion from what she learned. "I suppose your people do that too? Tickle fish, I mean?"

"Odd did," the woman said, lighting the fire with embers she carried in a gourd. She blew the smolder to full life, then met his eyes with her own clear gaze; her irises were brown, in keeping with her dark complexion. "No other man of the tribe could, except perhaps by chance. Many tried, though."

Sith rose and lifted a leather bottle off a rack on which several similar skins hung. She handed it to Corylus. "It's kvass," she said. "You must be thirsty."

He worked the wooden stopper out and sucked a careful taste from the bottle. It was sour—rancid, even—but the sting of alcohol was sharp on his tongue. He held his breath, swallowed, and then took another swallow.

Blinking, he closed the skin and handed it back. "What is it made from?" he asked.

"Reindeer milk," Sith said, her eyes narrowing slightly. "Don't your own people make kvass?"

"We don't have reindeer," Corylus said truthfully. His

stomach growled, brought to life by the drink and ready for more. He didn't think filling it with fermented milk was a good idea right now, though.

"We'll have reindeer sausage," Sith said. "Pemmican, that is, dried and chopped with myrtle berries." Frowning, she said, "Are all your people hunters, that you don't keep reindeer? You don't look like a hunter."

"We have sheep, though I'm not a shepherd," Corylus said. "And I'm not a hunter either, though I've hunted some." He grinned. "And fished," he added.

By being honest but not dwelling on the differences, Corylus hoped to keep off the subject of where he came from. He wasn't sure how he *could* explain that, honestly or otherwise.

Sith set three pieces of stream-smoothed quartz on the edges of the fire, then ran a sausage onto a hornbeam skewer. She dug the bottom of the skewer into the ground so that the sausage wobbled over the flames. A bucket of leather stiffened with willow withies stood nearby. It was half full of water and bruised grain.

Most of the children were still watching, but the tribe's adults were largely about their own business. Many of the women were fixing meals. The two older women who shared a fire in front of a double-sized hut occasionally turned a flat glance toward Corylus and his hostess.

"Frothi's other wives," Sith said, looking at them. She smiled faintly. "They're angry at me for his choice. Nerthus knows that it was no choice of mine, and they know it too; but they don't dare blame Frothi."

"Is this going to be a problem for you?" Corylus said carefully. He began polishing the hornbeam staff with his hands, as much for the soothing feel as because the wood benefited from the exercise.

"I don't care," Sith said. She lifted a piece of hot quartz with birch pincers and dropped it into the bucket to warm the contents. The second and third rocks splashed in also, raising the liquid toward the rim of the bucket. That done, she broke up the remainder of the trout into the porridge.

Looking at Corylus, she said, "Tell me about Odd. Tell me what happened to him."

"I found Odd's boat floating upside down in the river," Corylus said cautiously. "He was strapped into it; he'd drowned. I built a cairn with rocks from the streambed over him before I came seeking his people."

Sith looked at the large hut, not the women cooking in front of it. "Odd wouldn't have overturned his kayak, not even in a winter storm," she said harshly.

She swung the bucket one-handed and placed it midway between them, offset to his right side. She handed him a spoon, of ivory rather than horn. The handle was carved into curves that reminded Corylus of the patterns of trout swimming near the surface.

"Odd's spoon," she said. "He made its pair for me."

Sith took his hand in hers, dipped his spoon in the porridge, and guided it toward his mouth until he took over in embarrassment. Only when Corylus had swallowed did she begin to eat.

"What's the porridge made of?" Corylus asked. "Ah, it's very good."

Which it was, though he was hungry enough that he'd have relished boiled mulehide at this point. This tribe clearly wandered with its herds, so he wondered if the grain had been bartered from more settled folk.

"Food grasses," Sith said, gesturing toward the prairie. "Don't your people gather them?"

"Something like that," Corylus said. "Though we don't travel so much, so we plant seeds in patches instead of foraging." He smiled wryly. "Most of us don't travel," he added.

"The trout adds much to the soup," Sith said, plucking the skewer from the ground and offering the sausage to Corylus for the first bite. "Odd wouldn't have stopped to fish on his way back, so I'm eating better tonight than I expected to."

The flavor of the pemmican sausage was like nothing Corylus had eaten before. The dried meat must have been mixed with tallow, and there were probably spices besides the myrtle berries Sith had mentioned. He chewed slowly. Once he got past the initial notion that it was musty, it was extremely good.

"Ah . . . ," he said. He raised his eyebrow in question. "A vision told me that Odd had a flute?"

"He left the flute with me," Sith said, lowering the sausage and looking toward something beyond the northern horizon. "He was a wizard. This morning, Frothi came and took it. I knew then that Odd must be dead, so I didn't care anymore. About the flute or about life."

"I'm sorry," Corylus said softly. He tilted the bucket so that he could spoon up the last of the porridge from around the rocks. He focused on that so that he didn't have to look at the woman's face.

"Frothi was always jealous of Odd," Sith said, giving Corylus the rest of the sausage. His stomach was warm and pleasantly full. "Frothi could play at being ruler of everything—except of his brother. No one ruled Odd, but Odd didn't want to rule anything except himself. And now he's dead."

"I . . . ," Corylus said. "A vision told me that Odd is at peace, Sith."

"Is he?" she said with the same lack of emotion. "Perhaps I'll be at peace one day too, Publius Corylus."

She took the spoon from him and set it on a mat with her own. "Come," she said. She stepped into the hut and tugged him gently with her.

"Sith?" Corylus said. "I don't . . ."

He didn't know how to finish the objection. He didn't *want* to finish the objection.

"Come!" she repeated. She knelt and lifted her tunic to her waist, then gathered the bunched leather again. "Do you think I care?"

Corylus entered the hut and dropped the flap behind him.

CHAPTER XV

It was barely an hour after dawn. Four men, one of them Bearn, whom Corylus had seen at Frothi's side, entered the camp from the south. Each of the others carried a variety of small game, largely hares and grouse, rolled into the nets they'd used to catch it.

"That's the last of the hunters," Sith said. "The men fishing in the Ice River arrived in the night. Now Frothi can hold his council."

Though Bearn averted his eyes, the hunters were looking at Corylus with interest. He waved. Hercules knew what they thought of the gesture, but at least it was better than standing like a prisoner tied to a post for archery practice.

"Is Frothi calling a council because of Odd's death?" he asked.

Sith looked at him. "Frothi is calling the council to deal with you, Corylus," she said. "Since he's afraid to face you alone."

Corylus turned. As he'd expected, Frothi was glaring at his back. The chief spoke sidelong to Todinn, who held a horn hollowed from a section of mammoth tusk. He lifted it and blatted with far less music than the hairy elephants managed when they called to one another. People quit their tasks and rose from where they were sitting.

"Come," said Sith, touching his arm as she joined the

movement down into the shallow crater. "You faced down Frothi yesterday. Perhaps you can do so again."

"Sith?" he said. People were eyeing the two of them, not hostilely but certainly without any sign of fellow feeling. Again he had the feeling that he was being led into the arena to entertain the citizenry. "Would the men fishing on the river have buried Odd if I hadn't? Or brought his body back to you? Ah, to the tribe, I mean."

"Odd went to the Isle of Dreams," Sith said. "No one but a wizard would have dared to do that, Corylus. Our people don't fish that part of the river."

She looked at him. "You went to Odd, or he drew you to him," she said. "Like called to like."

The bowl was several hundred feet across; the gentle slope of the sides made it a natural amphitheater. The grass of the interior was shorter and obviously less diverse than that of the surrounding prairie.

Corylus thought the air had a tinge of sulfur, but that could have been a trick his mind was playing on him. After living in the shadow of Vesuvius, he knew a volcano even when it must have long been dormant—and he knew the bite of a volcano's breath.

Corylus held the hornbeam staff in his right hand and let the fingertips of his left run along the smooth wood. He felt a cool, sturdy woman gazing through his eyes from a vast distance. The staff must be very old.

Sith intended to go to the middle of the arc of spectators, facing Frothi and his three henchmen. Nemastes stood with them, but he kept slightly back from the men of the tribe. His hulking servant squatted on the ground well behind him. The Stolo was worrying a rack of reindeer ribs; at regular intervals a crackling announced that he had just crushed more of the bone between his great molars.

Corylus deliberately took Sith with him to the right

end, where the old women had been relegated. For him to succeed, the whole tribe had to be able to see him. A place on one end of the arc was the best way of achieving that.

The tribe was assembled. Todinn raised his ivory horn again. Before he could sound it, Corylus cried, "People of the tribe! I come to you for justice! I ask you to make over to me the flute which Odd gave me but which Frothi unjustly holds!"

There was general consternation: folk gasped or muttered to one another. Todinn paused with his lips on the trumpet, then lowered it. He looked at Frothi, but the chief was too consumed by anger at Corylus to notice anyone else at the moment.

"The goods of my brother Odd are mine—*if* Odd is really dead!" Frothi said. In sudden decision, he reached under the pegged closure of his deerskin shirt and came out with a curved black bone a foot long. He waved it over his head.

At first Corylus thought the instrument was made from the bone of a man's calf, though the color puzzled him. The joint on the upper end was wrong for a human, though: it was more like that of a lizard which walked with its legs splayed out.

Frothi swept the crowd with his eyes, but his henchmen and Nemastes were staring at the stranger. The Stolo dropped the remaining ribs and glared also, hunching forward. He bared his teeth again; Corylus thought he heard a rasping growl, like that of an agitated lion.

"Odd is certainly dead, Frothi," Corylus said. "As I who buried him know, and as you know for better reason yet."

The acoustics of the bowl were excellent. Spectators on the far end edged forward from the slope so that they could look at the speaker, but their faces weren't scrunched up in frustration at not being able to make out his words.

"Odd is my brother!" Frothi said. His face had gone pale, then flushed again. "If he lives, I'll give the flute to him on his return. If he in truth is dead, the flute is mine by right of kinship."

"Aye, Frothi," called a man unseen in the crowd. The words were spoken toward the slope, but the echo was clearly audible. "Your wife is his widow!"

There was laughter. Frothi's eyes became unfocused, and the flute in his hand trembled with rage.

"People of the tribe!" Corylus said. "I buried Odd's body. For that duty, his spirit gave the flute to me. Do you doubt me, Frothi?"

He pointed his left arm toward the chieftain. Pitching his voice so that everyone in the bowl could hear him, he said, "Then call Odd from his tomb! Call him here, and he'll repeat the gift his spirit made to me! And perhaps, Frothi, your brother will do another thing as well. Call him and see!"

Corylus wondered what would happen if the chief did call his bluff by summoning Odd. Nothing, probably. Odd was certainly dead, and the sun this morning was too bright to be dimmed by phantoms. But though Odd had been buried, his vengeance was nevertheless alive—especially in the eyes of Sith as she looked at her husband.

Frothi's henchmen exchanged concerned glances. Bearn leaned close to his chief and whispered something that Corylus couldn't overhear.

Nemastes stepped between the two tribesmen, thrusting them apart by the force of his personality. "No!" he said. He held the ivory talisman in his fist under Bearn's nose. "You must not give the flute to this stranger!"

Bearn held javelins and a throwing stick in his left

hand. He snatched one of the flint-pointed darts with his right and raised it as if to stab.

Nemastes muttered something which sent the henchman staggering back. There was a general cry of anger and dismay from the assembly. Women snatched their younger offspring and scrambled back, while the men fitted javelins into the knuckles of their throwing sticks. The Stolo stepped in front of his master, growling openly.

"My people!" Frothi said, raising both his hands empty. He'd slipped the flute back out of sight within his shirt.

Nemastes tried to whisper in his ear. The chief shook him angrily away. *He doesn't like the foreign wizard giving orders either,* Corylus thought with a smile.

"My people!" Frothi repeated. "I will give the flute to this stranger—if you and the gods desire it!"

Corylus stepped forward, holding his open left hand out. The stick was in his right hand, vertical at his side. *It can't end so easily!*

But maybe it was going to. Nemastes retreated, though he held the talisman up. Was he preparing to call the ancient wizard from out of the ivory again? The Stolo, whining uncertainly, backed with him.

"A moment, stranger!" Frothi said. "My people—the gods must state their will, must they not? The stranger must undergo a trial!"

Corylus felt as though he were running on ice. So long as he set his feet squarely each time, he would be all right. If he lost his balance by even a hair, however, he'd go down and never rise again.

"What trial do you propose, brother of Odd who was drowned?" Corylus said. He wished that Pandareus could see him now, using rhetorical training in a contest that probably meant his life. His enunciation was perfect, and he projected his voice so that it filled the bowl.

"You say that my brother drowned in the Ice River, stranger?" Frothi said. He'd regained his composure. "Is that so?"

"Yes," said Corylus. Sith was at his side, trembling like a cold flame. "And his body is buried on the river's bank even now."

"Will you fill a cup with water from the river at the place where Odd was drowned, then?" Frothi said. "If you do that, I will give you the flute. Do you agree to the trial, stranger?"

"It's a trick!" Sith whispered. Corylus brushed her aside in irritation, lost in the moment. *Of course it's a trick! But it's the only way.*

"I accept your trial, Frothi!" he said. "But be sure of this: when I have completed that trial, the flute is mine as your brother wished. Justice and your own people will make sure of that, and I will make sure of it too."

"Very good!" said the chief triumphantly. "You know where the river is, you say—so here is the cup. We're standing in it, stranger! Fill this cup in the plain from the Ice River!"

The spectators hooted with approval. By playing a clever trick on a stranger, Frothi had won the tribe's renewed support. Bearn slapped the chief on the back; Todinn and Gram hugged him from the other side.

"I warned you!" Sith said, her voice an angry rustle like a viper in dry leaves.

The only face that wasn't filled with cheerful delight was that of Nemastes. The wizard eyed Frothi with a mixture of fear and anger. He turned when he felt the glance of Corylus and fled up the slope toward the camp.

"I'll be back to claim my flute, Frothi!" Corylus said. "And it may be that your brother will return with me!"

Corylus had no idea of how he could succeed in filling the crater from the river miles to the north, so the look on the chieftain's face might be the only triumph he got out of this business. That was a real triumph, though.

ALPHENA WAS HUNGRY. Maron had found them plenty of fruit to eat on the way, but nothing really felt like food in her stomach except bread.

The faun had killed and eaten several small animals as they went along too. He'd offered Alphena a piece of something she'd decided was a bird, but he'd laughed when she asked if he was going to cook it first. *She* certainly didn't know how to build a fire.

It had to be a bird, because women didn't have wings and no *real* woman was only six inches high. Still, Alphena wasn't sure she'd have been able to eat that meat even if it was cooked, and she really wished that Maron hadn't sucked the bones clean with such loud enthusiasm as they paced along.

"What's that ahead of us?" Hedia asked. "It's a building, isn't it?"

An hour ago they'd come out of the forest; now they were on grassland. The loamy soil was easier to walk on than stones hidden in the leaf mold of the forest, but Alphena didn't care one way or another: her army-pattern boots protected her feet from any surface. Her stepmother wore light sandals and was probably glad of the change, though.

"That?" said the faun. "Oh, that's a tomb—a wizard's tomb, they say, but I don't know anybody who saw it built. Nobody really knows."

He laughed. "You won't find a chamber with feather mattresses for you to sleep on, Hedia," he added. "Nor banquet table for you with all manner of cooked meats, girlie. Cooked! Cooking drives out all the flavor!"

"I don't care about meat," Alphena muttered. "I'd just like a round of wheat bread and a little oil to dip it into."

The faun had already faced front again. "And I don't

like to be called 'girlie,'" she said, though she knew he wouldn't pay any attention even if he had heard her.

She'd thought the slope-sided structure ahead was a natural formation, like the cliffs of Capri. It was at least two hundred feet in diameter, too large to seem artificial at a first glance.

When Alphena shaded her eyes with her hand, though, she saw that it was built almost vertically of stone blocks from the mounded earth at the bottom to at least fifty feet above, where the slope slanted back sharply. The face of the structure was carved with a molding like a door in the middle. In the center was a cross with a loop instead of the top upright.

"That's an ankh on the door," said Hedia in surprise. "You say it's a tomb? Was the person buried there Egyptian—or a priest of Isis, perhaps?"

"I wouldn't know," said Maron. "A wizard was all I heard."

"That can't be a door, can it?" Alphena said. "Isn't it too big?"

"No, you're right," Hedia agreed. "It must just be decoration. The real entrance would be in the mound, probably hidden."

"Why would anyone want to go inside a building anyway?" the faun said in grumpy disdain. "We'll stop in the palm grove, though. There's a well, and you can have some dates if you like."

He grinned over his shoulder to Alphena. "And you, girlie? Sometimes there's mice in the palm groves. Delicious little things, and you can hear them calling for their mommies as you swallow them down. Would you like me to catch a few for you?"

"No thank you, Master Maron," Alphena said stiffly. He was mocking her. She wanted to make him beg forgiveness at the point of her sword, but that wasn't a very practical way to deal with a guide. The alternative was to be primly ladylike.

Hedia turned to Alphena and nodded approval; Alphena found herself smiling in response. Hedia had probably been surprised to learn that the deportment teachers she'd provided to Alphena had actually had an impact.

Palms and a scattering of succulents with tough gray skins grew near the base of the tomb. The grove was to the right of the mound as they approached; Alphena couldn't say south or east, because there was no sun, just the uniform illumination above.

The sky had been growing dimmer for some time, though. She wondered if there would be stars or a moon when it became darker still.

"Something's moving in the palm trees," Hedia said. Her voice was clear, but she sounded more as if she were bored than sounding a warning.

"Is there, now?" the faun said, taking the long club off his right shoulder. He sauntered forward; his body was more obviously taut than it had been. "Well, we'll see them off, won't we?"

Alphena stopped uncertainly; she drew her sword. She willed herself to see the movement that Hedia had noticed, but in truth she saw nothing but faint shade and the succulents.

"Come, Daughter," Hedia said. "We don't want to crowd him, but we don't want to be too far away either. In case something has circled behind us."

Alphena jerked her head around. There was nothing behind them. The sky seemed noticeably darker. She wished they could have a fire.

"All right," she said, nervous and frustrated. *She* had the sword, which she was well trained to use. Even so, she felt comforted that Hedia was with her.

What could Hedia do if another sphinx attacked them? Alphena grinned despite herself. Like as not, Hedia would figure something out.

A woman came toward them out of the grove. Though the sky was the pale violet shade of early evening, her eyes flickered like emeralds.

"She's not human!" Alphena said.

"No, she's not," said Hedia in a grimly ironic tone. "She's *far* too attractive to be human."

"Well," said Maron, his voice huskier than it had been a moment before, "at any rate, she doesn't look hostile."

The woman—the nymph—was tall and slender except for large breasts which didn't sag the way they should. Her hair was probably black, but it seemed to catch highlights from the sky. She smiled at Maron, but the only sound she made was the whisper of her feet on the sand.

"It may be a trick!" said Alphena.

The faun laughed and continued walking toward the nymph. He twirled his club out at his side, making dips and curlicues with it. He must be remarkably dexterous when you considered that his baton was merely a length of sapling which didn't even have the bark smoothed off.

"Well, it could be!" Alphena muttered angrily.

"I suppose it could," said Hedia, taking her arm. "But I don't believe it any more than Maron does. That sort doesn't have room in their tiny brains for anything as complicated as treachery."

Alphena looked at her in surprise. "You've met these, *these*, before?" she said.

"Only the human variety," Hedia said drily. "I doubt there's much difference, though. Come, let's find the well."

"Look at her!" Alphena said. "She's holding him by the *cock*! She's *leading* him!"

"Yes," said Hedia. "Ordinarily I've heard that statement used figuratively, though in this place it may be more common than it is in Carce. Or even in Baiae."

She tugged Alphena's arm gently. The faun and the nymph had sunk out of sight behind a screen of succulents at the edge of the grove.

"We'll be better for a drink of water," Hedia said. "I don't think Maron will be ready to leave for some while. He has a great deal of stamina, that one—I suspect."

Alphena followed her stepmother into the palms twenty feet away from where the other pair had vanished. She didn't look in that direction, but she couldn't help hearing Maron wheezing like steam escaping from under the lid of a pot.

Three more nymphs drifted from the direction of the tomb. They were headed for where the faun and their sister lay. *They can't see him! Do they smell him?*

Alphena blushed, realizing that they probably *did* smell him. Smell them.

"Here, dear," Hedia said. "There's no well curb, but the water seems clean enough. I'll watch while you dip some up in your hand, shall we?"

Alphena knelt abruptly. She wondered if her cheeks would cool if she sank her face in the pool.

HEDIA WAS ANGRY, which in itself irritated and angered her. She didn't usually feel this way, not because she was—she smiled at the thought—unusually equable, but because she ordinarily either solved problems immediately or just as quickly moved them out of her life.

"Haw!" Maron snorted from nearby in the darkness. "Haw! *Haw!*"

"What's he doing?" Alphena asked plaintively. "I mean, he *can't* be, can he? How many times would that be?"

"Twelve," Hedia said. "But yes, I suppose he can. He doesn't just *look* like a goat, my dear."

The only real lights in the grove were the occasional flickerings of the nymphs' eyes, but the sky must not have been perfectly black. The palms stood in vague silhouette, and the girl's face was a study in pale misery.

There'd been rustlings in the leaves and whispers in the shadows ever since the light failed. Hedia wasn't cold, but she would have liked a fire. Even if it didn't illuminate whatever was making the sounds, it might drive them a little farther away.

A racking scream sounded. It seemed close as well as loud. Seconds later it echoed from the range of hills Hedia had noticed on the horizon to the left as they approached the tomb.

Alphena jumped to her feet, waving the sword. The sound didn't recur—for the moment. Hedia remained where she was.

The girl gave a shudder. She started to sheathe the sword, but after missing the throat of the scabbard twice, she continued to hold it in her hand.

"Hedia?" she said. "What are we going to do? Are we just going to wait?"

Hedia rose to her feet in sudden decision. "I thought we would, yes," she said briskly, "but I was wrong. I see another of those *things* headed this way. There may not be an end of them, and it appears that our guide"—she looked sourly in the direction of Maron; a swell of the sandy soil separated her from the faun, but his "Haw! Haw! *Haw!*" could be heard for miles—"isn't going to quit until his heart fails. Which would be perfectly all right with me, were it not for the fact we need him to lead us out of this place. So, because I've never known any argument to work on a male in a state of rut, we'll see where those females are coming from. It seems to be the tomb."

Nodding to make sure the girl was coming with her, Hedia strode toward the latest pair of lambent eyes.

First they had to walk around the pool they'd drunk from. It was about twenty feet in diameter and seemingly shallow, but the water hadn't been stagnant so it must be fed from a spring. There was a slightly smaller pool to the right, visible mostly as a smoothness where the soil around it was matte.

The female glided toward them; glided toward Maron, with them standing in the way, at any rate. "Can you speak?" Hedia demanded in the tone she would use on a servant who was trying to get away with something.

If the female could, she didn't bother to acknowledge it. Not only did green flames lick from her eyes, but her perfect body had a glow like burnished ivory brighter than could be a reflection of the light reaching the grove. The nymphs were as similar as frogs in a pond, but they weren't identical.

"I asked if you can speak, you bitch!" Hedia said, stepping sideways to block the female's progress. She was furious with Maron. She couldn't say that publicly—it made her face scrunch up even to admit it in her own mind—but she could certainly treat these gorgeous *creatures* as the sluts they were.

The nymph moved around her. Hedia wasn't sure how it happened: she was beside Hedia, then past, without apparently stepping out of her initial line. Her smile was biting, but Hedia knew the mocking laughter must be in her own mind.

Alphena raised the sword as though she meant to do something with it, but Hedia touched her shoulder and said, "No, she's not the problem. Killing a trollop isn't going to get us out of this place."

"Oh, I wouldn't have *killed* her!" the girl said in amazement. Her expression was if anything more horrified than it had been when she watched Maron going off with the first of the nymphs.

"Good," Hedia said as she resumed trudging toward the tomb. "Now, put the sword up so that you won't get in trouble waving it around. It's not a magic wand, you know."

Alphena successfully got the sword into its sheath this time. She looked crestfallen. "I'm sorry," she muttered. "I don't know what's happening. I don't understand anything at all!"

Hedia weighed the situation and the long-term results of whatever she said now—or failed to say. Because if she *didn't* respond to the girl's admission of weakness, she would pay for it in Alphena's resentment of her forevermore.

Forevermore might not be terribly long, of course, but Hedia wouldn't have survived if she hadn't always hoped for a good result. Smiling at the thought, she said, "*I* understand that I'm boiling with jealousy because that beast who's supposed to be our guide is so besotted with a crew of sluts that he's forgotten us completely. Which is exactly what you'd expect a man to do. Because they're *all* beasts, I'm afraid."

Alphena looked at her sidelong, obviously grappling with the possible implications of what her stepmother had just said. Hedia gave the girl a lopsided smile and put an arm briefly around her shoulders.

She said, "Don't worry, dear. You and I will take care of this business and get back to Carce where we belong. And nobody but the two of us will know anything about it."

If Hedia had misjudged her stepdaughter, she'd made a great deal of future unpleasantness for herself; but she almost never misjudged another woman. Her success in predicting men wasn't nearly as good. That, she knew, was because her mind was rarely in control when she was dealing with an attractive—or reasonably attractive—man.

They'd reached the side of the tomb. The sheer sides were even more impressive now than they had been from a distance. She didn't see an entrance.

"I think we should go around to the right, Mother," Alphena said in a determinedly calm voice. "The, ah, women were coming more from that way."

Hedia smiled with satisfaction at the way the girl was reacting. "Thank you," she said, turning to skirt the mound about ten feet out from the bottom. "I don't think we can assume that since those females are safe we'll be safe also, but I'm going to hope that's the case."

The darkness was disquieting. In Carce there would normally be stars and a lantern visible somewhere. Even during a drenching midnight rainstorm, the sky was likely to be lit by occasional lightning.

"There must be some light," Alphena whispered. "Otherwise we couldn't see the building even. But where does it come from?"

Hedia grimaced. She wasn't willing to say that she "saw" the tomb, but its presence beside them was blurrily separate from the lesser darkness of the sky. She opened her mouth to speak just to show she was listening. Before she got a word out, Alphena said, "There! There's a hole!"

Either the girl's eyes are a great deal better than mine, Hedia thought, *or we aren't seeing with our eyes here.* Since Alphena hadn't seemed unusually sharp-sighted in Carce before these things began happening, it was probably the latter.

Now that Hedia had been alerted, though, she noticed that the sandy soil had been thrown back not far in front of them. Alphena's hand hovered near the sword hilt again.

Hedia smiled wryly. In Carce she had disapproved strongly of the girl's fooling around with a sword: it wasn't just unladylike, it was unwomanly. That was a very different thing and one which offended Hedia's sense of *rightness*. She didn't claim a sense of decency, and certainly she'd been told by enough other people that she didn't have one.

Now . . . Well, the skill might still be unwomanly, but Hedia was rather glad that Alphena had gained it nonetheless. It was certainly more comforting than being with Varus, unless the monsters intended to hold a poetry-reading contest.

They stood side by side, staring into the hole, which slanted down toward the tomb. It looked rather like where a mole had surfaced in a garden, except that the opening was much too large.

"There's a light down there," Alphena said. Her voice was firm, but she gave the older woman a doubtful glance with the words.

"Yes," Hedia decided aloud. "It's . . . almost pink, wouldn't you say?"

Actually, it wasn't so much a color that Hedia saw in the light as a sense of *stickiness*. She would much rather not do what was necessary, so she did it immediately.

"Watch things up here," Hedia said, crawling in headfirst. "I'll be back as soon as I learn what's happening."

"I'm coming too!" Alphena said, as Hedia had very much hoped she would. Her voice was muffled because Hedia's body was in the way. It would make much better sense for the girl to stay guarding the entrance, but Hedia *really* didn't want to come down here alone.

The tunnel in the dirt was no more than ten feet long, though that would certainly be enough to bury her for life. She hiked her long tunic up above her knees and quickly scrambled the rest of the way to the stone at the end of the tunnel.

A hole had been ground through it from the other side as if a giant worm had been gnawing. There might be huge worms in this world, but the only thing Hedia had seen here was the nymphs. Surely they couldn't have been responsible for the hole and the tunnel beyond?

But this was where they must be coming from. Hedia wriggled through the hole, onto the floor of an arched corridor almost six feet wide and over eight feet high in the middle. It was made of blocks of rusty granite like those facing the exterior of the mound; the light, faint and diffuse, came from the rock itself.

Alphena's scabbard clinked on the stone as she squirmed through the opening and jumped to her feet. She looked around in concern. "What is this?" she said. "I thought we'd be in a room."

To the left, the passage ended in a blank wall; to the right, it curved to the left out of sight. "Well, my dear . . . ," Hedia said. She felt elated simply to have gotten out of the narrow tunnel alive; they were still entombed if the dirt collapsed behind them, but at least they wouldn't be instantly suffocated. "Let's follow the corridor and see if it leads us to one."

Their feet echoed on the dry stone floor. The quiet *whisk-whisk-whisk* of Hedia's sandals was almost lost in the ring of the younger woman's hobnails.

Alphena's feet sound angry, Hedia thought; and perhaps they were. Anger wasn't a bad emotion for a woman in a difficult situation. It had gotten Hedia out of places where panic and resignation—and especially resentment—would have done her no good at all.

"How far have we come?" Alphena asked in a little voice.

Hedia had been lost in musings. She glanced at the girl and smiled. Alphena held her hands primly before her with the fingers lightly interlaced. *Otherwise she'd be groping for the sword, and she doesn't want to seem frightened in front of me.*

"We've made at least half a circuit," Hedia said. "Of

course there may be another blank wall at the far end so we'll have to turn around and come back, but at least it's an alternative to listening to Maron grunting."

Her head was turned to the side, looking at her companion. Because they'd come so far without anything happening, the flicker in the corner of her eye didn't register as movement quite soon enough. Another flame-eyed nymph was coming up the corridor in the opposite direction.

Alphena cried out in surprise. The creature passed between them, gliding rather than walking. There wasn't room for the three of them to cross without touching, but Hedia had no physical sensation. Her mind was on fire with a surge of lust beyond anything she'd ever felt before, even the night Pansus had whisked the cover off the lantern during the orgy in his garden. The emotion was so intense that she staggered to her knees.

The nymph vanished around the curve of the wall, going toward the hole to the outside through which so many of her sisters had already passed. The floor of the passage was gritty, but her feet hadn't left marks.

"That was *awful*," Alphena whispered. "Are you all right, Mother?"

Hedia rose. "It was certainly disquieting," she said. Rather than start off immediately, she waited a moment to make sure that she was steady on her feet again.

She chuckled, grinning at the girl. "I could almost feel sorry for Maron," she said. Then, briskly, "Well, let's see where she was coming from."

They started in unison, but Alphena was on the inside of the curving passage and quickly became a half step ahead. She shortened her step then, but she didn't give up that half step—and Hedia certainly wasn't going to run to catch up.

"There may be another door," Hedia said. "Even a stone—"

There wasn't. The room at the end was an open circular expansion of the corridor. In the center was a stone bier, complete with pillow, on which an old man lay. No one and no thing else was present.

Hedia strode to the man and touched his neck. His flesh wasn't cold, but she didn't detect a pulse in his throat. The gods knew what was wrong with him, but Hedia had few options and very little time: she shook him by the shoulders.

"Wake up!" she said. "Waken! My daughter and I need to know what's going on here!"

The man's eyes opened and met hers. He gave a piercing scream and tried to roll off the other side of the bier. Alphena caught him. He saw her in turn and screamed again.

"Stop that!" Hedia said. "We're not going to hurt you, but we need some answers."

His mouth opened. Despite what she'd said about not hurting him, Hedia was going to slap him hard if he screamed again.

Instead the man's eyes widened in surprise. "But . . . ?" he said in a rasping voice. "Why, you're alive, aren't you?"

"Yes, of course we are," said Hedia. "There are some creatures, nymphs, in this place. We need to know how to get our guide away from them."

The man was short, slight, and nondescript. The sheen of his robe had made her think that it was silk, but touch proved it to be finespun metal. On his chest was an ankh. The chain from which it hung was gold, but the pendant seemed to be cold blue fire.

Hedia reached toward the ankh to see if it existed physically, then jerked her hand away. The internal light moved like a viper. Touching it might prove to be an equally bad idea.

"They're loose in the world!" the man said. "Oh my heavens! I'm so very sorry!"

He sat upright and swung his feet over the edge of the bier, but he didn't try to stand up. He laced the fingers of both hands on the upright of the ankh and raised it. As he did so, his face changed.

Hedia walked behind him around the bier and put her arms around Alphena. The girl was trembling.

The little man didn't speak, but the air trembled with portent. "What's he—," Alphena said.

The man spoke a four-syllable word. White light flared.

Hedia blinked. She was lying on the stone floor. Alphena hadn't fallen, but she looked stunned. The man was awkwardly trying to stand.

Hedia's skin prickled. She felt as though a thunderbolt had struck very close to her. Her senses were unusually sharp, however, and she bounced to her feet feeling full of energy.

"Alphena!" she said, taking the girl's hands in her own. She glanced toward the little man, her eyes hardening. *If she's been harmed*—

Alphena clutched her suddenly; her eyes cleared. "What was that?" she said. She sounded as though she'd been asleep.

"You've saved me," said the man. "I thank you with all my heart. If you hadn't rescued me, I might have . . . I might never . . ."

"Are they gone now?" Hedia asked. "The ones outside too?"

"Yes, they're quite gone," he said with a shudder. "That will never happen again, I assure you."

He shook his head and said, "I can't believe that they got out. I wonder how long it's been? It felt like eternity, and I suppose it almost was. Except for you."

"What were they?" Alphena said. "Demons?"

The man gave her a wry smile, then turned his head away. "They weren't intended to be," he said in obvious embarrassment. "They—but please, I appreciate what you've done for me, but you really must leave at once. I don't want anyone around me now. Especially not women!"

"I don't want to stay here either," said Alphena, looking toward the corridor. "Maron may be wondering where we are."

"Wait," Hedia said, putting her hand on the girl's arm. "We'll leave as soon as you tell us what was going on, sirrah!"

The man looked at her. She couldn't have described the change in his face, but she was suddenly reminded of his expression before he spoke the word that knocked her down.

"Will you give me orders, woman?" he said with a tiny smile. "But you have a right to know. Though it will be no benefit to you."

He touched Alphena's face lightly, turning her profile to him. He dropped his hand and smiled at Hedia again. She wondered how she had ever imagined that he was a helpless little rabbit.

"I studied for a very long time," he said, "and gained certain knowledge. I'm older than you might think."

Hedia looked into his eyes and immediately wished that she hadn't. What she'd thought at first glance were gray irises instead opened into infinite distances.

"At last I found this amulet"—he gestured toward the ankh, now hanging on his breast again—"and learned the ways of it. You should understand that until I gained all power, I had *no* power. *Do* you understand that, woman?"

"I hear what you said," said Hedia. "No one is really that powerless, though."

"Perhaps you're right," the man said, shaking his

head with a sad smile. "But I thought it was true, which is the same thing."

His face lost its weakness again. "With the amulet, I resolved to make a paradise for myself," he said. "So I thought. A living paradise for *my* mind alone. I knew nothing of women, you see, except that I desired them. And so in my ignorance I created"—he turned both hands upward and moved them apart: the gesture included more than the physical presence of the chamber and the tomb—"this. And found myself trapped in it, with the figments of my desires—as I imagined them to be."

Hedia nodded. "Thank you for the explanation," she said. "Daughter, we should be going. We have a great deal to do yet."

She and Alphena walked quickly up the corridor. The chamber and the man in it were lost behind the curve of the stone.

"I've sometimes wished that I had more power," Hedia said quietly. "But in truth, I've never been so badly harmed by a lack of power as I have by the lack of judgment to use the power I have. That would seem to be the general fate of humanity."

VARUS WALKED DOWN the cloud-wrapped path at the woman's side, picking his footing carefully. He forced himself not to look back. He wasn't afraid of what he might see—there was probably nothing but more mist like the fluff which cleared for ten feet ahead of them as they descended. He was remembering the myths of men who looked back as they returned from the Underworld and lost the prize they'd gone there to gain.

"You are not returning, wizard," the woman said, responding to his thought. "If you gain your wish, you will never return."

"There's nothing back there I need to see," said Varus.

"And I promised that I'd do this." He cleared his throat and added, "I don't care if I die, so long as I save the world."

The woman laughed.

Varus shook his head in embarrassment. It disconcerted him to be with someone who seemed to know what he was thinking. *He* didn't know what he was thinking himself, half the time.

He said, "But I admit that I'm afraid to die, Sigyn. I can't help being afraid. I'll still try to do whatever I have to when the time comes."

The woman looked at him. She never wore what Varus would describe as an expression, but he thought the curves of her face became minusculely softer.

"Sigyn was afraid to die," she said. "But when the time came, she died as all humans do. Even great wizards."

Varus stared in horror. His left hand gripped the ivory talisman, and the throbbing in his mind was briefly overpowering. *How could she be so callous?*

He suddenly stepped far enough outside himself to catch the irony. He grinned, then with difficulty swallowed a giggle.

You could always find humor in things if you looked in the right way. Poets—and lawyers—were trained to look for the way that suited their purpose in each particular case. Varus had been mired so deep in self-importance that he hadn't used his skills on his own situation—until a dead girl reminded him.

"Thank you, Sigyn," he said. "I'll do my best."

She smiled again.

The clouds below cleared in a rush, melting as though the sun had burned off morning mists. They were descending into the round valley Varus had entered when he pursued the sacred chickens a lifetime ago.

The present path was steep but nowhere nearly as

precipitous as the crater walls he remembered from the earlier visit. He and Sigyn would be able to run away rather than having to climb if the dragon pursued them—though of course the dragon wouldn't be slowed noticeably by the slight incline either.

There was no doubt that this was the same valley: the opening to the cave had vertical sides and an arched transom, like the passageways of an arena. It was unnatural and unmistakable to anyone who'd seen it before.

"If the fruit"—Varus lifted the bunch in his right hand—"doesn't poison the dragon quickly enough," he said, "I suppose I could take us back to the grounds of the Temple of Jupiter."

He looked at his guide. "That wouldn't help me get into the Underworld, though," he said.

"I do not belong in a temple," the woman said, "nor would your temple welcome me. But the fruit of the First Tree is the source of all life. It will not poison the Guardian. There is no place too harsh for the fruit to root and grow, spreading life."

"But—," said Varus. "Sigyn, will the dragon even eat the fruit? Or does he eat just meat?"

"The Guardian will eat anything, wizard," the woman said. "The Guardian would eat you and me."

They were halfway down the crater wall. The great lizard wasn't visible, but Varus had seen how quickly it could move after it appeared.

He looked at the woman. She had never set him a task that he couldn't accomplish. That meant there was a puzzle here; he *liked* puzzles.

He *didn't* like the thought of being gobbled by a beast he'd seen swallow a larger man whole, but that was the sort of thing that happened to epic heroes. Or at any rate, to the lesser folk standing at the side of epic heroes.

Patroclus, the bosom friend of Achilles, could die that way.

Varus chuckled. "I wonder if Corylus is Achilles in this epic," he said.

"There is no Achilles here, wizard," the woman said. He couldn't identify the emotion he heard in her voice. "You stand or fall alone."

They had reached the floor of the crater. Side by side, they walked toward the cave mouth, choosing a path through the brush.

"You're with me, Sigyn," Varus said.

"Sigyn is dead," she said harshly. And as she spoke, the dragon squirmed from the cave.

It started for them without hesitation. Its claws clacked and sparkled on the rock, and its breath smelled like the arena after a long August day of slaughter.

Now.

He ran two steps forward. A voice in his head reminded him that the one time he'd tried to throw the discus, it had sailed off at almost ninety degrees to the direction he'd intended. A gymnasium attendant had thrown himself flat, that time. If Varus missed by that much with the bunch of berries, the dragon would ignore them, at least until it had eaten the two humans.

He threw. The bunch arched high in the air, spinning over and over the twig it was attached to.

The dragon's forequarters lifted like a viper rising to strike. Its jaws, each the size of a rowing skiff, slammed on the berries like the release of a siege catapult. The creature rocked down as gracefully as a gymnast, then started for the humans again.

Help me! thought Varus. His inertia carried him forward, into the fog he'd first encountered in the vault of the temple. It was as thick as spun wool.

He heard the sound of laughter, female but cruel

beyond his previous conception. A form lurched across the path in front of him. The mist cleared enough for him to see that it was a spider; its body was pale white and the size of an ox.

Varus froze, then strode forward deliberately. He couldn't see anything through the fog. If he stepped off a cliff or into the teeth of another great spider—did spiders have teeth?—then *his* troubles were over.

The fog cleared. The old woman waited for him in a grove of oak trees.

It must be springtime, for the leaves had the bright flush of new growth and the insects hadn't been at them yet. She was tending a brazier which stood on three legs shaped like stylized goats; thin violet flames wavered from what looked like chips of quartz, not charcoal.

"You have come to see me again, Lord Varus?" she said. He took the deeper crinkling of her face as a smile, though he knew he could be mistaken.

"I need you, lady," he said. "I must destroy a dragon so that my companion and I can pass into the Underworld. I don't know how to do that myself."

"*All* knowledge is yours, Lord Varus," the old woman said. "You wear the amulet that was Botrug's and is now mine. But if you choose to use your power by imagining me—"

She lifted her right hand; her mouth opened to chant.

Varus was in the valley again, facing the dragon. He staggered; Sigyn caught him by the arm. He cried, *"Thou wilt burgeon in greatest abundance!"*

Her fingers felt cold. He didn't think he had touched Sigyn before. He straightened with a little effort.

The dragon stepped toward them. It was only thirty feet away, and its legs, though stumpy in comparison to the length of the body, covered ten feet with each pace.

Its foreclaws gouged the hard volcanic rock into puffs of dust and sparkling.

The creature paused and lifted its head slightly. Its right eye glittered like a ruby.

"You say the fruit isn't poison," Varus said. He started out in a whisper, but he had to raise his voice to be heard over the snorting gale of the dragon's breath. "But if the fruit grows as you say, perhaps he'll swell till he bursts."

"The Guardian cannot be harmed, wizard," the woman said. "Not by poison, not by bursting. The Guardian *cannot* be harmed."

"Then run, Sigyn," Varus said, holding himself straight. The dragon moved its head slightly; its right foreleg was still poised in midstep. "I'm going to stay here."

The creature's jaws opened slowly. Instead of presaging the final lunge that Varus expected, that was the only movement.

Tendrils of vine squirmed from the dragon's mouth, curling up and around. The creature looked surprised. Cocking its huge head, it clawed at the swelling foliage. A rumble came from deep in its abdomen.

"Sigyn?" Varus said. He didn't ask the question he'd formed: the answer was obvious. The fruit of the First Tree couldn't burst the dragon's stomach from inside, but neither could it be prevented from making its way up the creature's gullet.

As though the claws' touch had magical effect, the vine exploded into a torrent of greenery as forceful as a waterfall. Leafy vines wrapped the dragon's body, band after band of them. The bundle continued to writhe, but now very slowly.

The dragon's forelegs were lumps in a tube of green. A claw poked out, then was covered again by leaves.

"You do not sufficiently credit your own power,

wizard," the woman said. She smiled again and took Varus by the hand. "Come. You have opened the way for us to descend to our destinies."

Together, Varus and his guide entered the mouth of the cave. Her fingers were like ice, but he trembled for other reasons as well.

CHAPTER XVI

Corylus squatted on the bank of the Ice River, looking toward the Horn beyond. As before, a line of bitter smoke streamed from the cone to etch the white sky.

The water chuckled, curling past blocks of drifting ice and the roots of trees exposed by the freshet. The scene was as busy as the peddlers' kiosks filling the Field of Mars in Carce, though here the busyness was of hatchling insects, the birds preying on them, and voles scampering about to crop the young shoots uncurling from the roots of the grasses.

In the sky was a hawk, but it kept at a safe height to avoid Corylus. He looked around, wondering if the ravens were watching him. They weren't; or at any rate, they weren't from where he could see them.

Corylus rose with a sigh. He'd come by himself, though Sith had wanted to accompany him. He'd thought—he grinned: he'd prayed, really—that by musing alone and staring at the river, a solution to his problem would suddenly appear. That had never happened to him in the past, but the rules of this place might be as unusual as the matter which had caused him to be here.

Instead, spring in Hyperborea was much like spring on the Upper Rhine. Corylus felt his mind going back to his boyhood, when the problems—in hindsight—seemed a great deal more straightforward and trivial.

They'd seemed both knotty and serious at the time, of course. And while the task of diverting the Ice River into a bowl ten miles to the south might someday seem laughably simple, Corylus wouldn't have a future if he didn't solve it now. Frothi wasn't the sort to spare a stranger who had failed to meet his challenge.

The hawk screamed: it must be a harrier. Corylus couldn't make out the bird's markings against the pale sky, but its call was unmistakable.

Smiling faintly, Corylus settled at the base of Odd's cairn and leaned back against the stones. He was facing south, so the sun was fully on him. If he couldn't solve the problem himself, he would call on the being who presumably could: Odd's Vengeance. He closed his eyes and let the sun's warmth creep into his bones.

The hawk called again, but the sound touched Corylus only the way the ant tickling the back of his left knee did, or the delicate scent of the lingon flowers mixed with the grasses. Corylus hadn't been sure that he could relax under these circumstances, but he'd had a rough couple days. Quite apart from the physical labors, there'd been the stress of wondering what the Fates would throw at him next—and facing each next thing down.

He felt his mouth smiling. Confronting Frothi had if anything taken more out of him because there *hadn't* been a fight; that would have burned away the emotions which instead had continued to curdle his blood. Sith had done a great deal to settle him, but that had been strenuous too.

The soil Corylus sat on sighed, and the breeze and the sun toyed with his hair. Behind him, the river joked with the ice. Everything here was warmth and peace.

Frothi and the wizard had found Odd in his trance and drowned him; they could do the same to the stranger who claimed to be Odd's heir. Corylus didn't think they'd dare to try while the tribe—and especially Sith—were watching for something of the sort, but it didn't matter: Corylus couldn't dig a ten-mile canal by himself. If Odd's Vengeance came to him only while he slept, then he would sleep.

He heard giggling and turned. Girls stood in the grove of willows just upstream of where Corylus had built the cairn. When they saw him looking at them, one of them shook out her ash blond hair and said, "So, you're going to notice us after all, Corylus? We'd decided that you thought you were too good for us."

She stretched to her full lissome height, twining her arms together above her head. Her breasts were small, but the nipples thrust hard against the silk of her silvery tunic.

"I'm sorry, ladies," Corylus said, rising to his feet. He wasn't here to socialize, but neither was he going to be discourteous. "I hadn't seen you. I certainly wouldn't have ignored anyone as lovely as yourselves if I'd been aware of your presence."

He grinned. After all, he hadn't been accomplishing anything. He hadn't even managed to get to sleep.

"I'll forgive you," said the nymph who'd spoken, "if you'll give me a kiss."

"Give each of us a kiss," said a sister; other nymphs giggled. All ten or twelve sprites from the stand of willows were sauntering toward him.

Corylus had grown up in army camps. He was a good-looking youth and the son of an officer besides, so he was well used to getting offers of female companionship. The situation in Carce hadn't been a great deal different, though in the better parts of the city, women generally put a gloss of culture on their propositions.

"Ladies, you're all very lovely," he said, sweeping his smile around the, well, grove of women. "I'm flattered, and another time I'd do my best to respond, but right now I'm hoping the man buried here will visit me. I need to divert the river"—he gestured—"south, and I don't know how to do it."

"The wizard Odd is dead, Corylus," said a nymph. "He can't help you."

"He means Odd's Vengeance," the first sprite said. "But he"—she returned her gaze to Corylus; her eyes were slightly slanted and had a tawny luster—"can't help you either, dear."

"We can," said another sprite.

"*We can!*" the grove chorused together.

"Would you like us to help you, Corylus?" said the leading sprite archly. "For kinship's sake?"

"And for a kiss!" cried a sibling, but she broke into giggles and ducked away after she spoke. Perhaps the request had been a joke.

"We'll need help," said a sprite. "But surely all our sisters will join in, won't they?"

"We would!" cried a sprite.

"All our sisters will help Corylus," said another. "For kinship, and because he's so handsome."

"Ladies . . . ," said Corylus. He didn't understand what was happening. He was pretty sure that if he said the wrong thing—promised the wrong thing—to these tree nymphs, the result could be as bad as failure, at least for himself personally. "I would appreciate any help you can give me. But I need to know what I would pay for that help first, please."

"For kinship, Corylus," said the leader. "But you'll have to dance with us."

Corylus realized the landscape in which he stood and spoke had become slightly blurred, as if he were seeing it through a sheet of glass with a faint yellow tinge. The sprites were sharp and clear, and battalions of similar laughing women were coming from all directions. *What is happening?*

"Your ladyship . . . ," Corylus said. He had no idea of how to address a tree nymph, but erring on the side of courtesy was never a bad idea. "I'll of course dance with you, but I have other duties. If you please—I must be able to perform those too."

"We mean you no harm, Cousin," said the leading sprite. "We'll release you. But you must join the dance if we're to help." She offered her hand. "Come, dear," she said, grinning wickedly. "You won't regret it, and we'll enjoy it a great deal."

"I would be honored," Corylus said. He took her hand in his left, and another sprite took his right. Nymphs of all types and ages joined them, but the slender spirits of the willows were in the great majority.

They began to pace to a high, piping rhythm. Corylus wasn't sure where the music came from. It was as though grass flowers were singing and the breeze accompanied them.

Perhaps there was a pattern, but so far as Corylus could see, the dancers drifted like thistledown or bubbles on the surface of a pond. Sprites left the rout and others took their places. Some whirled away, linked hands with siblings, and waded into the river. The chill didn't seem to affect them. Others spun on their toes, digging into the soil. Sisters joined them, laughing and gesturing rhythmically in a serpentine line stretching southward.

Corylus danced with high steps, turning deliberately while he raised and lowered his arms. The conscious part of his mind recognized his motions as being those of the Salii, the dancers who performed with the sacred shield of Mars and its eleven exact duplicates; the original had fallen from the heavens. He wasn't copying the priests, though: his limbs were performing the evolutions that had flowed into them from the touch of the willow sprites.

Corylus felt sunlight and the moisture in the ground. The dance exhilarated him as wine never had. Not even his greatest triumph on the sports field could equal what Corylus felt now. He laughed and felt the world laughing in the voices of his companions.

The earth cracked. A split ran jaggedly through and beyond the dancing spirits. Prairie grasses waved and shuddered southward as the rock continued to break apart. The river chuckled and bounced into a new channel, directed by the nymphs linking arms in the former stream.

"There, darling kinsman," said a sprite as she squeezed his hand. "We've helped you, haven't we? As no one else could have done."

The haze between Corylus and the waking world was clearing, and the willow sprites were beginning to fade from his vision. *Maybe I've been asleep after all.*

"Thank you," he said. He wasn't sure what he'd seen and what he'd merely dreamed. "Did you . . . I mean, has the river really changed its course?"

Instead of answering, the nymph turned her head and called, "Canina? Come here, darling. Our Corylus is going to need a reed for his flute."

A girl with hair the color of verdigrised bronze minced over, her full lips in a pout. "Do you think you can give me orders, Salicia?" she said. Though she was speaking to the other nymph, her eyes watched Corylus sidelong.

"Of course not, darling," Salicia said mildly. "But he does need you, you know. I didn't think you'd mind helping him."

"I *don't* mind," Canina said. "I just don't like to see people getting above themselves."

She turned to Corylus and gave him a warm, false smile. "Take a lock of my hair, darling," she said. "Here, I'll step close to make it easy."

Corylus reached for his obsidian knife. Canina pressed

herself against him, almost pinning his arm to his torso before he got the knife out.

"Careful!" he said, feeling his body tense reflexively. He pinched a lock of the bronze hair against the flat of the blade with his thumb, then twisted the edge against the strands to clip them off.

"There," he said. "I've got—"

Canina took the lock of hair from his hand and tucked it behind his ear like a stylus. She kissed him on the lips, then stepped away with a triumphant grin at Salicia.

"Remember me, darling," she said.

Salicia didn't say anything aloud, but her eyes smoldered. Her fingers played with Corylus's neck for an instant; then she unbent and said, "Now, kinsman, I think you'd better join your human friends. After all, you've succeeded—because of our help."

"Yes, because of your—," Corylus said. Before he got the sentence out, Salicia too was kissing him. He started to put his left arm around her by reflex, but she vanished. The landscape was in sharp focus again.

He stood beside icy water bubbling raggedly southward. The east side of the new channel was lined with willow trees; roots had crept into a fracture in the bedrock and dug down, splitting it wide. Out in the Ice River, more willows had woven their roots and branches into a mat which diverted the current into the crack.

The shadows surprised him. Corylus glanced toward the sun and realized it was already the middle of the afternoon. His legs didn't feel as tired as they should if he'd been dancing for six hours, but he was lightheaded, the way that much exercise would have made him.

The tribe—it must be all or almost all the members, adults and children both—was streaming toward him. They weren't driving their animals. Frothi, unmistakable for his red-orange beard, was in the lead, but

Corylus could identify Nemastes and the Stolo also by their unique builds.

One of the women would be Sith.

Corylus lifted his pack. He must have succeeded in filling the "cup," the task that Frothi had set him, but that didn't explain why the tribe was rushing toward him in this fashion.

The plain rippled. The tribesfolk staggered, many of them thrown to the ground as it heaved up from behind them. Steam blasted skyward from where they had been camped. Corylus rode the shock wave with his knees flexed; a moment later he heard the hissing boom of the eruption.

He dropped the pack. Carrying only the hornbeam staff, he began jogging southward.

There was a louder crash when icewater flooded into the heart of the ancient volcano. This time fire shot upward instead of steam. The orange flames wrapped together into a squat giant, who lowered down from the heavens.

The fire god raised a blazing sword. The landscape rocked with his hellish laughter.

MARON WAS SLIGHTLY in the lead. When he stopped abruptly, Hedia put out a hand reflexively to keep from walking into his back.

"What is it?" said Alphena. "Ooh! Look at the flowers!"

Hedia *was* looking at the flowers. She could hardly avoid that, coming as she had from what was virtually a tunnel through the trees. The forest's foliage hadn't been uniform, exactly—out of curiosity, she'd begun to count distinct shades of green and had quickly identified more than she could note on her fingers alone—but it had become as depressing as a foggy night would.

Here were red and orange flowers, purple and yellow

flowers, and pink and white flowers. Their size and profusion were beyond anything Hedia had seen before.

Butterflies more than a foot across fluttered over the meadow, bearing stems down when they lighted to drink. Their wings were entirely golden, but the light showed whorls and points as though they were made of stamped foil. When the insects lifted, scales drifted away in glittering clouds.

"They're beautiful!" Alphena said, stepping farther into the meadow. She bent to sniff a flower, though the air was already sweet with mingled perfumes.

Maron shook his head as if to clear it. He'd been walking in a near stupor since they'd left the outskirts of the wizard's tomb. Hedia's smile held a touch of satisfaction: the faun may not have reached his limit, but he'd come closer to it than he'd probably ever expected.

"Come along," he said gruffly. "This place may be harmless now, but it wasn't always so. We're best away from here."

Hedia walked into the meadow. The great flowers bobbed about her waist, and the stems of the mixed grasses tickled her. The gorgeous insects fluttered off when she came too close, but they didn't seem to be inordinately afraid of humans.

There was—there had been—a house here. Two walls still stood to shoulder height, and the foundation course of the other two remained as an angled furrow through the flowers. The interior of what had been the building was overgrown, but Hedia glimpsed painted potsherds among the foliage.

"What's this, Maron?" the girl asked, walking toward the walls. Here and there a touch of painted plaster remained on the stones, but they appeared to have been set without mortar. "Who lived here?"

"Didn't I tell you to come away?" the faun said. He started out shouting, but the loud noise must have made his headache worse. He'd half lifted his club in frustration, but he relaxed before Hedia had to take a hand.

Still—

"Yes, leave the house alone, Daughter," Hedia said sharply. "The sooner we're back in Carce, the better I'll like it. We don't have time for sightseeing."

"Oh, all right," said Alphena. She sounded disappointed, but she knew perfectly well that Hedia and the faun were correct.

She turned; as she did so, her elbow brushed what looked like a giant primrose. The butterfly which had been drinking there rose from the flower and circled above her, showering wing scales like droplets of sun. Alphena's face went blank.

"Daughter!" Hedia cried, running to the girl.

Alphena collapsed into her arms. Her pulse beat strongly, but there was no consciousness behind her eyes.

ALPHENA FELT DIZZY. Starting to topple forward, she put an arm out to catch herself. Instead of sinking into the sod, her fingers came down on a gravel path.

The dizziness passed; she straightened. The field was covered with thistles, not flowers, and the building in front of her was whole. She looked around: Hedia and the faun were nowhere to be seen, and the forest behind her was now of oaks and beeches rather than unfamiliar trees.

The walls were covered with beige plaster and the roof was shingled—which Alphena had never seen before. In Carce roofs were tiled, while the poorer sort of huts in the country were thatched. The windows to either side of the door were shuttered, but the door itself was open.

The woman who lay on the floor of the single long room had been stabbed repeatedly. The wall behind her, plastered like the exterior, was splattered with blood.

Storage jars had been leaning against the wall. All but one had been smashed, spilling their contents—grain and oil and beer. The insides of the terra-cotta jars had been painted with black resin to seal them. Dried vegetables, hams, and flitches of bacon which had hung from the roof beams had been slashed down onto the general ruin.

Alphena looked back. The attack must have been recent, because the odors of beer and fresh blood were still pungent. The enemy was gone, however, or at least wasn't creeping up on Alphena from behind.

Should I bury the woman? Alphena thought. There weren't any tools inside, but there might be a shovel or pick in an outbuilding. She hadn't had time to look.

The woman's eyes opened. Alphena screamed, jumping back as she might have done if a spider had dropped from the ceiling onto her.

"Well, since you're here now, girl," the woman said, "you must do me a service before you leave."

"You're *dead*!" Alphena repeated.

The woman laughed. Blood that had oozed from her lips formed little bubbles during the horrible sound. She said, "Freyr's sword is in the celadon jar, girl. Take it out and cut my head off with it."

"I don't understand," Alphena said. "Why do you—"

"Do what I say, girl!" the dead woman said. "Do you want me to stand up and put the sword in your hands myself?"

"No . . . ," Alphena whispered, but she was speaking to the image in her mind rather than responding to the threat. She stepped into the house for the first time.

The transom was low because of the steeply peaked roof. When Alphena ducked to clear it, she felt dizzy again. Nothing changed around her this time, though.

She walked across the floor. Wheat kernels crunched beneath her boots; she tried to concentrate on that to take her mind off the stickiness of the blood. The woman's eyes followed her as she passed.

The undamaged jar was the same shape as the others, but it was made of pale green ceramic instead of terracotta. The wax which sealed the wide stopper had been impressed with a symbol Alphena didn't recognize: the series of spiky verticals could have been letters in an unfamiliar script.

She picked with her thumbnail at the wax; it had darkened with age and seemed as hard as the jar itself. Alphena thought for a moment, then found a fragment broken from another jar. She was careful not to get a bloody one nor to look back. She was very much afraid that the dead woman would have turned to watch her.

Alphena took a deep breath, then used a corner of the pottery to chip at the wax. She gouged out a thumb-sized chunk before the point of the shard broke off; she turned it and with a different corner broke out more.

The old woman laughed behind her. "You could smash the jar, you know, girl," she said. "Do you think it matters in this place?"

"I'm doing what you said," Alphena snapped. "Just be quiet, won't you?"

The woman laughed, but she didn't reply.

When Alphena had cleaned out the wax, she dropped what was left of the potsherd and tried to lift the stopper. It still resisted. She hit it with the heel of her hand. It loosened with a *clink*; then she could remove it.

The jar was empty except for a sword whose scabbard and belt seemed to be metal. Alphena lifted the hilt, expecting friction from the blade to bring the accoutrements along with it. Instead the sword slipped out alone, startling her with its beauty.

The room's only light came through the doorway, but the blade seemed to glow from within. As Alphena raised it toward the roof peak, a serpent of shadow ran from the rounded point to the hilt, then writhed up to the point again. She didn't know what metal it was forged from, but it wasn't heavy enough to be steel; it was perfectly balanced and looked sharp enough to cut a dust mote.

"What is this?" Alphena whispered. She had never seen anything so beautiful.

"It's Freyr's sword, girl!" the old woman said. "Just as I told you. Now, get on with it, won't you? Or do you want to stay here with me forever?"

Alphena turned, feeling her face go hard. She brought the sword back, judging the distance. The blade was longer than that of the infantry sword she normally practiced with, longer even than the cavalry-pattern weapon that it more closely resembled.

The old woman grinned. Alphena struck through her neck with a single clean blow, barely nicking the earthen floor the corpse lay on. Neck vertebrae crackled faintly. The sword edge was so keen that it could have whisked through cobwebs for all the effort the stroke required.

The head bounced away. The flesh sloughed off before it hit the floor the first time, and the skull crumpled to dust at the second. Where the body had been was a faint gray silhouette, rather like what would remain after a dummy stuffed with chaff had been burned.

Alphena felt herself slipping out of consciousness. She thrust her arm out so that she wouldn't fall onto the sword. Hedia was holding her, saying, "Daughter! Are you all right?"

Alphena opened her eyes; she was surprised to find that they had been closed. She was standing in front of the ruined house, and her hands were empty.

"Where's the woman?" she said. Had she been dreaming? "Hedia, was there a woman here? A dead woman?"

Hedia stepped back but continued to hold Alphena by the shoulders as she decided whether the girl was all right. Only then did she release her and say, "You walked toward the house and seemed to faint. There isn't anybody else, alive or dead. Now, are you ready to go on?"

Alphena looked from her stepmother to the interior of the ruin. "Wait," she said, stepping inside. "Give me just a moment."

"Are you mad?" Maron said. "This is a dangerous place, a very dangerous place. I'm compelled to bring you safe to the path to the waking world, but I can't do that if you won't listen to me!"

"Did something happen when you stumbled, Daughter?" Hedia said. "If so, then we *really* need to get away from here."

Hedia was trying to hide her concern, but Alphena heard it in her tone. Not long ago she wouldn't have noticed anything in her stepmother's voice except anger—filtered through Alphena's own resentment.

"Please," the girl said, "just a moment. I'm all right, really."

She worked a large piece of jar from the dirt and began using it as a trowel. It was a fragment of rim, thicker than the shell of the jar and well shaped to her grip. The soil filling the ruin had been blown in by the wind; though light, the roots of grasses bound it and made it hard to remove with no better tool than Alphena had.

Hedia knelt beside her. "Alphena?" she said. "What's wrong?"

"Both of you, come along!" Maron snarled. "Must I force hellebore down your throats to cure your madness? Were it not for the compulsion, I'd flee this place as quickly as my hooves could take me!"

"Really nothing, Mother," Alphena said, scraping furiously now that she'd broken through the matted roots. Dust flew. "It's just that I want to see if—"

Her potsherd clinked, breaking on something harder. Alphena tossed it aside and brushed at the soil with her fingertips, uncovering pale green ceramic.

The celadon jar was still where she had seen it when she found the dead woman. Alphena had thought that if she found the jar, she would search for the sword where she remembered dropping it. Instead, the stopper was back in place. Its wax seal had dried to a stain on the ceramic.

"What have you found, dear?" the older woman said. "Is this jade?"

"Come away!" the faun repeated desperately. "You don't know what you're dealing with, either one of you!"

Alphena thumped the stopper with her hand to break the seal, then opened the jar. The sword was inside, just as she remembered. She grasped it, this time by the top of the scabbard, and drew it out.

The belt and sheath were of silvery metal which occasionally woke into rainbow highlights. Alphena drew the sword. Seen in open air the blade was the dull gray of tin, but a power beyond reasoned explanation lurked within it. The double edges were too sharp to make out clearly, even in the light.

"That's beautiful," Hedia said in a hushed voice. "However you came to find it."

"Put it back, girl!" Maron said. "You don't understand. Things of that ilk aren't for you!"

Alphena looked at him. "I think I was meant to have it," she said in sudden resolution. "Perhaps it was payment for a service I did someone."

She sheathed the sword, then wrapped the belt around her waist. It fit, though she had to wind the excess over itself.

"I'm ready to go," she said calmly to Maron.

The faun shook his shaggy head. "Only a madwoman

chooses to get involved with the gods," he said. He set off across the meadow at a quick pace.

AS SOON AS they entered what Varus had thought was a cave, he began to follow Sigyn instead of walking at her side. Illumination moved forward with her; at every step a further stride's length of rocky downward slope extended ahead.

The rhythm in Varus's mind had a fiery intensity. He thought the chant of the wizards had grown stronger recently, but he couldn't be sure. It seemed as much a part of him now as his skin or the color of his eyes.

The woman moved with the same dead calm as she did everything. A tiny smile played at the corner of her mouth, but Varus was afraid to read anything into that. He might have been imagining the expression anyway, because of a trick of the light.

The cave wasn't black but a gray which Varus found menacing rather than neutral. Anything beyond arm's length to either side of Sigyn's path remained shadow without form.

The illumination was dim, sourceless, and disquieting. The sound was odd also.

"Sigyn?" he said. "Our footsteps don't echo. How big is this cavern?"

"It is no more a cavern than I am Sigyn, wizard," the woman said. "And it is the size of all time."

The slope grew steeper. The woman turned sideways but continued to walk with apparent confidence.

Varus grimaced. He didn't want to look silly, but he wasn't any kind of athlete, and it wouldn't help if he missed a step and plunged into the nothingness beyond. He turned and continued down backward, gripping outcrops from the slope whenever he wasn't sure of his footing.

He grinned. The only person who could see him now

was his guide. He didn't imagine that she thought he was silly—or cared.

Varus heard cries as they went—crawled, in his case—deeper. He wasn't sure whether they were made by humans or animals; perhaps they were even of natural causes. He'd given up thinking anything was impossible, so it could be that what seemed to him wails of agony was really the sighing of the wind.

The slope flattened. Varus hesitated for a few steps more, then stood and resumed walking normally again. The light had color now, or he thought it did: a bluish tinge where there had been only gray.

This place was cold as well; cold mentally. His arms didn't have goose bumps, but his mind shuddered.

The woman stopped. Varus walked to her side and waited, wondering what to do with his hands. Eventually he clasped them behind his back for fear that he'd otherwise strike a rhetorical pose with his right arm lifted. He was nervous, and his reflex was to fall back into the forms he'd been trained to use.

The region of blue radiance expanded, stretching away on all sides. They were standing on a plain, rocky and as barren as the surface of the sea.

Varus was cold. He was as cold as death, and his mind throbbed in the rhythm of the dance. He couldn't see the slope they had descended.

"S-Sigyn?" he said. He swallowed. "What do we do now?"

The Cold replied, "PUBLIUS VARUS, YOU HAVE BROUGHT MY BRIDE TO ME. FOR THAT I GRANT YOU A GIFT: I WILL SEND YOU ON THE WAY TO WHAT YOU SEEK."

Varus licked his lips. His mouth was dry, but he was no longer afraid. He knew what to do, and the realization freed him despite the hammering pressure in his mind.

"Sigyn," he said. "You can leave here with me. This

isn't a place for anyone, not for *anything*. Come, we're going."

"DO YOU THINK YOU CAN BALK ME, HUMAN?" thundered the Cold through every atom of Varus's body.

He didn't speak. *I'm going to try,* he thought. His lips pursed to speak a verse to rip a path out of this place. He didn't think that he'd succeed, even with the help of the old woman, but Sigyn's fate wouldn't be on his conscience.

She touched his cheek with the fingers of her left hand. "You have removed the compulsion from me, Publius Varus," she said, "but the truth remains: this is where I belong. I will stay."

"Sigyn?" he said. He wanted to say more, but he didn't know what more he *could* say. The rhythm behind his temples almost blinded him with its angry insistence.

He felt the woman take his hands. "Go back to the waking world, Varus," she said, "but not as the tool of the Twelve. They lied to you for their own safety, and my husband supports them because of his perversity. Go as your own man."

She smiled. The ragged wound still gaped in her throat, but Varus no longer found it disfiguring. He supposed he'd gotten used to it.

"You will probably die," she said. "But you will find death preferable to fulfilling the task the Twelve set for you."

"What am I to do?" Varus said through the pain. His head might burst. He wished it would, spilling his life out with his brains on this cold stone. The pounding would stop then, *must* stop then.

"Do as seems right to you, Varus," the woman said. Her smile grew wider but softer as well. "Your instincts have served you well before."

"Yes, Sigyn," Varus whispered. He hurt and he was afraid, but he would go on. He was a citizen of Carce.

"Now," said the woman. "As you took the compulsion from me, so do I take the compulsion from you."

She kissed Varus on the forehead. The pounding stopped. He wavered, feeling as if all the bones had been snatched from his limbs. Sigyn held him, feeding strength through her cold hands.

She kissed Varus on the lips and stepped away. She had the same smile.

"Sigyn," he said, reaching toward her. He felt a relief beyond anything he could have imagined before this moment.

"That was Sigyn," she said. "But now and forever I am the Bride."

Her form faded, all but the smile; and at last the smile as well. In her place brightened a path of rosy light slanting upward.

CHAPTER XVII

"This is quite fast enough, Maron," Hedia said sharply as he started to lope ahead.

The faun turned with a petulant scowl. "Come!" he said. "The gate's not far ahead now."

Then, "I can carry you again, woman. Here, I'll do that."

He knelt with his back to her, his head turned over his shoulder. He placed his hands on his hips as before so that his wrists were ready to support her thighs. Alphena looked from the faun to Hedia, then back again.

"We will not," Hedia said. "We will walk as we've been doing, and if this gate is close by, then we'll get there shortly."

Maron glared at her, then burst into unexpected laughter. "Yes, great lady," he said. "I am yours to command and keep safe, as I will continue to do."

He held out his right hand to her and his left to Alphena. The girl made a moue and brushed the offer away, but Hedia touched her fingertips to the faun's for a moment before lowering her hand again. This wasn't terrain to stumble through linked to a neighbor, but she was willing enough to accept the gesture.

Alphena wasn't up to moving quickly either. The girl's footgear was more suitable for rough country, but it was heavy and would pull on groin muscles unused to hiking. Hedia's objection saved her stepdaughter from having to admit weakness.

There were red hills to either side, barren but wind-carved and not especially steep. The soil of the valley was largely sand that had worn from those rocks. The only vegetation was yuccas; they bunched their leaves in starbursts on the ground and sent up a single spiky stem from the center. On some of the stems were small yellow flowers.

Boulders ranging from the size of a man's head to the size of an ox were scattered across the plain. Bright green and ocher faces had been painted on several. As Hedia proceeded at the faun's side, faces appeared on other rocks as well. The features were stylized, with square mouths, four-pointed eyes, and a single thick brow.

"Mother?" Alphena said. "I think that rock just turned around. It's *looking* at me."

"It doesn't appear to have arms to grab us," Hedia said, keeping her tone carefully cool. She herself thought that the faces were appearing on what had been blank surfaces, not that the stones themselves were moving. "Maron, are these painted rocks dangerous?"

"Painted?" the faun said in an ironic tone. "But just keep away from them, why don't you? You can manage that."

Hedia looked at him appraisingly. Maron wasn't her servant, and she had to admit that the task of guiding and protecting her had been a considerable burden to him. Though she hoped there'd been what the faun considered fringe benefits.

She grinned wickedly but quickly hid it behind her hand. It wouldn't do for Alphena to see the expression and wonder.

"Mother?" the girl said. "What do we do when we get back to Carce?"

Hedia bent forward to look at her past the faun's

muscular torso. "I hadn't thought that far ahead," she said honestly. "Nothing until we've talked with Anna, certainly. And, ah, we don't know what else might have happened while we were gone."

She thought about Corylus having vanished, which the girl didn't know about. And Maron saying that her brother had smashed down the forest, including the giant centipede. She didn't—

Varus had disappeared when he chased the sacred chickens. He came back that time, and likely he would this time also.

Hedia chuckled. Aloud she said, "Alphena, dear, all that I'm really sure about is that we'll deal with whatever we find when we get back, just as we've dealt with the things that have happened to us here. The women of the Alphenus household are a force to be reckoned with, wouldn't you say?"

She was speaking to cheer the girl up, but part of her mind really did mean it. The other part quivered with formless dread, but *that* part had been terrified ever since she watched her stepdaughter vanish in the sunlit garden. It hadn't stopped Hedia from dealing with the situation, just as she'd said.

"Here," said Maron, halting before what seemed at first to be a curving field covered with tiny bubbles. "I have brought you both safely to the portal to the waking world. Is this not so, great lady?"

Hedia stared at the scene before her. The bubbles had fuzzy edges and were moving. The ground on which she and her companions stood faded when it should have come in contact with the plane of bubbles. They spiraled up and to the right, but when she moved closer she saw that they also curled down to the left.

"Maron, where are we?" she asked sharply. No matter how she turned her head or squinted, she wasn't sure that the spiral was a material object or an illusion of light.

"The path . . . ," the faun said. He took her right hand in his and swept it upward. "*That* path. Will take you to the world where you belong."

He laughed with some humor. "Do not take the downward path, Hedia," he said. "That goes to a place from which you will not return, not even with the help of those you called upon to bind me."

"Can we walk on it?" Alphena said. "It doesn't look solid."

Hedia took a deep breath. She and Maron both ignored the girl. The time she had spent in this place had been a life separate from the one she had lived for the previous twenty-two years—eventful though they had been.

"Then yes," Hedia said, her eyes holding the faun's. "Maron, you have guided and protected us as you were compelled to do."

She stepped to the faun and kissed him passionately while rubbing herself against his own hard body.

She stepped back. "Thank you, dear beast," she said, her voice husky. "Perhaps we'll meet again."

Maron laughed harshly. "Perhaps we will, great lady," he said. "Go back now to your waking world."

A little taken aback by his expression, Hedia gestured Alphena ahead. The girl looked doubtful—*Does she think I'm using her to test the footing?*—but stepped toward the path.

Maron strutted in front of Alphena and took both her wrists, swinging her to the side. "Go to your world, Hedia!" he crowed. "You and I are done now!"

"Release my daughter," Hedia said, hearing her voice rise despite her attempt to sound calm. "If you like, I'll stay with you for a time, dear. That's no hardship, is it?"

"I was compelled not to hurt you, great lady," the faun said, his tone slipping into the gutturals of lust. "There was no such compulsion about the virgin. Though as you said, there needn't be harm in what I intend for her. Maybe I'll even send her up to you when I'm done with her."

Laughing like the demon he was in fact, Maron bent the screaming, struggling girl over so that he could grasp her ankles with the same hands that held her wrists. He lifted her overhead, helpless as a straw doll, and poised her over his rampant member.

Varus had lost track of time and distance. The path took all his mind and concentration, the way versification did when he was deep in the moment. Part of his intellect told him that he should be wrung out from the effort of climbing seemingly forever, but instead he felt exhilarated.

The wizards of the Horn, the Twelve, were no longer in his mind. Each rosy step Varus took had a lively sharpness. He was happy, if only because pounding misery no longer gripped him.

In that joyous state, Varus stepped from the glow into a destination that had completely escaped his mind. He stopped with his foot raised, at a momentary loss for where to put it when the path no longer sloped upward. He was in the hall of the Temple of Jupiter Best and Greatest, and it was nighttime.

Lanterns hung from their sconces, casting yellow light on the pillars, the drapery, and the stiff earthenware form of the seated god. An aged senator, Sempronius Tardus, lay slumped on a couch facing the round table on which his dinner sat. He was an antiquarian friend of Alphenus Saxa and, as Varus knew, a commissioner for the sacred rites.

Around the dinner table and elsewhere in the big

room sprawled attendants—Balaton and the temple staff as well as the servants who must have come with the commissioner; they appeared to be sleeping. Varus supposed they'd been drugged, but a spell might have been involved instead.

He felt a touch of vertigo and rubbed his eyes. The lamplight wavered. All the light he'd seen since Oannes accosted him in the Grove of the Muses had been flat, sourceless, and constant.

Pandareus lay on the floor, midway between the entrance gates and the statue of the god. A helix of green flame flowed up and down between the teacher's ankles and throat. His eyes stared at Varus. Though he was obviously straining, no words came out of his part-open mouth.

Nemastes knelt, before the statue of Jupiter, Varus thought; but then he saw the triangle of three small fires on the floor in front of the Hyperborean. In their midst was a human skull.

Nemastes was working a spell. It had nothing to do with worship of the greatest god of the Republic.

Sigyn had told Varus to follow his instincts. He would do that because there was no better alternative—and instinct told him to oppose any and every action that Nemastes took.

"Nemastes!" Varus said, walking deliberately toward the wizard. He gripped the ivory talisman with his left hand. "Your brethren on the Horn sent me to you."

The wizard jumped to his feet and turned toward Varus. He had cast off the singlet he'd worn until now. Nude, he looked only marginally human; his genitals were tiny, more like those of an infant than a grown man's.

"Fear me, boy!" Nemastes said in a high-pitched voice. Varus hadn't heard him speak in the past. "You see your teacher, helpless against me. Run away now or you will be bound like him for eternity!"

He's bluffing, Varus thought. He took another step. Nemastes threw a handful of softly shining objects toward him.

Snake ribs! Varus thought as they pelted him, light taps and quite harmless. Nemastes shouted a word that human ears could not register.

One end of the green flame lifted from Pandareus's body. The coils abruptly unwound and writhed toward Varus.

Varus kicked at the serpent of fire. It slid up his leg and around his waist. He kicked vainly again and toppled paralyzed to the floor not far from his teacher.

Nemastes stared at him in satisfaction. "If my siblings sent you," he said, "and I suppose they did, since I see you have the head of Botrug . . . If they did, then they picked a poor tool to save themselves."

The Hyperborean squatted and resumed his chant toward the skull. One of the stones in the statue's plinth was glowing with its own pale light.

Varus could feel the coil of vivid green loop up and down his body; his skin felt brittle beneath its touch. He could breathe, but he couldn't move his arms or legs. He could still speak, though—

"Nemastes!" he said. "They're coming for you. You can't escape your brothers!"

Varus didn't know that, nor did he know anything else that could give him hope. He suspected that it was a threat the Hyperborean might believe, though, and that it might throw him off his stride.

Nemastes shouted a word that made the lanterns wink. A stone of the plinth powdered, vanishing like a bubble in a marsh. The wizard reached into the cavity it had left. He came out with a curved black bone which was pierced for fingerings.

Rising, Nemastes fitted a short reed into a hole in the knuckle end of the flute. Looking at Varus again, he said, "This is Odd's flute, boy. Have you any conception of how long I've waited to hold this? But the wait was worth it. All power in this world is *mine*!"

"Till your brothers come for you," Varus said. The cold from the helix of fire was seeping into his bones, but he continued to fight it. "You're doomed and you know it, Nemastes!"

"Spurius Cassius told me where he'd hidden this," the wizard said. Varus had never seen his face without an unpleasant expression, but the grin this time seemed exceptionally nasty. "He didn't know how to use it, but I do. In exchange, *Lord* Varus, I gave him your sister. He's pleasuring himself with Lady Alphena in Hell right now, I believe."

Varus lunged against the bonds of light. They continued to slip over him like greased copper; there was no give. The cold sank deeper, through the youth's muscles and into the marrow of his bones. *I'll never move again, and I'll never be warm.*

Nemastes raised the flute. "I've seen Odd use it!" he said. "I have Odd's power now!"

He's lying, Varus thought. He was sure of that, though he had no conscious evidence for his belief.

Nemastes put his lips to the reed he'd inserted. Varus shouted, "You'll die for a fool if you try that, wizard! You'll die and know you'll die!"

Nemastes blew, starting on a high note and wobbling down the scale. Varus wasn't sure whether it was music or if the sound was a side effect, like the ringing of iron as it was beaten on an anvil.

Light itself contracted in a violent convulsion. The interior of the temple glittered like an array of crystal prisms. There were thousands of identical *everything*—except the Hyperborean wizard alone, standing in the center and playing with the order of the universe.

Varus stood beside the old woman on a mountaintop;

she held a sprig of mistletoe. Snow lay all around, but
the two of them were on bare rock. The scene being
acted inside the temple was far below but as clear to
him as the wrinkles on the woman's face.

"Nemastes has power," she said. Her voice quavered,
but there was iron in it. "But not judgment. He thinks it
shows patience that he has waited ten thousand years,
but he has not waited long enough."

"I have to stop him," Varus said. He looked at her in
concern. "That's right, isn't it? Whatever Nemastes
wants isn't for the good of men."

"How is a phantom to advise a wizard of your power,
Lord Varus?" the old woman said. He didn't think she
was being ironic. "You have the knowledge and the ability to remake the world as you choose it to be."

Varus shook his head in horror. "Lady, not I," he said.
But it seemed that there was no one else.

Nemastes continued to pipe. The statue of Jupiter had
withdrawn into earthen silence; it neither watched nor
commented on what was taking place in its temple.

He's afraid! Varus thought. For a moment he told
himself that he was indulging in wishful thinking, but
closer observation of the wizard's strained face con-
vinced him that he *was* afraid. Though his flute sang
with the force of a tornado, Nemastes was a charioteer
who had lost his reins but feared to leap from his ca-
reening vehicle.

Around him twelve nodes in the yellow-green haze
began to thicken. The Twelve had arrived, at least as
observers; with them were the demons from the rocks of
the Horn. They began to dance in slow, horrid majesty
as before, to the rhythm that had ruled Varus for what
had been in its way a lifetime.

This time Varus was outside it and thought he could
smile. When he curled his lip, however, the result had
nothing of humor in it.

"They are not here," said the old woman, glaring in disgust at the dancing Hyperboreans. "They are not of the waking world or of this world either; they created their own place by walling off the Horn from any existence beyond their own."

"They're watching, though," Varus said. "Why are they doing that?"

He was frightened, but that was in a calm fashion now. He expected to fail and expected to die, but he was going forward anyway. He wished he could ask Corylus if that was what soldiers did, but he didn't suppose he would ever see his friend again.

"They are gloating, Lord Varus," the woman said. "Nemastes and his siblings are not human, but they are enough like human beings to share that trait."

She looked at him sharply and said, "But you do not gloat, do you?"

About what? Varus thought. *About how great a poet I am?*

Aloud he said, "No, your ladyship. I think that's discourteous."

Varus saw the circling dancers from the peak where he stood with the old woman and simultaneously from where he lay on the temple floor. He considered them with a new feeling of contempt. That relaxed him almost as much as Sigyn's kiss had.

The Twelve were prancing bullies, no different from Piso and his cronies in class. Varus had seen Corylus handle the students. Gaius Varus could deal with Hyperborean wizards.

That's why I'm with the old woman, he realized. His lips pursed to ask his companion to help him. Before his lips formed the words, Nemastes' skirling flute moved into a quicker tempo. Beneath the temple, a pit was opening. It grew in a world parallel to that of Carce, but it moved toward the temple with the speed of racing horses. There was movement in the depths, the way the sand on the floor of an ant lion's lair stirs before the creature strikes.

"Nemastes is a greater fool than any but you could have fathomed, Lord Wizard," said the old woman. "He has freed Surtr, but he does not know how to direct the god against his siblings. They had hoped to send the fire demons out the easy passage through Vesuvius. By twisting the path which the flute tore, however, the Twelve are loosing Surtr's legions in the heart of Carce."

Varus stared transfixed. He knew that the dance was syncopating the raging music of the flute, but his understanding was at the visceral level on which the rhythm had toyed with him.

Nemastes continued to play desperately. He was like a swimmer who has the strength to get out beyond the breakers, but not enough more to fight his way back. Varus felt sorry for him—

And choked a laugh at his own expense. The old woman had been right that he wouldn't gloat over a fallen enemy, but this was carrying courtesy beyond a sane level. And of course Nemastes' death would be followed by the death of all life in Carce and the whole waking world.

"Sibyl," Varus said, giving his guide and mentor the title he had long known must be hers, "help me and help the world."

She smiled like the sun and her mouth opened. On the floor of the temple Gaius Varus cried, *"Where the twisting passage lies, the Wizard knows!"*

ALPHENA PRIDED HERSELF on her physical strength, though she didn't usually think about it in those terms. It was more a matter of sneering at other women—including her stepmother, sometimes aloud—for being soft and weak.

The present journey through a dreamworld had forced her to revise her estimate of Hedia's softness, and all illusions about her own strength vanished the instant Maron gripped her.

Alphena screamed and tried to pull herself free. The faun's muscles didn't budge, and his fingers were like steel clamps on her wrists. Her hands were going numb.

Alphena opened her mouth to cry "You're hurting me!" but she caught herself before more than a tongue-muffled moan had come out. She wouldn't lower herself by pleading!

Besides, she knew it wouldn't do any good.

Proud of her resource, Alphena clamped her legs together and locked her ankles. Maron slammed her heels to the ground and bent her torso over her legs. Her scream wasn't at all muffled this time: youth and exercise had kept Alphena flexible, but this brutal manipulation happened whether or not her muscles and sinews were ready to stretch that far, that fast.

Guessing what was to come, Alphena kicked her legs to the left. The faun threw her over on her left side, pinned her left ankle with his right hoof, and then jerked her left wrist down so that he could grasp that wrist and ankle in the same hand.

She hadn't believed anything could hurt as much as this did. For an instant she was aware of nothing but whiteness that buzzed like a hive of bees in her skull. When her vision cleared, Maron gripped her arms and legs as easily as he might hold two lengths of worn rope. He raised her high.

"Do you want to watch, Hedia dear?" the faun cried, his voice raw with lust. "Watch, then! I like it that way!"

Hedia got up from the ground: the faun must have knocked her down when she tried to interfere, though Alphena didn't remember that happening. She wondered if she'd blacked out while she was being manhandled.

Maron's face seethed with desire that had more of cruelty than love overlying it. The skirt of Alphena's short tunic flapped as she hung suspended in the air. *Perhaps it'll get in the way and—*

The faun's member stood like an ivory battering ram, fully extended from its sheath. If he—when he—pulled Alphena down on it, it might not rip the woolen fabric but it would certainly carry the skirt along into her. The pain would make her forget the strain on her joints.

"Mother, *help*!" she shrieked, but she knew there was nothing Hedia or anyone could do. Except, as Maron had said, to watch. Alphena hurt too much even to feel her normal disgust at the thought.

"*Now*, virgin!" the faun said. Hedia stepped behind him and seemed to pat his ribs.

Maron's mouth opened and his tongue protruded silently. He stumbled forward a step and then another. His hands spasmed, hurling Alphena free; she hit the ground near the base of one of the yuccas. When she tried to stand, her groin muscles protested. She fell back with a squeak of further pain.

The faun fell prone. His mouth opened and closed. Blood cascaded down his right buttock and leg, matting the fur; it pooled on the ground beneath him.

Maron's hooves hammered the dirt, as though he was trying to run while lying on his belly. His head and hooves arched; then his body went flaccid. Though his eyes remained open, they were beginning to glaze.

Hedia stepped to the corpse, holding in her bloody hand the knife that Alphena had thought was a toy. She wiped the blade on the fur of the faun's left thigh, then gathered a fistful of the loose soil and rubbed her hands with it. Last she finished cleaning the knife with a fibrous yucca leaf.

There was a six-inch cut in the faun's right side and back, just below the ribs. The blade of Hedia's knife was no longer than her little finger, but when thrust *there* and pulled, it must have sliced the right kidney in half.

"M-Mother?" Alphena said.

"Yes, dear," Hedia said. "Are you all right? Can you walk now?"

"I think so," the girl whispered. She tried to stand, gasped, and lurched to her feet. "I'm all right. I'll be all right."

"Good," Hedia said, tucking her dagger away again in its ivory sheath. "Because I think the sooner we get out of here"—she nodded to the path rising into the fuzzy infinite: it reminded Alphena of the milky stain across the night sky which myth said was the River Eridanus—"the better off we'll be. There's nothing about this place that makes me want to extend our stay."

"No," whispered Alphena. She forced herself to walk forward. After she started moving, further steps were an ache and memories, but no longer fresh stabbing pain. "I can leave now."

She lifted her sword slightly to be sure it was free, then let it fall back in the scabbard. She'd been so proud of the weapon, so sure of what she could accomplish with the gleaming blade.

She'd done *nothing* to save herself. The sword and all her training had been a waste of time!

"Hedia?" she said. "Mother."

She stopped and swallowed. The faun's corpse drew her eyes no matter where she tried to look.

"Yes, dear?" Hedia said patiently. *She* must *know what I want to say!*

"Mother," Alphena blurted. "I thought you, well, *liked* him. The way you kissed him and, and *everything*!"

"Yes, dear," Hedia said calmly. "I rather did. But in this world, a woman must often do things she would rather not. In the waking world, I mean, but in this world too."

She put her hand on Alphena's shoulder. "Ready to come now? Here, I'll start and you follow if the footing is firm."

"No, we'll go together," Alphena said primly, taking her stepmother's hand. "We *are* together, after all."

The path of bubbles felt like polished marble underfoot. They climbed deliberately, Hedia obviously measuring her gait by what Alphena could manage without pain.

After a time, the girl glanced over her shoulder. The path curled back without end. She didn't see the world they had just left, nor the faun's sprawled body.

"My sword wasn't any use," Alphena said. "I was so proud of what I'd be able to do with it."

"Well, dear," the older woman said. They were still hand in hand. "There are different kinds of training. Mine was more useful than yours for the situation in which we found ourselves."

Hedia cleared her throat. "Daughter?" she said. "It's often better not to bother men with things that they wouldn't understand. Do you know what I mean?"

Alphena looked at her. Hedia's profile was as sharp and clean as a cameo. She was beautiful, as coldly beautiful as this pathway of glitter and stars.

"Men?" Alphena repeated. "You mean my father, don't you?"

"I mean 'men,' Daughter," Hedia said with a wry smile. "But yes, your father is a man in his own fashion." She paused, then added, "A very dear man. I wouldn't want to hurt him in any way."

"I understand," Alphena said. She felt sad—not for Saxa, who would be safe and happy in his own world if they could only rid him of Nemastes.

Alphena felt sad for herself. She'd been such a *child*, but she was happier then than she would ever be again. She thought back to how the world had looked to her only days before, when she had pretended she was the equal of any man because she trained in the gymnasium.

"We won't hurt my father," she said. *But when next I see Nemastes*, she thought, *I'll see if this sword is good for something after all. For what he did to Saxa, and for what he did to my own innocence.*

"FROTHI!" CORYLUS SHOUTED. The chief and the rest of the tribe were two hundred feet away. "I have fulfilled the task you set for me. Now, give me the flute which Odd your brother made mine!"

Steam bright with sparks shot from the reborn volcano. Corylus poised on his toes. The earth shock came seconds before the sound. It knocked down several of the tribesmen, but Corylus, facing the blast, rode it easily.

"Give me the flute or even worse will happen, Frothi!" he said. That was a bluff. Oh, worse things were certainly going to happen, but that had nothing to do with whether Publius Corylus was holding the flute. Channeling ice water into the heart of a volcano was very like rolling a boulder off a cliff: what happened afterward was out of human control.

"No!" Frothi shouted, fitting the base of a javelin into his spear thrower. He straightened, stepped forward on his left foot as his arm drew back, and strode into his release of the missile.

The dart snapped toward Corylus in a flat arc. The chief probably hadn't been an active hunter for many years, but his aim was still deadly. Corylus raised the hornbeam staff and *tick*ed the javelin harmlessly to the side. There was no great trick to that, but it was a good test of dexterity and timing. Arrows were much harder to deflect, but even that was possible perhaps one time in three.

Corylus grinned as he continued to walk forward.

You practiced with blunted arrows, though, unless you were too drunk to have much chance of succeeding anyway.

"Give me the flute, Frothi!" he said.

Nemastes had been at the chief's side; the Stolo kept a pace back from its master. The wizard stopped and turned, gesturing his servant brusquely to the side so that he had an unimpeded view of the crater.

Orange fire and dense yellow smoke blasted upward. Nemastes dropped to his knees and placed the ivory talisman on the ground in front of him.

This time the blast knocked everyone in the tribe down. Even the Stolo dropped to all fours, but the wizard rode it as though he were kneeling on rock.

The tribesfolk turned to stare, even before they rose to their feet. Steam shrieked and with the crackling of rocks smothered the children's wails.

Frothi rolled to his feet. He shot another javelin at Corylus, who again batted it away with equal practiced skill.

People joined hands and began to wail "Surtr! Surtr!" in what Corylus decided must be a prayer. They knelt, bowing in supplication to the crater from which they had fled.

The pillar of sulfurous smoke spread into a flat top like an anvil two miles in the air. Though the sky was otherwise clear, lightning began to dance between the cloud and the ground in its shadow.

The air shuddered as though a thin silk curtain had been drawn across the line of Corylus's vision. In place of the rising smoke, he saw a god of yellow fire holding a sword. The god laughed, and the earth roared.

Demons in the fire god's image boiled out of the pit and began to advance. Grass, trees, and the rock itself swelled upward in curling flames.

"People of Thule!" Corylus cried. He didn't understand the situation, but he understood what the situation would mean for ordinary folk if they were trapped. "Run to the east! Run now! Don't be caught on this peninsula!"

Frothi shot his last javelin from fifty feet away; Corylus touched it almost absently, sending it like the others to quiver with half its length buried in the turf.

Had the chief heard him? He seemed lost in the terror of the moment. The wizard was about his own business, and Frothi's three henchmen knelt praying with the rest of the tribesfolk.

"Run!" Corylus repeated. He knew only one of the tribe well enough that she might listen to him. "Sith, lead your people east, get them *away* from here! Otherwise they'll be trapped by the, by the lava!"

He'd almost said "by the demons." There was little to choose between his vision and the reality for those caught in the path of blazing rock, however.

The volcano belched again. For an instant, Corylus saw sprays of red-orange lava burst skyward and fall back in sequence: to the left, to the right, and then mounting a full thousand feet in the center. When the curtain slid back, the fire god roared. He flexed muscles of flame and lifted his blazing sword overhead.

Demonic miniatures of the god climbed from the fiery cauldron and marched in all directions, devouring the landscape as they marched across it; moments before they had been sluggish billows of lava, rolling their black crusts under fresh orange fire as they lurched from the volcano's throat.

Corylus walked on at a deliberate pace, unaffected by anything the chieftain did. They were now within twenty feet of each other. Frothi was a powerful man. Though he'd spent his javelins, he had a long flint knife and a pick of sharpened reindeer antler which was weighted with stone.

Corylus was sure that with his hardwood staff, he could deal with the chief and two more like him. Even if he'd been unarmed, he would have gone on. He had turned the Ice River into the crater as the chief had demanded, and in doing so he had ripped the chief's world apart. Frothi *could* not stand against him in this moment.

Frothi screamed in rage like a big cat. Reaching under his tunic, he came out with the black bone flute. He flung it at Corylus's face.

Corylus caught it in his left hand. Frothi ran—not toward anything, simply away. His gait was shambling and graceless, like that of a wounded bear.

He must not be looking where he's going, Corylus thought. Then, *He must be* blind. *He's running straight toward the lava*.

But that didn't matter now, because Corylus had the flute which Odd had ordered him to get. Odd—Odd's Vengeance—hadn't said what to do with the instrument when he got it, but that question didn't require deep thought.

Regretfully, Corylus dropped the hornbeam staff. The flute was a section of thighbone, though he couldn't guess at the animal it came from. It had been cut to something less than its full length, but one knuckle—what had been the knee joint, not the hip—remained. It was drilled through to the core from which the marrow had been sucked.

Corylus found the length of hollow reed behind his left ear, where the nymph Canina had tucked a lock of her auburn hair. He fitted the reed into the hole drilled for it, then lifted the flute to his lips.

He'd never played a flute; it was an art favored by specialists who generally doubled as male prostitutes, *not* the sort of thing a good-looking youth in an army camp wanted to be found studying. He'd never even played a panpipe of reeds stopped with wax, a different and much simpler instrument. What was he supposed to do—

"Here, silly boy," said Canina, suddenly at his side. "Goodness, darling, you're handsome but you're *quite* helpless, aren't you?"

Despite the situation, Corylus felt a shock of outrage. His mouth opened to snap, "In my family, we *hired* flute girls!" The absurdity of his reaction struck him as so funny that he almost started to giggle, which would have been equally inappropriate.

And there was nothing to say anyway. The tawny-haired nymph seemed to reach not around but *into* him. With his fingers on three of the stops he put the reed to his mouth and blew.

Corylus didn't understand what his lips or his dancing fingers were doing, nor did he hear the music. He was watching himself and the whole scene from above as though he were an equal of the fire god who roared and blazed from the pit of the volcano.

The flute song rang across the landscape. The demons marched relentlessly, leaving bubbling rock behind them for their fellows clambering from the pit to follow. Their blight spread in all directions. A yellow brimstone haze hung over the devastation.

The cairn of black rocks on the bank of the Ice River ruptured. *More earth shocks,* Corylus thought, but the stones he had placed with such difficulty were bursting from inside. The corpse got up, smiled at the stranger who had buried him, and stepped from the scattered tomb.

"I was lucky in who found me," Odd's body said. He was beside Corylus, facing the lava. There had been no motion, just *there* and then *here*. "Or perhaps someone picked you to find me. I would thank that One, if I knew whom to name."

Corylus lowered the flute. "Vengeance?" he said.

"No, I'm Odd," the other said. "Back again."

He stood as Corylus had buried him: bootless, cap-less, and wearing a wry smile. Corylus liked him instinc-tively, but nobody who understood Odd's smile could doubt that he would be a bad enemy.

Frothi already knew that: he was stumbling to cer-tain death rather than face the man whom his brother's vengeance had sent to him. And as for the wizard Ne-mastes . . .

Nemastes knelt, chanting over the ivory head. He held his arms before him with the palms outward in bar. Lava hissed and spat as it rolled north, closer each mo-ment to the wizard and the tribe praying behind him.

Nemastes shouted a word that glanced off Corylus's consciousness; his mind could not grasp the shape of its syllables.

The ancient shaman stepped out of the talisman. When Botrug appeared, the silk curtain fell again. Cory-lus saw the lava as squat sizzling demons whom Botrug threw back with a word and a gesture.

The shaman gave a gurgling laugh. The demons rose to their feet and started forward again.

Spots of blue as hard as congealed starlight formed in the air behind Nemastes, arrayed in a semicircle. In a further moment they swelled to become the Twelve, Ne-mastes' siblings. They looked at him with the murder-ous greed of cats eyeing a caged lark.

Nemastes glanced over his shoulder, then faced the fire god and his minions again as though the Twelve were of no concern to him. Their faces were death's heads, and they began to dance.

"I'll take the flute," Odd said, giving Corylus a hard grin. He held out his hand. "Not that you haven't done a good job, my friend."

"Right," said Corylus, glad to get rid of it. He didn't

like the feel of the instrument. Just as he understood things when handling objects made of wood, he got blurred impressions from this length of thighbone. He wasn't sure he'd have been willing to blow it had it not been for the reed mouthpiece.

He picked up the staff and immediately felt better. The nymph of the hornbeam watched him with gray eyes, stern but comforting.

"Here," said Odd, offering the reed to Corylus. He'd replaced it with one of his own. "You may need this later. You never can tell."

His grin could have been etched on a diamond. "Now, friend, get my people out of the way as you started to. There isn't a lot of time, even now that I've returned."

Odd put his lips to the mouthpiece and began to play, his fingers lifting and lowering on the stops. They moved like the legs of dancing men; they moved like the Twelve, dancing to exert their power over the renegade sibling who had robbed and betrayed them.

Willows still lined the channel which they had cracked in the rock; they quivered. As one they lifted their roots from the turf. In graceful undulations they began marching eastward. They moved no faster than sheep, but they were sheep headed for the byre in the evening with udders aching to be milked. Slender trees waved branches in farewell toward Corylus.

Frothi had finally seen where he was running. Fire demons were closing in on three sides of him.

He drew his pick and chopped at one, apparently trying to cut his way through. The deer antler flared white at the demon's touch.

Several demons—or billows of molten rock? It didn't matter—converged on Frothi. Though neither the flames nor the brief scream surprised Corylus, the gush of steam made him queasy.

But he had a task now. He strode forward, grasping

Gram and Todinn by the collars and lifting their heads to gape at him.

"Run, you fools!" Corylus shouted. "Get your families, get everybody to the east before the lava arrives! Odd is holding it back!"

He looked for Sith. She was already chivying women and children toward safety. Her glance met that of Corylus, but it was just that: a glance and a nod. They both had their duties.

And Odd had his. The fire god's horde met the icy tones of his flute and rebounded like storm-tossed waves from a breakwater. Demons snarled and wailed, striving to smash their way through to devour the striding trees and terror-numbed folk of the tribe.

"Go on, get moving!" Corylus said. "No, Bearn, take that little girl! Carry her! Or by Hercules, I'll break both your knees—"

He swished his staff through the air. The men of the tribe generally still carried their spears and daggers, but they were no more willing to fight Corylus than they would stand against the divine horror driving his legions from the reborn volcano.

"—and I'll carry her myself. Come on! Odd thinks you're worth saving, so you *will* be saved!"

The lowering shadow of Botrug kept the demons back in a semi-circle before Nemastes, but the lava was beginning to lap around to either side. Nemastes continued to chant where he crouched, but his eyes darted to left and right. He was looking for a place of safety, which the talisman could not provide for much longer.

The tribe had begun moving quickly. The folk were staying together, the strong helping the weak. They were barbarians, but they were nonetheless human beings— at least after Corylus had reminded a few of them.

It might have been better if the tribe had started running at once instead of falling in prayer, but that was a human choice also. For that matter, if Odd hadn't appeared to play the flute, running would have been no more useful than prayer. Lava would have cut the escape route before any but the strongest males reached it.

Corylus quirked a smile. Prayer hadn't brought Odd back—Publius Corylus, with help from a relation on his mother's side, had done that. But who was to say that prayer hadn't brought Corylus to this place? He didn't have a better explanation himself.

And it very much seemed that he would live his remaining however many years here, in Thule. Perhaps he would found a line and grow famous as the man who told fantastic stories about a dreamworld he called Carce.

He wouldn't be fathering children by Sith, though. While Odd played, the young woman was fitting a boot to his lifted right foot; its mate was already on his left. She must have brought the boots with her, along with a cap of reindeer hide neatly decorated with dyed bone splinters.

Trees from farther west marched past with swaying grace. Corylus saw birches, willows, alders, and a few splendid spruce trees which must have come from the headland whose fogs implied a warm ocean current.

He supposed he'd best be getting along himself. The lava or fire demons would devour him as surely as they had Frothi—or would a hazel sapling which didn't heed the flute's call to flee.

Corylus looked toward the tribe, disappearing over the highest swell of ground to the east. His eyes flicked toward Sith and Odd—and were held by Odd's penetrating glance.

The burly wizard continued to play. His flute had thrown up a wall before the fire demons. They climbed atop one another in their thunderous desire to reach the trees and men they watched escaping. If Odd stopped, the rush would sweep all before it for a mile or more, up to the bank of the Ice River.

But Odd nodded meaningfully, and the note of the flute changed. The air beside Corylus began to rotate like that of a basin emptying through a pipe. Everything beyond it in the present blurred, but at the heart of the vortex he could see the roofs and temples of Carce as they appeared from the top of the Capitoline Hill.

A fair exchange: Corylus had returned Odd to his world, and Odd was returning his savior to Carce. Smiling with not only triumph but joy—which Corylus hadn't felt in some while—he waited for the opening between worlds to spin wide enough to pass a human being.

The Twelve wheeled like skeletal vultures, waiting in certain knowledge that their prey would soon fall. Greed and excitement shone in their evil faces.

Nemastes shouted urgently, his tone very different from his singsong above the talisman. The demons bulged toward him, but he resumed his chant in time. Botrug drove them back again, though it would not be long before the ends of the encircling lava closed behind the wizard.

The Stolo obediently turned and shambled toward Odd. The creature hunched forward and spread its arms wide as it advanced. With its bared fangs, it looked like a huge spider advancing on its victim.

Odd had already begun to sidle eastward. He moved as quickly as he could, but he couldn't both run and play. Sith shouted and put herself between her lover and the monster.

The window to Carce was wide enough for Corylus to jump through it. Odd was repaying him: they were quits now.

Except that friendship didn't work that way. Corylus, the soon-to-be storyteller of Thule, shoved Sith out of the way.

"Go on!" he said, poising his staff. "Make sure Odd doesn't stumble. I'll take care of this one."

"Publius Corylus," Sith called urgently. "Shall I bring you spears?"

"Hell take you, woman!" he said. "I'm busy! Take care of your man!"

Corylus spread his legs slightly, working the balls of his feet into the turf. He wished he were wearing cleated boots, both for their grip on the soil and the very useful punch of their iron-shod soles. He held the hornbeam staff by the end in both hands, the right leading. This would do.

Nemastes rose like a stork lifting from its nest, abandoning the ivory head on the ground behind him. Elbows flailing, feet splaying to the side, the hairless wizard galloped toward the gate to the world Corylus had come from. He was uncoordinated and looked ridiculous when he flung himself toward the vortex, but he vanished into its haze. As he did so, the gate collapsed on itself like a sand sculpture.

When Nemastes stopped chanting, Botrug's shadow vanished like raindrops on the sea. With the shaman gone, the demons burst into the salient, but the Twelve swooped even more swiftly onto the talisman. For a moment the cabal of wizards was a sapphire bubble surrounded by red bubbling lava; then the Twelve were gone. In the instant before fire engulfed the place where they had been, the turf was empty. The ivory miniature of Botrug had disappeared with the wizards.

The Stolo didn't seem to notice that Nemastes had abandoned it, but it slowed its pace when Corylus stepped into its way. Its shoulders dipped and it began to sidle to the left, though it still advanced.

It isn't contemptuous of me, Corylus thought. That was a pity.

He stepped toward the Stolo, lifting his thumb-thick

wand slightly. He could wish for a heavier staff, but the gray nymph watching him from a distance through time was a comforting presence. She understood, and she would not fail him.

The Stolo snatched at the end of the wand. Corylus slashed down, smacking the side of the creature's left knee. A human's joint would have broken, but the Stolo snarled like a rock slide and rushed forward. Instead of dodging, Corylus brought the wand backhand across the creature's face, turning it away from him. Its flailing right arm missed his head by the width of a hand. The fingernails were black and as powerful as a bear's claws.

The Stolo whirled. Corylus was planted. He brought the tip of his wand down on the creature's right thigh with the strength of both his arms behind the strike. The Stolo took a step toward him and blatted in surprise: the blow had pinched the muscles across the top of the thigh against the massive bone and numbed them. The creature's leg collapsed; it sprawled on the turf.

Corylus lifted his wand, then slammed it against the back of the Stolo's neck. The *cr-crack!* was doubled: the sound of hardwood against bone mixed with the *pop* of vertebrae crushing under the blow.

The Stolo's limbs went as flaccid as raw tripes. Its mouth opened and closed. Corylus fell to one knee, gasping. He planted the wand vertically on the ground and clung to it for support.

"Come along, darling," said a cheery female voice. "You don't want to stay here when Surtr's on the march. Take my hand."

He looked up. A young woman, slender and pretty with a roguish tilt to her eyes, held out her hand. When he blinked, he saw the branch of a silver birch which seemed to have drifted from the grove striding along at the end of the great exodus of trees.

"Come!" she repeated, squeezing his hand. Corylus

lurched to his feet, guided by the nymph's touch rather than compelled. Yes, he did have to get going, though the future for a youth raised to civilization was bleak, even if he survived. Better than being cooked alive by lava, he supposed, though the choice in his mind wasn't entirely one-sided.

"Thank you, mistress," he said, but the nymph was handing him on to a sister—a cousin, better; an alder nymph—well ahead. Corylus felt motion, but his feet weren't touching the ground. The landscape rolled beneath him.

Surtr thundered, waving his fiery sword, but Corylus had nothing to fear from the fire god and his legions now. A cancer was burning into the landscape; it already covered a third of the peninsula below the Ice River. In a few places lava had reached the sea, throwing up curtains of steam to roil and dilute the sulfur haze.

Odd's music had drawn a line as straight as a plumb bob's in the path of the oncoming demons; but as the wizard marched at the back of the tribe, the western end of his barrier was giving way. Smoke and fumes marked the passage of lava over prairie from which the trees had fled.

Far away, separated from Corylus by more than distance, Sith lifted her arm in farewell. He would have waved back but the nymphs had his hands and he was moving with breathtaking speed.

"*My,* you're a pretty little fellow," said a thick-bodied ash nymph, taking him in turn. "Oh, if Fraxina were just the *least* younger, she would *dally* with you, boy!"

She bussed him on the cheek and sent him on to the smiling beech waiting to receive him. The beech handed Corylus to an oak, a huge matriarch who spread across ground that a forester would have given instead to a grove of a dozen trees more useful for timber.

There were no oaks in Thule—it was too far north.

The forest had made Corylus its own, and he was experiencing time and space as it did.

He lost track of the nymphs who patted, hugged, or kissed him as they passed him on to the next smiling kinswoman. A slim, straight girl with green eyes grinned at him from a hazel coppice and said, "Well met, Brother. Mother would be proud of you." Then she too was behind him.

Corylus didn't have the breath to speak, nor did he stay at any point of his passage long enough to exchange a real question and answer. *Where am I going? When will it be when I get there?*

"Now be well, darling," said a nymph with a smile and shaggy locks. "Don't forget my sisters and me, will you?"

"I won't—," Corylus started to say. He stood on firm soil beneath a grove of cypresses. The moon, just past full, was at midsky. Lights within the temple to his left gleamed through clerestory windows and the open double doors in the front.

Corylus was on the Capitoline Hill, beside the Temple of Jupiter Best and Greatest. He heard shouts and the sound of fighting. Empty-handed—he must have left the hornbeam staff behind in its own time—he ran toward the steps into the temple.

That was what his father and mother would have expected.

CHAPTER XVIII

Alphena was holding her stepmother's hand as they stepped together from the ramp of stars. They were back in the waking world. The noise, the foul yellow light, and the smell of brimstone made her clutch the hilt of her sword.

They'd come out between two pillars on the right side of a large hall. Alphena had never been here before, but she recognized the seated statue of Jupiter from his beard and the brass thunderbolts in his right hand. The size made this the temple of Jupiter on the Capitoline, where her brother had prophesied to Corylus and their teacher, Pandareus.

Varus lay trussed in glowing cords toward the back of the room, where the great statue sat. On the mosaic pavement near him was Pandareus, rising stiffly into a sitting posture. *Where's Corylus? The others are here.*

Nemastes stood at the foot of the enthroned statue, wearing a desperate expression as he played a black bone flute. Twelve demonic simulacra of the Hyperborean wizard rotated slowly in the air about him, staring avidly down.

Alphena saw the Twelve clearly, but they weren't in the same world as she and her brother were. A pit of sickly light filled most of the center of the hall; it seemed to slant down to the center of the earth. Up that slope crawled figures which might almost have been men. They were squat and terrible, and their bodies were formed by licking flames.

"*Where the twisted horn is hid, the Wizard knows,*" Varus shouted. The cord tying him shifted from green to the colors of a rainbow. It moved and changed hue when Alphena tried to focus on it. "*Under the heaventouching tree that is the world, the tears from Othinn's eye fall on it!*"

A demon crawled from the pit. It was no taller than Alphena herself, though its torso rose in almost straight lines from its hips to shoulders as wide as those of Saxa's new German doorman. Its face was brutishly human until it smiled, displaying not teeth but interlocking fangs.

The creature seemed to shimmer. As it moved, Alphena saw what she had thought to be skin was a transparent membrane which enclosed licking flames. Spreading its abnormally long arms, it stepped toward Varus.

A metal lantern lay on the floor beside Pandareus. He flung it, striking the demon in the chest. Instead of bouncing off, the bronze sheeting burst like a thunderbolt. The grinning demon continued forward.

"Get my brother free!" Alphena cried, drawing her sword and placing herself in the demon's way. She didn't expect to do any good, but if an old Greek scholar could try to save Varus, then a healthy young woman with a sword had to do *something*.

The demon's chest quivered as though it were laughing, but Alphena couldn't hear sounds well over the roaring chaos from the pit. The only thing she *could* hear clearly was the phrase Varus was chanting; that must have been more than sound. Had her brother become a magician?

Behind her, Hedia bent over Varus; either she'd heard Alphena's demand over the cacophony or she'd come to the same conclusion on her own. Hedia wasn't somebody who needed to be told the obvious.

Alphena shuffled forward, though the demon also continued to advance. She wished she had a shield, but the way the lantern had burned suggested that the creature's gripping hand would turn laminated wood into an inferno. She didn't know why she hoped for better from the blade of her sword; perhaps because there was nothing else to hope for. That was a good enough reason.

The demon made a quick snatch for Alphena's face with its left arm. She responded the way Lenatus had trained her to do if an opponent attacked with his spear high: she swiped her sword sideways, chopping the demon's hand off. The blade went through the creature's arm as easily as it would have through water.

Fire gushed from both edges of the wound. The hand flexed, then in an eyeblink drained to a glistening patch on the stone floor. The demon's body flailed, spewing flames like the flue of an overstoked oven. It lost shape and shrank in on itself as it tumbled, still blazing, into the pit from which it had climbed.

Two more demons appeared over the rim. Alphena thrust one through the face. It curved back into the depths, its head a roaring torch, but its right hand had swept close enough to singe the hairs on her lower leg. She'd forgotten how long the creatures' arms were, so her instinctive response had almost been fatal.

Her sword gleamed like sunlight. The other demon hunched onto the temple floor. Alphena slashed at the creature's elbow. It twisted quickly to snatch the blade from her, so her edge sheared its hand and forearm, opening them wide. A flaring bloom sucked out the demon's life, leaving only a slick gleam on the stone.

Demon flesh made no more resistance to this blade than fog would. Alphena panted, dizzy from exertion and the reek of sulfur that the demons brought with them. *I can do this! I am good for something!*

Alphena looked into the pit. A demon near the rim

reached for her ankle. She took its hand off at the wrist but jumped back instead of watching the creature bounce down the slope as a fiery pinwheel: two more demons were so close that they would have had her if she'd hesitated.

Beyond those two, stretching down into the hazy depths, were thousands more. Thousands of demons, and likely thousands of thousands besides crawling up from deeper yet.

Alphena took a quick glance behind her. Hedia was fussing over Varus, but the fetters of light still bound him. Alphena started to snarl a curse, but she bit the words off. She'd seen her mother respond to a crisis. If Hedia was having trouble cutting Varus loose, then very likely anyone would have had trouble.

And besides, Alphena didn't have time to worry about what other people did.

She'd given back a step when she saw how close the pair of demons were. A hand reached over the rim of the pit, its claws shrieking against the stone.

Alphena thrust, taking off a finger and sparking a divot from the floor. Her blade sang, but its edge remained sharp as sunlight. She backhanded the blade through the face of the other demon.

That one simply dropped toward its oncoming fellows, but the first tried to continue climbing. It stumbled and fell when the scintillant roar from its missing finger devoured its hand. Destruction was working up its arm before the last of the fire drained out. Its casing gleamed on the stone like a slug's trail.

More demons were coming. Infinitely more.

Alphena poised, her left arm advanced slightly to balance the weight of her sword. Her brother couldn't move, so she was going to stand here until he was freed or she was killed.

Or perhaps she would kill all the demons, too many

for her even to count. That didn't seem likely, but right now it didn't seem likely that Varus could be freed either.

Three demons came at her together. Alphena had her rhythm now; she would nick each one and it would bleed into a fiery spectacle. *These* wouldn't get past her.

Eventually a creature from the hordes climbing upward would turn Alphena, daughter of Gaius Saxa, into a stench and a few scraps of charred bone; but not yet. She thrust, and slashed, and thrust again; and more demons shoved their way past the blazing torches of their fellows.

UNDER OTHER CIRCUMSTANCES Hedia would have reacted vividly at being ordered around by a chit of a girl, but this wasn't the time for it. Besides, Alphena had jumped into the path of a fire demon without being told. Hedia wasn't sure she'd have been willing to do that even if there was no one else available. The girl could be forgiven for blurting something silly in the heat of the moment.

Hedia knelt at the side of her son. Whatever Varus had been doing, he seemed healthy enough now. He'd lost his toga during the ceremony before all this started to happen, but his tunic wasn't torn or bloody.

Hedia knew she herself must look a fright. The first thing she'd do when it was over would be to take a bath. And she'd have these clothes burned, including the slippers that she'd worn through! Why, she didn't know when her feet could be pampered back to normal.

Part of her mind laughed at herself—her worst enemies wouldn't claim that she was either stupid or lacking in self-awareness. Another part really was worried about her appearance, however. It wasn't the part that was in control, though; not now or ever.

The ligature holding Varus wasn't a shimmering rope, and it didn't have a knot. Colors rippled along it in a fashion that subtly reminded Hedia of the way a snake slithered—but this snake had its tail in its mouth. She tried to grip it, then jerked her hand away with a shout. *It bit me!*

But it hadn't, or anyway no more than the prickle that she sometimes got from touching an amber bead. It was not knowing what was happening that had made her react as though a viper had struck out of the dark.

Hedia closed her hand on the binding again, feeling only a slick coldness this time. She gripped as firmly as she could, but the colors raced along the shape undeterred. She tried to lift it away from Varus so that she wouldn't nick him with her blade; it didn't budge.

Shapes like reflections of Nemastes quivered in the air. She couldn't see them clearly, though she was sure they were there. They reminded her of when she'd walked into the garden and seen Alphena disappearing. These bald, lowering figures had the same almost-presence to her eyes as Persica had had at that moment.

Grimacing, Hedia jabbed her dagger's needle point at the fetter, planning to lift the blade and saw through the upper half while she tried to figure out what to do with the rest. Keen as the dagger was, it glanced off as though from polished granite.

The boy seemed remarkably calm for someone who was bound in the path of monsters which would destroy him as soon as they'd disposed of his sister. Brave as Alphena was—and skilled, judging by Hedia's glance as the sword the girl had insisted on digging up sliced through a pair of demons—it could be only a matter of time before they bore her down.

Varus's left hand clutched the ivory head he'd been wearing since his poetry reading. He paid no attention to Hedia, though a flick of his eyes as she bent over him showed that he wasn't in a trance. He was chanting the same stanza over and over: *"Where the twisted horn is hid, the Wizard knows!"*

Was Varus the wizard? If so, Hedia certainly wished he'd do something to end this, *this*!

If she couldn't cut the shimmering bonds, perhaps she could pull Varus out of the way. Suiting her action to the thought, she grabbed him by the feet and tried to drag him toward the nearer side aisle. He slid easily on the polished mosaic floor, but her slippers didn't grip well either. In struggling at the unfamiliar task—this was the sort of thing that *servants* did for her, by Hecate!—she almost stabbed her son through the ankle. *This is no good!*

Hedia dropped the boy's legs in a flash of insight. She'd been so focused on freeing Varus that she hadn't been thinking about the *real* problem: the demons. *Nemastes is calling them with that hellish flute music!*

Hedia turned abruptly and paused, swaying. She supposed she'd moved too quickly after her long climb up the ramp; that, and maybe the brimstone stink of the air here in the hall, were making her dizzy.

Collecting herself, Hedia strode toward Nemastes with crisp, steady steps instead of risking a fall by trying to run. The wizard continued to play, watching her. He backed up a step, pressing against the shoulder-high plinth that supported the god's throne. His expression was anguished.

"Give me that!" Hedia said. She grabbed the flute with her left hand. She'd thought it was made of black wood, but the feel showed her it was bone.

Nemastes held on to the instrument, but she'd pulled it away from his mouth. "You mustn't!" he said. "I can turn back Surtr if I can only find the tune! Surtr will destroy your whole world unless you let me play!"

"Give me the flute!" Hedia repeated, trying to jerk it away from him. "You're raising these demons, you barbarian!"

He tried to push her away. Hedia stabbed him in the left armpit; she'd almost forgotten that she still held the little knife. Nemastes bawled and tried to grab her arm. She jabbed him in the face. Her point skidded upward from his molars; a severed flap of his cheek sagged away.

He let go of the flute and put his hands in front of his face for defense. Hedia pressed close and stabbed him repeatedly in the chest. She lost track of how many times the blade punched in; she even forgot what she was doing.

There was no science to this, none of the calculation with which she had killed the faun. Hedia was white with fear and anger, striking blindly at the thing that she was afraid of. She gripped the flute in her left hand, but she'd forgotten about it.

"Surtr . . . ," Nemastes whispered. He coughed a bubble; it burst, smearing his face with blood. Foam oozing from his punctured lungs covered his torso. He slipped into a sitting position, his back against the plinth, then toppled onto his side. In death, the wizard looked even more like a stick figure than he had when he was alive.

A hand touched Hedia's left shoulder from behind. She whirled, her bloody dagger poised to strike.

CORYLUS HAD TRADED his sandals for the boots he'd taken from Odd's body. They were gone now, along with Odd's bandolier of equipment. He ran toward the Temple of Jupiter Best and Greatest, feeling the stone flags of the building's plaza cool on his bare feet. From inside came roaring and the shrieks of the damned.

The double doors at the top of the staircase were ajar. As Corylus slipped between the valves, he heard the cypress nymph call, "Good luck, Cousin. And be careful!"

Corylus stepped into an angle where worlds met. The hall of the temple was a faint outline overlying a vast pit of sour yellow-green light. Demons—the same squat fire demons he had seen marching across Thule—were climbing out of the abyss, by handfuls at present but with unnumbered legions following.

Above circled the Twelve like vultures, watching and waiting above their sibling Nemastes as they had done in Thule. That time they took the head of Botrug. Now—who knew? Perhaps they wanted the talisman back from Varus's clutch.

The pit was the present reality, but the Temple of Jupiter still existed as a sort of crystal scaffolding over it. At the edge of the chasm, Alphena faced fire demons with a sword which, to Corylus's amazement, cut them apart. The weapons he'd seen in Thule had ignited like chaff, even the stone dagger Frothi had used in his last moments of life.

Behind Alphena sprawled Varus, tied with rainbow loops. Pandareus, faceup with a bloody welt on the forehead, lay nearby; at the base of the seated statue of Jupiter, Hedia in a torn tunic struggled with the wizard Nemastes.

Skirting the pit—and, in the waking world, keeping to the edge of the hall, just inside the pillars separating the side aisle—Corylus ran to Hedia's aid. When he found a weapon, he'd try to help Alphena or perhaps cut Varus loose, but for now his task was clear.

As Corylus reached the struggling couple, Hedia stepped back. The wizard fell against the dais, then slumped to the floor. His chest was a mass of blood, and his face had been brutally sliced.

Corylus touched Hedia's shoulder and said, "Your ladyship?" She whirled, cocking back the little dagger in her hand. All he could see of the weapon was its point, glinting like a serpent's fang through the gore.

"Hedia!" he said. She was all blood too. Her face and hair were spattered, her silk tunic was stiff with it, and her right arm to the elbow dripped red . . . but it wasn't her blood. Hedia was all right; physically, at least.

Corylus thought he'd seen hell when he looked down into the pit, but the look in the eyes of this cultured, attractive woman froze him. He'd been reaching for her right wrist, just in case, but his hand stopped.

Hedia's expression became human again, changing as completely as water differs from ice. She held out the flute—Odd's flute!—in her left hand and said, "Here. Do you know how to play this? I don't think anything else can help this"—she gestured generally with her right arm; some of the blood was still wet enough to fly off in droplets—"*affair*."

"I might," said Corylus. They were shouting to be heard over the roar from the pit; it sounded like the shore of the German Ocean during a winter storm, but there were keener, crueler noises within the brutal thunder.

He examined the flute, ignoring all else that was going on around him. It looked exactly the same as it had when he'd played it in Thule; though of course *he* hadn't played it, not really.

Smiling, Corylus plucked out the reed that Nemastes had fitted to the knuckle end and replaced it with the one he'd stuck behind his ear when Odd returned it. He lifted it toward his lips, whispering, "Canina, are you still—"

"And why wouldn't I be, Cousin?" the tawny nymph said. She ruffled his hair with one hand. "The sun still rises and the rain falls, don't they? Here, let's see what we can do."

Canina reached *into* him as before. He felt his fingers shifting on the flute, touching the stops. His head bent slightly, and his lips began to play.

Corylus couldn't hear the music, but he heard the nymph in his heart laughing. Light flooded the hall, as clear as the sun glinting from ice. In it, risen from the pit and brandishing his flaming sword, stood Surtr just as Corylus had seen him dominating the landscape of Thule. The fire god roared, but now his raging cruelty held an undertone of fear: though Surtr was a deity, the cool light of the flute cut him.

Cut him, and bound him. The pit and the creatures crawling up its slope froze into crystal while Canina played through Corylus's lips. His fingers moved with elegance on the stops, movements that mimicked the high steps of the Twelve as they danced. But the Twelve—

Corylus lifted his eyes to where Nemastes' siblings were circling. He half expected them to descend the way they had in Thule when Nemastes abandoned the ivory head.

The Twelve still hung in the air, but their pattern had shaken into wild chaos like the play of raindrops on a pond. There was power in their movements, but they no longer directed that power.

Corylus's lips played and his fingers danced. Alphena dropped to her left knee. She gasped through her mouth, expelling her breath in racking sobs. Her right arm lay on her thigh; her hand kept the sword forward, waiting for demons to burst through the barrier enclosing them. Until then, she would rest.

The ropes of shifting light had dropped away from Varus. He sat cross-legged, still holding the ivory head in his left hand as he recited. It didn't seem to have occurred to him to run away now that he could.

In a way Corylus supposed that it didn't matter—from what he'd seen in Thule, there was no real escape unless Surtr was stopped. Still, he didn't want to watch his friend incinerated if the flute player ran out of breath and strength. Most likely Corylus wouldn't have long for regrets in that case, however.

Corylus couldn't grin while his lips were pursed on the reed, but he smiled in his heart. Canina was a good companion for however long he could hold out, cheerful and unflagging. His fingers or lips might cramp, or he might simply fall asleep and not even feel the demons whose release doomed him and the world, but the nymph would remain faithful for—how had she put it? For as long as the sun shone and the rain fell.

Surtr bellowed in balked fury from the high clouds. Soon enough the god would be loose, but for now the icy trills of the flute bound him. Corylus played, and he smiled.

WHEN NEMASTES' SPELL bound Varus, he fell with his face toward the statue of Jupiter. There the wizard fitted a reed to the flute and began to play. Ice shivered through Varus's mind when he understood what Nemastes was doing.

He realized that the wizard didn't understand it himself, because he couldn't possibly have wanted this result. The notes of the black bone flute gouged deep into the cosmos, opening layer after layer until they finally cut down to where Surtr crouched in white-hot splendor. That wasn't Nemastes' intention, but the Twelve were twisting the music to their ends rather than his.

Surtr didn't so much swell as come into focus. His figure rose, piercing the crust of the world and the very clouds in his blazing magnificence. The fabric of the cosmos eroded, spilling down into the pit which spread at the god's feet. His fiery minions began to climb toward the waking world, mindless and inexorable agents of destruction.

"Sibyl?" Varus said as his body chanted. "What do I do?"

"You have opened the way, Lord Varus," the old woman said. "Follow it, and when you reach your goal, act as you will know to do."

That's not very helpful, he thought; which was silly,

when he really thought instead of reacting in his mind. Varus continued to see through the eyes of his body lying on the floor of the temple, but there was now a path leading down from the cloud-wrapped hilltop on which his soul spoke with the Sibyl. Varus followed it.

He remembered Sigyn guiding him on a route much like this one; now he was alone. His lips drew tight as he thought about Sigyn. He wasn't responsible for her state, but he wished he'd been able to do more for her. And there were the others he'd touched and who had touched him, and whom he couldn't help either.

That wouldn't have bothered him in the past—he wouldn't have thought about it in the past. Gaius Alphenus Varus hadn't been cruel or even callous, but he'd been almost completely detached.

Varus stepped into the cloud; his skin felt damp, but this time the fog was warm, almost hot. He walked on with long, firm strides, even though he couldn't see where his feet would come down.

The Sibyl had told him that he'd opened this path. If it was open, then he was fine; if it wasn't—if it ended in a chasm and he fell to his doom—then he had done a bad job and deserved to die.

Perhaps the waking world deserved to die also, for having picked an inadequate representative. Would a cause of action before the praetor—presumably the praetor for foreign cases—lie against the agent, Gaius Varus, who had failed in his fiduciary duty?

Varus smiled faintly. It helped to imagine Sigyn at his side. His fancies had amused her.

Varus could hear himself chanting the stanza from where his body lay on the temple floor: *Where the twisted horn is hid, the Wizard knows! Under the heaven-touching tree that is the world, the tears from Othinn's eye fall on it.*

Were the verses from the *Sibylline Books?* Their rhythms

were wrong and he didn't think the words were even Greek, though they were easy enough for his tongue to form and perfectly clear to his ears.

The fog that surrounded his spirit suddenly cleared. To his surprise, he was walking through a forest glade instead of down a barren rocky slope. The buttress roots of the largest trees looked like high, slanted walls. Vines clung to their trunks and dangled from branches hidden in the foliage.

Concealed among the vines were cords of silk as thick as Varus's little fingers. He forced himself to continue walking while his eyes traced the strands up to the webs—he'd thought *web* but there were at least three— they supported.

Hanging from branches, each front pair of legs on the frame of its web to feel any tremor in the silk, were the spiders. Their bodies were striped green on brown, and each was the size of a calf. They could drain a man— certainly they could drain a very young man, soft and bookish—and leave him as dry as a ruptured wineskin.

Huge as these trees were, they were not the World Tree of the verse. Varus had farther to go unless the spiders were to be his end and the end of his world. The path led between two of the impossibly thick strands of silk. He walked on, his steps measured and his eyes almost blind with his fear.

I am a citizen of Carce; I will be steadfast in the face of my enemies. I am a citizen of Carce.

Varus passed under the web and the monster which had woven it. He was into the forest again, continuing to descend.

The path became mud which the feet of those who had walked it before him had cut deeper and deeper. Before long he was following a slick-walled clay track no wider than his elbows. The trench was already twice his own height, and he was still going down.

In the temple, the wizard Nemastes coughed his life out. His eyes glazed, and the spell which had wrapped the youth Gaius Varus drained away as Nemastes' blood did. It didn't matter to Varus now, but his body twisted upright with the help of its right hand. The left hand held what had been the talisman of Botrug until the Sibyl's greater power had displaced the ancient shaman. He continued to chant.

Something cried out ahead in a series of rising, rasping shrieks: one, and the *next*, and the *NEXT*. Varus's right foot kicked the heel of his left, an excuse for the stumble which he might have made anyhow.

I can't get away! The walls are too high and too greasy!

But Varus didn't intend to go anywhere except straight ahead, so it didn't matter. If there was a leopard waiting in the pathway, he would go through the cat or the cat would kill him; it was that simple. *I am a citizen of Carce; I will be steadfast.*

Varus grinned. It was easier to be brave while walking toward a leopard which might not exist than toward a giant spider which had been undeniably real. As real as anything in this world was, at any rate.

There was no cat in the trail, and the shadows on the gully's high rim could have been thrown by clouds. The sky was a narrow ribbon of brightness. *How long have I been walking this path?*

The trail entered a tunnel marked by two great pilasters carved from living rock. They slanted slightly inward, turning the entrance into a narrow trapezoid instead of a rectangle. Something was carved on the high transom, but the angle and orange splotches of lichen prevented Varus from reading it.

He grinned wryly. He very much doubted that the words would have made him feel better.

Varus was still going down. The only light came from the entrance, and he lost that very quickly. Sometimes he thought he saw purple-outlined groins which arched across the tunnel's high ceiling, but they were probably just a trick of his eyes.

After a time—he'd lost track of duration—Varus heard water trickling. He couldn't judge distance or even direction, but it pleased him to hear a sound that wasn't of his own direct making. His sandals scuffed the stone path, but they raised no echoes.

He wondered where the water came from and where it drained. Perhaps he was going to an underground—Underworld—lake, there to . . . what?

Where the twisted horn is hidden, the Wizard knows.

This wizard knew nothing but to keep going on, going down. Varus walked briskly as if he weren't afraid of what waited in the darkness. He was as frightened as he would have been if he'd been flung from a high place onto the rocks below. Fear wouldn't have helped him to fly to safety then, however; and he wouldn't allow it to turn him from his course now.

Varus had reached a different level of the Underworld. The darkness was still complete, but he felt it breathing; the air was hot, and sulfur bit at the back of his throat. He thought of Surtr looming above Carce as his demon legions marched upward.

The body of Gaius Varus was in the Temple of Jupiter while his soul walked here in darkness. This was the place where the fire god waited. This was the place where Surtr *existed*, though Nemastes the Hyperborean had summoned his semblance to scour the waking world with lava and clouds of sulfurous poison.

Was this what Varus's knowledge had brought him? A path to the flaming death that would shortly visit all the world—but for the Wizard, a quicker route so that he didn't have to watch what his failure had brought on all life besides?

Varus thought of Sigyn's cold hell. That would be

worse. He wished she were walking at his side; for the companionship, but for her sake as well.

Varus's path was rising, or he thought it was; he knew that his long trek in darkness could have disoriented him. His stride was firm and from the outside would have looked confident; if there had been anyone to watch, and if they could have seen anything in this lightless, lifeless place.

In the Temple of Jupiter Best and Greatest, Hedia knelt beside Pandareus. She had brought a bowl of mixed wine from the Senator's table. With a napkin she had dipped in wine, she was wiping the teacher's brow.

Hedia glanced at Varus—at his body, chanting the verse of power—nearby. Their eyes met, but there was no real connection because Varus's soul—his soul smiled in the darkness—was in another place. She went back to nursing the injured teacher.

Alphena had risen to her feet. She was pacing back and forth, working the stiffness out of her legs. She snapped her head around at each turn, keeping her eyes forever on the pit. She was ready for the moment that the demons would break free of the hedge of sound.

But for now, Corylus played. With the eyes of his soul, Varus saw the shadow of a woman standing so close to his friend that half the time he thought they were one.

The flute's song was a continuous sapphire wave, coiling about and freezing back the fire demons. It couldn't stop them forever. Nothing could stop them forever, for Surtr was a god and they were his minions. But while Corylus played, they were not free to ravage Carce and through Carce the world.

You're a good soldier, my friend Corylus. The Republic is lucky to have men like you, from whom the rest of us can learn our duty.

Varus saw light ahead of him. He felt an urge to run, but measured paces had brought him from Carce to this sight of his goal. He continued to walk in the appearance of glacial calm; and in ten steps more, or perhaps twenty, he stepped into a cold wind.

The sky was the color of watered milk, and the sun was low on the southern horizon. The ground was a bare slope of rocks reeking of sulfur. Open water lapped the shore of the island, but the sea beyond the wizards' barrier was a crinkled mass of pack ice.

Varus stood on the lip of a tall volcanic cone. On the strand below him, manlike figures danced with capering demons for partners. He had come to the Horn, the home of the Twelve.

This was where he had first seen the Twelve in a vision. They danced as they had done when they made Varus their slave, but their spells would not help them now. The Wizard whom the Twelve created had returned, not to rule but to destroy them.

Far to the east were hills, snowbound but brushed with the green of spruces and stippled by slender hardwoods which would bloom again in spring. Between the mainland and this volcanic island was a strait whose swift currents washed even the far shore clear of the ice which otherwise covered the surface for miles in all directions. The slumped basalt columns of the cliffs on the mainland had been shattered when the sea flooded onto molten rock.

Surtr was great, but when the Horn became an island the fire god had not been driven to exert his whole strength. This time, Surtr was not in control: the Wizard was.

"*Out I go at once,*" Varus shouted, "*flinging wide the doors!*"

He felt the rumble through the soles of his feet. Pebbles—cinders flung from the fires in ancient times—began to patter down the slope, their bonds shattered by the new tremors. The Twelve had closed the twisting ways to the Horn with their spells, but the Wizard had walked them. Now he opened those passages to the heart of fire.

The ground gave a violent shudder. They were coming. The legions of fire were coming.

The Wizard bestrode the Horn like a god. His left hand clasped the ivory talisman and his head scraped the clouds. The Twelve called to him in prayer, not command.

"I have no fear as I welcome my kinsmen!" the Wizard shouted.

The rim of the volcano crumbled as the fire demons tore it away in their haste to reach the outer world. Sulfur clouds belched up, wreathing the giant figure of Varus. He was beyond any human concerns.

Orange-red lava or red-orange demons pushed and bubbled from the crater, cascading down the steep slope to the sea. The Twelve waded into the water, but Varus knew they could not go far: the barriers they had set to bar entry to their fortress were now the walls of their prison.

The lava hissed and thundered in its descent. The demons whom the Twelve had forced to their will laughed as they continued to dance. Surtr's legions swept through them, mixing as completely and harmlessly as water with wine. The Twelve's minions were blue sparks in the red-orange sea, whirling in slow evolutions, and the Wizard heard their laughter.

Varus did not laugh. The Twelve had used him as they used the demons. They would have made him the instrument by which they destroyed all men, for which they had to be utterly destroyed: more thoroughly even than Carthage.

But the only pleasure Varus felt was the sense of a duty well performed. *I am a citizen of Carce. I have been steadfast.*

The wave of lava splashed into the sea, boiling it away and pushing farther out. The roar would have deafened human ears. Steam and sulfur mixed in a foul, clinging blanket which hid everything but the screams.

These screams continued for longer than the Wizard would have guessed; but when they ended, Varus sat on the floor of the Temple of Jupiter Best and Greatest. The ivory head of Botrug was in his left hand, and his friends were around him.

Nemastes lay dead by the statue of Jupiter. The Twelve had vanished, as had Surtr and the pit which had reached down into the fiery core of the world.

Corylus lowered the bone flute, looking dazed. Alphena stumbled toward him, holding her sword to the side instead of trying to sheathe it in her present state. Hedia was helping Pandareus to his feet, and the temple servants seemed to be coming around also.

Gaius Alphenus Saxa pushed through the front door. Immediately behind him followed a company of servants led by Lenatus and Corylus's man Pulto. The two old soldiers carried bare swords in defiance of the laws of the Republic.

"Varus!" Saxa said. "What's happened here, my Son?"

Varus stood and staggered into his father's embrace. He knew it would take him some time to decide how to answer the question, though.

EPILOGUE

Alphena felt drained. She'd trained hard many times in the past, but she'd never felt like this before. The exhaustion was more a matter of her soul than of her body, though when she moved she found that all her muscles—especially her thighs and her pectorals—ached.

Servants had intercepted her before she reached Corylus. She shouldn't have run to him anyway.

"Your ladyship!" said Agrippinus, looking more agitated than Alphena had ever seen him before. He held a gold-banded ivory baton which would probably make an effective weapon—in the hands of someone other than the majordomo himself. "Your ladyship, what are you doing with a sword here in the temple?"

"I'll take care of the girl, buddy," said Lenatus, stepping close to Alphena and crowding the majordomo back with his outstretched arm. "Look to her mother, why don't you?"

"You buffoon!" Agrippinus said. "She has a sword, don't you see?"

"Yeah, by Hercules, I surely do see," growled Lenatus. "Which is why I'm telling you to leave her to me, got it?"

The trainer had slipped his own weapon out of sight. When he and Pulto burst into the temple, their cloaks had been wrapped around their left forearms to give them some protection if they had to face enemies with swords of their own. As soon as it became clear that the fighting was over, the swords were sheathed again and the cloaks concealed them.

"Lenatus, you trained me," Alphena gasped. Her head was spinning. The air was clear now, but the stench of sulfur had flayed her nostrils while she faced the demons. "May Juno the Mother bless you for training me so well!"

Her tunic was charred just above the knee, and there was a long blister on the flesh beneath that mark. One of the creatures had almost gotten its grip when it snatched at her. She didn't remember that happening, but the injury was inarguable. Reaction to the burn might explain why she was remembering events that now seemed to be delirium.

"Is this a real sword?" Lenatus said, surprise replacing concern in his voice. "By hell, what *is* this? Pulto, come here. What kind of metal—"

His face blanked as he remembered whom he was talking to. "Your ladyship, I apologize," he said; he was contrite but he was still a free citizen of Carce. "I spoke without thinking. But please, may I take a closer look at this blade?"

Pulto waved away Lenatus's summons. He stood with Corylus, watching over the youth much as the trainer did with Alphena.

She smiled wearily, wondering what Corylus was telling his servant. Alphena didn't know how she could explain what had happened—if in fact it had happened outside of her dreams.

Hedia was talking earnestly with Saxa. Alphena came to a sudden ordering of priorities. The blade was clean and her hand didn't tremble anymore, so she sheathed the weapon smoothly.

"Yes, you can look at the sword, Master Lenatus," she said. "At leisure, when we're back at the house. But for now, do you have something to put on this burn? I'm not sure how it happened."

The trainer turned and bellowed to a servant keeping out of the way at the front of the hall. The fellow trotted over, opening his case of medical supplies. *Trust an old soldier like Lenatus to prepare for the aftermath of a fight as well as the fight itself* . . . .

But first—

"Mother Hedia?" Alphena called in a clear voice that everybody in the hall could hear. Her father and stepmother broke off their conversation to look inquiringly toward her.

"Thank you!" Alphena said. "I wouldn't have survived without you, Mother."

She seated herself on the floor, stretching out her leg so that Lenatus could get to it with a jar of ointment. His blunt fingers were gentle, though in the past she'd seen how much strength there was in his hands if he chose to exert it.

Alphena didn't know what Hedia would tell Saxa or what Saxa would choose to do; she couldn't control that. But she wanted both of them, particularly her father, to know that Lady Alphena stood shoulder to shoulder with her stepmother.

HEDIA MET HER husband's eyes again when it was clear that Alphena had said all that she intended to. Too often when people were tested, they learned—and those depending on them learned—regrettable things about themselves. Fortunately, that turned out not to be the case with Hedia's daughter.

"Has she been hurt?" Saxa said. "What's Lenatus doing?"

"I don't think it's serious," Hedia said calmly. It *couldn't* have been serious, not the way Alphena had been dancing around until Corylus and his flute controlled the demons.

"She may have been bumped, my lord, but our daughter is a very sturdy young lady."

And still a virgin, but she wasn't going to discuss that directly with her husband.

"And you, my dear?" Saxa said. "Are you all right? You look . . ."

Hedia grimaced. "Yes, I do," she admitted. "Well, after a bath and a change of clothes, and burning these"—she flicked her tattered tunic—"since they're not even worth saving as rags"—*and I don't want to be reminded of them*—"then I'll be fine. It's not my blood, you see."

She swallowed. She had to be very careful how she phrased the next part.

"I may have been dabbed when I bandaged Pandareus," Hedia said. "He'd been knocked down by the ring of a lantern that was, well, thrown at him. But most of it"—she met her husband's eyes with her straight, cool gaze—"came from Nemastes. He attacked Alphena, and I fought him off. And killed him."

"That was what happened just now, before Pandareus summoned us?" Saxa said. "But dear—you were gone for days. And Alphena too."

"My lord and master," Hedia said. She took a deep breath. "There were difficult times, but we came through them—and the man responsible is dead. I would rather not revisit the things that happened."

Especially with my husband. For his sake more than her own, but for hers as well.

Saxa sighed and rubbed his forehead with the fingertips of both hands. "I apologize, my dear heart," he said softly. "I brought Nemastes into your lives. I didn't think he could be a swindler, since he had as much gold of his own as anyone could want."

He paused, peering at Hedia again. "But he was merely trying to abduct my daughter?"

"Yes, dear," Hedia lied calmly. "I'm sorry, but that appears to be the case."

She glanced at the wizard's body and rather regretted it. She had no qualms about having killed him, but the corpse was so *messy*. She had been grappling with Nemastes while she stabbed him, as she couldn't help remembering.

"My lord?" she said. "Will there be problems? For me? Because I killed Nemastes?"

"There will not be an inquiry into a noblewoman's protecting her daughter against a barbarian rapist," said Saxa with a rasping intensity Hedia had never before heard in his voice. "If you like, I can request that you receive the thanks of the Senate for safeguarding the chastity of Carcean womanhood."

Hedia blinked. "No!" she said. "No, please, my lord. The less talk there is about this—"

She looked around the hall. The temple servants were all awake, though they seemed to cluster about Sempronius, the commissioner of the sacred rites. She'd used his wine to clean the teacher's scalp and her own gory arms. Pandareus wore the dinner napkin as a bandage too. Nobody seemed willing to object to what Hedia had done—or even to refer to it.

"Well," she concluded lamely, "I'd like to forget it. If . . . if you permit me to, my Husband?"

Saxa didn't speak for a moment. He must have rushed out of the house, because he wasn't wearing a toga. *He never appears in public without a toga.*

"My Wife," he said formally, "I asked you before: are you all right?"

Hedia took his hands in her own. His fingers felt hot and pudgy.

"My lord and master," she said, holding his eyes with her own. "I may be a little worse for wear, but as you know I was never a hothouse flower. I'm still the woman you married, Saxa. Is that"—she couldn't help it: she turned her face away as she forced out the last of what she had to say—"still good enough for you?"

"Yes, my Wife," Saxa said. "My little sparrow."

He embraced Hedia awkwardly, because he was an awkward little man. Her heart swelled with love and pride.

"I'm glad to see you," Corylus said, clasping hands with his servant, "but how did you happen to be here, Pulto? And Saxa too. *I* didn't know I was coming here an hour ago."

"Well, it was Pandareus," Pulto said, nodding toward the teacher, who was talking to Varus. The youth was in good shape, but Pandareus wore a serviceable bandage on his head. "He sent messengers saying that you and their ladyships"—Pulto dipped his head twice this time, indicating Alphena and then her stepmother—"were coming here. I guess he must've told your pal Varus too, though he didn't say so. Anna wanted to come, but you know—she doesn't get around quick anymore. And besides, I thought it might be more a job for me."

His hand patted the sword under his cloak. The blade sang softly.

"I don't mind telling you," he went on, "I was glad to see Lenatus come along with old Saxa. The Senator, I should say. But you seem to have had things in hand without us."

Pulto frowned. "Only—is that a flute you've got there, master?" he said doubtfully.

Corylus looked at the pierced bone in his left hand, then met his servant's eyes. With a hint of challenge, he said, "Yeah, this is a flute, Pulto. I haven't forgotten I'm a soldier of Carce, but you know—sometimes that takes a flute instead of a sword. Or even a hornbeam staff."

"Ah!" said Pulto, looking away in embarrassment. "Well, I didn't mean anything, master. There's a lot of gentlemen who play the flute, I'm told; only they're mostly Greek, but that's all right too. I don't doubt that whatever you been doing this past couple days, it would make your father proud."

Corylus suddenly remembered that all Pulto knew was that his young charge had vanished and had suddenly reappeared—with a flute but without explanation—in the temple of Jupiter on the Capitoline. He hugged the old soldier. That wasn't proper behavior for a master and servant, let alone a youth and a middle-aged man, but it was the best way to express his feelings toward Pulto.

"Thanks, old friend," he said. "My father felt better knowing you were backing him, and so do I."

"Well, old One-Eye was wrong, wasn't he?" said a harsh voice from above. "A fine place we'd all be if Corylus here had taken his advice."

Corylus looked up. A pair of ravens perched on a crossbeam above them.

"You know One-Eye," said the other raven. "Go straight ahead with a sword and kill everything in front of you. That's *his* notion of wisdom."

"How did they get here?" Pulto said, looking at the ravens with a scowl of wonder.

"You can hear them?" Corylus said in surprise.

"Hear them?" said his servant. "Hell yes, how could I *not* hear that croak, as oftentimes as I've heard it before? But on the borders, not right here in the center of Carce."

"Choosing this young warrior for his agent," said the first raven. "*That* was wise, I'll grant."

"As it turned out," replied the other with a hint of disagreement. "It's only in memory that you can be sure what is true wisdom."

"You say!" said the first with a harsh laugh. "But yes, wisdom must be built on memory."

Pulto glanced about the floor. *Looking for something to throw at them,* Corylus realized.

He put his hand on his servant's shoulder and said, "I think they're good luck, given the way things worked out tonight. Let's let them be, shall we?"

"Huh?" said Pulto. "Oh. Well, sure. If they want dinner on that bastard's eyes"—when he glanced toward the corpse of Nemastes, his hand went unbidden to the hilt of his now-concealed sword—"*I'm* not the man who's going to stop 'em."

Pulto looked at Corylus. "Can we get back to the apartment now?" he said. "Anna is going to be wondering how things worked out. You know how women are, boy."

Corylus thought of Alphena facing the demons which boiled from the pit and Hedia stepping back from the dying wizard, her arms bloody to the elbow. "Women are just fine, old friend," he said. "But yes, I'd like to get a proper meal in me and to sleep in my own bed."

He paused for a moment. "Pulto?" he said.

"Master?"

"Pulto, you said my father would be proud of me," Corylus said, "and I think he would. But I think my mother would too."

VARUS LOOKED AT the ivory talisman. He had to force the fingers of his left hand to open, because they'd been gripping it so tightly. The crude carving of Botrug looked back at him; but when the lantern light fell just the right way, he saw an old woman smiling through her wrinkles.

Or perhaps he was looking at a reflection of his own face. If he squinted, that was what he seemed to see. Shaking his head in wonder, Varus dropped the talisman down the neck of his tunic again.

A gaggle of servants stood close to Varus but were afraid to approach him. Pandareus stepped through them and said, "I'm glad you got free, Lord Varus. It must have happened after I knocked myself silly."

"Sir?" said Varus, noticing his teacher's bandage for the first time. Blood had seeped through it on the left side of his forehead. "Did you slip and hit the floor?"

"No," said Pandareus, smiling wryly. "I threw a lantern at a demon. When the lantern exploded, a piece hit me in the head. I seem to be even less suited for physical heroics than I realized when you and I were trying to escape the dragon that chased us."

He cleared his throat and added, "I'm glad to see you back, my student. I was concerned about you and about Master Corylus as well. I knew nothing about the women until I was told that you both and they would be in this temple tonight, facing great danger."

"Master?" said Varus. His left hand traced the dimples of Botrug's eyes beneath the fabric of his tunic. "You were told? By the stars, do you mean?"

"In a manner of speaking," Pandareus said deliberately. "It was in a star chart, yes. The meaning seemed quite clear to me as I looked at it. But I saw the chart in a dream, and the sage Menre brought it to me."

"And you came to help us, master?" Varus said. He spoke before he thought and regretted the words as they came out of his mouth.

"Yes," said the little old man in a worn tunic. "I sent messengers to your father and Corylus's servant—"

We need to reimburse him for the cost of public couriers! Varus thought.

"—but I was closer, so I arrived ahead of them. I didn't see that I would be able to accomplish anything useful, but I had put you both in danger."

He grinned wryly. "I was correct that I couldn't help,"

he added. "But since I survived, at least I don't have to remember that I didn't try."

Varus straightened. "You didn't put us in danger, my Teacher," he said formally. "And speaking for myself . . ."

He took a deep breath. For a moment he felt as though he were again breathing the clear cold air of the clouds above the island of the Twelve.

"Master Pandareus," Varus said. "The cosmos is wide and more accessible than philosophers would have us believe. The education and intellectual rigor which you work to instill in your students fitted me to act in that cosmos and to return to my home."

Instead of answering immediately, Pandareus looked about the hall. Corylus and his servant were walking toward the door. Corylus caught Varus's eye and raised an eyebrow; Varus nodded his friend on. They would meet tomorrow to discuss this, but not now. At the moment Varus wasn't in shape to talk more about what had happened.

Hedia and Alphena stood side by side, holding hands. Each reached across the other placing right hand in left, so that their arms were interlaced. Their apparent closeness was as much a surprise as any of the other things which Varus had seen since the afternoon of his poetry reading.

The women would probably like to leave also, but Saxa was speaking forcefully to Sempronius Tardus, who as commissioner tonight was in charge of the temple. Saxa appeared to be blaming his fellow senator for what had happened. He couldn't really believe what he was saying—Nemastes was scarcely the fault of Tardus—but it was a better direction in which to turn thoughts than a more truthful one. This would all be hushed up quickly, by the commissioners for sacred rites and by the unanimous Senate.

Varus smiled. It was a pleasure to watch his father

dealing ably with a crisis. There were more ways to protect Carce than to stand in the middle of the Tiber bridge, facing the massed Etruscan armies.

"Teacher?" Varus said, since Pandareus still hadn't spoken.

Pandareus met his gaze again. "I've never doubted that there were many things in this world which I didn't and couldn't understand," he said. His smile was wistful but still a real smile. "However I didn't expect so many of them to be"—he gestured with both hands—"so close to me, so to speak."

"Yes, master," Varus said. "But education allows us to meet the unknown and deal with it."

"Education and also courage, I would add," Pandareus said. "But you citizens of Carce have never lacked for courage, have you?"

He sighed, then smiled broadly. "In any case, I certainly hope that you're correct about being able to deal with the unknown. Because the star chart Menre showed me also indicated that something is approaching us from the waters to the west. And it is no more our friend than Nemastes was."

Turn the page for a preview of

OUT OF THE WATERS

DAVID DRAKE

Available in July 2011 from
Tom Doherty Associates

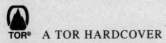

TOR® A TOR HARDCOVER   ISBN 978-0-7653-2079-7

CHAPTER I

Varus sat upright at his father's side in the Tribunal—the patron's box—over the right edge of the stage in the Pompeian Theater, jotting notes in the waxed memorandum book on his lap. Staring at him from the vast bowl of the theater was an audience of thousands: perhaps twenty thousand all told, including the slaves standing—they weren't allowed to sit—in the aisles and the surrounding colonnades.

It was disquieting to look out at so many human faces, though he knew that only a handful of them were even vaguely aware of Gaius Alphenus Varus. Indeed, very few of the spectators would pay any attention to his father, Gaius Alphenus Saxa: senator of Carce, replacement consul, and destined governor of the province of Lusitania on the Atlantic coast of the Iberian Peninsula.

The spectators didn't worry Varus as much, though, as the vision forming in his mind: a very old woman, seated on a throne. He wasn't sure if she really existed or if she ever had existed; but he knew why he was seeing her.

Varus was too well schooled in philosophy to lie, even to himself, about his father's personality. Saxa was a cultured and well-read man, but not a particularly wise one. He had chosen to commemorate his consulate by putting on a mime written for the occasion: *The Conquest of Lusitania by Hercules.*

The replacement consul sat on his gilded, high-backed chair, beaming with pleasure. If the emperor had been present, the Golden Seat would have been his. The Tribunal wasn't the best place from which to view the three-hundred-foot-wide stage, but it *was* the best place in which to be seen by the audience.

The citizens of Carce would probably have preferred watching exotic animals being slaughtered by the hundreds and perhaps even convicted criminals being devoured by cats and bears, but Saxa was wealthy enough that the present spectacle was keeping the audience in its seats.

Varus had once imagined he could become a great poet, one whose readings would fill a hall and might even fill this theater. His first public performance had been a disaster, not so much in the eyes of those attending as in his own.

On that occasion, the audience had been of freedmen and hangers-on of his father's wealthy friends, sent as a courtesy. They had expected to be bored. Varus himself was too intelligent and too well taught . . .

He glanced over his shoulder toward his teacher, Pandareus of Athens; the scholar nodded crisply in reply. He sat in the Tribunal as a mark of Saxa's gratitude.

. . . not to understand how bad his epic was when he heard the words coming out of his mouth.

Under the careful direction of two handlers each, the Cattle of the Sun—big animals with bright bay hides—were marching across the stage. Though they had been gelded and their horns sparkled with gold paint for this show, they were of the same Iberian stock as the bulls which not infrequently gored to death the lions and tigers set to fight them in the arena.

While even more dangerous animals sometimes appeared on stage, these steers were nothing to have loose in the belly of the theater. That was especially true since the seats in the orchestra were reserved for senators and their families.

A steer bellowed peevishly and lashed its tail. The actor playing Hercules stood at the back of the scene on a "rock"; he twitched noticeably. It was unlikely that an angry animal would crash through the spiked iron fence protecting the orchestra, but one certainly might knock down the mountain of plaster on a wicker frame and then start in on the actor who had been standing on it.

The audience would love it, Varus thought, smiling faintly. He wasn't the sort of aristocrat who sneered at The Many, the common people; but even at seventeen he was enough of a philosopher to be wryly amused by the difference between his tastes and those of his fellow citizens of Carce—including the tastes of many who were just as wellborn as the Alphenus family.

Varus gestured Pandareus to slide his chair up a few inches. The Greek had been careful to take a subordinate place rather than imply his equality with citizens of Carce, but that had now been established. Varus wanted to talk with his teacher, the only person in the box who shared his own passion for truth.

Saxa had a capacious mind, but it was like a magpie's and his learning was slanted toward the marvelous. The more remarkable a report was, the more likely he was to believe it.

Varus preferred sober facts. His smile quirked again. It disturbed him that some of the events he'd recently seen—and participated in—were more amazing than the fantastic myths which charlatans retailed to his father.

Pandareus advanced his chair to the railing. He and the others in the Tribunal sat on backless folding chairs with fabric seats. They were identical to the chairs of the senators in the orchestra, except that the frames were of oak or fruitwood instead of ivory.

Apart from the senators, free persons in the audience sat on stone benches. The wealthier had brought cushions, while the poor made do with a cloak or an extra tunic. This mime was scheduled to last all afternoon, so even a toil-hardened farmer visiting the capital needed something between his buttocks and the stone.

Pandareus followed his pupil's eyes to the slaves in the gallery and murmured, "I wonder how many of them are Lusitanians themselves? It's supposed to be a rather wild province, of course. If there are any of them here, they may not have enough Latin to realize that they're supposed to be looking at their homeland."

The last of the cattle stamped and clattered off the stage below the Tribunal. An actor dressed as Mercury with a silver helmet and winged sandals cried, "Behold, the treasures of Lusitania, now yours by right of conquest!"

The first of what was obviously a long line of donkeys followed the steers. Instead of ordinary pack saddles, the animals were fitted with shelves which displayed silver and gold plate, bronze statuary, silks, and expensive pottery. Some of the dishes were decorated blue on a white background, products of the same Far Eastern peoples who produced the silk.

"Master?" Varus said as a question occurred to him. "There were twenty cattle. Is there some literary basis for that? Because frankly—"

He lowered his voice, though there was no likelihood that Saxa on his right side could have overheard.

"—I would have expected my father to provide more, just for the show."

Pandareus allowed himself a pleased smile. "As it happens," he said, trying to keep the pride out of his voice, "your father's impresario, Meoetes, asked me the same question while he planned the mime. I told him that annotations by Callimachus on Euripides' claim that the 'cattle' are actually a metaphor for the twenty letters of the Greek alphabet which Heracles—"

He used the god's Greek name.

"—brought to replace the alphabet of Cronus. Meoetes was doubtful, as you surmise, but the senator insisted on accuracy over spectacle." He coughed and continued, "Since I couldn't give any guidance on the loot of Iberia, I believe they decided to, ah, spread themselves."

Varus grinned again, feeling a rush of unexpected warmth toward his father. Saxa had not been harsh toward his son and daughter—he wasn't a man who could be harsh to anyone, even a slave; though of course he had foremen and stewards who could do what they thought was necessary. Neither had Saxa showed any interest in his children, however.

That had changed very recently. Saxa appreciated the real erudition which he was honest enough to know that he lacked himself. He had learned that Marcus Priscus, a member of the Commission for the Sacred Rites and reputedly the most learned man in the Senate, respected Varus' scholarship and regarded Pandareus as his equal in knowledge. That had raised son and teacher enormously in Saxa's estimation.

Alphena, Saxa's sixteen-year-old daughter, had gained status for an even better reason: Hedia, Saxa's third wife and the children's stepmother, had taken the girl under her wing. Hedia was lovely and could be charming, but she knew her own mind—and got her way in everything that mattered to her.

Varus wouldn't have believed that his tomboy sister would ever want to act like a lady, let alone that she would be capable of doing a creditable job of it. The fact that Alphena was here in the theater, wearing a long dress with a silk cape over her shoulders, was almost as remarkable as other things that had happened in the course of the past week.

Almost. Varus had seen the earth open and demons rise from the blazing rivers of the Underworld. He had seen that, or he thought he had seen that; and it had seemed that he himself was the magician whose chanted spell had dispersed those demons and sealed the world against them.

Varus prided himself on his intellect; intellectually he knew the things he recalled could not be true. Unfortunately for logic and reason, his teacher recalled the same things. When a scholar of the stature of Pandareus accepted the evidence of his eyes over common sense, a mere student like Varus was left with a dilemma.

The line of mules moved steadily except when one stopped, raised its tail, and deposited dung on the stage. Pandareus leaned forward, watching with more interest than he had shown for the splendid goods themselves.

"How will they clean the stage after the performance, Lord Varus?" he said. "That is, I understand there are to be eight hundred mules. If even a small portion of such a herd . . . ?"

Varus laughed. He wasn't a frequent spectator at Carce's mass entertainments, but he obviously got out more than his teacher did. He said, "They hold beast fights and hunts—"

So-called hunts, that is. Archers and javelin throwers behind metal fences shot corralled animals until they had no more living targets.

"—here also. Channels from the Virgin Aqueduct divert water over the stage and the cellars beneath to wash detritus into the sewers."

He met his teacher's eyes and added, "I don't believe that will be part of the performance though, as this mime doesn't include Hercules cleansing the stables of King Augeas."

They smiled together. Varus was proud to be able to make literary jokes with his teacher, and he suspected that Pandareus was pleased to have students who actually appreciated literature as something more than a source for florid allusions to be thrown out during a speech. Of the ten youths studying with Pandareus at present, only Varus and his friend Corylus could be described as scholars.

Varus let his eyes drift over the audience to where he had spotted Corylus while the jugglers and rope dancers were performing before the mime itself began. Publius Cispius was a Knight of Carce, entitling his son Publius Cispius Corylus to a seat in the first fourteen rows at any public entertainment. Corylus was in the fourteenth row, so that his servant, Marcus Pulto, could sit directly behind him.

The elder Cispius had capped a successful military career with command of a squadron of Batavian cavalry and had been knighted on retirement. He had purchased a perfume business on the Bay of Puteoli with the considerable money he had made while in service.

By ordinary standards, Cispius was wealthy—but Saxa was wealthy by the standards of the Senate. At Varus' request, Saxa had invited Corylus to watch the mime with them in the Tribunal. Corylus had refused, politely but without hesitation.

Part of Varus deplored the stiff-necked determination of a sturdy provincial not to look like a rich man's toady. There was no question of anything of the sort: Varus just wanted his friend to sit with him at this lengthy event.

On the other hand, if Carce's citizens hadn't been so stiff-necked and determined, the city would not rule all the land from Mesopotamia to the Atlantic, from the German Sea to Nubia. Logically, Varus would admit that being without his friend's presence was a cheap price to pay for an empire.

In his heart, though, he wasn't sure. Corylus was a

soldier's son and destined for the army himself. He had grown up on the Rhine and the Danube, where mistakes meant not embarrassment and expense but death in whatever fashion barbarian ingenuity could contrive. Corylus projected calm.

Varus needed calm right now. He wasn't really watching the stately procession of treasures across the stage. That vision of the wizened old woman seated on a throne in the clouds was becoming sharper in his mind.

She was the Cumean Sibyl, and she prophesied the approach of Chaos.